MEASURING TIME

Helon Habila was born in Nigeria in 1967. He won the Caine Prize for African Writing 2001 for the opening section of his first book, *Waiting for an Angel*, which then went on to win the Commonwealth Writers' Prize for Best First Book, Africa Region, in 2003. He was previously Writer-in-Residence at the University of East Anglia and now teaches creative writing at George Mason University, Washington DC.

measuring
time

HELON HABILA

PENGUIN BOOKS

PENGUIN BOOKS

Published by the Penguin Group
Penguin Books Ltd, 80 Strand, London WC2R 0RL, England
Penguin Group (USA) Inc., 375 Hudson Street, New York, New York 10014, USA
Penguin Group (Canada), 90 Eglinton Avenue East, Suite 700, Toronto, Ontario, Canada M4P 2Y3
(a division of Pearson Penguin Canada Inc.)
Penguin Ireland, 25 St Stephen's Green, Dublin 2, Ireland (a division of Penguin Books Ltd)
Penguin Group (Australia), 250 Camberwell Road, Camberwell, Victoria 3124, Australia
(a division of Pearson Australia Group Pty Ltd)
Penguin Books India Pvt Ltd, 11 Community Centre, Panchsheel Park, New Delhi – 110 017, India
Penguin Group (NZ), 67 Apollo Drive, Rosedale, North Shore 0632, New Zealand
(a division of Pearson New Zealand Ltd)
Penguin Books (South Africa) (Pty) Ltd, 24 Sturdee Avenue, Rosebank, Johannesburg 2196, South Africa

Penguin Books Ltd, Registered Offices: 80 Strand, London WC2R 0RL, England

www.penguin.com

First published in the United States of America by W. W. Norton and Company, Inc. 2007
First published in Great Britain by Hamish Hamilton 2007
Published in Penguin Books 2008
1

Measuring Time is a work of fiction. Characters, events, and organizations are either
the product of the author's imagination or, if real, not necessarily portrayed with
historical accuracy.

Printed in England by Clays Ltd, St Ives plc

YA

ISBN: 978-0-141-01007-6

www.greenpenguin.co.uk

Penguin Books is committed to a sustainable future
for our business, our readers and our planet.
The book in your hands is made from paper
certified by the Forest Stewardship Council.

For Adam, Edna, and Susan

acknowledgments

Thanks to my editors on both sides of the Atlantic—Alane Mason in New York, and Simon Prosser and Juliette Mitchell in London—for working with me from the first, and rather unsightly, draft to this final one. All persisting errors and imperfections are mine alone.

Thanks to my friends and family in Nigeria for your constant, even if distant, support and encouragement. To the University of East Anglia for continuing to provide a stimulating environment to me long after my fellowship—thanks to Jon Cook, Val Striker, and Katri Skala for their friendship and kindness.

Thanks to Bard College and Chinua Achebe for that one year in America; it really made a difference. To the Arts Council England for the grant, which gave me time and freedom to complete this book. Thanks to Fati and Nuhu, to Juliette and Marco, to Dorothy and Tony, to Rita and George for being such excellent friends. There are other friendships and kindnesses too big and too numerous to mention, and to them I say only: God bless.

For permission to quote from Okigbo's "A Shrub Among Poplars," I wish to thank his daughter, Obi Ibrahimat Okigbo; and for the quotation from Reverend John Hall's *Religion, Myth and Magic in Tangale*, I thank the publisher, R. Koeppe Verlag.

measuring time

We are all prompted by the same motives, all deceived by the same fallacies, all animated by hope, obstructed by danger, entangled by desire, and seduced by pleasure.

SAMUEL JOHNSON
The Rambler

It is so hard to find out the truth of anything by looking at the record of the past. The process of time obscures the truth of former times, and even contemporaneous writers disguise and twist the truth out of malice or flattery.

PLUTARCH
Parallel Lives

part one

the king of women

THEY HAD decided a long time ago to make life hard for their father. He had broken their mother's heart, and though the twins had not been born then, some women in the village still hum the song, popular many years ago, about Lamang's philandering before and after he had married their mother. The song, a ballad that grew in detail and complexity with each rendition in the moonlit village square, called Lamang the "King of Women / Owner of ten women / In every village from / Keti to the state capital." The refrain described how women stood longingly on their doorsteps as he passed, and how mothers locked up their daughters at night to save them from "the handsome ravisher," and ended with the lines:

> Mother sighing with longing
> Daughter sighing with longing
> Ah, King of Women, show some mercy

The song mentioned one woman especially by name, Saraya, the "black beauty." She was his first love, but she had married someone else, a distant cousin preferred by her family to Lamang's penniless charms. But according to the song, and to village gossip, the relationship had not ended with her marriage—there were trysts in neighboring villages, secret visits at night, suspicious shadows behind the compound wall. Saraya's husband, a truck driver, died in a road accident one year after the wedding.

The twins were almost thirteen when they first heard the stories of their father's early love life, and their mother's heartbreak.
They overheard two of their loquacious aunties whispering about
how the twins' maternal grandfather, known by all as Owner of
Cattle because he owned more head of cattle than any of his
neighbors, had called Lamang into his room one day and asked
him to marry his daughter, Tabita.

"Musa," the old man said to Lamang, which was Lamang's first
name, though everyone called him Lamang because of his striking resemblance to his grandfather of that name, "marry my
daughter and I promise you will not regret it."

Tabita was the most beautiful maiden in the village, but her
beauty was marred by a sickly disposition. She had been born a
twin, but her twin sister had died at birth, then her mother had
died when she was only five, and now her father thought the best
way he could make her happy was to marry her off to the most
sought-after bachelor in Keti. Owner of Cattle had no male
child, and Lamang, a shrewd businessman even then, had immediately seen the financial benefits of such a marriage. He said to
the old man, "I love your daughter, I will be happy to marry her,
but I am only a poor student, how can I take care of her in the
style you've brought her up in?"

First the old man waived the bride-price, which Lamang wasn't
in a position to pay anyway, and then he gave him twenty head of
cattle as a wedding gift, and promised to make him his heir. A
month later the marriage between the beautiful but sickly girl
and the village playboy was solemnized in the village church.

There were other versions of the story, but though the details
varied—some said more head of cattle might have been involved
as dowry, others said less, some said Lamang had actually
seduced the poor girl and got her pregnant and that was why her
father agreed to pay him to marry her, to avoid the scandal—
what all the versions agreed on was that the wedding made
Lamang a rich man. Five months after the wedding his in-law
died, leaving him everything, over a hundred head of cattle.

Lamang promptly left the Teachers' Training College where he was a student and went into business as a cattle merchant, buying cattle cheap from the nomadic Fulani herdsmen and transporting his live cargo to the big coastal cities, Lagos and Port Harcourt, where he sold it at more than four times its cost. Before long he was among the richest men in the village.

Fifteen months after the wedding Tabita died. Many years later, when he wrote his mother's story in his book of biographies, *Lives and Times*, Mamo, the elder twin, tried to capture in words the night she died—it was also the night he was born.

He wrote of the darkness, and the rain that fell for two days without abetting, of the cornstalks in the yard shaking and sinking to the muddy ground under the weight of the fierce wind and the rain and darkness, of the small square room in which Tabita lay in a narrow bed, sweaty, fainting, her hands grasped tightly by the midwife who was seated on the edge of the bed. A single lantern, fighting valiantly against the wind that leaned with both hands on the wooden door and the darkness that advanced and withdrew playfully in umbra and penumbra, revealed the other occupant of the room: Auntie Marina, who had arrived two days earlier from a neighboring village to be a witness to the birth of her brother's first child. Lightning flashed through the window like a camera capturing this grim tableau of parturition and expiration. Tabita screamed and thrashed about and in a lucid moment just before she died, she contemplated how life had given her all she had wanted with one hand and then taken it away with the other: she had married the man of her dreams, but he was in love with another woman, and life had given her a child, but she knew she wouldn't live to see it grow and run in the field, like other children, seeking the sun.

She died without knowing she had given birth to not one child, but two children. Mamo came out first, then his brother LaMamo, who had to be dragged out by the midwife. This accounted for his slightly elongated head.

The shrill cries of the babies above the rain and thunder

brought Lamang from the next room, where he had been pacing, waiting. He stood at the entrance, his eyes taking in his wife's sprawled motionless figure on the bed, the petrified midwife whispering, "She is dead, she is dead," and the twins in Auntie Marina's hands. She lifted the bloody bundle and approached her brother with it, but he lifted his hand, stopping her. With one last look at the sweaty, still figure on the bed, he pushed open the door and walked out into the rain.

Poor Tabita was buried the next day, under a baobab tree in the village burial ground. It was a lonely burial. Lamang did not turn up—most people assumed he was too heartbroken to come, but some, those who still hummed the song about the King of Women, said he might have been with his lover Saraya, and couldn't be bothered.

In her retelling of the same events to the twins, Auntie Marina never dwelled too much on the unhappy aspects of the story; she had a light touch, skimming and flying over the surface, always aiming for the folktale's happy reversals of fortune and resolutions. And so the sound of thunder that roared outside as Tabita's spirit left the room became angels' trumpets welcoming the ascending spirit; the furious flashes of lightning became guide angels' torches lighting the path to a new celestial home. Then there was the dramatic run in the dark—not desperate and clumsy as in real life, but a dignified hurry, with the twins swaddled and cozy in a blanket, all the way to her brother's, Uncle Iliya's house, where she first broke the sad news to Auntie Amina, Iliya's wife. She then gently revealed the mewling contents of the blanket and said to Auntie Amina, "Take them, poor orphans, they are now yours. If only I had any milk in these shrunken breasts, I'd take them with me."

The twins stayed with their uncle Iliya for the first three years of their lives, believing him to be their father, his wife their mother, and their cousin Asabar, whose meals they shared, their brother. But after three years Lamang came and shattered their illusion, he took them away—that was the day the seed of their hatred for him was planted, and when they grew older and began to hear the song about the King of Women, and about his maltreatment of their mother, the seed sprouted into a tree.

Lamang, for his part, never took much interest in his children; he left them in the care of their aunt Marina, who had been staying with him since the breakup of her marriage, and the village widows who occasionally dropped in to help with the housework and to generally advertise their availability to the once again eligible Lamang. He smiled at the widows and flirted with them, but he remained single. He couldn't marry his Saraya because after her husband's death she had suffered a stroke that destroyed her memory, leaving her only sporadic recall of the faces around her: her daughter, her brothers and sisters, and Lamang himself. Sometimes she'd look at him as though he were a perfect stranger, smiling politely at his words, but her eyes would be blank. It seemed fate, for once, had taken Tabita's side.

fever

WHEN HE was four, Mamo was discovered to have inherited his mother's blood disease, and it was, for the first time, given a name: sickle-cell anemia. He would make a lengthy reference to this in his biography of his mother, explaining in detail the chemistry and the biology of the disease. He also painted a picture, mostly in indigo and blue, of his earliest memory of his illness, and he described the occasion as "similar to being born again," and also "like emerging from some cave" where he had been dwelling in silence and darkness. He wrote:

I was in my father's room, lost in the huge four-poster bed, and everywhere was shadowy and blue, I felt like a dolphin coming up for air. There was a strange woman seated beside me, smiling and muttering: "You will be fine, Twin. You will be up and about in no time."

She had a kindly face; she looked like a sea spirit, riding the waves with me, helping me to stay afloat. Her nose was aquiline; her head scarf was a severe turban, beneath which a few gray wisps peeked, but her eyes were soft and soothing; there was also an air of sadness about her, as if she had known loss and heartbreak. She laid a piece of wet cloth on my forehead, cooling the red-singeing fire in my head. She smelled of outdoors, of fresh grass and the earth after rain.

"Mummy," I muttered, mistaking her in my fever for my mother returned. I closed my eyes. She was there when I woke up again—

hours or days or years later. She told me I had been in a coma and everyone feared I wasn't going to come back, but she said she had known I would return, that I was a fighter, like my mother.

"You knew my mother?"

"Yes, I was fond of her."

"Who are you?"

"She is our auntie Marina and she will be staying with us," LaMamo said, jumping onto the bed. I was happy. The room was dark; I wanted air, and sunlight. As if she could read my mind, she went and opened the window; the light came flooding in, throwing the room into focus. The door opened and my father came in, there was a man with him—he was a real doctor, not the village quack, Dr. Shangle—he had a stethoscope around his neck. He came and put his hand on my forehead. I shrank away. He smiled. He lifted my eyelids and peered into my eyes, and then he patted my cheek.

"You will be fine," he said and rejoined my father by the door.

". . . sickle-cell anemia." The doctor's words carried to me, whispery, conspiratorial, grave. I didn't understand what it meant, but I knew it was me they were talking about. My head ached. I turned to my auntie. She was also looking at the doctor, but she threw me a quick smile and sat down again.

"It is a disease of the blood, hereditary," the doctor went on.

"His mother had it," Lamang said gruffly.

"Not only her. You also must carry a trace of it, that's the way it works."

"His brother is a healthy, strong boy. He takes after me," Lamang argued. The doctor paused a moment, then he went on. "There's no known cure. He will either learn to live with it or . . . most people suffering from it die before they reach their twenties."

"He will recover, Doctor," my auntie said. "The good Lord will not abandon him."

Auntie Marina saved me from early death, she taught me how to live with it, how to deride it, even. She did this in a very simple way. She was a magician, a witch with words. She could conjure up mountains and undersea kingdoms with words. I stayed alive from

day to day just to hear her next story. She was Scheherazade, I was
the king, but she told stories to save my life, not hers—at least that
was how I saw it.

But of course much later I came to realize that no one can really
save another's life, and if someone does, it mostly happens more by
accident than by intention. The stories she told us and the neigh-
borhood children in front of the mud kitchen, far into the moonlit
night, she told not only to entertain us, but also to push back the
time when she'd have to go to her lonely bed and stare at the bare
wall that mocked her nightly with images of her failed life: her abu-
sive husband who had infected her with gonorrhea, and who, when
she couldn't give birth, had married a younger woman to whom she
had to defer, turning her into a maid in her own house. Cleaning-
cooking-farming, and there were also the nightly beatings. And
when she couldn't take it anymore there was the long tearful trek
with only her nanny goat for company and her bag on her head,
from the neighboring village where she lived to her brother's house.
My life is linked to hers like it is linked to my brother's, in a straight
and uncomplicated line. There are no mysteries, no shadows—just
light.

Auntie Marina never told the same story twice, unless the twins
asked her to—she seemed to have an inexhaustible stash somewhere on her farm from which she daily replenished her store.
One story the twins never tired of hearing, and which their auntie never tired of telling, was the wedding story. She described
the flow of relatives to Lamang's compound as if they were water
from a broken dam, and the two cows that were slaughtered, and
the sacks of rice that were cooked, and how for more than a week
after the wedding people still routinely stopped at the house to
eat because the food just refused to disappear. Lamang had
invited the best musicians and dancers from the state capital to
entertain his guests, turning the road in front of his house into

one big dance hall. And the bride—the whole village had agreed that they had never seen a prettier bride. Tabita was only seventeen, and the bloom of youth sat on her cheeks like a rainbow on the sky. Auntie Marina would point at the wedding picture on the living room wall: Tabita in a plain white cotton wedding gown, the veil raised and resting on her head, and Lamang, with a "follow-me" haircut, in a three-button suit, both of them smiling at the camera. They were alone, without groomsmen or bridesmaids, inside the old mission compound; behind them was the old church with its sloping thatch roof.

"See how she smiles happily," Auntie Marina would repeat over and over.

And so Mamo came to think that it was these stories that kept him alive. He imagined the stories insinuating themselves into his veins, flushing out the sickle-shaped, hemoglobin-deficient red cells that clogged the nodes in his veins and caused his joints to swell painfully. It was the stories and not the folic acid tablets that he swallowed daily, or the green vegetables and liver that were staples in his sickler's diet, or the special care not to get bitten by mosquitoes; it was his auntie's stories slowly working their magic in his veins, keeping him alive.

But with time, under the harsh daylight of reality, even Marina's words of magic lost their spell—and as they grew older the twins saw that in the wedding picture the glow on their mother's cheek hid an incipient dark tinge of sadness and apprehension, and their father's smile had a nervous sneer at the edges, and though the couple held hands, they leaned away from each other, looked away from each other, as if both were looking into the congregation for deliverance. Lamang was certainly looking for Saraya. And Tabita? Her old, foolish father, perhaps— or the angel of death, whose ominous wings were even then already circling over her.

hate thy father...

IMMEDIATELY AFTER he had discovered how different he was from his brother and from everyone else around him, and how tenuous his hold on life was, Mamo began to view things in a new way. Life gained more urgency, driven by a hot but sometimes purposeless rage; he began to learn the art of prioritizing. To help himself focus he began keeping an imaginary diary, the contents of which only his twin brother could fathom, and in it, in bold letters, he wrote his first priority: *HATE THY FATHER, MAKE HIM PAY*. Not that the twins had the means to make their father pay, but they tried their best whenever he was back from his endless business trips to the state capital and Lagos. They'd drop the occasional scorpion into his shoe, or misplace his car keys just as he was about to go out. Once or twice they had contemplated poison, but some unclear, unnamed terror had deterred them from that exigency. In any case, they preferred the death of a thousand cuts to the single bullet in the head.

The first time they put a scorpion in his shoe, Lamang's foot had swollen to twice its size, forcing him to stay indoors a whole week. Auntie Marina turned the house inside out looking for more scorpions. The kids solemnly helped her take out the chairs, and the carpet, and the table, but apart from the now-dead scorpion in the shoe, no other scorpions were uncovered. The second time, months later, the twins grew bolder. They went into their father's bedroom while he was in the bathroom and hid the scorpion—big, black, and pregnant—under his pillow. They

waited all night to hear the howl of raw pain from Lamang's bedroom, but nothing happened. The next morning he came out,
looking refreshed, and left for the city. The twins frantically
searched for the scorpion, but they didn't find it; for days they
went about with apprehension, avoiding dark corners and over-
turning the cushions before sitting down.

They lost interest in scorpions when Mamo discovered his
second priority. They had just turned thirteen. One night, lying
side by side in the open field, gazing up at the clear, dry-season
skies, the twins saw a plane pass, its wingtips blinking with light.

"Who are they?" LaMamo asked idly.

"Famous people," Mamo replied. And with that the solution to
his unavoidably short life on earth flashed before him, vivid as
the light on the plane's wingtips.

"We could be famous. That way people would remember us
even after we are dead," he whispered to LaMamo. From that
day, CHEAT DEATH, BE FAMOUS became the second com-
mandment in his mental diary. If he might never live to be
twenty—even that was being too optimistic; the two other cases
of sickle-cell anemia in the village apart from himself had both
died before the age of sixteen—then quick fame was his only
assurance of immortality.

"How?" LaMamo asked.

Mamo was silent. He did not know how. But he knew the
answer would come to him eventually, just as the idea itself
came, with the clarity of a meteorite streaking across the firma-
ment. They grew more restless as they waited. LaMamo had no
doubt that his brother would eventually come up with an idea to
make them famous. In the meantime, to keep their goal in focus,
they took to plane spotting. They'd stand on the highest hill, not
far from their house, and watch the planes flying past—some
days the planes passed, some weeks they wouldn't—and they'd
imagine themselves up there surfing the clouds, on their way to
some faraway, interesting place, famous, without a care in the
world. Sometimes their tall, gangly cousin Asabar would join

them on the hill. Like them he was also in the grip of a burning, mysterious rage; the twins had sold him their gospel of fame and escape. He brought magazines from his father's collection, and Mamo would read out to the other two the more interesting essays and stories, skipping the more difficult English words, about distant cities and famous people. They'd look at the pictures of women and skyscrapers and cars and stores and run their hands over the glossy paper, and then they'd sigh with longing.

how they killed the dog

THIS WAS the year they killed the old witch's dog.

Their restlessness had led them up a mango tree in the mango grove behind their compound. School had closed early that day because a new Mai was being installed. The Mai was the foremost traditional ruler in Keti and the fourteen smaller villages making up the Keti District. The last Mai had died suddenly a year ago, and today, after months of debates and horse-trading by the kingmakers, a new Mai had been elected and the entire village had gone to the palace square to witness the coronation.

Mamo and LaMamo and Asabar had the whole grove to themselves.

It was the loud barking that gave Mamo the idea. They were high up in the crooks of the topmost branches, their legs dangling in the air, their mouths yellow with mango juice. He stopped gnawing on a mango seed and said, "You know, dogs can see spirits and ghosts."

LaMamo looked at him and said, "How do you know that?"

"I read it somewhere, in a book."

LaMamo couldn't read very well. Mamo went on, "You can see things too if you rub dog's rheum in your eyes. You know, distant places, underwater people, and spirits, all those beings Auntie Marina talks of in her stories."

Asabar said, "I don't think I like the idea."

But LaMamo was captivated by it.

"Let's get Duna," he suggested. Duna was the old witch's dog, and it was perhaps the most vicious dog in the whole village. They looked each other in the eye and they agreed: to get Duna's rheum they'd first have to kill it. They got down from the tree and picked up their school bags in the grass and set off for home, totally immersed in trying to figure out the best way to kill a dog. Asabar casually slinked off, suddenly remembering he had to run an errand for his mother.

The twins continued to debate the best way to kill Duna. Halfway home Mamo hit on a solution.

"Batteries!"

"What batteries?" LaMamo asked, puzzled.

"We poison it . . . with the black stuff in radio batteries."

"How do we do that?"

"Come."

Mamo was running, his bag flying behind him from its strap, his spindly legs jumping high over the thick grass undergrowth. Their compound was a few yards from the edge of the grove. Their father and their aunt Marina had both gone to the palace square for the coronation and they wouldn't be back till late in the afternoon when the sun hung low and red over the hills. They found used radio batteries in the garbage pit behind the out-house. *Tiger Head Battery, For Long Life*. They spread out old newspaper pages on the ground and cracked a battery open over them. When the black carbon powder poured out onto the paper, the pile looked disappointingly small.

"More. It is a mean big dog," Mamo said, pushing another battery onto the paper. When they had enough, they carefully poured the black powder into leftover bean cakes they had found in the kitchen. This stage was easy; by now the outer skin of the akara were tough and membranous, and didn't crumble when the boys made a tiny hole in each and hollowed out the insides; they poured in the powder a pinch at a time.

Soon they were back in the grove. The old witch, Nana Mudo, lived alone with her dog on the other edge of the grove. Her house was a single mud hut fenced in by a wall of straw and

sticks; she spent the daylight hours seated on a log under a
tamarind tree outside her house. The tamarind trunk was
human-shaped; people said it was her husband, trapped in there
by her witchcraft. A footpath leading to the market passed before
her house, and though she was blind she could tell who was
passing from the footfalls and would call out their names and
harangue them with gossip. Duna was always beside her, a huge
gray ridgeback that loved to growl and chase after passersby, children especially, while the old woman encouraged it gleefully,
"Go, catch them, Duna, get them. Ha! Ha!"

Many a parent had come to complain, his tearful, dog-bitten
child in tow, only to be greeted by her wild cackles, her sightless
watery eyes shining, her toothless gums pink and crooked. "Tell
your spoiled brat to stop calling me 'Old Witch'!" Nana Mudo
would scream at the parent.

As they approached the old woman's house, they perfected
their plan.

"You will play bait. Stand so the dog sees you. Wave and throw
stones at it. When it gives chase, you run and climb up the tree,
where I'll be waiting. It will stand barking under the tree, and
that is when I'll throw down the akara. Any questions?" Mamo
asked.

"What if it doesn't come after me?" LaMamo was smiling, his
eyes shining with anticipation. His brother looked the opposite;
his feet dragged, and his hand that held the akara was sweaty and
limp.

"It will," Mamo said shortly. They chose a tree in the center of
the grove. It was small but leafy, easy to climb, and a fair running
distance from Nana Mudo's house. LaMamo did a few test runs,
jumping from the ground and grabbing a lower branch with both
hands, then swinging up into the tree.

"Easy, let's do it."

The grove was quiet and eerie—this was July, the mango season was almost over, and not many people came to the grove at
this time of the year. In the muddy ground beneath their feet last

season's mango seeds had already begun sprouting tender shoots. Insects and tiny frogs flew out of the grass as they passed. It was hot; moisture hung in the air, trapped beneath the mango leaves. Mamo used his sleeves to wipe his forehead every minute or so. She was seated in her usual place, on the log under the huge and gnarled tamarind tree with her faithful dog stretched on the ground beside her, its huge tongue lolling out of its mouth.

"You . . . you know what to do?" Mamo asked. His mouth was dry and he kept licking his lips.

"Stand in view, throw stones at the dog, make sure it sees me, and then run."

Mamo returned to the tree to wait. He did not wait long. A few minutes later he heard a deep barking, then the sound of feet racing through the grass, and then LaMamo appeared running, almost flying over the undergrowth, dodging trees. The ridgeback was a blur behind him, a gray ball moving faster than the eye could register. Then with a sinking feeling Mamo saw that LaMamo had missed the tree—the trees all looked the same anyway—he was running around in circles, his eyes searching desperately, the dog snapping at his heels.

"Here . . . here . . . here!" Mamo croaked. Without thinking he dropped out of the tree and started jumping about, waving his arms frantically. LaMamo saw him and made straight for him, breathing hard through his mouth; they both jumped as if on springs and grabbed at a branch, and they were up and safe. The enraged dog rushed at the tree and stood on its hind legs, scratching at the trunk with its front paws, jumping up, all the time barking, its fangs bared, saliva dripping out.

"Where are the akara, where are the akara?" LaMamo shouted at his brother, breathing hard, laughing, high on adrenaline. But Mamo couldn't get his hands to move, they were shaking uncontrollably. He was staring down into the dog's wild yellow eyes, mesmerized.

"There," he croaked, pointing with his mouth at the parcel in the crook of a branch above his head. LaMamo reached up, took down the parcel, and threw it down at the dog. Duna charged at the parcel, its body quivering with rage, then, scenting food, it stopped barking and poked its snout into the parcel. The twins leaned down from their perches, eyes fixed on the dog. Suddenly the dog looked up and growled at them, once, and then it lowered its head into the parcel and began swallowing the bean cakes hungrily. As soon as the parcel was empty, the dog resumed barking up at the tree, but the poison acted swiftly—the barking grew weaker, and soon the dog seemed to have lost all interest in them. It turned and headed for home, staggering from side to side as it went. Then they heard the old woman's voice calling the dog. It sounded close: "Duna! Come here, you crazy dog. Duna!"

The dog made for the voice, wagging its tail weakly, but it did not get far. It stretched out in the grass, and after a few thrashes and turns it went quiet. The twins looked at each other.

"Do you think it is dead?"

"It should be. It finished all the akara."

They spoke in whispers.

They cautiously descended from the tree. Now the old woman came into sight, tapping in front of her with her walking stick, all the time calling, "Duna! Duna!"

"She can't see," Mamo whispered to his brother needlessly. Soon she was out of sight, her voice growing fainter as she went. They ran to the motionless dog and stood over it, undecided what to do next. They were shocked and momentarily checked by the sight of the dog, dead on its side in the grass.

LaMamo knelt down and felt the dog's gray coat with his hand. It was still warm.

"Let's get the rheum and go."

"How?"

Mamo hesitated, and then he said, "Rub it into our eyes." He shrank as his brother reached for the dog's eye and scraped the rheum from the edge with his index finger, then carefully rubbed it into his eyes. LaMamo looked up, his eyes clammy with the rheum, and saw the look on his brother's face.

"Come on, let's hurry and get out of here," he said impatiently as he scraped at the dog's other eye. Mamo knelt beside his brother and presented his eyes.

The rheum turned out to be a disappointment—initially. In order not to reduce the rheum's potency, they avoided washing their eyes that night as they took their baths before going to bed.

The children's room was next door to Auntie Marina's: it was her duty to keep them quiet when their father wanted some peace, to wake them up when they overslept, and to make them sleep when they stayed up late. But on the night of the dog rheum there wasn't much noise from the children's room. They shut their door soon after supper; each went to his bed and lay shivering with anticipation. They left the lantern on low. Mamo was the first to drift off into a fitful slumber, muttering in his sleep, tossing and turning, and so LaMamo was the one who heard the gentle tapping at the window, the one overlooking the grove. Tap . . . tap . . . tap . . . it came again and again, regular, insistent. He froze under the bedsheet, eyes fixed to the window.

"Mamo . . ." he croaked. "Can you hear that . . . ?"

Eyes still fixed to the window, he tumbled out of bed and stealthily crossed the room to his brother's bed. He grabbed his brother's arm and shook him awake.

"Can . . . can you hear that?" he stuttered. They listened: far away, dogs howled into the night, voices of women returning late from the market carried on the air, then the tapping came again: tap . . . tap . . . tap . . . regular, insistent, the glass louvers amplifying the sound till it seemed to be issuing from somewhere right inside their heads.

"It . . . is only a branch knocking against the window," Mamo said, trying to conceal the tremor in his voice. He was glad when LaMamo slipped into the bed beside him, but they did not go back to sleep immediately. They lay in the gloom of the lamp, their eyes tightly shut, their limbs stiff as if with rigor mortis, their ears focused like radars toward the tapping on the window. When they finally fell asleep, they dreamt that it was raining outside—which indeed it was—and as the deluge raged the world grew darker, till not a ray of light could be seen, save when bright fissures of lightning lit up the air suddenly, to be followed by thunder. In the mango grove the water was shoulder-high; bodies floated past the window, their dead eyes glowing like lamps.

First was their mother, her mouth opening and closing as she passed by. She was trying to say something, but water kept filling her mouth, drowning the words. She struggled against the strong tide, but it took her away, her sad eyes still fixed on them, glowing, turning the muddy water translucent, silvery. Next came the old woman with Duna on a lead. She was cackling wildly, struggling to control the demented dog, fighting the flood to get to the window, and all the time the dog barked and barked, the sound bloodcurdling. Now she was at the window; she hammered at it with her walking stick, tap . . . tap . . . tap, till gradually the glass began to crack under the insistent hammering.

The twins woke up screaming. The scream became louder when they found out they could not see; they had gone totally blind. They scrambled out of bed, kicking their legs out of the sheets, knocking against each other, knocking into the table, beds, chair, each other, the walls, in their desperate search for the light. The rheum had glued their eyelids shut.

"Mamo, I can't see!"

"Me too!"

Then they heard Auntie Marina's voice outside the door. They threw themselves at her, sobbing with relief, when she opened the door, and at last their eyes opened and they saw the clear morning sun rays behind her, bathing her as she stood on the threshold.

That day Mamo's whole face became bloated from an eye infection; he lay on the sofa in the living room, writhing with pain. LaMamo sat dolefully beside him most of the time, fetching him things without being asked, feeling guilty that he had escaped unscathed from the dog adventure while Mamo got the infection. But his turn came the next day; it was as if the ghosts they had so wanted to see were having their revenge at leisure. LaMamo fell out of the flame tree behind the kitchen, hard on his left wrist, and got a fracture.

For weeks the twins dreamt of the dead dog, lying on its side in the grass, its eyes open, staring at them accusingly. They'd wake up at the same time and huddle together in one bed, shivering and looking at the closed window, waiting for the morning, till eventually sleep overpowered them.

"Do you think she knows?" LaMamo asked.

Auntie Marina had asked them about the dog a day after the event: "Nana Mudo's dog died yesterday, have you heard?" She looked directly into their eyes when she asked the question, as if she could see into their souls. "No sin ever goes undiscovered," she always told them. Now she said it with more frequency, especially in the evenings when she sat them down for prayers.

"Oh, Lord, have mercy on us sinners," she'd shout out in her strong, breaking voice. The twins would stare at her closed eyes, and at each other, nervously.

"Oh, Lord Jesus, save us from scorpions as we sleep in our beds tonight, and poisonous vipers, for we are your children. And when we eat our food, let it not be poisoned by the hands of the enemy. . . ."

in the harmattan season

SOME OF the rage left Mamo with the death of the dog, though he continued running in his sleep long after his brother had stopped. Sometimes it was the dog chasing him, sometimes it was the deluge threatening to drown him, at other times it was his eyes dilating, big as balloons, so that he could feel the pain in his eyes even after he had woken up shivering and screaming. His brother would sit helplessly by him to wait out the night. Mamo fell ill more often, one illness seeming to flow without break into the next. In November the cold dry harmattan wind began to blow. The wind, blowing from the Sahara, always had a way of sucking the vitality out of him, making him fall ill more frequently than in other seasons. He drank the bitter concentrate from neem leaves prepared for him by Auntie Marina every evening, swallowing most, throwing up the rest, and he ate folic acid and blood tablets without noticing the repulsive taste anymore.

By now LaMamo's fracture had healed and the splints around his wrist had been removed. He could draw sketches of Mamo as he lay in bed reading on good days, swaddled in sheets and shivering on bad days. In the sketches his face had a gaunt, empty look, but sometimes LaMamo would try to make him look happy, smiling, not so gaunt, his eyes staring toward an imaginary light streaming in from the window. At the end of each cycle of illness, when Mamo felt a bit stronger, his auntie would urge him to take a mat outside and lie under the flame tree, to rinse his lungs with the fresh clean air. At such times, he'd make a conscious effort to entertain his brother in turn and he'd read aloud from whatever book was at hand, Wilbur Smith adventure novels mostly, till his head began to ache.

Sometimes Asabar came to keep the twins company, he and LaMamo would kick a ball back and forth, taking turns to play goalie, but increasingly Asabar would turn up drunk, staggering and talking loudly about how unhappy he was. He had discovered the pleasures of alcohol. Auntie Marina would shake her head in disgust and give him a long sermon on the evils of drinking, and how all drinkers would end up in hellfire.

"But this is hell, Auntie . . . Life in this village is hell . . . Tell her, Mamo . . . sorry, not you . . . you are sick . . . but LaMamo, tell her how terrible. . . . I am tired of going to the farm . . . and school . . . and . . ." And he'd go on and on. To stop him, Auntie Marina would disappear into the kitchen to return with a bowl of rice, or tuwo, and hand it to him.

"Stop! Stop!" she'd scream as he began to dip his dirty hands into the bowl, and make him wash his hands before eating.

"See how scrawny you are?" she would mutter as he gobbled down the food. "See what sin does to you?"

Lamang didn't seem bothered by his nephew's drinking. He had always treated Asabar with more levity than he did his own children. "It is youth," he'd say, "he will grow out of it."

After eating, Asabar would go into the living room, where Lamang always sat listening to the news, and from outside the twins would hear their voices raised in conversation, Lamang's voice ringing out loudly in laughter as Asabar begged to be taken along on one of Lamang's business trips to Lagos.

"Take me as an assistant, or a bodyguard, Uncle. You travel a lot, you need protection, and you don't even have to pay me. After all, I am your nephew, we are family. . . ."

Lamang would laugh some more, then he'd tell Asabar, "Come to me when you finish school. How many years have you left?"

"Next year I'll be through. All of us . . . the twins . . . we will be free."

Harmattan is the harvest season.

Auntie Marina had a huge field of sorghum, which had started life as a small rocky patch of clan land belonging to Lamang, but for which he had no use and had handed over to her. Over the years she had expanded the tiny patch through dogged negotiation and complex deals with neighboring farm owners. Every year at this time the house was invaded by a gang of relatives from the neighboring villages come to help Auntie Marina with her harvest. This year four of them came. The twins knew them all by name, but the exact familial ties with each of them, patiently mapped out for the twins' benefit each harvest season by Auntie Marina, were too confusing to follow. The youngest was only twenty, but he already had a wife and a child. He had a reed flute and last year he had spent the after-work hours teaching the twins how to play it. This year it was only LaMamo who was available for the flute lessons. Mamo, still convalescing, kept to his room, watching the men through the window. They were quartered in the round mud hut that stood not too far from the kitchen, next to the flame tree.

The main house, facing the kitchen, was a big, rambling L-shaped structure. Lamang had built it incrementally. His father had left him a compound of only two mud huts, and to these he had added the shorter part of the L when he was getting married, fourteen years ago. It was a squat and rectangular structure consisting of two rooms and a living room, and it had square zinc windows and heavy wooden doors: the effort of local builders more used to working in mud and thatch. But in its time it had stood out among the surrounding thatched structures as a piece of architectural magnificence, one of the few in the whole village. Then five years after his wife's death Lamang had added the

longer part of the L; Auntie Marina was living with them by now
and the children were growing up fast and needed more room.
Also, he had now firmly established himself in business and
could easily afford the expense. The new house had louvers on
the windows, netting to keep out mosquitoes, and a veranda at
the front where Lamang sometimes sat on hot dry evenings to listen to the radio. The old wing and the new wing met in the living room. The children and Auntie Marina occupied the new
section, but Lamang kept to the old wing with its memories of
his early years. He loved to remind his children that only through
hard work could they hope to progress in life, using the house as
a metaphor.

Through the window Mamo would watch the men as they
returned from the farm, tired and dirty and hungry, but glowing
with the happiness of honest manual labor. They would sprawl
out under the trees and on the veranda, their hoes at their feet,
exchanging anecdotes from incidents at the farm. Now they were
gathered under the flame tree, skinning a rabbit. On the way
back from the farm LaMamo had surprised the rabbit and had
bashed in its head with his hoe; now he was eagerly reenacting
how he had pinned down the rabbit with one hand and had
brought down his hoe with the other hand. Mamo decided to
join them, but when he went to them he immediately noticed a
lessening of spontaneity in the conversation and a forced attempt
to accommodate him. When he realized that they felt sorry for
him, for his illness, he decided to keep away. He'd watch them
through the window and interact with them only when he had to.
They would be gone soon, he reminded himself patiently, they
never stayed longer than a weekend.

the play's the thing . . .

AFTER THE harvest, when he felt stronger, though still too weak to follow his brother to the soccer pitch, Mamo took to following his aunt to church to watch the drama rehearsals. He'd sit with the other kids at the back of the church. The kids, all younger than him, had tagged along to watch their mothers and they always fell asleep halfway through the rehearsals after tiring themselves running up and down the aisle and pews. Sometimes they'd fall off the flat wooden benches to the floor and their eyes would snap open to look around in confusion, and then they'd climb up again to return to sleep. The drama group had fifteen members, with Auntie Marina, the oldest of them, as leader. The women were mostly in their forties and fifties, with only two or three in their twenties and thirties. They joked and exchanged banter as they mimed and sang and danced. Mamo would watch them, especially the younger ones, their skin glowing with Vaseline, their hair newly braided, and sometimes when they came close to him he'd catch their scent of soap and wood smoke and fresh air. One, especially, had him enthralled; her name was Abiyatu, and she was the youngest of them. She was big-boned and tall and she exuded an animal energy that had Mamo's eyes following every step she took, every swing of her hips, every jiggle of her breasts, with voyeuristic intensity that left him fearing for his young soul, especially when he looked up to see the blue-eyed Jesus hanging over the door looking down at him. Abiyatu, being the newest member of the group, had to work harder than the rest to memorize her lines, because the play had no text. The lines, like folk wisdom, were handed down through apprenticeship. Unfortunately for Abiyatu, the person she was replacing had left rather abruptly and without handing down her lines.

Christmas was over a month away, but the church drama group always began preparations early. They performed the same play each year, yet each year they approached the performance with the enthusiasm of a new discovery, and each year the audience applauded and cheered with undiminished enthusiasm. It was the story of the arrival in 1918 of the village's first missionary, Reverend Nathan Drinkwater. The characters were: Drinkwater himself (played for the past eight years by Auntie Marina), his wife, Hannah Drinkwater (played for five years now by Amina, the assistant pastor's wife), and his two daughters (these were nonspeaking roles, most of the action being between Drinkwater and the "natives"). The climax came when the reverend stormed the village's central shrine to knock the peaceful-looking idols from their stands and then, Bible in one hand and idol in the other, he angrily turned and faced the surprised crowd outside, eyes blazing, advanced to the front of the stage, and shouted, quoting Joshua 24:15, "Choose for yourself this day whom you will serve . . . but as for me and my household, we will serve the Lord." Then he hurled the idol into a bonfire. Curtains. Only there were no real curtains, since the play was always staged in the open space in front of the church, with the church doors serving as exits.

Watching the frustration and the perplexity on Abiyatu's pretty, heart-shaped face gave Mamo an inspiration. The next day, he came with a notebook and wrote in it as he watched the women moving up and down the stage. By the end of the week he had written down each character's lines in the order in which they were delivered, then he went to the actors and hesitantly presented them with the lines.

"I wrote down your lines, I thought it'd make things easier.

And we can print it if you like. You don't have to improvise year after year."

At first the women weren't sure what he meant, but when he stutteringly read out the lines to the smiling, indulgent matrons, their eyes widened with comprehension, admiration. Like all true Christians, they were in awe of "the word," the written word, because in the beginning was the word and nothing was made that was made but through the word. They touched his head and said how clever he was, and when Abiyatu threw her hands around him in gratitude, his heart sang out, *Hosanna*, Auntie Marina smiled proudly and said the Lord had touched him and that in the future every group that performed the play would remember him because his name would be acknowledged on the printed text. He gave the play a title: *The Coming*.

But on Christmas day, as he stood in the audience watching the performance, Mamo saw instantly how poor his version of the play was. These women, in their forties and fifties, not by any means the most mentally agile age, now faced with having to be word-perfect, had suddenly lost their confidence and went about in a wooden, self-conscious way, and although the audience still cheered and laughed good-naturedly when the white man tried local food for the first time, and shed tears when his wife rescued abandoned twins, Mamo could see that the raw, unpremeditated vitality had gone out of the performance.

He was standing next to a girl of about his age; she was dressed in a pretty pink skirt and blouse. He had seen her earlier in church, at offering time when everyone had to step forward, in family groups, to put their offerings in a huge bowl before the altar, and he had thought how pretty she looked. She was obviously from the city. At Christmas families living in cities made the pilgrimage to spend time with the extended family.

"I . . . wrote the play," he whispered to her.

She turned and looked at him directly in the eyes. He felt uncomfortable. He felt excited and foolish. He wanted to keep talking to her, on and on, but his tongue lay heavy in his mouth.

She seemed to be debating whether to reply or not, then she said, "No. I have seen it before. It is from our history."

"I didn't mean I created it. I worked with the women to write it down on paper. Their leader, that one, is my auntie Marina."

He could see the disbelief and amusement on her face, so he handed her the sheets of paper in his hand; they were cyclostyled copies of the play, and they all bore his name on the last page: *By Mamo Lamang*.

"I am Mamo Lamang."

It was harmattan and cold, but he felt the sweat gathering under his armpits as he waited for her to look up at him and make a comment. The crowd cheered the burning of idols; the Reverend Drinkwater stood in center stage dressed in khaki shorts and shirt and heavy gum boots and wide hat and made his famous speech. When his wife Hannah came out of the forest clutching a pair of abandoned twins, Mamo said, "I am a twin. And this place where we stand was the evil forest where twins used to be dumped. This was where Reverend Drinkwater built the first mission."

Now she looked impressed.

"My name is Zara," she said. Then she added, "I am also writing something, a story, but it is not easy. My father said writers are geniuses." She was almost speaking to herself.

"I can look at it if you want. Are you going to be in Keti for long?"

"One week."

She turned and pointed through the crowd at a group standing beside a white car. "Over there are my father, mother, and sister."

"That is my house." He pointed. He felt certain he was in love.

the miraculous visitor

THE FOLLOWING year the twins finally solved the pending riddle of how to get famous, and that new knowledge would forever
change their lives. In an instant the mist of childhood and inno-
cence was blown away by the gales of time and experience. They
solved the riddle with the return of their uncle Haruna from the
Biafran war. Uncle Haruna was their father's youngest brother.
He was only sixteen in 1967 when he left Keti for the war front,
and after the war when he failed to return, his comrades swore
he had been killed in one of the very first skirmishes of the war.
Some of them even mentioned the battle in which he was killed,
and how his body, and that of hundreds of others, was abandoned in the heat of battle, left for wild animals to feed on.

But then in 1977, exactly seven years after the war, he
returned to Keti.

Mamo was home alone that day, convalescing from another
bout of fever. He had stepped out to the gate and was staring idly
into the dusty street. It was March, the dry season was coming
to an end, the air already carried the fresh, stirring odors of rain
from far away; dust devils swirled up into corkscrew funnels, lifting up twigs and pieces of paper and chasing them around and
around in circles. Mamo saw a man appear before him. He had
seen him approaching in the distance, walking in his direction,
but then the man had stepped off the road and out of view, and
now he was standing before Mamo. The man looked wild, his
hair was knotty and thick, his beard and mustache joined at the

sides of his mouth to form a circle. His clothes were tattered and looked as if he had been living in them for a long time. His lips, protruding from the hair-fringed O, were badly chapped and they bled when he spoke. At first Mamo couldn't make out what he said. He reached into his pocket to give him a coin, thinking he was a beggar—but then the man spoke again, louder. "Is this Musa Lamang's house?"

"Yes," Mamo replied, taking a step back, repelled by the strong smell coming off the man.

"Are you his son?"

Mamo hesitated before answering, "Yes."

"You must be one of the twins, then." There was an attempted smile on his face; he licked his lips as he spoke.

"I . . . am your uncle, Haruna. I . . . I . . . went to the war." His voice shook when he spoke and he closed and opened his eyes as if to concentrate all of his energy for this conversation.

"My uncle . . . ?" Mamo began, uncertain, and then stopped. The man was rocking on his feet: back and forth, back and forth, as if manipulated by an invisible hand, as if about to fall.

"Do you want to sit down? Should I get you some water?" Mamo asked, reaching out his hand instinctively. "My father is not home."

The man continued to smile, licking his chapped lips, but now he looked crestfallen, as if on the verge of tears.

"Come in and sit down." They went in, side by side, Mamo's arms ready, not touching the man, but waiting to catch him if he fell. The man collapsed on the first step of the veranda and dropped his tattered jute bag next to his feet. "Water," he sighed.

Mamo went to the kitchen and returned with a bowl of water. The man's hands shook, spilling water on his grimy shirt. He finished it all and put down the bowl by his side. There was a spot of blood on the rim.

"I . . . I . . . am so tired," he said, his eyes closing; he slowly stretched out on his back on the veranda step. "I've . . . traveled . . . for so long . . . so far . . ." He fell asleep before he finished the sentence. Mamo stood over him, staring at the upturned, bearded face, the open mouth with the yellow, rotten teeth inside. His father was away on a business trip and Mamo wasn't sure when he'd return. Auntie Marina wouldn't be back from the farm till late in the evening. LaMamo was at the soccer pitch— not that he'd be any less confounded by the situation than Mamo was. The best person to turn to, Mamo decided, was Uncle Iliya.

Even if this is my uncle Haruna, Mamo thought on the way to Keti Community School where his uncle Iliya was the principal, *I doubt if even his brothers and sister would be able to recognize him.* The face behind the beard had looked so tired and emaciated that he was sure it looked nothing like it must have looked ten years ago. He remembered nothing of his uncle. Mamo had been only four years old when his uncle left for the war front. All he knew about him came from family stories. In the stories Haruna was always idealized as a hero who had bravely given his life for his country. Nothing bad was ever said of him. Auntie Marina always talked wistfully of how kind he had been, how helpful to their old parents, and how old he would be now if he were still alive, and the tears would trickle down her face briefly, then she'd sigh and say, "God knows best."

Mamo felt the excitement mount in his chest, and for a moment he forgot how weak he was and he half ran all the way to the school located a few yards beyond the church. If this man was really Uncle Haruna, then today would be an exciting day; it was like a dead man returning to life.

Uncle Iliya was in a classroom teaching. Mamo stood at the classroom door where he could be seen. The students all turned to stare at him curiously. When his uncle saw him, he excused himself and came out, a frown on his face.

"Is everything okay?" he asked, taking Mamo's hand and leading him away from the door.

"A man just came to the house; he said he is Uncle Haruna."

"Haruna died in the war," Iliya said.

"I think you ought to see him first. I think he is telling the truth."

"Where is he now?"

"At the house."

"You left this strange man alone in the house?"

"He is ill."

Uncle Iliya went back into the class and talked briefly with his students, then he came out again. "Let's go."

The man had not moved an inch from where Mamo had left him. His head rested on his right arm, his bag lay at his feet, the flies buzzed joyfully over his open, bleeding mouth. His snores had grown deeper, whistling through his nose, making his heavy mustache rise and fall. Uncle Iliya climbed the steps and stood over the stranger, turning his head this way and that way to get a good view. He stood like that for a long time, and Mamo stood to one side, watching him, waiting. Then at last Iliya straightened up and took a deep breath.

"It is him," he said. Then he added, "But we must wait to hear what Marina will say."

He climbed up the stairs into the living room. Mamo followed him, a thousand questions burning his tongue like pepper. Uncle Iliya left the door open and the curtain raised; he sat facing the door, keeping the outstretched form in view. A puzzled frown played on his face, and each time he shifted in his chair he'd mutter to himself, "I don't understand this . . . it doesn't make sense. . . ."

Mamo, seated beside his uncle, asked at last, "What's going to happen now?"

"The poor man, whoever he is, needs medical attention. His legs are swollen, sore, look at his face. I only hope he doesn't die on us. But I can't do anything until Marina is back. Do you know when your father will return?"

"No."

Iliya fell silent, his eyes still intent on the sleeping man, and whenever the man shifted he'd get up and hurry to the door, then

return to his seat when the shifting subsided. At last he began to
speak distractedly, not looking at Mamo. "I didn't even know he
had gone to the Biafran war. . . . I had gone to the same war a
few months earlier. . . . He was only fourteen when I saw him
last. . . . I was living in the city then . . . all I remember of him is
that he was really close to Marina, even though they had different mothers. . . . We all had different mothers. . . . I remember
him always hanging around Marina. . . . He was rather weak as a
child, so I was surprised when they said he had gone to war. He
was our last-born, and everybody spoiled him silly, especially the
women—there were many women in our house. My father . . .
your grandfather . . . had three wives, he was a hardworking
farmer, at one time he had more goats than anyone else in the village, but his children kept dying—he fathered almost eleven
children, but only five survived. Of the survivors, I am the eldest,
then Marina, then your father, then Pandi, who died when he
was fifteen—then Haruna. Pandi and Haruna had the same
mother, she wasn't a very happy person, her heart broke when
Haruna went off to war, and then Pandi died, she died soon afterward." Uncle Iliya spoke as if he were reading from a prompter;
as if he could see the past he spoke of displayed on a screen in
front of him.

"My war ended in 1968. I was shot in the arm." He lifted his
empty left shirtsleeve. "I spent the remaining months of the war
in a military hospital in Kaduna. It was a terrible time, I saw more
deaths and more suffering than I had seen in the Second World
War."

"It is him, all right," Auntie Marina said after taking hold of the
man's right hand and pointing at a long scar inside his wrist.
"This is where he cut his hand on my wedding day."

But by now it was clear that there was something wrong with
Uncle Haruna—he didn't seem to be able to remember much.
He didn't say much; the tears simply ran down his face when he
woke up and saw his sister and brother standing before him.

When they asked him where he had been, what had happened, a vacuous look entered his eyes, and the more he tried to focus and to remember, the more agitated he became, and the tears flowed more freely. They left him alone, putting it down to fatigue. Marina prepared a bed for him in the mud hut next to the kitchen, and Uncle Iliya brought him some clothes. His old clothes were burned in the garbage pit near the outhouse. He took a bath with scalding hot water, then he ate, and almost immediately went back to sleep.

"What if it is some madman claiming to be Uncle Haruna?" LaMamo whispered to Mamo.

"It is not. The scar on his wrist proves that," Mamo said with a proprietary air. After all, he had discovered the man. He had told and retold the story of how the man had appeared in front of him as if by magic, and how he had boldly taken the man in and given him water.

"You are a brave man," everybody told him. "You did the right thing."

Lamang returned that night and met the excitement. He went into the hut where his brother slept and when he came out there was a big smile on his face. He said, giving one of his grand hand gestures, "It is him, no doubt. This calls for a celebration."

The next day half the village turned up for what Lamang called a celebration party and Marina called a thanksgiving party. Food was plentiful; a goat was slaughtered, and women came in and out of the kitchen bearing plastic plates of rice on trays and distributing them to the men, who were seated on benches and on mats under the trees and on the veranda. They shook hands with Haruna, looking into his eyes and exclaiming, "It is a miracle, nothing like this has ever happened before in Keti."

Dr. Njengo was seated on a stool, holding Haruna's leg in his hands, dabbing the wounds with antiseptic before bandaging them. He and Haruna were seated before Haruna's new abode, the hut to the left of the kitchen before which the women sat on mats and stools, chatting and eating. Njengo was not really a doctor. As a young man he had been a bag carrier for Dr. McGraw, a Scottish doctor and amateur botanist who had come to Keti to study the medicinal herbs of northeastern Nigeria. He had started the first clinic in Keti, where he treated minor complaints free of charge and had chosen Njengo as his bag carrier because Njengo's mother, Iya Tabak, was a healer and she knew each herb in the bush by name and by use. Njengo was going to be her successor in the business because he had the gift, but when the white man left—after he had made thousands of drawings of plants with detailed notes on each—Njengo had gone into the clinic business for himself.

Uncle Haruna was now surrounded by his ex-army buddies and childhood friends, who formed a semicircle around him, each trying to put in a word about the war, about the past, but Haruna, seated on an armchair, his bandaged feet raised onto a stool before him, only looked from face to face, a fixed smile on his lips, not saying anything, nodding vigorously to each recollection. He had shaved and rested, but his eyes still looked tired. Without the beard his cheeks jutted out of his face, making him look gaunt and hungry. The hair on his head was more white than black.

Toma, or "One-Leg," as he was called because he had lost a leg in the civil war, was the raconteur, and now his voice rose high over other voices as he re-created the past. The compound fell quiet. People drew nearer, and though many of them had heard Toma's civil war stories many times before, today they listened with a new ear. He said, "It began with rumors of killings. The year was 1966. We heard from travelers and on the radio that the Igbo leader, Ojukwu, was planning to divide the country in two, and already the name of the other country was on everyone's lips: Biafra. And then the riots began in faraway towns like Kano and Kaduna—everywhere the Igbos were being hunted down and killed—every day they left the north in busloads for their hometowns in the southeast with what little of their possessions they could gather. There was also a reverse traffic—northerners fleeing the Igbo lands in fear for their lives. And even in remote, unimportant Keti the fires of violence were being lit.

"The Keti Igbos had been here for as long as most people could remember. They had intermarried and prospered, and they even had their own chief, Mr. Eme, who had the biggest shop in the market, where he sold dresses and shoes and all sorts of men's clothes. I remember the day the violence came to Keti. That day the town crier announced that all children should be kept indoors because the streets were not safe. Everyone could see it but the Igbos themselves. One man, his name was LaMasa, when he heard the crier, ran to Mr. Eme to warn him, but Mr. Eme did not believe him, he reported him to the police as a troublemaker and he was detained. The fights began at exactly six in the evening. This is how it happened: Mr. Eme had a local friend, his name was Ando, and that day Ando went to visit Eme as usual. Mr. Eme had a gun, a rifle, which he always kept on the floor beside his chair in the living room. Well, as they talked Ando suddenly swooped down and snatched the gun, he rushed out with it to where a crowd was waiting. It had all been planned. That was how Mr. Eme was killed. Yes, I was there, I saw it with my own two eyes. It was not a pretty sight, I tell you.

"Haruna here was with me. Eme was stabbed and clubbed to death. His broken body was left in the gutter that ran before his house. The people had gone totally wild. It was as if they were a different people. Eme's brother, John, was hacked to death in the shop—he was just closing the shop for the day when the people fell on him. That was the day the fights began in Keti. It went on all night. Some of them managed to escape to neighboring villages, some were hidden by friends, but most were killed."

Toma went on, "About a year after the killings, after the civil war had started and many of our older brothers had gone off to join the army, Haruna and I were wandering around in the village when we ran into the district officer and his entourage of policemen. The DO stopped us and gave us five shillings each and told

us if we wanted more we should report to the council tree early
the next morning. His man took down our names. We reported
to the council tree early the next day, and from the council tree
we were all taken to the Mai's palace where seven trucks waited
to take us away. A clerk read out our names, and when you heard
your name you'd be given ten shillings and told to board the
truck. There were over two hundred of us, all from Keti and the
neighboring villages. Most of us were under fifteen, but nobody
bothered to find out our age. From the palace we were taken to
the state capital. We were in the state capital for a couple of
days—that was where we took our medical and physical tests.
We that passed the test were taken to Bauchi, where we stayed
for about two weeks. We were so excited we didn't even have
time to think of the war that awaited us. We were young, we had
money in our pockets, and we were seeing the world.

"Then one day the army trucks came to take us to Kaduna,
where our training would begin with the Fifth Battalion. From
Kaduna we were sent to Lagos—that was where our original
group was separated. Haruna and I were posted to the Federal
Guards at the Dodan Barracks. We didn't get to the front till
months later. By then the war had progressed deep into the
Biafran territory. Benin and all the midwestern states had been
recaptured by the federal troops. We were in Benin for two
months, and then we went on to Asaba, from Asaba we went on
to Omarina, from Omarina we moved on and on.

"Now let me tell you of my first day at the front. It was at
Omarina—a small, insignificant town, but we had to take it to
progress farther. We went to the trenches in the evening, when
the sun was almost setting and the dense jungle around had
become dark and heavy with mist and shadows. We relieved the
soldiers in the trenches and waited for the enemy to make the
first move. There were two men to a trench, each trench five feet
away from the next one. The enemy didn't attack till early in the
morning when the shadows and mist had started lifting from the
trees—that was when we heard the guns. A funny thing happened

at that moment—one of the men in the trench next to mine, a young boy, really, younger than me, started shouting and asking for permission to go into the bushes to relieve himself. He really had to go. Our commander, a young lieutenant who had been at the front before, turned on him furiously and told him to do it right there in the trench. I can't forget it, he was crying and mewling like a cat as he took off his belt and pulled off his trousers and did his business right there. The rest of us hardly noticed him. The fighting was on.

"The villages were always deserted by the time we got there, though once in a while we found the old and the sick who couldn't escape. Sometimes we only found piles of corpses. Sometimes a few people would come out of the bushes and give themselves up voluntarily, forced out of hiding by hunger. My most lasting memory of the war happened in 1970, when I lost my leg. We were in Ughelli and that year it rained like it had never rained before, for months and months, nonstop. We couldn't go into our trenches because the ground was flooded up to knee level; the wounded had to be taken away by canoe. We were days and days in the water and mud, like fish. We had to make a sort of frame with tree branches, four sticks stuck in the mud upright, then more on top across to form a surface on which we'd lie, that was how we slept, but only when the fighting eased, which was not often. The rest of the time we were in the mud with the snakes and rats. I still remember the rats. Our legs rotted inside our boots. When you removed your boot it'd come off with large layers of your sole. Many men became cripples because of that. Some just went mad and dashed toward the enemy trenches, screaming, and were cut down. Others shot themselves in the head with their own guns.

"I lost my leg on a mission. Three of us were sent to blow up a bridge. We, er, we failed. Our sergeant was shot, the other man, a private like me, was taken prisoner. I was lucky—I was shot in the leg, but I escaped by lying low for a whole day in a crag in the riverbank. I was able to get away in the night."

The party was the highest point of Haruna's return; after that everything gradually settled into humdrum routine. He woke up, he bathed, he ate, he slept, and some days, mostly market days, Toma and his other civil war buddies would bring a jar of beer and they'd drink together and sing war songs and laugh. But Uncle Haruna's mind refused to remember anything that had happened before the day he turned up in Keti. The doctor from the hospital who came on occasion to see him said Haruna's mind had withdrawn into itself and would eventually recover with time.

The twins would stand on the veranda, leaning over the half wall, watching their uncle's face, wondering what he thought of as he sat before his hut, smiling at anyone passing. They were amazed at how swiftly his hands moved as he shelled peanuts or made rope in the evenings with Auntie Marina. Beside him stood a basin of water in which he soaked the hemp before taking it out and running the length through his hands, squeezing out the water, feeling the fiber for breakages before bringing the ends together and twisting. He did it so easily, as if his hands were seeking to prove that though his mind may have forgotten the past, the hands hadn't. Sometimes, mostly at night, bits of memory would come back to him, then all night he'd pace up and down in his room, talking loudly as if there were another person in the room with him, and then finally there would be silence. The doctor said he was losing his mind. After such recollections he hardly ate the next morning, he'd sit and stare into space, not smiling as usual, and gradually everyone got used to his sporadic moodiness and learned to ignore it.

But what impressed the twins most was how everyone in the village still talked about him, about his adventures; imaginary exploits and heroisms were attributed to him by even those who had never seen him. Most of the people simply referred to him as "Soja." And they'd stop the twins and ask them, "How is Soja today?" "Give Soja our regards."

This was the kind of fame they dreamt of.

One day, when he was alone in the house with his uncle, Mamo went to him and pulled a stool and sat down facing him. He dipped his hand into the sack of peanuts beside him and began to shell.

"Good afternoon, Uncle," he said.

"Hello, Twin."

"Tell me about the war," Mamo said, smiling.

"The war," he said, mirroring Mamo's smile. But wariness had crept into his face; Mamo had seen this happen before whenever anyone mentioned the war.

"Yes, the Biafran war."

His face assumed a distant look; his hand slowed down in its rhythmic shelling.

"Did you shoot people?"

He said nothing, and when Mamo got tired of waiting for his reply, he got up to leave.

"I had a friend, you know. We traveled together. Chris."

Mamo stopped and turned back. He had spoken, clearly. The last time Mamo had heard him speak this clearly was when he appeared at the gate in his tattered clothes and with his lips all broken and bloody.

Mamo returned to him and said, "Where did you go to?"

"Africa."

After a long pause, Mamo asked, "Who is Chris?"

But Haruna had returned to shelling peanuts, the vacuous look back on his face. Mamo knew it would be useless to try to make him talk. And that was how Haruna's life droned on and on, shelling peanuts and weaving rope and staring into space, till he committed suicide six months later. There was nothing interesting or spectacular about the occasion—he woke up, he ate, he made rope, he ate, he slept, then early the next morning Auntie Marina found him hanging from the flame tree in the backyard. She cut him down and put him on his bed face up, as if he were merely sleeping, with the sheet up to his chin, before going to call Lamang.

It was at the burial, listening to the graveside orations delivered by Haruna's friends and family, about his kindness, and his loyalty, and above all his dedication to his fatherland, that the twins finally decided on what to do.

"We could be famous as soldiers," they told each other. And in their eager, fifteen-year-old minds they saw themselves on some distant battlefield, surrounded by dead bodies, some of which they had killed, and only themselves standing, masters of all they surveyed; and far away in the villages, which they had liberated from some evil tyrant, hidden by dusk and the smoke of battle—the villages all resembled Keti—the women waited to welcome them with garlands. Then, after achieving fame and wealth, they'd return to Keti as living legends.

But the months passed and still they waited, scared to take the bold step of running away from home. They waited until one day when they saw an advertisement in a newspaper their father brought home, hidden somewhere in the center. Mamo came across it as he idly turned the pages: the army was recruiting in the state capital. Accompanying the text was the picture of a young soldier, his uniform ironed to a crisp, his gun slung over his shoulder carelessly as if it were only a walking stick.

It was time to go.

the bridge at the abattoir

THEY LEFT home on a rainy morning in September. The dawn was as dark as midnight, they could hear the rain and wind twisting and uprooting the cornstalks in the yard outside their window. Their room was in semidarkness, illuminated by a single candle, which flickered and almost died out whenever LaMamo opened the window louvers to peer out into the darkness.

"It won't stop," he kept muttering. "This is the kind of rain that goes on for days. I told you we should have left earlier. . . ."

"Hey," Mamo said, rising from the bed and putting his ear against the door, "listen."

Footsteps, then the sound of the front door opening. Their father was awake already, most likely on his way to the toilet in the backyard.

Saying goodbye to their father was not a part of their plan.

By now the distance between the twins and their father was at its farthest, and because of that, they realized, there was really nothing they could do to hurt him. He only spent about a week at home every month, and whenever he came back he'd look at them with astonishment, as if remembering suddenly that he had two sons. He always struggled to remember their names, and when he did remember, he invariably mixed them up even though they were not identical. The only person they would have said goodbye to was Auntie Marina, but they knew that if they did, her tears, like chains, would tie them to the earth, and they wouldn't be able to fly. They left her a note.

It was almost five A.M.; they had planned to be out by four A.M. to catch the bus that stopped twice daily at the village, at six-fifteen A.M. and again at six-fifteen P.M., on its way to the state capital. The bus stop was on the other side of the river, about thirty minutes' walk—maybe forty minutes in the rain.

"We wait," Mamo said, going back to the bed and flopping into it. Beside him was a canvas bag containing all their travel gear: clothes, a change of shoes, a pouch full of his medicines, a few tattered books, and their school and birth certificates. In Mamo's pocket was their entire savings, three hundred naira, secreted from money given to them by relations, their father's business friends, and occasionally by their father himself when he was in one of his expansive moods.

"We will surely miss the bus," LaMamo said. He went and threw open the window. Mamo shielded the candle flame with his palm. Behind the low compound wall was the mango grove— it was invisible, covered in foliage and shadows and the solid sound of rain on leaves and earth.

"Then we leave in the evening."

"No, we leave now. We can still make it."

LaMamo picked up the bag and was out the door in a second. Mamo hung back a little longer, looking around the small room, at LaMamo's paintings and sketches stuck on the off-white walls with long strips of cellophane tape, the few novels on the table against the wall, the two identical wooden boxes under the beds with their clothes in them, a carton in a corner filled with old books and other odds and ends. A twinge of panic gripped him, but it passed and he joined his brother in the hallway. Outside, it was tar-black, and they had to feel their way down the veranda steps and into the rain and mud. Though they couldn't see, they knew when they passed the mud kitchen to their right, and the hut next to it, and when they got to the gate their hands unerringly found the handle. Outside the compound the wind was fiercer; they stood against the wall, facing the dark wet grove through which they must pass to get to the road. The rain pelted them, the water seeped into their shirts at the collars, and soon, despite their plastic rain-coats, they were wet to the skin.

"We should have brought a flashlight," Mamo said.

"I can go back and get it—" LaMamo began, but Mamo had already started moving.

"It is too late. Let us hold hands so that we don't get sepa-rated."

But holding hands made progress difficult, for even when they were finally out of the grove the darkness didn't abate—all open spaces in the village had been solidly planted with corn and sorghum; it was what the village survived on before the major harvest from the bush farms in September and October. They burrowed through the wet, head-high plants in a single file, with LaMamo in front and the elder twin behind, using his brother's back as a shield against the leaves and rain. Whenever lightning pierced the sky they saw all around them cornstalks lying flat on the ground, broken and uprooted by the wind.

Most of the footpath was now a gulley in which a river ran, gurgling and seething in the darkness. The church building to their right hulked in the dark, leaping into detail whenever light-ning flashed; the branches of the huge neem tree in front of the church hall twisted and turned in the wind like arms reaching out to grasp. The house after the church was their uncle Iliya's. A few feet to the front and left of the compound, right by the path, was a small hut nestled under a sycamore tree. A window opened and closed in the wind, a light shone in the window. Their cousin, Asabar, who was part of the escape plan, was wait-ing for them. Through the narrow window they could see his thin, fully clothed form sprawled across his bed, his mud-covered shoes dangling over the edge.

LaMamo banged loudly on the door. After a long while Asabar croaked, "Who is it?" He sounded drunk.

"It is us, the twins. Open the door."

Asabar threw open the door and stood in the entrance, swaying from side to side, peering at the two forms that quickly
pushed past him into the room. A paraffin lantern splashed its
sickly yellow glow around the room. Asabar was wet, his shirt
slick with mud—he must have just returned from outside where
he had fallen in the mud many times.

"It is raining," Asabar shouted at the top of his voice. "It is raining, raining—"

"You've been drinking," LaMamo said angrily. He turned to his
brother. "We can't go with him, he is drunk."

"What . . . but?" Asabar spluttered, looking from one twin to the
other. "What do you mean, I can't come with you? I am not . . .
very drunk."

"Don't you know how serious this is? Can't you stay sober for
just one day . . . ?" LaMamo went on angrily. "We are leaving
home, it is raining, and we are almost late for the bus, and . . .
and . . ."

"And . . . and . . . and . . . so what?" Asabar mimicked and burst
out laughing, swaying and leaning against the rough red mud
wall.

"The rain will sober him up," Mamo said.

They left. Asabar didn't take much with him, just a shirt and a
pair of trousers in a plastic bag. He was babbling, going from one
twin to the other, pulling at their arms as he spoke, oblivious of the
rain, which had slowed to a drizzle by now. The twins ignored him,
walking fast, their faces lowered, forcing him to stop talking in
order to catch up. A little distance from the house, he turned and
stared back at his father's compound, now faintly visible in the distance, and then he covered his face and dramatically sobbed into
his hands. "Bye, my hometown, my mother, brothers, sisters. I may
never see you again in this life. . . . Tomorrow by this time we will
be in the city, in the army, and after that . . . after that . . ."

"Keep going," LaMamo said.

"Yes . . . after that we will keep going!"

Mamo wrote many years later that as soon as they left Asabar's room he had felt deep inside him that something was going to go wrong. Each step they took he expected the wind bearing a huge tree to knock them into darkness, or some heavenly fire to fall on them and incinerate them. None of that happened, though— until the river.

The Keti River ran from north to south on the eastern side of the village, and this morning it roared with liquid rage. The tall reeds and sugarcane stalks on both banks were flat on the ground, half buried in mud. The narrow footbridge that provided the only passage across the river in the rainy seasons now lay on the opposite bank, its iron and wood and concrete uprooted and scattered in the emerging light of dawn, as if a giant hand had played with it before throwing away the bits in boredom.

"The bridge is gone," Asabar said, pointing at the broken concrete pillars rising from the riverbed. The rain and blustery wind had started to sober him up. The footbridge had been the short- est path to the bus stop, about ten minutes' walk on the other side. The other bridge—the motor bridge—was almost thirty minutes' walk away from here, and then it was another twenty minutes from there to the bus stop. They couldn't make it before the bus left. They stood on the bank, listening to the water—in the rising light their wet faces looked suffused with frustration.

"We'll get the evening bus," Mamo said slowly, resignedly, speaking almost to himself. "Before noon the water level will have dropped, and then we can ford it."

They decided to wait in the old abandoned abattoir not far from the river. Mamo led the way through the wet elephant grass to the huge empty building. The abattoir had been the last local government chairman's attempt to catapult Keti into modern times. The building consisted of a cavernous central hall where the butchering and quartering used to be done. There were over- head tanks, water taps, conveyors, and a slaughter line capable of processing over twenty cattle per hour. But only a year after the commissioning of the building by the state governor, the butchers had quietly deserted it and returned to the old meat market. They said the new abattoir was too far from the village center, and they had lost most of their customers because of that. Now the structure stood lonely and derelict, most of its removable fixtures "borrowed" by the villagers to use in their homes.

"Look out for snakes," LaMamo said as they stepped into the gloomy hall. Asabar halted at the door and declared, "I will wait out here on the steps."

The twins soon joined him on the steps, discouraged from venturing farther into the hall by the darkness and the eerie scurrying and slithering sounds made by rodents and reptiles. The rain had stopped by now. Far away beyond the trees and cornstalks and reeds that were gradually emerging as the clouds frittered away in the sky, they could hear the roar of water in the river and the frogs and the chirping insects. To the west the village lay not more than two miles away on the foothills, slowly coming into view through the rain mist.

They had not been on the steps more than an hour when Mamo started to shiver, his forehead wet, not with water but with sweat. He pulled the raincoat tighter around his narrow shoulders and hugged his knees to keep warm.

"Listen," Asabar said, raising his hand, cocking his head. "The river is quiet."

LaMamo stood up and descended the steps; he turned his ear toward the river. "You are right."

It was almost eight A.M. now. Out of view from the footpaths, they could hear the voices of farmers on their way to check the extent of damage to their crops. Asabar stood up and joined LaMamo, but as Mamo made to join them, his knees buckled and he fell back onto the hard concrete step.

"Are you okay?" LaMamo asked, rushing forward.

"I feel awful," Mamo said, his voice betraying his frustration. "I am feverish . . . but I'll be fine." He was cold despite the sheen of sweat on his forehead; his teeth chattered audibly when he spoke. LaMamo went and slowly sat beside him, dropping the canvas bag between his legs.

"Maybe we should go back now," he said, looking at his brother, concern and disappointment conflicting with each other in his voice.

"I will be fine. You two will just have to support me when we cross the river, that is all," Mamo said. But soon he could not even sit down. His leg and arm joints were on fire, his belly heaved with nausea; he stretched out on the cold step, all the while muttering to the two standing over him, "Just give . . . me . . . one . . . minute."

Asabar looked toward the river, then back to LaMamo. "What do we do now?"

"We take him inside. It is cold out here."

They helped Mamo to his feet and into the building; he slumped to the floor and onto his side as soon as they set him down against the wall.

Asabar and LaMamo sat on either side of him. None of them was a stranger to Mamo's sickle-cell anemia, and in their hearts they both knew that this might well be the end of their adventure. The most important thing now was to get him home before he grew worse.

Asabar asked, "How long does the attack last?"

"It is called crisis."

"How long does the crisis last?"

"It depends."

LaMamo absently punched the bag between his outstretched legs. He opened the bag and took out a shirt and a pair of trousers. "We need to change him into these dry things."

As they stripped him to his underpants and changed him, Mamo grunted and sat up. "I feel better already."

When Asabar stepped outside, LaMamo said again, "We are going back. We will plan for another day. I am sure the army will recruit again next year. . . ."

"I said I feel better already," Mamo said stubbornly, looking at the open door through which Asabar had disappeared. "I'll be fine before the evening bus comes." He took out some tablets from the sachet in the canvas bag and began to chew on them.

Asabar returned. "You can see the farmers if you stand by the window." LaMamo joined him at the window. They could hear excited voices coming through the trees and tall grasses.

"They are going to see the washed-out bridge."

They went back to their earlier positions and sat. Above them, in the cusps of the massive iron girders, house martins had built their nests, from which they'd swoop down twittering and fly out of the gaping window with uncanny accuracy. The empty, vandalized doors and windows exaggerated the size of the giant hall. Mamo closed his eyes and hallucinated about goats and cows being slaughtered; he heard the hall fill with their terrified cries, amplified a million times by the hollow, cavernous space, he saw blood splattering against the walls as the slaughterer efficiently slit their throats. He opened his eyes and suddenly his head was clear and he could see the tiniest details in the room: the insects crawling in the dark corners, the line of light on the tables and walls, even the old, forgotten bloodstains on the floor; he could smell the feces, the sweat, the blood, the urine. Gradually the air was warming up; by afternoon the sun would have boiled out the water from the earth and leaves and pools and the moisture would hang in the air, making everyone sweaty and sluggish. Mamo was propped up on one elbow, his face shiny with sweat, trying very hard to mask his pain; LaMamo was staring up at the birds in the girders. They waited.

An hour later Mamo was flat on his back, gasping through his parched, cracked lips, his head turning from side to side with the pain in his joints. LaMamo removed his shirt and began to fan him, all the time muttering, "We need to get help. . . ."

Asabar watched, saying nothing. When he got tired of sitting and watching, he went to the window and stared out toward the river. LaMamo suddenly stood up and joined him at the window, and without a word he jumped out through the window and headed toward the river. Asabar turned toward the prone, writhing Mamo behind him, and then he called after LaMamo, "Where are you going?"

"To the river," LaMamo called back over his shoulder, not slowing down. He disappeared behind the tall grass and a while later he was back, his shirt in his hand, soaked and dripping with water. He pressed the shirt to his brother's searing-hot forehead. After a while Mamo opened his eyes and sat up.

"Listen," he mumbled, "I will be fine. I will just lie here and wait till it gets cooler and then I will go home. But I want you to go on. There's no need for all of us to return home. . . ."

Asabar said nothing, but he kept looking at LaMamo, waiting for him to agree or disagree with his brother, but his eager eyes were ablaze with his preference; he paced up and down for a while, then he went outside. LaMamo stood up and followed Asabar to the head of the steps. A vulture, its wings hanging wet and heavy by its sides, stooped on the last step, drying off. LaMamo viciously threw a stone at it and watched it scamper into the bush in short ungainly hops; he went down the steps, then back up again, a huge scowl on his face. They heard Mamo's steps behind them and when they turned he was leaning against the doorframe, hugging it for support, his face contorted.

"This is—" LaMamo began, but his brother cut him short.

"Don't argue, just go. I really don't mind. Just go now . . . and when you are settled and have a place . . . then I will join you."

"Well . . . okay," LaMamo said dully. He rushed into the abattoir and came out with the bag. He took out Mamo's things and handed them to him.

"Keep all the money, you'll need it more than me," Mamo said. He was now seated on the top step, his face downcast, and the others could see how hard he was trying to hold back his tears. They shook his hand solemnly and started quickly toward the river. He watched them till they disappeared behind the trees, and then he lowered his head and let the tears roll down his cheeks.

A while later he looked up, startled by the sound of quick footsteps. He composed his face, hastily wiping away the tears, thinking it was some farmer on his way home. But it was LaMamo standing over him. He also had tears in his eyes. Mamo stood up and silently the twins embraced, then LaMamo said, "I will send for you as soon as I am settled. I promise. Don't fall sick again."

Mamo watched his brother disappear through the grass, and in his mind he felt like a prisoner, imprisoned by the village with its vast hills and valleys and rivers. He felt certain, more than ever before, that he was doomed to die young.

He sat on the steps till the sun had gone down behind the hills and the air had turned chilly and the birds and insects had started singing their goodnight songs, and then he stood up and started for home.

the silent listener to
every conversation

CHRIST IS THE HEAD OF THIS HOUSE, THE UNSEEN GUEST AT
EVERY MEAL, THE SILENT LISTENER TO EVERY CONVERSATION.
The words were engraved on a blue plastic plaque above the living room door; they were gilded with lush leafy vines twisted
around each letter, while a red apple, its skin waxy and tempting,
formed the full-stop at the end of the sentence.

As a child, soon after he had learned to read, Mamo had built
a narrative around the words on the plaque: he'd imagine a fam-
ished, ghostly Christ hovering unseen as the family ate, occasionally stretching a nail-scarred hand over a family member's
shoulder to pick up a piece of chicken, or an akara, from a bowl.
Sometimes, mostly when he lay sick with fever, his delirium
would cause him to imagine footsteps outside the door, and the
silent-listener Christ standing with held breath, an ear against
the keyhole, silently listening.

Lamang noisily cleared his throat and asked, "Where did you
think you were going to?"

"Timbuktu," Mamo answered dully, uttering the first thing
that came to his mind. A week had passed since the day at the
abattoir, and this was the first time he had emerged from his
room, the first time his father had confronted him on that subject. For seven days he had lain in his room, feverish, throwing
up anything Auntie Marina forced him to eat, ignoring his
father's restless pacing in the hallway and Auntie Marina's gentle

but insistent questions about his brother's whereabouts. At night his febrile dreams were filled with images of the roaring river, the broken bridge, the tumbledown abattoir with vultures screaming shrilly on its doorstep, and then the river again, bearing away his brother, faster and faster, and no matter how fast he ran on the bank he couldn't keep up with the water's swiftness and he had to stand helpless and watch his brother disappear under the tumbling waves.

Last night he had not had the dream; in the morning the fever had abated and he felt strong enough to go to the bathroom and take a bath. After the bath he had forced down a mushy concoction of beans and spinach cooked in palm oil, which Auntie Marina always made for him when he was convalescing. Now his father had summoned him to the living room for a talk. They had sat quietly for over ten minutes, Lamang pretending to be going through a book in his hand, letting the tension mount. This was his tried and tested third degree, guaranteed to turn the twins to jelly before he even began to speak, but today Mamo hardly noticed the heavy silence, the stony frown, the menacing sound of foot-tapping under the table. His mind was blank, his mouth sour with the fever's aftertaste, his eyes yellow and fixed on the plastic plaque on the wall behind his father.

After a long silence Lamang repeated, "Timbuktu?"

Slowly, mechanically, Mamo improvised: "We wanted to travel . . . by boat . . . on the Niger, like Mungo Park . . . but in the opposite direction, from Bussa up to Bamako, then by land to Timbuktu. . . ." He avoided his father's eyes as he spoke. Out of the corner of his eye he saw his father's expression change from surprise to anger to bewilderment.

"Mungo . . . who?" Lamang said at last when Mamo fell silent.

"Park. The explorer. He was a—"

"I don't care," Lamang said, now unable to keep his voice down. "Just tell me where your brother is."

"On his way to Timbuktu."

"Why?" Lamang finally asked, his voice losing its harshness.

"We just wanted to go," Mamo said, almost convinced by his own story. He could already picture his brother and his cousin in a canoe on the wide, shallow Niger, a magnificent sunset behind them. Lamang was silent for a long while, and Mamo waited, enjoying the perplexity on his father's face. A contemplative frown gradually spread over Lamang's face. It was as if he were seeing Mamo for the first time.

"Well," Lamang said finally, attempting a small, carefree laugh, but his voice was angry, aimed to hurt, "you are lucky you didn't go far, with your weak and useless body, otherwise we would now be telling a different story. What do you think people would say if you had died out there? They would blame me for not caring for you, for driving you out of my house. Tell me, is there anything that you lack in this house? Is there anything I haven't provided for you and your brother?"

We have everything, Mamo felt like answering, *except your love*.

"But why am I asking you all this? It is not as if you have the mind to understand what I am saying. Anyone stupid enough to want to go to Timbuktu by boat is . . . is . . . has no mind. Now listen carefully, I am not angry with you, I just hope you have learned something from all this, and we won't have any more trouble from you in the future. What I want you to do is to send word immediately to your brother, tell him the same thing I told you, that I am not angry and that I won't punish him for running away. Just tell him to come back immediately. Do you understand? Immediately."

Mamo could see how hard his father was trying not to bang on the table, not to lean on his toes as if ready to pounce. "I don't know how to get in touch with him," he said dully. He was thoroughly enjoying the thrust and parry with his father and it was all he could do not to let his triumph show on his face.

"But surely you have some means of getting in touch. Did you not make plans . . . ?"

"No. We parted in a hurry. He said he would write."

Lamang moved impatiently in his seat, and lines slowly

appeared on his forehead as if planted there by a brushstroke. At last he said, "Write? Write? When? You . . . the elder . . . I thought you had some sense. . . . Now he is gone, and you know how stupid he can be. I blame you for this . . . just remember that. If anything happens to him, it is on you. . . ." Lamang abandoned all restraint and banged on the table with his fist as he shouted the last words. Beneath the door Mamo saw a shadow thrown by Auntie Marina's feet—she was waiting outside, poised to jump in and intervene if things got physical. He was her favorite, just as LaMamo was Lamang's favorite. On the rare occasions that Lamang had deigned to notice his children, it was LaMamo he noticed. He'd sometimes brag to his friends about the striking resemblance between them. In the picture on the table, the only family picture in the house, taken when the twins were five years old, Lamang held LaMamo on his lap, Marina sat to the left with her scarf almost covering her face, and Mamo's face was a speck over her right shoulder. From very early Mamo had learned to keep his sick and awkward body in the background, learned to observe from the sidelines. He often thought of himself as the real silent listener to every conversation.

He kept to his room after the interview, perfecting his already faultless art of avoiding his father. His illness lingered, but this time it wasn't only sickle-cell anemia—there was also a mental torpor that refused to be shaken off. He felt a nagging sense of guilt whenever his father's words came back to him, playing as the soundtrack to his recurrent dream of the river bearing his brother away: "If anything happens to him, it is on you. . . ." He had never had many friends before, just his brother and Asabar, but now, really alone for the first time in his life, he realized just how much he had depended on his brother for companionship. He ate very little and read ravenously, sometimes picking up a piece of paper on the ground as he passed, stopping to read it before moving on. His father would look up with a waiting expression whenever Mamo passed him in the living room, as if expecting some news of LaMamo, and at such moments Mamo felt tempted to confess the truth, but he always stopped himself in time. To confess would be to forgo his position of superiority by sharing his knowledge with his father. He didn't want to put his father's mind at rest; what would be the point of that? For once he wanted to be the torturer, his father the tortured. After all, he was sure his father was not concerned about his son's fate in faraway Timbuktu, only with what people would say about his son running away.

asabar

ASABAR RETURNED exactly one month and two days after that rainy day at the abattoir. It was late afternoon and Mamo was in his room engrossed in a book, straining his eyes in the wavering candlelight, when he heard Auntie Marina's voice outside his door. "Go in. He is in there."

Then the door opened and Asabar emerged from behind the flimsy curtain.

"Asabar?" Mamo shouted, jumping out of bed, grabbing his cousin's arm, and shaking it vigorously. "Asabar!"

Asabar did not display the same enthusiasm. His face was hangdog; his sensitive poet's eyes looked hollow and exhausted, as if he were haunted by memories of a harrowing experience.

"I came back," he said before Mamo could say anything more. He went and sat on the chair by the table, twisting his body so that he faced the center of the room where Mamo stood.

"Where is LaMamo?"

"I left him at the Chad border. He was going to join the rebel army in Chad. I returned because I . . . I . . . just wanted to come back."

"The Chad border," Mamo repeated, waiting to hear more. He went and sat on his bed.

They had reached the state capital late that day, Asabar said. They spent the night in a shed at the bus station, and early the next morning they reported to the army barracks where they met other young men eager to join the army, but they had been unceremoniously sent away by the recruiting sergeant when he saw the dates on their birth certificates. The sergeant had bunched up the certificates in his huge fist and waved them in their faces, his mustache bristling with annoyance.

"So you tink say you fit come here waste army time, abi? You dey craze? We say we want eighteen years minimum, and you come here with sixteen years minimum—you tink say army job na for small pikin? Oya, get out before I count three. One . . . two . . . Are you still there? I go handle you o . . ."

They loitered about the state capital for two days, slowly recovering from their disillusionment, uncertain what to do next. They even contemplated returning home, but then LaMamo came up with the idea of traveling up the River Niger. "We used to dream about doing that someday, Mamo and me," he said to Asabar. "Now we can do it for real." He shook Asabar by the shoulder. "We are free, there's no one to stop us. Think about it, Asabar, think."

They took a night bus to Kaduna, but while in Kaduna they abandoned the plan of going up the River Niger. An old trader they met on the bus had laughed at them when they revealed their plan to him. "The river, to Mali. *Haba kai!* You must be a pair of dreamers. No one travels by boat nowadays. Besides, most of the river has dried up. Why don't you go to Chad, from Katsina? From there you can get to Mali by road, it is not too far. I have been that way myself before."

They stayed two weeks in Kaduna, sleeping with the street boys in rough shelters at the bus station at night, admiring the buildings and the cars and the incredible mass of people in the streets by day. Their money ran out very quickly and they survived by working as market hands, helping to load and off-load cattle and corn from trucks, cleaning the animal enclosures, and fetching water from the impossibly deep wells for the water troughs. It was the hardest work either of them had ever done in their lives, but they had no option. They ate once a day, in the evenings, buying millet porridge and akara at the roadside food stalls. It was at one of the food stalls that they overheard a group of three starry-eyed Fulani boys talking of going up north to Chad to join rebel soldiers. They were also adventurers like the two cousins, eager to travel and see the world beyond their little villages. One of them, Idrissa, sounded more educated than the others. He said the money in the army was good and the fighting minimal, and in any case it was not a life sentence, since one could desert at any time one wanted. But by now Asabar was homesick, and the thrill of the escape had long worn thin. When he suggested to LaMamo that they return, LaMamo only looked at Asabar with disgust, which shut him up immediately. Each day LaMamo was becoming more and more aggressive and unpredictable. Sometimes he'd go off by himself and Asabar wouldn't see him again till late at night when he returned to the shelter.

The three youths, Idrissa, Jabbo, and Saleh, told them that there was a small border town north of Katsina where scouts from the Chadian rebel army came monthly to recruit young men. On the truck to Katsina—full of Hausa traders and their goats and chickens and sacks of kola—Asabar's thoughts were as glum as the landscape fleeing past on either side of the road. The roadside villages of thatched mud huts with cattle enclosures behind them were few and far between. Here the earth was bare of greenery, and only sand dunes stretched for miles and miles around; once in a while a desolate, stunted neem tree or cactus would pop up as if in a bid to lend the landscape some color and variety. The landscape only changed when night fell: it became bleaker.

From Katsina they walked on foot to a border village called Iyaka. Their timing was uncanny. They learned from local sources that a scout would be in the village in two days' time. LaMamo was almost delirious with excitement. "At last," he shouted, shaking hands with Idrissa, hugging his cousin, "at last."

In his mind Asabar began to rehearse how to tell LaMamo he was returning home, while all the while he prayed that something would happen to unjoint their plan. But nothing did: the recruiting scout did come as promised. They met him in a thatched mud building, which served as a bar and bore the rather grandiose name El Duniya Hotel, scrawled in chalk on a wooden board before the entrance. The bar was located in the heart of the sandy wasteland, far from the village itself, and was run by a surly Igbo man who banged the drinks on the wooden tables and glowered at the customers as if daring them not to pay. The drinking space was a square enclosure at the back of the mud building, with shaky wooden chairs before shaky wooden tables packed closely together. A small, noisy, smoky generator supplied electricity.

They waited for twenty minutes before the scout came in.

"There he is . . . I think," Idrissa whispered, pointing at the entrance.

The man stood briefly at the entrance, and for a while his face was clearly illuminated by the green lightbulb above: olive-skinned—an Arab or Berber—short hair matted to his head as if he had just taken a shower or used too much oil to slick his hair, a scar deforming the left side of his face from forehead, just missing the eye, to upper lip.

"How old are you?" was the first question he asked Asabar and LaMamo. He spoke in French and Idrissa attempted a translation. He ordered a beer for each of them.

"I speaks English," the scout said, impatiently interrupting Idrissa's hesitant translation, looking very interested. "We likes people speaks good English. How old is you?"

"Almost sixteen," said Asabar

"Eighteen," said LaMamo. He wasn't going to be turned down again on account of age.

"No problems. Is not how old you is, but how strongs," the man said, smiling. "Tomorrow we leaves. We goes to Chad, if you survives Chad, after many monthses, we goes to Libya for more trainings. Comes here by six A.M. tomorrow."

That night Asabar told LaMamo he was returning to Keti.

"This is beginning to sound too dangerous," he said. "We could get killed."

LaMamo was angry. He accused his cousin of cowardice, but Asabar was past caring. By morning LaMamo had cooled down a bit and the two were once more on speaking terms.

"When you get home, tell Mamo I am fine, tell him I will write to him soon," he said, looking almost sad.

Lamang stared straight ahead, his face stony, listening to Asabar repeat his story. He had just returned from the state capital; his black leather case lay on the floor beside him, his cap was still on his head, his white caftan looked as fresh as when he had put it on in the morning. He listened, not saying a word. The only thing he said after Asabar's narration was, "Chad, Libya," and then he sighed.

the wilderness years

MAMO'S SECOND chance to leave Keti came a year later when, one day, a letter with his name on it arrived from the state university. He had been offered a place to study for a degree in history. He wrote a letter accepting the offer that very day, and a month later he was attending classes. And it was as a student that he discovered the kind of anonymity he'd always wanted. The busy city streets and the large student community hid him from view; no more did his father's burning glare follow him around; he was just one among thousands of young, eager faces from all parts of the country lugging books to class and the library every day. He missed Auntie Marina, who had in the past months tried all she could to ease his loneliness with her constant presence and solicitous words, but unsuccessfully; he was too old now to hide in the fantastic architecture of her stories and songs. LaMamo's absence, though never talked about, haunted the house like a ghost that went from room to room, denying them rest.

He missed his brother, and often he'd begin a sentence aloud, calling his brother's name before catching himself, and then he'd marvel at the fact that a time had come in their lives when they were not together. Gradually he began to lose his feeling of joy at his newfound anonymity, and because he didn't have much talent for making friends, he walked around the campus alone, like a waif. He spent most of his time in the classrooms and the library, reading any book that took his fancy, from Plato to Fanon.

He was at the university for only two years, and in those years Mamo returned home only when he needed money for his medicine. During the short breaks when other students eagerly left for home with their parents who had come from all parts of the country to pick them up, he hung out with a group of stragglers who had turned the school hostels into a sort of home, only going to their real homes at the end of the session when their accommodation permit expired. The first year went well, and it seemed as if his new environment was acting as some kind of therapy and he hardly fell ill that year, but then toward the end of his second year things changed drastically: he fell ill just before the sessional exams.

It began innocuously with a slight headache, which he cured with aspirin in the hope that it was nothing but the result of reading late the night before, but the next day it returned, sharper, and again he tried to suppress it with aspirin, determined to endure in silence and not see a doctor till after his exams, which were only two days away. But on the morning of the exams he woke up vomiting, and he had to go to the school clinic for treatment. The clinic occupied three rooms in a row in a rectangular block building. The first was the waiting room, the middle was the doctor's room where he met and treated the patients, and the last was the ward with three narrow beds where seriously sick patients were kept before they were moved to the state hospital.

It was the rainy season, which also meant malaria season, and the clinic was filled with students waiting to receive malaria treatment. Mamo sat in line and when his turn came and he tried to explain to the doctor that his case wasn't malaria but sickle-cell anemia, the old doctor, who should have retired ages ago and who still held the job because he was somebody's relation, looked at him crossly and said, "Young man, are you trying to teach me my job?" and gave him the routine malaria shots of chloroquine and Piriton.

The Piriton knocked him out as soon as he returned to his room and he slept the whole day. The next day he collapsed in the bathroom and had to be carried back to his room. His room-mates tucked him up in bed and rushed off to class to write their exams. When they came back in the afternoon they found him sprawled out on the floor unconscious, his legs and arms swollen. It was the severest crisis he had had since he was a child. His roommates brought him home that night in a char-tered taxi, which Auntie Marina paid for. Unfortunately, when they went back to school none of them remembered to inform the exams office that Mamo had missed his exams due to illness, and so when the results came out a few months later his name was on the list of withdrawn students.

Mamo would come to refer to these years—the years following LaMamo's departure and before Zara's reentry into his life—as his "wilderness years." They were filled with shadowy shapes and fears that left him confused and unable to think clearly. Even his mental diary of hate and fame, which used to give him focus, now only seemed stupid and childish, and he hardly visited its pages again. But he still thought about death, even though, now at twenty, he seemed to have been overlooked by its angel. He was never oblivious to its darting hooded shape, which he some-times caught at the edge of his vision, and never deaf to its con-stantly droning wing beats. His idea of fame was less assured now than it had been before the escape attempt when everything had appeared so clear and simple. Now he knew that his uncle Haruna, despite all the pomp and celebration that had greeted his return, and all the long speeches at his graveside, was not really famous, he was just tragic. But Mamo still believed that fame could give him immortality, only now he didn't know how to achieve fame.

He missed his brother. They had been two parts of the same thing: LaMamo had been the leader who always came up with the wild, edgy ideas, which would then be reviewed and tem-

pered by Mamo's less assertive, reflective nature. But now Mamo
had to do everything by himself, and he was finding it hard to
cope. The letter La Mamo had promised to write had still not
come. He missed the letter even more now that he didn't have
the school library to ease his loneliness. Sometimes, when he
was unable to sleep at night, he'd cross the room to lie on his
brother's bed, and somehow that soothed him.

Only two things happened in these years of wilderness to bring
some kind of spark to his days. One was Asabar's return in the
first year, but that spark did not last long. Asabar did not provide
the companionship Mamo wanted; instead he changed into a
garrulous, drunken, brawling character, always boasting in the
village brewhouses about his days in "the Chadian rebel army
with my cousin LaMamo." Mamo learned to avoid him as much
as possible.

The second spark occurred in the third year when LaMamo's
letter finally arrived. It was full of disconnected ideas and bad
grammar, but it made perfect sense to Mamo as he eagerly ate up
the lines with his eyes. It was two pages long and it repeated
Asabar's account of the journey to the Chadian border and the
meeting with the recruiting scout, then it talked a bit about life
in the Chadian rebel army—but it did so with impatience, as if
to show that the writer's real ambition had been not just to
remain in Chad, but to follow the road to Libya, and after that to
wherever it might lead. He said he was with the rebels only seven
months before five of them were selected to proceed to Libya.
Here the letter became more settled, more detailed:

*A month after we come to Libya I was made a group leader—
there are almost 20 groups, and each groups with 20 people,
men and women and some of the women are really beautiful
too and from different African countries, Arabs and blacks. My
duties as a leader are to lead the cross-country running every
morning, to take charge at drill, and to make sure every one is
happy and to report everyday to the captain. I am not so good*

*at the class work—I wish you are here to help me with it like
you use to do when we are in school.*

*It is a tough life here to be a soldier, and even though I miss
you, I am glad you did not come because it will be bad for your
illness. Sometimes we climb the mountains with 20 pounds on
our back, and sometimes we trek ten miles in the desert in the
heat with only one liter of water.*

*I am not complaining though because we also learn many
good things here—I now know all the names of African countries by head and the names of important cities and there pop-
ulation and some of there histories also I can read map and do
so many things. Our teachers tell us how important it is to get
education if we are to become future African leaders. At night
we have the political classes—important people come all the
time to speak to us. They talk about African freedom, about
capitalism and socialism and esploitation of people by other
people and how Africa must be free, and we as volunteers must
be wiling to even give our lives to save Africa. It is really
important because we cannot continue to live like slaves even
after independence from colonization—look at many African
countries, even our country Nigeria, our leaders are just pup-
pets of the Western powers. That is what Charles Taylor says to
us. He is one of the people that come to speak to us. Soon
Gaddafi the President of Libya himself will come here. But
soon we will be leaving the camp to face a real action—we
have been here almost over one year now. I hope you are fine,
and Auntie Marina, and I know that one day I will come back
home so that we can leave together when I have a place of my
own. Give everybody my greetings. You can't write to me
because I cannot give you my adress here and even this letter I
posted it by smuggling it out and we will be leaving camp soon
to face action, but I will write to you again.*

Your brother,
LaMamo

PS
I have included a sketch of the camp and the desert here, and the hills in the distance. The view of the hills sometimes reminded me of the hills at home.

Mamo did not show his father the letter. As far as he was concerned, his father had not shown any sign that his son's absence was a cause of pain to him; in fact, he had not mentioned it again since after Asabar's return. Mamo folded the letter and kept it in a book by his bed to read on the nights when he couldn't go to sleep.

light fantastic

IN 1982 electricity came to Keti, and it was also the year that Lamang decided to go into politics. The military, after decades of systematically running the country into the ground, had at last handed over power to the civilians, and one of the first promises made by the local politicians was to bring electric power to Keti. And surprisingly they kept their promise. After only a few weeks the villagers, especially the well-off, began to discover that electricity, apart from providing power, could also be a status symbol. They did this by installing two, sometimes three lightbulbs on cross poles before their houses, literally setting the entrance to their houses alight, and then leaving the bulbs to blaze, day and night, till they expired. The villagers called this prodigal display "electric power."

But it was Lamang, with his businessman's eye, who first saw how electric power could be converted into political power. First, instead of the fifty-watt electric bulbs sold in the village shops, he bought the longest fluorescent tube he could find in the supermarkets in the state capital and strung it up on a cross before the compound gate, and then he bought a television box, a twelve-inch black-and-white Sony, and turned the front of his house into a free viewing center for the village.

Mamo was returning from a long walk in the dusk when, as he came out of a turning that led to the compound gate, he saw a large crowd right before the gate. Half of the crowd was seated on the ground, forming a semicircle, as if readying for a group photo, all facing the flickering TV screen, chattering excitedly, pointing at the moving, speaking, singing images. The TV rested on a wooden table, a power cord feeding it from somewhere inside the house. Mamo stood on the fringe of the crowd, his eyes not on the screen but on the excited faces: they were neighbors and passersby and all sorts of idlers. The men stood while the children sat in the front, jostling and pushing for the best positions. Most of the people were seeing the magic box for the first time. The man next to him wasn't even jabbering—his mouth hung open, and every once in a while he gave an excited giggle, clapping his hands loudly.

On the grainy, wobbly screen a couple danced a ballet, and when the man lifted the woman and threw her up into the air, catching her deftly as she descended, the crowd cheered. The enraptured man beside Mamo nudged him roughly in the ribs and said, "Look at their hands, see how soft their palms are."

"Yes."

"I bet they've never done a day's hard work in their lives, eh? Now, if you threw a hoe before them they'd take off, they'd think it is a snake. Ha! Ha!"

Mamo turned and went into the house.

△ ▽ △

There were voices in the living room. Mamo recognized his uncle's voice. Uncle Iliya, Asabar's father, was deep in conversation with Lamang, and the two hardly looked up when Mamo passed them on his way to his room. But soon their voices began to rise, and from his room Mamo could tell that his uncle was getting impatient with whatever Lamang was saying.

"Then what did you call me for? I thought you wanted my advice."

"Of course I do," Lamang said.

"Well, that is what I am giving you, take it or leave it."

"I just want to do some good to the community. . . ."

"Then stay a businessman. I don't see why you have to be a politician also. As a businessman there's so much you can do. What's the matter with you, why are you so restless, why can't you settle down, marry, have a family?" Uncle Iliya said with anger and with resignation, as if this wasn't the first time they were having this conversation, as if he already knew what his brother's answer would be.

Uncle Iliya was Lamang's senior by five years, he was the only person Mamo knew who could talk to his father in that tone of voice and get away with it. Mamo had heard that it was Uncle Iliya who had dissuaded his father from marrying Saraya after Tabita's death—Lamang had been willing to marry her, even with her strange illness. Iliya had pointed out to him how the whole village was talking about the two of them. There were even rumors, which were of course nonsensical, that she had used witchcraft to kill both her husband and Tabita, and that if Lamang married her the village would turn its back on them and that would be the end of them both. He had advised him to find someone else, not only for his sake, but also for that of his children. The argument had worked on Lamang because he was an ambitious man and anything that could turn the community against him, and so stand in the way of his upward mobility, must be avoided—but up to now he had been unable to find a replacement for Saraya.

"I am telling you of my intentions because you are my brother and I didn't want you to hear about it first from other people. Our country is changing. Look around. All over people are forming political associations. I haven't joined any of them all this while because I wanted to see if the military were really serious when they handed over power to the civilians. It's been two years now and I believe democracy is here to stay. This is the time to get involved," Lamang went on. "The military are gone for good. Next year there will be the second general elections, and I intend to be one of those elected."

"Good, then I wish you luck," Iliya said, bringing the conver-

sation to an abrupt end. Mamo heard the creaking of a seat and
then footsteps approaching his room. He quickly got off the bed
and stood at the window, poised, his eyes on the curtain in the
doorway.

"Can I come in?" his uncle asked as he stood in the doorway.
He was over six feet tall, a veteran of both the Second World War
and the Nigerian civil war, and people said that the injection
given to soldiers to make them bold and fiery-tempered still
worked in his blood, but Mamo had only heard of that fiery side,
he had never encountered it firsthand. To him, his uncle was the
gentlest, most intelligent man he had ever known.

Iliya's empty left sleeve was folded to just below the stump.
His eyes looked around the room, at the two beds, the table, and
the sketches on the wall. He went to the table and picked up a
book. "What are you reading?"

"A novel."

Iliya put down the book and perched on the edge of the table,
the wood creaking and wobbling beneath him. "Marina told me
that you sit all day in your room, doing nothing but reading and
falling ill. Is that all you want to do with your life?"

"I don't fall sick deliberately."

Mamo lowered his head and sat down on the bed—his uncle
went and sat on the other bed, LaMamo's bed. On the bed frame
the words VONO in red shone against the black background.
Mamo still fantasized, in his moments of dejection, that Iliya was
his real father and that Lamang was his uncle, and that one day
everything was going to be explained and ironed out—after all,
for the first three years of his life it was Iliya that he and his
brother had called father. Iliya had never stopped acting the part
of father to the twins, to Mamo especially, for whom he felt a
special fondness. Once, when Mamo was only six, he had said to
him, "Since you'll be spending more time than other people in
bed recovering from illness, you must learn to love books, they
will save you from boredom." He had then gone on to tell him the
story of how birds got their wings. He said at first all birds were

created wingless, and then the creator gave them a big hump on the back, but at first they found the hump too heavy to bear and they tried to throw it off. When they couldn't, gradually they got used to it, and finally they realized that if they unfurled it and flapped it, they could fly.

Now Iliya asked, "How old are you now, twenty-one?"

Mamo nodded.

"And do you know that most people with sickle-cell disease die before they are twenty, and isn't that a reason to be thankful? Don't worry too much about your brother, I am sure he is having fun wherever he is. Or would you rather have him in the village going about brawling and drinking like Asabar? I wish a thousand times that Asabar had not returned." Iliya fell silent, staring at the open window, and Mamo could feel the bitterness flowing from him in waves. At last he sighed and continued, looking Mamo directly in the eye, speaking slowly.

"You have a very good mind. It is up to you what you do with it. You can also go on a journey, like your brother, but a journey into your own mind. You'd be surprised at the things you will discover."

He stood up. "Do you have any plans to go back to school, or for work?"

"No. I don't."

"Well, I have an offer for you. Our history teacher has left us for a government job in the city. Why don't you come and take his place? The pay is not much, but at least the job will take you out of this room every morning."

Mamo had never envisaged himself as a village schoolteacher; it never featured, not even as a brief detour, on the map of his dream of fame and immortality. It was a mark of how far he had matured in the last few years that he saw immediately the sense in his uncle's offer, but he still hesitated.

"I am not sure I am qualified to teach history."

"It is not hard, believe me. And you did spend two years at the university. I will leave it to you to decide. Let me know what you've decided, but the opening won't wait forever."

widows and politicians

THEY MET once, sometimes twice, every week, in the evenings, in Lamang's living room. Once the meeting had started, Mamo would be trapped in his room, because to go out he'd have to pass through the living room crammed with his father's politician friends discussing campaign strategies and political allies, and this he never had the boldness to do. He preferred to wait till the meeting was over and the men had walked out to their cars parked under the mahogany trees outside and had driven off to the state capital from where they had come, before rushing out to get some air, or to the toilet to release the pressure in his bursting bladder. Outside by the gate the TV viewers would be out in full force—recently Lamang had taken to feeding them, a plate of rice and a bottle of Coke for each person. "Munching while watching," Lamang described this new development to his friends, his face lighting up with pride. His friends would shake their heads enviously and say, "Ah, see how the people flock to you."

From his room Mamo could hear the voices in the living room clearly, and now, after days of seeing them arrive and leave, and hearing them debate, he could match some of the voices to their owners' faces. There was the oily-voiced, equivocating Alhaji Danladi, who listened more than he spoke, and the clownish Emmanuel Dogo, who acted as secretary, and the shrill-voiced Gidado, who never seemed to have an original opinion but would always support and expand on whatever Danladi proposed.

Now the host, Lamang, was speaking, his deep baritone slowly

prevailing over the others. It began confidently, with a joke to
ease the way, and then it soared eloquently and began to elaborate on just what needed to be done: "I am talking of practical
things, things that affect our everyday life. Take water, for
instance. . . ." Now the voice paused, and Mamo imagined his
father looking at the faces seated around him, one arm half
raised, a smile on his face, conscious of his importance. "Ninety
percent of our people, in this local government, are either full-
time or part-time farmers, and so their greatest fear, our greatest
fear, is that of drought. But what if we assured the people that
we could solve that? What if we can guarantee that never again
would they have to worry about drought, like that of 1973?"

"And '76," someone contributed, "don't forget the drought of
1976."

"But how can you do that? Don't tell me you will hire rainmakers and witch doctors . . . ha-ha." This was Emmanuel Dogo's
waggish contribution. There was general laughter, deep male
voices; some of the laughter was forced, calculating. Interspersed
amid the male laughter were a few female voices. The widows.

There were three of them today. Mamo had seen them arrive
separately earlier on, all wearing their best *buba* and wrapper,
their head scarfs tall and stiff on their heads. They'd be seated
discreetly on the outside of the semicircle of men, or hovering by
the door, refilling empty water cups, going out to the kitchen now
and then to return with plates of goat-head pepper soup or some
other snack on a tray, batting eyelashes as they came in, finger-
ing their permed hair beneath their scarves as they passed in
front of the men, and the men would pause momentarily from
their arguments as the women passed, to savor the whiff of soap
and perfume—and soup. The three women were the remainders
from a larger group of widows who had hovered hopefully around
Lamang after his wife's death. On days like this they'd politely
but firmly take over the kitchen from Auntie Marina to cook for
the TV viewers and the politicians, hoping by this to catch the
elusive Lamang.

"No. No rainmakers," Lamang resumed, his voice almost curt, emphasizing the seriousness of his proposal, but of course there'd be a small smile on his lips to acknowledge the humor in the last question. "I am a practical man, I always think positive. Look at me, today I am the biggest cattle merchant in this state. I saw the opportunity a long time ago before anyone else, I saw the big demand for beef in the densely populated coastal cities, and how people there were willing to pay almost anything to get good meat. I saw what that meant in business terms, I did not hesitate, I seized the opportunity. That is the kind of approach I want to bring to politics, to our party. Supply and demand. I am going to use the same formula: get water from where it is abundant and transport it to where it is scarce."

Lamang allowed the murmurs to go on for a while, and then he cleared his voice. "Gentlemen—and ladies, of course, ha-ha!—I can hear you asking: But how can he do that, could you transport water in trucks like you transport cattle, and even if you could, could you transport enough from your source to supply a whole village, a whole local government, in time of drought? Well, I have a practical, scientific answer, not black magic and witchcraft like some here may want to propose. . . ." And here he paused to let the crowd appreciate how he had cleverly turned the joke on Emmanuel Dogo, before proceeding.

"As a businessman I travel a lot, and on my travels I meet all kinds of people. That is how I came to learn about reverse osmosis. I can see some of you already looking at your neighbors in puzzlement. Don't worry, I have it all written down here and I'll give it to you to read as soon as I finish speaking. But don't be overwhelmed by the huge scientific term. It simply refers to a process for purifying salty or unclean water from the sea and pumping it inland in pipes, et cetera. It is the same system used by ships on the ocean when they need fresh water. Imagine if we can sink our pipes in the River Niger, or in Lake Chad, or even in the Atlantic, and using reverse osmosis, we'll purify the water, and then we'll use giant engines to pump it inland whenever there is drought in our region, or to store in our giant reservoirs to use later as we wish. Gentlemen, this is the age of science and modernity; things like this are not impossible if we have the will and the money. This is the time to move our whole country and our people forward out of the dark ages. Think positive. Think supply and demand."

There was a long pause, and then Mamo heard one pair of hands coming together, and soon more hands joined in. He could imagine the men getting up and shaking Lamang's hand, patting him on the back, repeating the strange but impressive words "reverse osmosis" with awe, and the widows basking in reflected glory. There was more clinking of cutlery and glasses, and then much later the sound of footsteps as one by one the men left for their cars and the long drive back to their homes. The widows remained and Mamo heard their soft, syrupy voices outdoing each other in congratulating Lamang on his brilliant speech.

Outside, the sun would be low over the hills, setting. It was dark in the room already, but Mamo didn't bother to turn on the light—there was something comforting, cocoonlike, in the soft darkness. The women should be heading off to their lonely houses by now, but none of them wanted to be the first to leave. They were still gushing nonchalantly, but beneath their colored eyebrows they'd be keenly watching each other, each waiting for the other to give in and depart first. And Lamang would be lapping it all up, sprawled on the central sofa, a woman on each side of him—the unlucky third would be alone on the seat facing the sofa, leaning forward as much as possible, reaching out to pat Lamang on the knee with each sentence, with each burst of laughter.

Mamo sometimes wondered if his father had sex with the widows. They were allowed in his father's bedroom openly, to clean, sometimes to chat—but they always left the door open, as if to say, *See, nothing indecent is taking place*. But there were days when he had returned and found the door shut, and a woman's voice inside talking in low tones to his father. Yet there was some-

thing almost asexual about these women in their forties and
fifties battling loneliness and midlife crisis with powdered faces
and painted lips and cheap perfumes sent to them by their
grown-up daughters married to civil servants in the city, trying so
hard to capture the fading bloom in their lives before it finally fell
off the stem. Suddenly he felt an urge to get up, to go out and
feel the cold, bracing harmattan wind in his face. His mouth felt
as if it were stuffed full of cow dung. He got off the bed and as
he stood up he felt the floor move and he had to press against the
wall to steady himself, then the vertigo passed and he went out.
He passed the living room quickly, avoiding his father's gaze,
smiling politely in response to the chorus of endearments from
the women:

"Hello, Twin, come and say hi . . . see how thin you look. . . ."
This was Rabi, a teacher in the Women's Teachers' College. The
rouge and powder on her cheeks made her look jaundiced. She
was seated on Lamang's right, pressing her left breast against his
arm, pulling away discreetly at Mamo's entrance.

"Your hair is so bushy, Twin, you need a haircut, dear. . . ." This
was Doris, the eldest of the widows, in her early fifties, her
twisted mouth hinting at a bitter past, an unhappy present; she
had three children, all in their twenties. She was the unlucky
third in the single seat directly facing Lamang. Her severe head
scarf made her look even older than her age; her huge sagging
breasts seemed to be pulling her shoulders downward.

"Where have you been hiding, Twin . . . ?" This was Asabe,
forty-five years old, mother of five. She was the prettiest: petite
with long slender arms and surprisingly firm-looking breasts. She
was the shiest, always lurking out of sight, letting the others do
the talking while she nodded enthusiastically, her lips always
parted, ready to laugh agreeably.

Mamo went down the veranda steps slowly, one at a time. He
stood on the last step, looking up at the dying sun for a long time,
enjoying the slowly rising heat below his shirt. His father's voice
came clearly to him, ". . . His brother is my spitting image, taller,

strong. He is right now in the army, abroad, a fine young man, not like his brother . . . weak . . . too weak . . ."

Mamo felt the heat rise and rise under his shirt, until he sweated. He went to the kitchen and fetched some water from the earthenware pot; he went back into the sun and poured the water over his head, then, still dripping water, he went and parted the living room curtain. His father and the women looked up, their faces curious, waiting for him to speak.

"I am actually taller than LaMamo," Mamo said slowly. The words came out painfully, a ball of air raking his chest. He was facing his father defiantly, unblinking. "He is five-nine, and I am five-eleven."

His father looked surprised for a while, then he turned to the women and laughed out loud and long, as if trying to cover his son's lapse in manners. "But you walk with your shoulders bowed; you must learn to walk straight. Think positive."

He went out for a walk. It was a Monday, market day. The streets were busy with people returning from the market: traders still counting their money, women hurrying home to feed their children before they fell asleep, drunks walking hand in hand, weaving from one side of the road to the other, singing lustily at the tops of their voices. Sounds of drums and *goge* rode high on the air from the neighboring brewhouses. The village's dusty central street was lined on either side by mahogany trees, which towered into the evening sky, their branches meeting overhead and shaking gently in the mild wind; egrets and bats cackled madly in their dark foliage. Hanging in front of the neighborhood's only provision store, smoking cigarettes and listening to loud disco music, were young boys with prematurely disillusioned eyes— they were the local counterculture, eager for experience, trying to appear sophisticated in hand-me-down jeans and T-shirts, feeling trapped by the hills and the trees and the farms and the poverty. Mamo passed through the dark and silent churchyard with its huge neem trees and gravestones. He shivered as he passed the gravestones. Cases of ghost-sighting in the church-yard had been reported by terrified villagers, only they weren't sure if the ghosts were those of twins that long ago used to be dumped here or that of Reverend Drinkwater, whose grave lay beside his wife's in the church's tiny cemetery. And perhaps because he was a twin himself, Mamo felt the presence of the spirits with a great intensity, felt them hanging in the air, stifled, sad. He never passed here without reminding himself that but for the accident of being born many years later than the abandoned twins, he'd have shared their fate.

The sun was still visible over the hills. It was a fluke sun—the dull red orb should have long been blocked out by the foggy harmattan dust this late in the day—but still it lingered lazily, defiantly. The hills circled the village in a horseshoe from west to south, and the scrubby vegetation that covered the hilltops and the stunted trees that slanted on the slopes were now desiccated and leafless from the harmattan wind.

A few brushfires were visible at the top of the hills. December was the hunting season, when the grass on the hills was tinder-dry; hunters would set it ablaze to chase out the rabbits and squirrels and monkeys that lived there. They'd chase them to the summit with their hounds; late in the evenings they'd return with their kill in sacks, or ostentatiously slung on poles, their dogs behind them. At the foot of the hills was the village burial ground, with its headstones and crude wooden crosses looking as if they had sprouted from the clayey red earth. This had been the village burial ground for generations: new graves straddled older graves, new bones mingled promiscuously with ancient ones.

uncle iliya, uncle haruna, and okigbo

MAMO TOOK up his uncle's offer the month he turned twenty-two, and on a bright Monday morning he began his life as a village schoolteacher. The Keti Community School was the only school in Keti not owned by the government. The idea for the school, initiated by Iliya, was to give the village's secondary school dropouts, and those that hadn't passed their "O" levels, a second chance. The emphasis was vocational, with subjects like carpentry, brickwork, basketwork, metalwork, and photography forming a major part of the curriculum, although students who showed aptitude for academic work were encouraged and assisted before being referred to the appropriate schools to sit for the General Certificate of Education exams. Originally, the school had been planned for teenagers between fourteen and seventeen, but now there were more students in their twenties and thirties than teenagers, all eager to learn, to get a certificate. At the school's inception there had been a total of fifty students, but this year their number had crept up to over two hundred, and all of them, on this Monday morning, were standing in neat rows, staring up at the teachers.

Uncle Iliya, dressed in khaki trousers and a spotless white shirt, was conducting the morning assembly; he addressed the students in his calm, even voice, telling them of their duties not only as students but also as citizens, and when he had finished, the Christian religion knowledge teacher stepped forward and said the Christian prayer, after him his Islamic counterpart said the Muslim prayer, and then the assembly was over.

Mamo had his first class at nine A.M.

"Good morning, sir," the students sang, standing up as he entered. He stood at the door, thrown off-balance by the loud and lusty greeting, unsure what to do next, but at last he said, "Good morning, class. Sit down."

Last night Mamo had spent hours trying to make notes for this class, using his old secondary school textbooks and notes as guide, but halfway through he had thrown the notebooks away, astonished at the amount of irrelevant material he had had to learn in school. There were less than fifteen students in the class; history was apparently not one of the popular subjects. The craft classes were the favorites, followed by English and economics. Uncle Iliya had only recently added history to the syllabus because of his belief in what he called "comprehensive education." He went and stood at the window, looking out at the dusty harmattan morning, aware of his students' restless chair-shifting and whispers.

"My name is Mamo Lamang."

He wrote his name on the blackboard. Then beside his name he wrote the question: *What is history?* The infinitesimally tiny chalk particles floated on the air in slow motion, taking a whole eternity to settle on his hands and face, to waft into his nostrils.

Immediately hands went up. "It is the story of the past."

"Not entirely true, it is also about the future," he replied.

"It is the story of a people and how they came together to form a nation."

"Partly true, but nations have been formed without consulting with their future citizens. Nigeria is a good example."

"It is the story of a people's wars and migrations."

He listened, looking at the eager faces, their different skin tints, their different haircuts, their nostrils, their shirts and shorts. The voices rose and rose as he kept shaking his head to each answer. Finally there was silence.

"Sir, what is history?" This voice was hostile. It was one of the older students in the back row, his eyes defiant, a thin beard covering the lower part of his chin.

Mamo shook his head and said abruptly, "Class over. I expect more intelligent answers tomorrow."

He walked out and quickly made for the staff room. Two teachers were there, Mr. Bukar, the physical education teacher, and Mrs. Rhoda, the home economics teacher.

"Ah, our new teacher. You are out early. What happened?" It was Mrs. Rhoda. She was a popular character in the village because of her high-strung, argumentative temperament, and also because of her liberal use of lipstick—her nickname, Ms. Lipstick, given to her by the students, had found its way into daily use in the village, but behind her back. Today she was wearing a vividly crimson brand of lipstick, she had added it on rather thickly, and it gave her rather thin lips the look of a knife wound slowly clotting. By the end of the day the red would be all over her teeth and smudged around her face.

"Nervous on your first day, are you?" Mr. Bukar said. He was a huge man and had once been famous in the village as a soccer player, but he had gradually run to fat as he grew older and developed a great love for the local brew. He stank of it even this early in the morning. His tiny red eyes followed Mamo to his seat, his hollow, meaningless laughter hanging in the air.

"It is a very good day," Mamo said as cheerfully as he could. The others continued to look at him, not sure what he meant. At last Mrs. Rhoda laughed brightly and shuffled the papers on her desk and said, "A good day it is."

At the end of the first period two other teachers came in, chattering loudly. Mamo had been introduced to all of them earlier by his uncle, before the assembly. The school had six teachers in all—apart from the headmaster, who also taught—and four of them, including Mrs. Rhoda and Mr. Bukar, were permanent and had been with the school from the beginning. The other two permanent teachers were the English teacher, a hypochondriac who

only turned up at work once or twice a week and talked about her
ailments all day, and the recently departed history teacher whom
Mamo had replaced. The two nonpermanent teachers were student interns from the Advanced Teachers' College in the state
capital.

In the staff room, between classes, Mamo mostly kept to himself, burying his face in a book. At first he taught only one lesson
every day, always in the first hour of the school day, but by the
end of his second month he was so bored that he offered to stand
in for the habitually absent English teacher. But even then he
found himself with enough time to stare blankly at the broken,
sagging ceiling overhead, and the lizards in the cracks in the
walls escaping the scalding noon heat outside, and the broken,
potholed floor beneath his feet, and if all these failed to distract
him, there'd be his colleagues lamenting over their debts, their
farms, their children, their slowly disappearing prospects in life.
Mr. Bukar wanted to return to school someday, to the university,
to study psychology; Ms. Lipstick was desperate to pay the debts
she had accumulated during her daughter's wedding three years
ago; one of the interns, whose name was Agnes, but who was
called Langalanga by the students behind her back because of
her tall thin figure, spent her free time crying into her desk
because her fiancé had jilted her; the second intern, Adamu,
soft-voiced, baby-faced, was obviously in love with Langalanga,
and he spent most of his time holding her hand and trying to
console her.

Mamo would listen to them silently, and when he couldn't
take any more he'd go to his uncle's office to have a chat, if his
uncle wasn't too busy. Iliya had a brilliant, searching mind that
went to the heart of issues. He had books on almost every subject, and after reading a book he would give Mamo a summary
of it, after which he'd give his own opinion on the subject,

sometimes going totally against what the author had suggested. "The worst thing you can do," he'd say to Mamo as they sat in the tiny office surrounded by books and files and wooden chairs, "is to ever accept anything at face value. Don't agree with what a man says because he has lived longer than you, or because he claims that is our way, using history as evidence to back his claim. Some have accused me of promoting Western ways and making young people forget their tradition and culture. They point out to me the evils of modernity—as if tradition itself is devoid of evil. You will come across such people; my advice is, don't listen to them, get education. If you want to follow tradition, follow it because you understand it, not because some old man told you it is our way. The youth must be encouraged to ask, why is it our way? If the elders can't answer, then forget it. The rest of the world has science and commerce and prosperity. What do we have? Culture. Most cultures and traditions are devised by society to help it survive a particular threat at a certain time, and once that threat is over, that culture becomes anachronistic."

Mamo said, "But how do you distinguish good from bad culture?"

"The bad one is the one that can be replaced easily. Like the killing of twins. See how easily that was removed, because the mothers didn't want it, the fathers didn't want it, and certainly the twins didn't want it! Some traditions simply lose their relevance and they die off by themselves. For example, on the faces of some older men you will see the deep marks that once distinguished us from our neighbors. Perhaps the most important use of these tribal marks was to distinguish friend from foe on the battlefield. But that was when wars were fought with clubs and spears and stones. Now that you can shoot down an enemy from many miles without even seeing his face, tell me, what is the use of tribal marks in such an instance?"

Through the open door Mamo could see out across the yard to the neem tree under which the carpentry students were busy cutting and planing wood. They were crowded around the work-table, keeping out of the merciless noon heat.

"Are you, then, saying that there is nothing such as culture, tradition? Because tradition by its very definition is something that lasts, that never goes out of fashion."

Iliya lifted his absent arm, as if to emphasize a point, as if momentarily forgetting that there was only a stump there. "I am not saying that. I am saying that when you examine the motive behind most customs and their champions today, you will see that they are rigged to serve the interest of some elite, some self-styled custodian of our culture. I can't remember who said this, but it is true: 'The difficulty lies not in new ideas, but in escaping from old ones.'"

"What of religion? You do go to church every Sunday."

"I do, but I don't hold the same view as other Christians that only through Jesus Christ can one attain salvation. . . . I believe that you can equally be saved through other religions, Islam, Buddhism, et cetera. Most of the people who go to church, or go to mosques and synagogues, do so not because they have critically examined their faith and found it better than other faiths, they simply do so for social reasons: some because they are born into it, some because it makes more business sense, some because they marry into it. If you had been born an Arab, chances are today you'd be a Muslim. Be wary of those who try to exclude. The truth is complex and various. Exclusion is never the answer. It is what gives rise to fascism and all sorts of racial and religious fundamentalism. We are pure, you are not; we are superior, you are inferior."

After the conversations, Iliya would ply Mamo with books, sometimes up to a dozen at a time, and Mamo would lug them home after work and he'd spend his evenings and weekends reading and making notes and elaborating lines of argument to try on his uncle the next day.

Uncle Iliya was also a lover of poetry, and among the books Mamo took home from his office would be a few poetry collec-

tions, from Dennis Brutus to Wole Soyinka to Okot p'Bitek to
Agostino Neto to Léopold Senghor to Kofi Awoonor to Christopher Okigbo. He became particularly captivated by Okigbo when
he found out how the poet had thrown away his poetic career to
become a soldier in the Biafran army, and how he had died at the
front. He found himself mentally, and at unguarded moments
audibly, repeating the poet's lines:

> For he was a shrub among the poplars
> Needing more roots
> More sap to grow to sunlight
> Thirsting for sunlight
>
> A low growth among the forest

In the staff room, the mindless banter between Ms. Lipstick
and Mr. Bukar, the droning complaints of the English teacher,
and the furtive looks exchanged between Langalanga and the
male intern, would force Mamo to recede into his mind, to
build an invisible wall between himself and the rest of the
room. One of the ways he did this was by developing elaborate
imaginary stories around people and events. He called it the
"what-if" game. His favorite subject was the poet Okigbo. He'd
say to himself: *What if the poet isn't really dead? What if, like
Uncle Haruna, he simply wandered away from the battlefield?
What if he and Uncle Haruna wandered away from the battlefield
together?*

And from here the game would take on a life of its own, using
as fuel the most airy and adventitious references from real life.
He remembered how his uncle had once, enigmatically, mentioned the name Chris. What if it was actually Chris Okigbo he
was referring to? What if they had really met at the front? And
here the game would assume a cinematic/poetic license:

On a dark, smoky day at the front, in 1967, Uncle Haruna and
his comrade Toma and one other person, a sergeant, had been

sent on a bridge-destroying mission. Uncle Haruna had gone ahead of the others to reconnoiter the ground across the bridge and was immediately taken by an enemy scout party. Toma and the sergeant waited and when he didn't return they assumed he'd been killed, as earlier they had heard the warning gunshots fired over his head by the Biafran scouts.

And now he was on his knees, his hands bound behind him. He had been brought before a rather youngish Biafran captain. The Biafrans, about ten of them, had turned the space under a huge iroko tree into a sort of temporary camp. Haruna couldn't be sure if there were more of them in the thick bushes surrounding the iroko—men kept disappearing into the bush and reappearing again. They all looked rather bedraggled, their uniforms and equipment looking makeshift and depleted. The captain kept glancing up at the sun, shielding his eyes as he did so, as if waiting for some kind of sign, or as if he wished he were somewhere else at that moment. At last he looked at Haruna, and for a moment his eyes looked almost compassionate, then they turned steely.

"My name," said the captain, in English, "is Chris Okigbo. In real life I am a poet." Here he paused and laughed as if amused by some secret irony. Then he went on, growing serious: "You picked a very bad time to get caught. We are on the retreat at the moment, we have lost touch with our headquarters, and we have no resources to deal with a prisoner. The easiest thing would be to put a bullet through your head and get it over with. . . ." But then, as if distracted by some telepathic message, the captain went quiet, and then he abruptly turned and disappeared into the bush, leaving Haruna with a sergeant, one from the original group that had captured him. Haruna heard the captain talking to someone out of sight, and then he returned, followed by a corporal. It was at that moment that the earth opened up and they all went hurtling down toward its center—Haruna wasn't sure which came first, the fiery explosion, the hurtling fall, or the great crack on his head. But he was falling, falling through tree branches and severed arms and legs, all the way screaming. All went dark and silent. Hours later, or minutes or seconds, when he opened his eyes he found the captain bending over him, his mouth opening and closing but making no sound. Much later, when his ears had stopped ringing and he could make out the captain's words, he heard the words, "We are the only two alive— we might be the only two left in the whole wide world. I see a sign in that. Are you injured?"

Haruna extricated himself from under the pile of leaves and branches and stood up. He wasn't injured.

"Let's go," Okigbo said, and they left. They just walked, not certain where they were headed for, instinctively avoiding the fighting, deeper and deeper into the forest.

They ate when they could, they slept when they got tired, they didn't talk much, and they just luxuriated in their newfound freedom. After a day, or a week or a month, the war became only a memory in their minds. At last they came to a village, and when they asked where they were, the people told them, "Cameroon."

Another country.

They looked at each other and continued walking. It was not certain how they came to own a van, but they used it to continue traveling. By a silent agreement they never talked about the war again, they just drove. They went from town to town, from country to country, and one day they found themselves on the easternmost edge of Africa—they were in Dar es Salaam. Then they headed north to Egypt to see the pyramids, then south, then north, then west: Mali, Guinea, Congo, Botswana, Senegal, Morocco, Kenya, they kept going. On the way they passed other wars, other kinds of peace. They witnessed births and weddings and festivals and deaths and burials. Then, exactly ten years after they had begun, Haruna told Chris, "My friend, the time has come for me to stop. I am home." He had recognized where they were; to his left were the green hills of Keti.

Alone in the van, Okigbo composed these lines to the hills before moving on:

Alone again, I see the green hills of
Keti rear up before me, forelegs raised,
Beckoning, like horses at a durbar—
Below them my crusty old friend, road, also beckons.
. . .

Haruna seemed to float as he went down the strange, yet
familiar street. His brother's house was over there, right behind
the mahogany trees. A boy of about fourteen stood at the gate,
staring dreamily into the hills, as if waiting to see someone
descending. It was March, the dry season was coming to an end,
the air already carried the fresh, stirring odor of rain from far
away; dust devils swirled up into corkscrew funnels, lifting up
twigs and pieces of paper and chasing them round and round in
circles. Haruna staggered as he veered off the middle of the road
and approached the boy by the gate; he seemed to realize, for the
first time, how tired he was. The boy was looking at him, his head
bent slightly; his eyes ran over Haruna's wild hair and gaunt face
and then went down to his torn shoes. The boy looked as if he
was recovering from an illness, he looked bony and stooped
around the shoulders, but the resemblance to his father,
Lamang, was quite striking. As Haruna stood before him, licking
his lips in preparation to speak, the boy reached into his pocket
nervously and brought out a coin and proffered it.

Haruna looked at the coin. He licked his lips again and said,
"Is this Musa Lamang's house?"

By the middle of his second year at the KCS, Mamo became
increasingly aware of the difficulty his uncle was going through
just to keep the school running. Owned and financed by the
community, the school just managed to stay afloat on its shoe-
string budget. Iliya daily resisted the temptation to increase
school fees. As the days went by, he talked less and less about

politics and culture and more and more about the importance of
keeping the school going. He'd explain to Mamo the precarious
situation of the students: they were the children of peasants,
grandchildren of peasants, who were suddenly thrust into a modern system that required them to pass exams in order to get anywhere. But most of them were unable to pass the standard
school certificate exams because the village schools were sub-
standard, the teachers could barely read themselves, and so the
students always failed, ending up as village layabouts, congregat-
ing in the evenings in front of the village shop to sit on upturned
Coke crates and smoke cigarettes and sip whiskey and listen to
disco music that the Igbo shop owner always played on his bat-
tered cassette player. Some would grow into adults with permanent bitter expressions on their faces. In some the bitterness
would trickle into the heart and find vent in petty crimes. The
community school offered them an alternative.

Then one day, as if to finally upset the fine balance Uncle Iliya
was maintaining in holding the school together, a letter came
from the state Ministry of Education.

"I can't believe this," Uncle Iliya said as he ran his eyes over
the letter. Mamo waited to hear what it was all about. He could
see by the way his uncle's lips were pressed tightly together that
this was bad news.

"They want to close down the school." He read out: " 'Unless
you raise general standards, yours will be one of the private
schools around the state whose continued existence the government will be forced to review.' What exactly do they mean by
'review'? What do these idiots know about general standards
when they send their kids to private schools in London and
America, and now . . . 'The conditions are: 1. A minimum
amount of one hundred thousand naira must be present at all
times in the school's bank account; 2. A teacher/student ratio of
one to fifteen must be maintained'—by their calculations I need
to employ at least ten more teachers, how can I do that, just tell
me—'and 3. More classes and facilities—' "

He put down the letter and shook his head. He bowed down his head in thought, and he seemed to have forgotten that another person was in the office with him. After a while Mamo got up quietly and left him.

Back in class, burdened by the weight of his uncle's worries and uncertain about the continued existence of the school, Mamo faced his pupils with a new sense of urgency. He pushed aside the lesson plan and began talking about things at random. In his ramblings he tried to make sense of life and its unfairness. He found himself repeating the phrase from LaMamo's letter about "future African leaders." He had been impressed by the way his brother had used it so matter-of-factly in his letter, as if becoming a "future African leader" were a thing expected of every African as a matter of course. He said to his students, "If we are to go far, if we are to be the future African leaders . . ."

He wanted to ask questions, not really to teach. He wanted to encompass all of history in one lesson, one hour, one sentence; he wanted to talk about the Berlin Wall, about Vladimir Lenin, about the slave trade and the American Civil War; about how their country, Nigeria, came to be named; of Martin Luther King; of Mandela on Robben Island; of the pyramids and the pharaohs in Egypt; about Plato and Aristotle and the Roman emperors; of Marie Antoinette and how she thought bread and cake were really not much different; of Hitler in his bunker and how ultimately good triumphs over evil; of Napoleon on St. Helena; of Chaka the Zulu king; of Mansa Mūsā; and of how all of these things affected them directly; how a victory over tyranny and injustice anywhere and at any time was also a victory right here, right now. He wanted to tear off the roof and break down the walls and say to them, *See the horizon, there over the hills? That is not the real horizon, there are a myriad other horizons, and you can see that when you climb the hill and stare into the vast open fields beyond, and they only multiply as you approach them. That is the true meaning of history.* But he lacked the words and the confidence to say it all. He often felt

like a fraud when he stood before the eager, expectant eyes. He
felt too young, too inexperienced.

△ ▽ △

The months rolled by. Mamo witnessed his first, then second
graduation ceremonies as two sets of final-year students left, and
fresh ones came in. The interns, Langalanga and Adamu, who
were now engaged to be married, left and were replaced by two
new girls. Despite these flurries of events, Mamo felt the passage
of time keenly by its slowness. It made him restless, and this
restlessness was heightened by the letter he got from LaMamo at
the end of his second year as a teacher. The letter bore a Malian
stamp. Like most of LaMamo's letters that were to follow, this
one didn't bother to fill Mamo in on what had happened since
the last letter. But the passage of time was evident in LaMamo's
voice: clearly he was no more the young, eager hopeful; he
already sounded like a veteran of many battles and experiences.

June 1985

Dear brother,
I am writing from a small village on the border of Mali in the
Sahara desert—a war has been going on here for a long time.
Its between the Tuaregs and the govenment. The Tuaregs feel
that they are oppressed and they want to be free. Everywhere
people want to be free and I think its right. We are fighting on
the side of the Tuaregs, but I don't think we are going to win,
is sad. There were sixty of us volunteers when we first left the
camp in Libya, but in the pass two years many have died, oth-
ers have deserted (AWOL), and now there is only twenty of us.
Sometimes when there is no fighting I lay on the sand and I
see the stars in the sky and I know that death is evrywhere

around me—yesterday the government forces came and raid our camp in the night—I was lucky, many died. I was covered in limbs and blood.

I remember last year, we fought agianst a terrible warlord. He was a magician, a wizard who control the soul of his soldiers when he sent them out to fight. He took their soul from their bodies and they become zombie, they fight without fear because they are not human, they keep coming and we keep shooting and they keep coming. They fell on the ground like grasses, but they keep coming. We grew sick of shooting at them. They said the war-lord had turned their soul into birds, and has kept the birds on a baobab tree at the gate of his village, and whenever one of the men, the zombies, is killed, a bird will fly away into the air, never to return. They keep flying. We finally captured him and in his village there was jubilation. The women kissed us and hugged us and they say he has been killing there husbands and sons for many years now with his magic, he wanted to control the whole country, the whole of Africa. He was a very wicked man.

I have a new friend now—his name is Samuel Paul. He is from Liberia. You will like him, he is quite, and he love reading all the time, like you do. His story is sad. He join the army because of his family which where all killed in a church on his sisters wedding day. It is a sad story and he cries whenever he remember and he swears one day to revenge on the tribe that have kill his family and the people of his village in northern Liberia. They have entered the church, twenty of them on the day of the wedding, and started shooting—he wasn't killed because he hid behind the church altar, but he can hear his sister scream as they rape her before they kill her, and his mother begging them not to kill his sister, and the husband begging them not to rape his wife. There was blood in the church evrywhere, even the pastor killed because he belongs to this tribe.

Samuel Paul wants me to go with him to Liberia because we

are now strong friends, but that will mean deserting our own army—there are only 20 of us left from the first 60 people. But he said who are we fighting for anyway, the others are asking the same question. We are volunteers, so we fight wherever our leaders tell us to, our purpose is to set Africa free and get freedom for all black people in the world. But many of the remaining 20 are talking of leaving, we have been fighting for almost five years now, and many are dead, and Samuel Paul says it will take more than us to set Africa free. I wish you are here with me, you'd have enjoy seeing the people here when there is no fighting—the Tuaregs are like Arabs or Berbers, though some are darker than you or me, there langage is Tamashek, and their name means "abandoned by the gods" in Arabic, they drive on horses and camels and they live in the Sahara. It gets hot in the day and cool in the evening, their are oasis with small gardens and many kind of flowers. They love to sing when there is no fighting and the women and men will dance for us and in the evenings we roast goats and lambs to eat and couscous and sometimes we even forget that we are soldiers.

I will write again soon, tell Auntie Marina and Asabar and everyone I am fine and I send my greetings.

Your twin brother,
LaMamo

PS
I have skeched the oasis and the desert and camels on the back of this letter to give you an idea of how it is hear in the desert. In the night it get cool and peaceful, and it sometimes reminds me of home.

zara

WHEN HE wrote the biography of Zara many years later, Mamo would begin it not from the day he first met her, on Christmas day the year he turned fourteen, but from the day after, Boxing Day, when she turned up at the front door with her manuscript. When she had told him the day before that she was writing a story, and that she'd bring the manuscript for him to go through, he hadn't known whether to believe her or not. But she came. She wore a long leopardskin-patterned skirt and a blue blouse, her hair held by a blue plastic clip at the back of her head.

"I brought the manuscript," she said, waving a hardbound notebook in her hand.

"Come in," he said when he finally found his voice.

LaMamo was sprawled out in the sofa, singing loudly along to a Bongos Ikwe song on the radio. His mouth fell open when he saw Zara, and he sat up, looking at Mamo questioningly.

"My brother, LaMamo," Mamo said.

"Oh, the twin brother," she said and she went to LaMamo and shook his hand. He patted the space beside him and she sat down. Mamo, still a bit flustered, watched in silence as his brother quickly engaged Zara in a winding chat about twins and writing. Mamo listened, his mouth heavy, unable to contribute more than a yes or a no. It seemed that his brother, just like himself when he saw Zara the day before, had fallen in love. Mamo slowly stood up and said, "I'll go to the other room to look over the manuscript. I'll be back."

From the bedroom he couldn't hear what they were saying in the living room; their voices were just murmurs broken every once in a while by loud laughter. He knew that his brother, when excited, was a coin in motion, spinning and spinning to give the illusion of a million sides. He engaged her in subject after subject, making her laugh out loud—moving forward and backward like a hummingbird. Mamo felt the tears of frustration cover his eyes and he couldn't read the words on the manuscript. Much later, when he came out, Zara looked up at him and asked, "Well, do you like it?"

"Yes," he said. "It is really interesting."

She waited to hear more, but he silently handed her the A4 pages. The twins walked her halfway to her home. She promised to write when she returned to the city, and she did, a letter each on their fifteenth birthday. Mamo wrote a short reply and helped LaMamo to compose a lengthy, chatty reply. After that she never wrote to Mamo again, but for a whole year she wrote to LaMamo, always with a PS: *My regards to your brother.*

Mamo wrote in Zara's biography many years later that when he looked up as Iliya entered the staff room and announced a new teacher, Zara's face was the last thing he had expected to see standing next to his uncle, a polite smile on her lips as she looked curiously around the staff room. Earlier that morning the headmaster had informed the teachers that a new member of staff was coming to work with the mathematics teacher, and that she was volunteering her services for free.

She was stunning, that was what Mamo noticed first. She was dressed in a long black skirt and a lilac blouse, her head was bare, and her thick shiny hair fell around her cheeks, framing her oval face, and falling onto her shoulders almost carelessly. She looked as if she had just stepped off the plane from some far-away, interesting place. There was something familiar about her face, and Mamo was sure he had seen it before. Now they were in the center of the staff room. She was looking at Mamo, as if also trying to recall where she had seen him before.

"This is our new member of staff. Her name is Mrs. Zara Dogo. Most of you may not know her, but you would have heard of her father, Mr. John Lamemi, our former state schools inspector. She will be working with the math teacher."

He took her around and introduced each teacher by name. When he got to Mamo he said, "This is Mamo, he is my nephew, he teaches history, and sometimes English."

"We have met before," she said, smiling, "but he might not remember me, it was long ago."

Uncle Iliya looked from Mamo to Zara and said, "Er, well, that is good, then. Feel free to ask any of us for assistance if you need anything."

They left together.

the flame tree

ZARA CAME to see Mamo at home the next day—a Saturday. It was a busy day at the Lamangs' house. Lamang was in his room getting ready to go to the Victory Party's convention in the state capital. Today he was going to be named the party's state chairman; it was something he had campaigned for since the day he joined the party two years ago. All the party dignitaries from around the country would be at the convention, and most of them might afterward follow him home for a congratulatory dinner. Last week painters had worked day and night to repaint the entire house in green-purple-green, the Victory Party's colors. Even the brand-new leather seats in the living room were in green and purple.

A group of Lamang's friends was gathered on the veranda, waiting for him to come out; looking up at them from the foot of the steps was another group, made up of beggars and hangers-on, chanting their support for the Victory Party. Occasionally one of the men on the veranda would dip his hand in his pocket to bring out a coin and throw it at the beggars. Outside the gate, by the cars, drummers waited, drumming, for the men to come out and give them money.

To escape the noise, Mamo had taken a chair and a book to the flame tree in the backyard, but now Asabar had discovered him and was giving him a long, winding lecture on politics. He listened patiently as Asabar vituperated against the opposition party, the New Victory Party. He paced the space before Mamo as he spoke. Asabar was now Lamang's assistant. He had gone to Lamang a few months after his tail-between-the-legs return from the Chad border and reminded his uncle, "You said you'd give me a job after I graduated." Lamang had looked him up and down and said, "Well, I like your spirit. You are a fighter, and you value family. I'll make you into a politician—that is where the future is."

He was officially leader of the youth wing of the Victory Party, Keti local government, and his job was to daily drive around the village streets at near zero miles per hour in the party truck, its open back filled with the youth wing members, blaring the party song and campaign slogans from the speakers. He had taken to dressing in a camouflage combat jacket and trousers and thick army boots. The jacket, a bit too large for him, rested on his scrawny shoulders like a cape; the trousers' side pockets bulged with cigarette packs, pocketknives, key holders, and other odds and ends.

"They have no respect, I tell you. For two hours they parked across the road from our party office with their speakers pointed directly at our office, blaring their party's song."

"It is a free country, they have a right to be wherever they want," Mamo said.

"No, you don't understand party politics," Asabar said, waving his hand impatiently. He was drunk, and when he was drunk he had a habit of talking at the top of his voice, his face contorting pugnaciously. "Are you supporting the New Victory Party? I mean, just look at their name; couldn't they get something more original? Are you not with us?"

Loud cheers came from the direction of the veranda. Lamang must have appeared.

"They'll leave without you—I am sure they are looking for you now," Mamo said, lowering his head into his book.

"Are you trying to get rid of me, is that what you are doing?" Asabar's voice rose higher, and he stepped closer, pushing his face next to Mamo's. "You . . . you . . . don't understand me, you don't respect me. LaMamo was different, because me and him, we are both soldiers, we fear nothing—" He interrupted himself in midsentence. "Anyway, so I said to your father . . . Uncle . . . I said to the chairman, let me go with the boys and talk to them—but he wouldn't let me. I said just for one minute. They want trouble. Because in a few months elections will be here. We have to show them we are ready for them. . . . But he said let them be. But next time . . ."

That was when Zara appeared behind the kitchen, looking around hesitantly. Asabar saw her first and he stopped talking and stared. Mamo followed his cousin's gaze, and then he stood up, unable to disguise his surprise.

"Hello, Zara," he said. "Welcome. This is my cousin, Asabar. He was just leaving."

"Yes," Asabar said, taking the hint, squaring his shoulders. "We are going for a very important meeting. Mamo, remember what I told you . . . and also, I want to talk to you when I come back. It is important. I have to talk to you."

"I'll see you tomorrow."

When his cousin had gone, Mamo offered Zara the chair and said, "Sit down. I'll go and get another chair."

"Is someone having a celebration?" she asked when Mamo returned.

"Just my father and his politician friends."

They fell silent. He wanted to ask her what she came for, but he kept quiet and waited for her to speak. Yesterday, after the general introduction, she had left with Uncle Iliya before Mamo had a chance to speak to her.

Now she was staring up toward the hills, her eyes almost closed, breathing in deeply. Mamo thought she looked pretty with her head raised like that, her eyes closed, her brows furrowed. She said, "God, I have almost forgotten how fresh the air can be here in the village. Last time I was here was four years ago, for my father's funeral."

He said to her, "So, have you finished that novel yet?"

"I see you still remember." She laughed, turning to him, shaking her head. "I was too busy doing other things."

"What things?"

"The usual: university, youth service, marriage, motherhood, and divorce."

He had not heard of the divorce, or the child. She was twenty-five, one year older than him. He wanted to say that she was rather too young to be a divorced mother, but he kept quiet.

"Do you always come here to read?" she asked, looking up into the tree, and at the outhouses against the far wall and the chicken coops and the goat enclosures. It was a huge compound, encircled by a wall of gray concrete blocks.

"No. There was too much noise in the house—I didn't know where else to go to."

"Good, because I actually came to invite you to my place; it is quiet there."

"You came to invite me?"

"Well, actually I need assistance. I have so much unpacking to do, and it would take me ages to do it alone. I have been to my cousins' place, but none of them lives here anymore. One is married in the city, one is actually a nurse in Brunei, and one is dead. I have been so out of touch." She said the last softly, speaking to herself.

"And then you thought of me . . . I, who am still alive and available."

She laughed. "I didn't mean it to sound that way."

"I know."

"Where's your brother, LaMamo?"

"He has gone abroad, to see the world."

"Really? I wish I could do that, go off to see the world, and never bother about coming back."

He waited for her to say more about his brother, but she didn't, so he said, "He was in love with you. He still has your letters."

She looked at Mamo and there was genuine surprise on her face, then she smiled and said softly, "I see."

"Shall we go?" he said after a long, awkward silence.

Outside, she pointed at an old Peugeot 504 GL parked under a tree. "I inherited it from my father. It's the first car he ever bought. I left it in the garage here and had almost forgotten about it. Now I am glad I didn't give it away."

The car had bad shock absorbers, and when it bounced over boulders and potholes on the dirt road that led to the house, the impact was felt sharply on the seats and the dust rose from the floor. Opening the windows didn't help because that only let in more dust. The house was at the eastern end of Keti, next to the hospital quarters, and it stood in its own grounds, surrounded by a high wall; its big iron gate was opened by a one-eared young man who looked at Mamo suspiciously as Zara drove in.

"That is Yam, the caretaker."

"What kind of name is that?"

"Remind me later to tell you about it, and about how he lost his ear. Maybe you'll write a play about it someday. Do you still write plays?"

"No."

The front and sides of the house were overgrown with grass, as if it had been uninhabited for a long time. A naked lightbulb hanging from a socket over the front door cast its light valiantly into the afternoon brightness. To the left were the boys' quarters, which consisted of a room and a toilet. In front of the room was a veranda on which Yam now stood, looking over at Mamo and Zara stolidly.

Inside was musty and cobwebby; the seats and tables were covered by cardboard cartons. She went and threw open a window and stood there, staring into the overgrown backyard, and then she turned, shaking her head, waving her hand around the room. "The family house, looking rather neglected. No one has been here since my father's death; my mother hates the village, my sister can't bear to be away from her husband, and I . . . I love it here . . . this is the only place where I can think clearly . . . but I was busy." She stopped speaking abruptly and pointed to a chair. "Find a place, sit down, but be warned about the dust," she said. Most of the cartons were open, displaying framed photographs, clothes, books, pots and pans, and other bric-a-brac. She dropped her bag on one of the cartons and headed for the fridge in a corner. "A drink? I have only water, I am afraid. I could send Yam for some soft drinks, though."

"Water is okay."

He pointed at the cartons. "Looks like you plan to stay here a long time."

"I don't know . . . long enough to sort out my affairs."

He went and opened another window, which looked onto a different section of the backyard, a garden shady with mango and orange and guava trees. She left him and went into the bedroom and returned later in jeans and a red T-shirt. Her bare feet on the cushion raised a cloud of dust as she climbed up to fix a picture to the wall.

"Let me do the pictures," he offered, taking the nail and the hammer from her. "You do the kitchen."

There were pictures of her family: her father, her mother, and her sister, who looked so like her, but slimmer, and her eyes lacking the abrasive energy that always blazed out of Zara's. In one of the pictures Zara stood in a wedding gown next to a handsome young man in an army captain's uniform, their hands together holding a long military sword over a huge cake.

"My ex. His name is George Dogo." Her voice was flat, giving no indication of what she felt about him.

"How many kids?"

"Just one, Sam . . . Samson." Now the voice was softer. She was rummaging in the cartons on the table as she talked, her back to him, but for a moment she stopped and opened her handbag and handed him a passport picture of a young boy smiling sunnily into the camera.

"One year old—he is with my in-laws. They took him away from me."

"Sorry," he said.

"Sorry for what?" She was all feisty now, her stare hardening. He opened his mouth to speak, but she raised her hand and stopped him. "Look, it wasn't exactly a bad marriage, we were in love at the beginning. We got married three years ago. I was in my final year at university. Everybody was happy, but then after the baby came we grew apart. He is a soldier, he loves to hang out with his comrades in the mess, leaving me alone with the baby, and for the first time in my life I had time to think—I saw my life stretching on and on like that, and I wanted out. I guess I grew up too fast; being a mother does that to you. Of course, he had other women, but that was not the main thing. The main thing was . . . he was so shallow. He was so damn shallow, but I was only twenty-two, for God's sake. I was just too damn young to see it."

Mamo stood with the hammer and a picture in his hands, not sure what to say next that wouldn't sound offensive. She was staring at him defiantly, as if waiting for him to say the wrong thing.

"I hope you won't swear like that in class."

She laughed, and her eyes looked grateful. "Enough about me. Tell me about the school; what should I expect?"

"Well, nothing much . . . but you can be sure of a nickname from the students. . . ."

"A nickname? What is yours?"

"They call me Future African Leader. . . ."

He smiled and shrugged when she sniggered. "I guess I do use that phrase a lot in my classes. But don't laugh too early, wait till you hear what they'll call you."

The next day he went to her. He didn't go in when she opened the door. He said, "Last night I dreamt of you. We went out for a walk, on the hills."

She smiled. "Well, do you want to go for a walk?"

"You mean . . . right now?"

"Why not? Let me get my shoes."

They stood as he had dreamt, facing the village below: the trees, the people like ants, the houses with smoke rising off the thatch roofs of the kitchens. But they did not hold hands as they had in the dream. They descended when the sun dipped behind the hills and they couldn't see the smoke rising from the kitchen roofs anymore. They returned the next Saturday. It was a hot and airless day, but at the top of the hill the breeze was strong and soothing; they sat under a stunted tree, their shoulders touching. Mamo nervously threw stones over the edge of the hill, saying nothing. Finally Zara said, "In your dream what did we do when we climbed the hill?"

"We kissed."

"I see."

He threw more stones, then he said, "My brother was crazy about you . . . he used to show me your letters. . . ."

"Oh . . . those were just . . . letters."

"But what of that day when you first came to the house, to show me your manuscript . . . ?"

"The day you ignored me completely?"

"I didn't, you and my brother were obviously—"

"I came there for you, to see you, remember? And your brother was only asking me about my sister. He had seen her at church and wanted to be introduced to her."

"That was it?"

"Yes."

They sat in silence, staring at a group of goats chewing grass.

"Were you jealous, of your own brother?"

"I guess I was. I was so jealous I never talked to him about you again. I felt so betrayed that day. . . .But I guess I've always been jealous of him, he has everything I don't have. He is always the strong and healthy one, and when we were kids, adults would always pat him on the head and say, 'What a healthy strong boy,' and when they turned to me the look on their faces would change. My fantasy is to have his body, with my mind, and then I'll be the perfect person." He managed a small laugh, trying not to sound too serious. "It is my inferiority complex acting up. Maybe I ought to see a shrink." He tried to laugh again, but the laughter stuck in his throat.

"It is normal. I also envy my sister. . . . She is everything I am not, she has the perfect husband and house, she has three kids, my mother stays with her, and . . . I am such a mess. But it is normal, there's even a name for it: sibling rivalry. We are perfectly normal, normal, normal. . . ."

"I think you are great," he said. "I admire you."

"Me too."

"You admire yourself?"

She smiled. "No, you. I always have."

She extended her hand and laid it over his, sliding her fingers between his fingers.

They walked through the gate as night fell. He stood with his hands on her shoulders as she took out her key and opened the door. Behind them, in the grass, frogs and crickets called out to each other and fireflies described brilliant trajectories in the air before subsiding into the grass. Inside, she turned on the light and pulled down the curtains, and then she went into the kitchen, asking him if he'd like anything to eat.

He shook his head, "No. I am not hungry."

"I have sand in my hair. I'll take a shower. One minute," she said, reaching out to touch his hand as she passed. He took her hand and pulled her into his lap.

"Oops," she said with a laugh as she lost her balance and fell against him. He kissed her on the mouth and ran his hand gently over her face, and all the time she stared directly into his eyes, as if searching for something. He felt her breasts against his chest. She brushed her nose against his and stood up.

"One minute," she said.

From the living room he could hear the sound of water running in the bathroom down the hallway. After a while the water stopped running. A door opened and then she called, "I've finished. Come here."

He stood up, and then he sat down again and took off his walking shoes. She was still in the bathroom when he got into her bedroom. He went and peeked into the half-open bathroom door. She was standing before the mirror with a towel covering her chest down to her thighs, reaching up to take out a bottle of body cream from a shelf. He asked, "Need any help?"

"No, I'll be out soon."

He returned to the bedroom and began to look idly around, feeling a guilty thrill as he ran his hand over her dresses and underwear in the wardrobe. Next to the window was a double bed with sheets the same light blue color as the curtain on the window. On the bedside table was a picture in a tiny square wooden frame. It was Zara and her son, hugging each other, smiling into the camera. She came out and found him with the picture in his hand. "Nice picture," he said.

"Me and Sam."

She stood beside him, still wearing the short towel.

"He is a pretty boy," Mamo said. "He looks like you."

The bathroom was still warm and misty when he went in to urinate. Her panties hung on the shower curtain. He washed his hands and when he came out Zara was lying on the bed, on her tummy. She was already dressed in a short purple nightgown, which exposed her long shapely legs from the knees. The light from the bathroom fell on her and from where he stood he could see the outline of her naked body under the flimsy gown. She turned and smiled up at him. He sat down beside her. They looked into each other's eyes silently. They both began to speak at the same time. They stopped and she said, "You go ahead."

"I wanted to say that you smell great."

She laughed and he could see in her eyes that she was as nervous as he was. He bent down and pressed his lips on her. She reached out her arms and pulled him down, hugging him tightly so that all his weight rested on her. When she let him go, he sat on the edge of the bed, looking down into her eyes.

"Talk to me," she said to him. He began to massage her neck and her back. She turned onto her stomach and buried her face in the pillow.

"What do you want to talk about?"

"Anything." Pause. "Your girlfriends."

"All of them?"

She nodded.

"But there are too many. It will take ages."

She lifted her face and looked at him. "You are joking?"

"Yes, I am joking," he said smiling. "I have no girlfriend at the moment. What of you?"

"I just got divorced."

"Still. . . ."

"None, nothing."

Now his hands were inside her gown, running up and down the broad of her back. He took out his hands and began to undo the buttons on the gown. She remained still, her face in the pillow. When he finally had the gown open, he bent down and kissed her back, running his lips down her spine.

She shivered and said hoarsely, "That tickles. Nicely."

He kissed her again, and as he drew back he saw a nasty-looking scar on her back. It was unmistakably made by a belt buckle. It was a square black ridge against the light chocolate of her skin, just beneath her left shoulder blade. He touched it, circling it with his hand, around and around until she looked up at him, a half smile on her face. She got up and went and turned off the light, leaving only the light coming in through the half-open door of the bathroom. With a shake of her shoulders she dropped the gown onto the carpet before returning to bed; her round, up-tilted breasts made him catch his breath sharply. She lay beside him, then she rolled over him, and now he couldn't control himself any longer. Almost shaking with desire, he threw off his pants and his shirt and he pulled her to him, burying his face in her breasts. She sighed and guided him in.

"It will be better next time," she said afterward when she saw the rueful look on his face. He nodded. They lay in the gloom, facing each other, her head on his arm, his other hand running up and down her back, from her buttocks to the nape of her neck. He let his hand linger on the scar again and asked, "What happened here?"

"My ex. A souvenir from our last fight." She sighed, and then she began to speak, dredging up memory. "You know, he was the second person I ever made love to. . . ."

"Oh, I am disappointed. I thought tonight was your first time," said Mamo, trying to sound lighthearted, to counter the new note of sadness creeping into her voice, into the room.

"No . . . oh . . . be serious. . . ."

"Okay, but you must tell me about your first time."

She laughed and shifted nearer, throwing a leg over him. "The first time, I was in my first year at university, I was eighteen. It was awful. He forced himself on me at a campus party. He was a complete jerk. I can't even remember his name or what he looked like. I spent the whole month after anxiously waiting to see if I was pregnant. But the incident cured me of the desire to experiment further with sex. I totally lost interest. I became the most serious student in class, what they call a teacher's pet. I was always first in, sitting in front, answering all the questions, and doing all the assignments. Then George came . . . in my final year. He was something totally outside my experience. I remember he came in his army uniform, to see his sister, she was my roommate, and she had been telling me about him, but I wasn't prepared for the full impact."

"He must be really something, then."

"Then, yes. The first time he came to our house, my mum and my sister all promptly fell in love. Then, he was a gentle man. He was kind to me, gentle and generous . . . it was great. Then things changed after the baby. That was when the money began to come in. . . . During the last military regime he was just a lieutenant, but because of his connections in the military—his father was a retired officer—they made him head a task force on petroleum. He bought cars and went away for weekends with his friends and their girlfriends, leaving me home with the baby. Those were terrible times, I feel sad even now talking about it. . . ."

"You don't have to."

But she went on. "The baby was what saved me. I remember one day we were both crying, at night, the baby and I, and I got so angry that I felt like strangling the baby. I actually stood over the cot, looking down at him, and then suddenly he stopped crying and smiled up at me. I knew then that I needed help. When I went to my mother she told me that was how military men behaved, that I had to be patient, that he'd soon get tired of running around and come home, and that after all he had bought me things, jewelry, and recently a car. But that was before the beatings began. I remember the first time he slapped me. I had caught him red-handed with a girl in his car as I passed them on the street. When I asked him about it later at home he just raised his hand and slapped me. It was a revelation; my eyes opened and I knew I had to leave. Things would only get worse. The next time was this one, with the belt. He was drunk, and when I told him I was leaving him he took off his belt and started swinging it. I don't know how I had the presence of mind to grab my baby as I ran out, but I did. I drove to my mother, and only when I got there did I realize how much I was bleeding. And even then my mother wanted me to return. I told her no, I was getting a divorce. She was angry, she said it would bring shame on the family, that maybe if I had been a bit more patient with him things wouldn't have gotten to where they were. She always accused me of being too strong-minded, not like my sister. She made it worse when one day she let George take the baby. I was away at the market; when I came back she told me that my husband had been to the house and had taken the baby away.

"I left her house that night. I didn't say anything. I just went

inside and took my bag and left. I moved in with my friend at the
Low Cost Estate. The next day, when I went to his house,
George told me he had sent the boy to live with his retired par-
ents in the village. That was six months ago. I haven't seen my
baby since then. I couldn't think clearly, so I decided to come to
Keti, just to give my mind space to think."

The next time was better. They were more relaxed, and she cried
as she came, her body shaking and bouncing on the bed. Afterward she broke into tears and kissed him all over the face, hugging him tight.

Later, he said, "My first time, I was fourteen. There was this
girl, Binta, the neighbor's daughter. For some reason she had a
crush on me . . . surprisingly, because usually my brother was the
one the girls went for. But she liked me, and she sent me letters,
simple, stupid letters, over which LaMamo and I would laugh.
But I never spoke to her; I always avoided her when I ran into her
alone, only speaking to her when my brother was with me, which
was most of the time. Then one day she came to the house. She
had timed it perfectly; I was alone at home: my brother had gone
to play soccer. She came into the room and got straight into bed.
I stood over her, watching her, feeling trapped. When I finally got
in beside her, and she groped into my trousers, my penis had
shrunken to a quarter of its size. I was so embarrassed. I bluffed.
I told her it was a result of my sickness, and that this always happened when I was ill."

Zara laughed. "You liar."

"I was so nervous."

"What happened, did you do it?"

"We did. But I had to get help from my brother."

"How?"

"Well, despite that first disappointment she did come back,
and the next time she came she met both of us at home. And
when I stepped out to the toilet, I returned and found them in
bed."

"She was with your brother?"

"Yes. I can still see the look on his face as I stood over them: he looked helpless, apologetic, and excited all at once. And for some reason I did not feel angry or betrayed. The look on his face was hilarious. And she . . . she didn't even know I was in the room, her eyes were closed and she was moaning and urging him on. I sat on the other bed and watched. It was only after they had finished that I noticed how hard I was. I was almost bursting out of my pants. She casually asked me if I also wanted to do it. I guess she wanted to pay me back for betraying me so horribly. I did not hesitate."

"So where is she now? Do you still see her?"

"She died two years ago."

"Oh, what happened?"

"It's tragic. She was a nymphomaniac, I guess. She really loved sex. She was two years older than us. All the boys in our neighborhood had had her. She just loved it. Then she got pregnant and when she couldn't make any of her many casual lovers accept responsibility, she ran away to the state capital to get an abortion. She didn't come back afterward. She stayed on, returning to the village only once in a while, mostly at Christmas. I remember how she'd come home at Christmas, her hair dyed pink or blue, or whatever color had taken her fancy at that moment, wearing high heels and miniskirts, strutting up and down from one neighbor's house to the next, distributing gifts. The fool thought she was so sophisticated. Then Binta fell ill, she wasted away. When they brought her home she was just a skeleton. She died a week later."

In the morning, after a quick shower, he stood by the window and peered out through a crack. Zara was curled up in the sheets, her eyes closed, the outline of her body clear beneath the sheet. She wasn't asleep. Through the crack in the curtain he could see into the dew-wet garden. The one-eared Yam was up early; he was bent, almost hidden in the tall grass, cutting it down with a scythe, and every once in a while he would stop to pick his nose, or stare at the blade, a big frown on his flat, lumpy face, as if not happy with the implement's sharpness.

"You were going to tell me how Yam lost his ear," Mamo said, not turning around.

"Where is he?"

"There, in the garden."

She threw the sheets off and came and stood behind him, sliding her arms around his waist—she was almost as tall as he was. Her naked body was warm from the bed.

"Do you remember, when we were kids, there were all sorts of stories about child kidnappers?"

"I do. Strange men from the south who lured away children with sweets to turn them into money. But they were just bogeyman stories to make us behave."

"Not so, according to Yam. One of them actually kidnapped him, and to avoid getting caught he turned him into a yam tuber—easier to carry too." She laughed.

"They could turn young children into goats too, and lead them away on a leash, right before the parents' eyes."

"But Yam was lucky. It seemed some bystander had seen him being turned into a yam—one minute he was standing there, the next minute this man had touched him on the head and he had dropped to the ground, a yam. The spectator raised the alarm, but the kidnapper insisted it was a yam he had just bought. Then one of the men had a brainstorm; he took a knife and scratched the yam with it, and behold, it began to bleed. This was no ordinary yam. The kidnapper was dragged to the Mai's palace, where he was forced to turn the yam back into a human being, but when Yam came back most of his left ear was gone, it was where the knife had scratched him, and so to this day everyone calls him Yam."

Later, as he put on his trousers and shoes, getting ready to leave, he said to her, "I hope I am not rushing you into anything you might later regret."

She shook her head; she had an amused, mischievous smile on her face. "Actually, I wanted you to kiss me the first time we went up the hill."

He shook his head and said, "Maybe it's the air up there."

the meeting

A MONTH after Zara's arrival at the KCS, Uncle Iliya got another letter from the Ministry of Education, and this time he summoned an emergency staff meeting to discuss it. The meeting took place in his small office; there was just enough space to sit all four teachers—the hypochondriac English teacher was absent—and the two interns after the boxes and books on the floor had been moved. It was a brief meeting. In a heavy voice Iliya briefly told them of the earlier letter from the Ministry of Education, and then he read out the new one and waited for comments. The second letter was mainly a repetition of the first, but this time with a definite deadline by which the school was expected to implement the "recommendations" in the letters or risk being "reviewed."

"Well, is there anything we can do about it?" Zara asked tentatively.

"No," Iliya said, shaking his head. He looked out through the door at the group of farmers returning from the farm, walking in a single file, their hoes hanging from their shoulders, their water gourds held by a string dangling from their wrists. He looked into the anxious faces of the teachers—Ms. Lipstick, Mamo, Zara, Mr. Bukar, the interns—and he made a visible effort to square his shoulders, which had been bowed since he got the letter.

"Let me explain, for those of you who don't know how the school is sponsored. The twelve clans contribute voluntarily whatever they can at the end of the year—our sons and daughters working in the cities send money every year to the clan elders, who then hand over the money to me. That is how we pay your salaries. Sometimes, at very difficult moments, I go from house to house, from family to family, soliciting for contributions. More than once special offerings have been made for us at the church. For the past couple of years I have been trying to get the local government to give a hand, but up to now we've only had promises. And now the ministry wants to finally shut us down."

The teachers were silent, but then Ms. Lipstick, in a loud, optimistic voice, with an asinine smile on her face, said, "We have to fight them, that is what we have to do."

All waited to hear her battle plan, but she subsided into silence, as if, having given the war cry, she considered her part done and it was now somebody else's turn to take it from there. But no one spoke; they all stared at the floor or through the door or window, each with his personal thoughts. At last Iliya said, "Yes, we will have to do that, we have no other option. In the meantime, we have to close down the school. Tell the students we are going on an indefinite break till further notice." He spoke sadly, gathering his papers as he did so, opening the drawers, looking around him as if he did not expect to return to the office again.

After the meeting Zara offered to drive Iliya home in her car. He was looking suddenly tired and old. Mamo went with them; he sat in the front passenger seat, his uncle sat in the back with his case next to him on the seat. The teachers stood in a row before the classrooms and watched the car drive away.

Zara drove fast, almost recklessly.

"Watch it," Mamo said as she swerved to avoid a chicken sand-bathing in the middle of the road. Dogs came out of the roadside houses to chase the car, barking madly, covered by dust.

"I can't believe this. These people are bloody morons," Zara said angrily.

Mamo frowned at her. *Your language*, he mouthed. He looked

in the mirror to see his uncle's reaction. Iliya was seated in a corner, the stump of his missing arm pressed hard against the door,
as if he didn't want to take too much space—he was staring out
of the window, deep in thought.

They all went in when they reached the house. They sat in the
living room in silence: Iliya slumped on the sofa, Mamo on a
chair by the window, while Zara sat in an armchair next to the
sofa. Uncle Iliya's Second World War picture hung over a window. He was clutching a rifle tightly to his side, dressed in khaki
shorts and shirt and knee-length woolen socks, his head covered
by a wide-brimmed Stetson.

He had run away from home at fourteen to the city, where, two
years later, he had joined the army. His father had been a struggling farmer and a hard taskmaster—in the rainy season he'd
send his whole family to the bush farm for weeks, with little
food, to survive only on what they could hunt or dig up. His
father was especially against his growing interest in the new
Christian religion. Iliya would hang around the mission gate,
joining the other kids whenever he could to listen to Reverend
Drinkwater talk about the lives of biblical characters—David,
Joseph, Naaman, Ruth, Esther, and, of course, Jesus Himself. As
soon as they could read and write, the reverend would make
them write their own biographies: about their ancestry, their
gods, their myths, and of their desire to be washed white by the
blood of Jesus. At last the conflict between the farm life, which
he hated, and the new religion, which he loved but which he
wasn't allowed to practice, became unbearable and he decided to
leave home. His chance came when the reverend was going on
one of his annual trips to Jos; Iliya followed him and his porters
at a distance—it was a journey of two days by foot to the state
capital, then half a day by truck from there to Jos. He remained
out of sight the first day, hiding behind a bush whenever the reverend's party stopped, but on the second day, weak and almost
fainting with hunger, he revealed himself. After hearing his story
the reverend agreed to take him along. In Jos he entrusted Iliya

to one of the missionaries as a servant—but after two years, he had joined hundreds of others to enlist in the West African Frontier Force. It was 1940 and the Second World War was in its first flush. They were sent to India and Burma in 1942. "That was where I lost my youth and my religion and my idealism; I had actually wanted to be a preacher. But after Burma I became a realist, a pragmatist." He had been appalled by the open racism toward the black soldiers by the white soldiers.

"When we got to India we were surprised to discover that a legend about us, most probably started by the British soldiers, had already taken root: we were cannibals and we were there to eat the enemy, raw. And whenever we went to bathe in the river the Indians, some of them actually darker than us, would follow us to see if we had tails. But the worst moments were still yet to come. I made a friend; a young man from the Ivory Coast, his name was Wilson. He was badly wounded during an engagement, and he and a few other wounded were to be taken by train to a hospital. But they disappeared on the way. We heard the rumors later that they had been thrown off the train into the Ganges by white officers because they were really not worth the bother. After that I lost my faith in people, in religion, in almost everything."

He saw that one could never depend on his fellow humans to protect him, or even to be just to him. One had to fight every inch of the way, and the best way to equip oneself for this lifelong fight was by getting an education. After the war he stayed on in Jos to get an education, only returning to Keti when he had qualified as a teacher and had started working in the state capital. His father was dead by then, and his mother was hanging on to life only because she was convinced she'd see him once more before she died—he was her only son. Education became his one moving passion in life, and when he retired from government service at the age of fifty-five he had convinced the community to start the KCS, which they did, and he had poured his whole energy into it, working without pay or rest. And now everything he had worked for and believed in was about to go.

Zara said, "Sir, I just want you to know that I'll back you all the way if you decide to fight this in court."

Iliya said nothing; he only sighed and shifted in his seat. At last Zara stood up and said she had to go. As she passed him the headmaster reached out his one arm and held her hand; he looked up at her and smiled. "Thanks, child, for everything. I don't know what your story is, or why you came to us, but it has been great working with you. Not many people will do what you did, working without pay. How long have you been here, two months?"

"Yes."

"Well, I hope you've been happy. I wish . . . I wish . . . " Iliya groped about broken-tongued, and when he couldn't find the right words he sighed and dropped her hand. Zara dipped her head and Mamo saw the tears in her eyes before she quickly wiped them away. He walked her to the car; she sat behind the wheel and leaned her chin on it, staring ahead. Mamo stood before the open door and stared at Asabar's former hut, which now stood empty; goats lay in the open doorway, chewing the cud meditatively. Asabar had moved to his own place at the edge of the hill when his drinking and wild ways became too much for his father to ignore. They watched half-naked children chasing each other around the sycamore tree, squealing loudly, scaring away the goats. The road ahead seemed to stretch on and on, the red earth shimmered and shifted under the scorching heat, once in a while a lone figure would appear in the distance and then disappear again, as if swallowed by the mirage. A group of five school kids appeared out of a turning, hand in hand, their uniforms patched and dirty, their feet bare. They were singing "African Rivers" and their voices rose high and clear in the hot air:

> Nile
> Niger
> Senegal
> Congo

Orange
Limpopo
Zambezi! O Zambezi! O Zambezi!

"Have you been happy here?" Mamo repeated his uncle's question, leaning his arm on the car roof.

"Yes, as happy as I can ever be anywhere, I guess. I am not a very happy person by nature."

"So, what now? Are you going back to the city?"

"Yes . . . I have decided to take my husband to court, over my son's custody."

Mamo went around and got into the passenger's seat. This was the first time she was mentioning this to him.

"Are you sure you want to do this? Things like this could get rather messy. . . ."

"I can't give up my child, not like this."

Mamo took her hand and they sat in silence. Finally she asked, "And you, are you going to stay on in the village?"

Mamo sighed. "Do you sometimes feel like there's this big sack you want to carry, and you know you can carry it, only it has no handle?"

"Every day." She rested her head on his shoulder. "Every single day."

"You could finish writing your novel."

"Sometimes I feel like I have run out of things to say."

He stroked her head, then he quoted, " 'The world is as new today as it was when first created, and what we have is not a shortage but a surfeit of things to say.' "

She sat up and looked at him.

"Herman Melville, or Thoreau, said that," Mamo said.

"It's so optimistic, so beautiful. I should write it down somewhere."

the decline of lamang

LAMANG'S DECLINE began the day he went to the state capital with his huge entourage, expecting to be crowned as his
party's chairman. Years later, when he wrote his father's biography, Mamo would handle this aspect of Lamang's life by quoting
the report of the event by the state's only newspaper, the *Trum-
pet*. It was as if he wanted to have revenge on his father by
immortalizing his worst moment in the starkest words possible.
The headline was bold and unremitting:

Reverse Osmosis: Lamang Loses to Danladi

*Today the Victory Party's hot favorite for the state chairmanship, Mr.
Musa Lamang, lost out to Alhaji Isa Danladi after a month-long
battle for the post. The members of the party today voted at the
party's annual convention going on at the state capital. The compe-
tition was so close that at first voting the candidates came out even,
and finally the members had to ask the candidates to make a brief
presentation about their vision for the party, and that was where
Danladi came out on top. It seems he had come well prepared for
such an eventuality. His first words were met with a loud ovation:
"I know how we can supply the whole state with water cheaply and
steadily using a technique called reverse osmosis." He then invited
a consultant whom he had brought specially from Lagos to present
the details. The consultant, an Indian engineer who owns a water
treatment company, took the floor and went on to explain to the*

audience in complex and impressive details the concept of reverse
osmosis. In brief, reverse osmosis refers to a technique of taking
water from the sea, purifying it, and pumping it into tanks and
reservoirs for domestic use. Danladi claims the same technique, but
on an industrial scale, can be used to supply the whole of the state
with water from the Atlantic.

"If we can pump crude petrol from Port Harcourt to the refinery
in Kaduna, there is no reason why we can't pump water. We will
create artificial lakes and rivers; we will turn the barren lands into
huge farms and green belts. Remember, money is not our problem,
but how to spend it."

At this point Lamang got up and walked out of the convention
hall in a huff without making a presentation. Some of the delegates
accused him of being a bad loser. But Danladi's presentation was so
successful that not only was he made the chairman by unanimous
decision, but the words "Reverse Osmosis" have been adopted as the
Victory Party's official campaign slogan from now on.

Lamang resigned from the party, but only after his repeated
petitions against Danladi's blatant theft of his idea had gone
unanswered by the party leadership. To the few loyal friends who
came to commiserate with him—the majority had deserted him
to Danladi's side—he was careful to appear unbowed by this set-
back; instead he was full of fighting words, promising a spectacular "comeback" soon. The widows stayed by him, perhaps
hoping to take him unawares now that he was weak, his defenses
down. They'd come mostly in the afternoons, separately, sometimes together, bearing food flasks covered in white antimacas-
sars; in the flasks would be pounded yam and pepper soup,
Lamang's favorite food, and as he ate he would anxiously deliberate on his change of fortune, and the widows would listen and
once in a while put in a word of counsel.

"I give the party two months, no, just one month, before they
regret choosing Danladi, and all the negative thinkers around
him, over me. They'll see him for who he truly is, an ingrate, a

double-crosser. This is a man I opened my doors to, and introduced to all the important members of the party—in fact, I
recruited him into this party. . . . I tell you, soon they'll see his
true colors, then they'll come begging to have me back. And you
know what? That is when I will laugh in their faces and send
them away."

"No," Rabi would caution, putting a hand on his shoulder, "you
mustn't do that. Just accept their apology and take the post."

"Yes," the other widows would chorus. "They will have learned
their lesson by then."

Lamang would laugh and after a while he'd shrug and con-
cede, "I guess you are right. The main thing is to serve."

One month passed, then two months, then three, but still the
much-expected delegates from the Victory Party headquarters
didn't come. Lamang hardly went out of the house, remaining
mostly in his room, listening to the radio, pacing up and down;
this routine was only broken by the widows' visits, because by
now even the few friends from his political meetings had stopped
coming. He still brought out the TV in the evenings, though not
as many people as before came to watch it.

measuring time

AFTER THE closure of the school Mamo found himself with time on his hands and without much means of using it apart from taking long walks in the afternoon. He took walks not only to kill time, but also to avoid his father's constant looming presence in the house, and the inane laughter of the widows whenever they came to visit. A few times he had contemplated going to his uncle and asking for a small loan to enable him to get a place of his own, a modest room somewhere, but he knew this wasn't the time to talk to Iliya about a loan, and so he took his long walks. Zara was not around to make the days more bearable; she had left for the state capital a week after the school had closed, promising to return the following weekend, but two weeks later she still hadn't turned up. Before leaving she had told him she was finally feeling strong enough to bring things to a head between her and her ex-husband. He had offered to help in any way he could, even if it meant asking his father for assistance, but she had shaken her head and said no, "I'd prefer you to keep out of this."

With no work to prepare for in the mornings, the hours seemed to have grown twice as long and Mamo would sometimes wake up in the morning and almost panic when he thought of the long, lonely day ahead of him—he'd sit on the bed for hours, his back propped up against the wall, watching the thin rays of morning sun streaming into the window. He missed the drab routine of meeting the students and listening to Ms. Lipstick and Mr. Bukar gripe about their lives. Outside, in the yard, Auntie Marina would be talking to the goats and chickens as she fed them. On good days he walked her to her farm and passed the hours under a tree reading a book or sleeping, but often he left her early, before the fresh invigorating morning air had turned hot and painful and hard to breathe.

He waited for something, anything, to happen, and as he waited he measured time in the shadows cast by trees and walls, in the silence between one footfall and the next, between one breath and the next, in the seconds and minutes and hours and days and weeks and months that add up to form the seasons. The rainy season ended in October, the wind turned dry and harsh, the leaves on the trees and cornstalks turned brown and brittle. Farmers brought home the harvest; the hunters set the hills on fire and chased the game up to the summit. At night the hilltops became incandescent with color—like a painting, the fires snaking around the contours of the hills, their orange reflected by the low clouds that hung over the hills like a backcloth.

He took his longest walks in the evenings. In his walks he was in no hurry to go anywhere. He'd go far into the fields, past the farmers grubbing in the dry raw red earth, past the Fulani herdsmen and their cattle and families and tents. Whenever he walked, he felt like going on and on, breaking into a run and flying away—but he always grew tired and returned home slowly, his head bowed and aching.

One day he went to the old abattoir. He felt a strange kinship with the tired, tumbledown building; it reminded him of his brother, and how their childhood dream of running away to achieve fame had burned brightest and then burned out, for him at least, in this dark hall. The building looked even more derelict than he remembered, the fetid smell was stronger, the mounds of garbage and animal droppings had risen higher, the rodents and reptiles had multiplied and the sounds of their scurrying in the dark corners had also multiplied proportionately, goats took afternoon naps in the enclosures and utility rooms. He stood at the window that faced the river—now that the rainy season was over the tall elephant grass had withered and the view to the water was clear. He could see naked children jumping in and out of the water that was growing shallower each year, screaming maniacally with pleasure, their wet brown skin gleaming in the sun. The children rushed out of the water and stood in the sand, pointing up at a plane passing overhead with a white trail following it like a tail.

He walked until he got to the main road, an A Trunk road leading to the neighboring state. He walked by the road, enjoying the violent rush of wind and noise that accompanied each speeding car. He and his brother had once seen a woman drop a handkerchief out of a car window. She was wiping her face with it and the wind had snatched it out of her hand and into the tall grasses. The small red car had not stopped and the twins had broken into a mad dash for the handkerchief, which was once again airborne. LaMamo dived and caught it, and then he stood staring and sniffing at it, as if mesmerized. It felt soft to the touch, light, its sparkling white now turning dirty where their grubby hands touched it. They rubbed it on their sweaty faces, imagining the woman's softness in its softness.

"Silk," they whispered.

The radio and books sustained him at night. He'd lie in the dark and listen to the voices from faraway Lagos or London or America or Germany discussing art or politics or architecture. There were also the late request programs when insomniacs like him would phone in with their marital woes, their sexual angst, their clinical depressions, and their congenital diseases. As he listened to the voices, with the moonlight coming in through the window, the loneliness didn't bite that sharply; he'd feel as if the people

on the radio were seated beside him, together forming a community of misfits, freaks, and solitaries, desperately reaching out to
touch flesh, to form a cycle of empathy. His bed was a time ship,
the radio was a component of it, moving him forward and backward in time, visiting history and people and places, until finally
the announcer's voice lulled him to sleep. Sometimes he'd jerk
awake again, the light through the window in his eyes and
Beethoven's Fifth on the radio—but it was not morning yet, it
was only the false dawn and it would grow dark again. The real
dawn was still hours away. It was at times like this that he'd look
across the room to his brother's empty bed, and his eyes would
fill with tears.

Once, Auntie Marina, on the way to the outhouse at three A.M.,
had found him seated in the living room, in the dark. He had
been seated there for hours, staring at a tiny chink of light coming in through a hole in the window. She started when she turned
on the light and saw him on the sofa.

"Twin, what are you doing, seated here all alone in the dark, is
something wrong?"

"No," he replied, "I am just waiting."

"Waiting? For what?"

"Nothing." He stood up and headed back to his room. "Just
waiting, that's all."

At moments like this he could actually feel the loneliness
curled up like a ball somewhere low in his abdomen. In his room
he brought out from under the bed a carton in which he and his
brother had always kept their stuff since childhood. It was full of
tattered books, most of which had been given to them by Uncle
Iliya, or which they had borrowed from friends and failed to
return. There were also pocketknives, buttons, and other childhood odds and ends. He unfolded a large piece of tracing paper
and spread it on the bed; it was LaMamo's impression of the
Seven Wonders of the Ancient World, which he had painstak-
ingly copied from a history textbook one evening while Mamo lay

recuperating from a crisis. The hills were in green, the rivers in blue, the people in pink and brown, the buildings in gray. The Hanging Gardens of Babylon, the Great Pyramid of Giza, the Colossus of Rhodes, the Mausoleum at Halicarnassus, the statue of Zeus at Olympia, the temple of Artemis at Ephesus, and finally, the Lighthouse of Alexandria. Once, they had dreamed of one day visiting all these sites.

He refolded the paper and returned to rummaging. He found the handkerchief, still white, still faintly smelling of the woman's heady perfume—or maybe it was just his memory of the smell. He spread it out on the bed and his mind went back to the woman. Long after the fleeting encounter they had continued to obsess about who she might be, where she might be going to, and if she was married to the driver. They had taken turns to masturbate in the hankie while images of the woman flashed through their minds. But gradually that fever had abated; she grew blurry and indistinct and finally disappeared.

He raised the hankie and ran his hand absently on it. A few weeks after LaMamo's departure he had discovered that the material was not really silk, just ordinary muslin. He had felt unaccountably scared after that—scared that all he had dreamt of being, the places he had dreamt of going, might not really exist in real life, they might be only figments of his imagination, like the silk, or the ancient wonders. That day when Zara had asked him what his future plans were, he should have told her, as he had told Auntie Marina, that he was waiting, just waiting. Once he had waited for death, and once he and his brother had waited for fame and adventure, but now he wasn't sure anymore what he waited for.

going to see the mai

HIS UNCLE sent for him early one morning and when he went he found Iliya already dressed in a long caftan with a hand-embroidered hat on his head, ready to go out.

"We are going to see the Mai," he said the moment Mamo came in. Mamo sat down and listened as his uncle unfolded yet another plan for rescuing the school from being finally shut down. He had written endless letters to the commissioner of education and then to the deputy governor and after that to the governor, but not one of them had replied. The letters had been long and full of details about the idea behind the KCS, and how important the school was to the students, and the need for keeping the education sector an open one where both the private and the public schools could function. If everything was taken over by the government, Iliya had argued, it could lead to monopoly and a slackening of standards, and even though the KCS did not have a hundred thousand in its bank account at the moment, that didn't detract from the good work it was doing. But not one of them had replied.

Now he said, "We are going to the palace to explain to the Mai what is going on. As the village's foremost traditional ruler he has the governor's ear, and if anyone can make the governor listen, it is him. And it is in his interest to have such a good school in the district, it is one thing he can point to and be proud of. I hope he knows that. I want you to come as the teachers' representative."

"Me?"

"Yes. You are the only one I can find at such a short notice."

Mamo listened and allowed himself to be infected by his uncle's desperate enthusiasm. In the past month, as he took his walks, or paced his room at night unable to sleep, or as he listened to his father's footsteps pacing back and forth in his room, he'd also imagine his uncle in his room pacing back and forth, measuring time with each step, and he'd feel the guilt and the powerlessness mount because there was nothing he could do to assist his uncle in his time of distress. He felt guilt because, though he believed in the school and its importance to the community, he did not have the sense of personal mission his uncle had regarding it, and not having it was like a betrayal of his uncle. Here at last was a chance for him to contribute to the effort, even if only as a silent listener.

The palace was in the village center, not too far away from the market. Today was Monday, market day—the streets were crowded with people, the cars and motorcycles moved an inch at a time, and the drivers had their hands permanently on their horns, adding to the noise and the heat and the general irritation. There were trucks off-loading merchandise brought by Hausa traders from Kano; there were Igbo traders with clothes and palm oil and imitation electronic products with names like Naiwa, Sonny, Samsong, etc.; Fulani herdsmen out on the town for the day swaggered in the center of the road, hand in hand, with long braided hair and trousers tight in the crotch and thighs and flaring at the ankles, their sticks slung over their shoulders. In the back streets the brewhouses were already filling up—loud *goge* and drum music pulsated above the roar of voices and motor engines, and for no reason Mamo suddenly remembered a proverb: that a drum is at its loudest and clearest just before it breaks.

The palace's main façade imitated a mosque's front view, with columns and horseshoe arches leading into a huge bare waiting room with a vaulted roof topped by a dome. Palace guards and attendants in multicolored uniforms lounged on mats in the cool interior of the waiting room, their backs propped against the wall, their mouths red with kola, and their eyes shiny with kohl, eyes which they lifted to the newcomers unsmilingly. Uncle Iliya looked at one of them impatiently and said, "Abu, is the Mai in today?"

The man, an elder in his sixties with badly wrinkled skin, grudgingly nodded, stood up, and wasted almost a whole minute shaking the dust off his robe before saying, "Follow me."

The waiting room opened onto a vast courtyard with a few cars jacked onto bricks next to the tall walls on either side. Mamo imagined the Mai's many wives and children on the other side of the walls, going about their business—and he wondered if they didn't feel a bit like prisoners sometimes. He had heard of how the compound behind the walls was like a town of its own, with several extended families living together, and how some of the wives never stepped out again from the day they went in until death—their death or the Mai's death. If the Mai died, the new Mai simply took over his predecessor's wives, unless he preferred to have his own choice. Facing them at the other end of the courtyard was the entrance to the Mai's lounge, where he received visitors; the entrance was of sliding glass, and as they climbed the steps that led up to the doors, Mamo could see faintly through the glass the outline of two men seated on a sofa, facing outside.

"Wait here," the old guard said and entered. He dropped to his knees as soon as he entered, approaching the Mai on all fours. Mamo thrust his hands into his pockets and took them out again. He was nervous. Soon the guard came out and waved them forward. "The Mai will see you now."

They took off their shoes before they went in, and for a moment Mamo was afraid his uncle would drop on all fours like the guard had done, in which case he'd have no option but to do likewise—but his uncle merely bowed from the waist as he greeted the two men.

"It is the headmaster—the Mai welcomes you, Headmaster," said the man seated beside the Mai. He was the Waziri, the Mai's vizier.

"Thank you, Waziri," Iliya said.

The Waziri waved toward the overstuffed ottomans in the center of the lushly carpeted room. As he stepped forward to sit, Mamo felt his feet disappear in the soft carpet—it was like walking on water. The Waziri and the Mai were actually not seated on the same seat, Mamo noticed. The Waziri was on a single seat drawn up against the Mai's big sofa, and they were huddled together, whispering—the Waziri was doing most of the talking, while the Mai occasionally nodded. The Mai had a big turban on his head, and its trailing part covered his chin and cheeks and nose. Mamo knew the face well, as he had seen it many times before, though mostly from a distance as the Mai passed through the street in his car, waving to the people lined up to see him. The face also stared out of photographs hanging in almost every house in Keti.

"Headmaster, who is the young man with you?" the Waziri asked, and Mamo assumed that was what the whispering had been about.

"He is Mamo. He is here to represent his colleagues, the teachers. He is also my brother's son," Iliya said, addressing the Mai directly.

"Your Highness, this is Mamo, Lamang's son," the Waziri said.

Mamo shifted in his seat, maintaining a constant smile on his face. He thought it would be amusing to see how the interview would go on, and wondered whether the Waziri was going to be the Mai's mouthpiece throughout. At the mention of his father's name, Mamo saw the Mai give him a sharp, interested look. Lamang was no stranger to the palace—Mamo knew that every year during the Muslim Eid feast his father sent two cows to the Mai. At last the Waziri said, "Well, Headmaster, it's been a long time since we saw you here. But they say the palace is like the marketplace, people must always return to it one day. What can the Mai do for you?"

"I am sorry, Your Highness, if I haven't been coming to greet you as much as I ought to, but you know me, I am a headmaster and the school takes up all of my time."

"The Mai understands, Headmaster. We are all proud of the great work you are doing with the school," said the Waziri, shifting in his seat, leaning forward. For the first time Mamo took a good look at the man, now that his eyes had adjusted to the poor light in the room: he was thin and writhy, like a snake, constantly shifting in his seat as if plumping the cushion with his buttocks, leaning forward, then back, then sideways to whisper to the Mai. On his head was a smaller version of the Mai's turban, but the Mai's was blue while his was white, as was his long caftan. His turban, however, had no trailing part to cover his lower face. He had a thin, long beard that he sometimes touched as he spoke or waited for an answer, and one of his eyes, the left one, was off focus. He looked as surreal as the wall mats behind him depicting scenes from Koranic legends: Abraham leading his son Ishmael, now a ram, to the sacrifice, while an angel in white lurked behind a bush noting Abraham's faithfulness. Another mat showed Adam and Eve, post-innocence, in the garden, their waists covered in leaves, apples in their hands, and above them the smirking human-headed snake, Shaitan, hanging from a tree branch.

"It is because of the school that we are here, Your Highness. But I am sure the palace is aware of our troubles, as nothing happens in this village that is hidden from the wise eyes of the palace. So I won't waste your valuable time with the details of the demand the Ministry of Education is making on us. I have here copies of the letters written to us by the ministry, and also of my letters to the ministry and to the governor and the commissioner of education," said Uncle Iliya, leaning forward and handing over the said documents to the Waziri, who placed them on the side

table beside his seat without even glancing at them. Mamo was
surprised when he heard a soft snoring sound coming from the
Mai, and when he looked he saw that the Mai had actually nodded off and his head was now tilted at an angle. Mamo looked to
the Waziri, who seemed not to be disturbed or embarrassed by
the Mai's sudden attack of narcolepsy. He simply cleared his
throat loudly, and at the sound the Mai's eyes snapped open and
he adjusted his position on the seat. He leaned toward the Waziri
and they conferred once more, then the Mai nodded and spoke
directly to Iliya.

"I'll look into this, Iliya, and I'll get back to you. But I want you
to know that since the coming of the new civilian administration
. . . there are so many changes going on and it will take a while
before things settle, so we promise nothing. But we will look into
it. What is a people without modern education?"

Mamo thought the Mai's speech sounded hollow and uncon-
vincing, as if he said the same thing to everyone who came to
him with a suit. After making the little speech, the Mai appeared
to subside back into sleep. The Waziri cleared his voice and said
to Iliya, "Well, Headmaster, the Mai has spoken. He will look
into it. He has given you his assurance and you know he doesn't
give his word lightly."

"Thank you," Iliya said, taking the cue and standing up. Mamo
quickly stood up too.

Outside, in the sun and air and dust, Mamo let his annoyance
show as he said to his uncle, "That was abrupt. Do you think he
will do anything?"

Iliya was quiet for a while, and then he said, "Our traditional
rulers are like politicians, you can't depend on their word. But we
are like drowning men, we have to exhaust all avenues." Uncle
Iliya sounded tired. He walked with a slow, listless gait, and
Mamo had to slow down in order not to leave him behind.

As he returned home he heard his father's loud voice from the
living room holding court with the widows and other friends.

Mamo sighed and paused at the door. Suddenly he decided to go to the state capital to see Zara. It was the fourth straight week since he had seen her last and suddenly he knew he couldn't wait any longer. He had never been to her place in the state capital, but he knew the address, and the capital was only an hour away. He went to his room to change and pick up a few things, and then he left without telling anyone where he was going.

part two

dear brother

Monrovia
January 1990

Dear brother,
First I must say happy birthday because tomorrow 15th of January you and I will both become 25 years old—though I know this letter will not get to you immediately. Some people they are medical workers of Médicins sans Frontières (or MSF) from France, they are going to Paris and they will post it for me from there. But still have a nice birthday whenever you get the letter, that is what I want to say first.

I've been in Liberia for over two years now, and so many things has happened, and not too many of them good. For instance if you remember my friend whose family was killed and because of him I am now in Liberia, well, he is dead. His name is Samuel Paul. We came together three of us from Mali then to Ouagadougou, we decide to leave the others in Mali with the Tuaregs because it was a fight that was not ending and we said what are we fighting for anyway? Samuel said in Liberia we can fight for money and be our own boss, and he also want revenge. So we came through Ouagadougou to his village in the north of Liberia. He has been away from here for five years and so much have change. All the house are empty, it seems so much fighting has been done here, the village is empty, and it smell of dead bodies, we even saw half-buried corpses in the bush. He showed us his house, it has been burned down by fire, and the church where all his family were killed. He cried when he showed us the church, he showed us where he hid that day behind the altar. This boy Samuel is younger than me, just about twenty and I can see how he missed his family.

When I saw him crying in the church I asked myself what all these fighting is for? I am a soldier for almost ten years now and I live by fighting but sometimes it doesn't make sense. It is just crazy. That's why I wish you are here because you have read many books and you know the meaning of things more than me and you can have explained things to me.

I am now writing from a house in a rubber plantation close to Monrovia, and there's a girl, her name is Bintou, that I want you to meet. Of all the women I have known she is the most beautiful and I tell her about you all the time. Her father is killed by soldiers and she has no one and it is now my duty to take care of her because I love her and after the war we will get married. But let me tell you step by step how I come to this place. After we left Samuel Paul's village which is in Nimba County of Liberia we decided to join a bigger group so that we can be safe and offer our service to them. There are so many different groups fighting here in Liberia. There are big groups like Charles Taylor, who I've seen before when he come to talk to us in the camp in Libya, and Alhaji Kromah, from the north, and Yomi Johnson, this man is said to be the most dangerous because he killed the Liberian President Samuel Doe like a dog in the street and made videos of the killing and is selling it for money on the streets. No one thought Doe could be killed because he had so much juju, but this Johnson has greater juju. There are also small groups, these are just hunters with guns and anyone who can get a gun. They don't believe in anyone or anything they are just fighting because they want to eat and they have nothing to do. Some of them are as old as

*ten years. It is terrible. There are also peace keeping groups the
ECOMOG mostly Ghanians and Nigerians from our country.*

*We decide to head south towards Monrovia the capital,
Samuel said that is where most of the action is. Here people
can make a lot of money by looting especially in Monrovia,
that is why we want to go there. In the first year we joined a
group of twenty rebels, they call themselves "Hit Squad" and
the leader agreed to have us, he is Major Kutubi a very unstable man, from the beginning I didn't like him, but we have no
choice. Kutubi's plan is to move and join the big group of
Charles Taylor because he believe Taylor will win the civil war
and become president and he Kutubi will be made a general
in the new national army. But our group instead of growing
only became smaller. We were in an ambush by another group
and Samuel Paul was killed, and other ten people, I escaped
narrowly. I lose one eye, I am sorry to tell you this because I
know it will be a pain to you, but it is true, I am used to it now,
and having one eye is really not too bad, it is like two eyes only
the empty eye still hurt sometimes.*

*I was left for dead beside my dead friend Samuel Paul, but
I was found by this French people from MSF. Their clinic is
in a classroom in the university in Monrovia which is now
closed because of fighting the city is not safe anymore and even
the MSF are scared for their lives. The whole country is dead,
all the villages are on fire and there is no food and there are
only dead bodies on the street. Only women and children can
be seen, all the men are soldiers fighting for survival. I almost
died but my eye healed after some weeks. Now I am alone I
have nowhere to go and really I don't feel like fighting anymore. I even began to plan how to return home. There are
many sick people here, hundreds of them everyday, and mostly
they are women and small children with cholera and infection
and many of the kids die and are buried in the field. Me and
one of the patients sometimes help the French men to bury the
dead and they give us food. This other patient is very interest-*

ing because he is not really a patient, he told me he used to be a lecturer at the university and that soldiers had killed his family and the MSF people have saved him like they saved me. He is not very old but is short, and thin like all people here because of the war and his teeth is brown and rotten and he is bald and he wear thick glasses. Sometimes I feel sorry for him, but he is the only one I can talk to. He is very educated and a professor, and he is always talking about why people fight each other, and the "political economics of war," and he said right now he is writing a history of the whole world through the wars people fought from beginning of time till now. Everyone calls him professor. He said there are many categories of war, but of all this categories only one is right, that is the war people fight to liberate themselves, and that every other kind of war is unjust and it is only war lords making common people to fight for them and get killed in the process. Sometimes he reads to me from a book called The Art of War. He said it is not a book about war but about how to avoid war. It is interesting. I am learning so much things since I met him.

Tragedy struck us when soldiers came to the clinic and started shooting. They killed one of the white doctors and many defenseless patients. Now I see the soldiers are Major Kutubi and seven soldiers. He sees me and said we must go together, I didn't want to go with him, but he just threw a gun to me and said, "Up, soldier, there's work to be done." They took one of the French men, his name is Charles, and he is very young, he is just a month in Liberia and he is journalist he is always interviewing the sick people and even me and the professor and taking pictures and always complaining of how he can't communicate with his newspaper in France. The phones are dead and there is no electricity. He is the one who told me that after the war he can get me a glass eye to wear and no one will know that my eye is of glass. The professor came with us. Kutubi is very excited. He said he has found how to make money by taking hostage, that he has a safe house in a rubber plantation outside Monrovia and already the farmer, an American, is his hostage, plus the farm foreman who is from Guinea, and his daughter and she is the one I mentioned earlier. He said the place is hidden and no one can find us and from there we can conduct business with the French government and tell them to give us millions to release the doctor, and also the American government for the American rubber farmer.

The rubber plantation is many miles big and it stands in the valley created by two big hills, there are miles and miles of rubber trees. The house stands at the foot of one of the hills, the one in the north. I must say how it reminds me so much of the hills at home. In the evening the birds and small animals can be heard calling to each other and a mist descend over the trees making everything look so peaceful. Kutubi had left two of his soldiers in charge of the owner of the plantation, he is a big American and his name is Mr. Turner. When we came back we found that one of the soldiers had shot Turner in the stomach. It seems they tried to rape the young girl, she is around eighteen, and when her father tried to stop them they shot him dead in the head, and the American also when he protested they shot him in the belly. So now her father is dead, her mother had gone to Guinea when the war started but she couldn't return because of the war, so she was only with her father and the American Mr. Turner who owns the plantation and now the father is dead and Turner is wounded. The father's body is dumped in one of the store rooms, and the American is on the floor bleeding, and the girl has been raped in the kitchen—that was how we found everything. Major Kutubi was very angry.

He shot both of the soldiers after asking them to bury the dead body, just like that. He said they had made him to lose money because if the American dies he will lose millions which the American government will pay him as ransom, and that the only good thing was that he had the French journal-

ist too. The major pointed the gun at the journalist and told
him to cure the American. But I can see how afraid Charles is
because he is very young and he has been in the country less
than one month. He began to protest and said that he didn't
know anything about medicine, and as he talk I saw the major
getting more and more angry and he was beginning to wave his
gun, the professor saw it too because he stepped forward and
said to the journalist, "I'll assist you, I've seen it done before.
The first thing is to knock out the patient with whiskey. Let us
take him to the bedroom. I can see bottles of whiskey all over
the place. Just get him drunk and operate."

   We sat in the living room and we can hear the American
screaming in the bedroom. The girl also went upstairs and
even though her clothes are torn and she looked terrible you
can see how young and really beautiful she is. I went out and
sat on the veranda steps. Outside the air is fresh and smelling
of rubber sap and you can see the clouds over the hills, they
look so close and as if they are leaning forward, as if they will
fall on you. Beside the main house there is another smaller
house, maybe one or two bedrooms, that must be the house of
the foreman the girl's father and now he is dead. The professor
and the journalist later join me and you can see the journalist
shaking and looking very white. The professor was joking
about him being scared of blood, and he gave him whiskey to
calm him down. Behind us one of the soldiers stands with his
gun, guarding the journalist so that he doesn't run away. When
he got drunk the professor started talking about his life history.
He was educated in Russia at the Patrice Lumumba University where he became a Marxist. But he changed his mind
from Marxism when the Berlin Wall fell down in 1989 and
when Russia started to become capitalist with the introduction
of Glasnosts. Then he became an African socialist. He believes
in Julius Nyerere and Ujamaa. He said in his book that he is
writing he will promote the idea of the single party in all of
Africa because that is closest to the African model—and that

*most people see multi-party democracy as a license to fight and
kill; he said Nyerere realized that long ago. He said that our
problem is that we have been divided along tribal and religious
lines by the former colonizers and now we are being devided by
multi-party democracy, he said what we need is more areas of
unity not division. He said also in Africa the traditional system
and our respect for elders has made us not to question the right
of those in office to loot and steal, he also said that the colonial system had taken all that is bad in our traditional system
and used it to keep the people down. Because of this brutality
the people never trust any government, we always see the
government as our enemy, because even after the colonial system has ended, the African rulers continue to use the same
system of dictatorship ruling as the colonial government. He
said that what we need is a political education of the people, and
that every government must create equal grounds for people to
grow to their full potential. He said that these wars will go on
until we reach that level. Have you ever thought about it, why
there are wars, or about this war in particular, about people
who make wars?*

*One day I shot the major. This is what happened. There is
a lot of food in the house, because the owner, the American
Mr. Turner has stock food in the store and many bottles of
whiskey. His plan was to stay till the war was over, he didn't
want to go back to America because of his farm even though
his embassy has evacuated all the Americans, like many people
he believe the war will soon be over, then later it became too
dangerous for him to leave. So we have a lot of food to eat.
Most of the time the soldiers drank the whiskey, and Major
Kutubi was only concerned with looting everything in the
house, he had filled the back of the Land Rover to the roof
with carpets and clothes and tv and video and all electronics
in the house. Everyday he asks Mr. Turner to give him the dol-
lars in the house, Mr. Turner gave him all, but he kept saying
it wasn't enough, now he threatens to kill him. Then he*

*ordered the girl to come down and cook some food in the
kitchen. We are now here over a week and all the canned food
and whiskey has almost finished. The girl has been hiding in
the bedroom all this time, helping Turner, and the professor is
the one taking food to her. Her name is Bintou. Sometimes I
go up to see how she is doing, but not always, because the
major doesn't like anyone talking to the American if he is not
there. I can see the American will soon die any way. Kutubi
dragged her to the kitchen and I can see her falling as she came
down the stairs because she is so scared, she is so thin because
she hasn't been eating and always grieving for her father and
fearing for her life. He followed her into the kitchen and after
a while we heard her screaming and she ran into the living
room. We were all soldiers seated there, nobody is interfering
even though she is on her knees begging and the major is
laughing and dragging her back to the kitchen. I didn't know
what happened but I suddenly saw myself standing up and
telling the major to let her go. I wasn't shouting just talking to
him and pointing my gun at him. He threw her down and
turned to me, he was laughing at me, with surprise and amusement as if he couldn't believe that one of his men could tell
him what to do. You remember how we used to feel when
father was going to beat us, our anger and fear and frusration?
That is how I was feeling as I saw him laughing and pointing
at me. "Shoot," he keep shouting, "are you afraid? Shoot. Your
bullet will only turn to water. I have strong medicine, how did
you think I survive this war? It is medicine." He is poking me
at the chest with his pistol, and everyone is laughing except the
professor and Charles and also the girl. When he started to call
me "Mr. One-Eye" I shot him in the eye. It was terrible, the
blood and brain and eyes just splattered all over the place and
everyone fell silent. I quickly assumed a defensive position over
the dead body, looking at all of them seated there. They are
about seven, and most of them are below twenty. Dirty and
thin and their clothes all torn, some are even wearing wigs and*

dresses because they say it is strong medicine, and some have
no shoes. No one said anything, but I can see that they think
I will shoot them, but I wasn't. I only told the girl to stop crying and to go upstairs and take care of the sick man. I sat down
and the professor stood up and went to the dead body and the
others followed him as if they really want to confirm that he
was dead even though blood is all over the floor. Then I went
outside and the professor came and sat beside me on the steps
and he said, "Now what?"

I know what he means so I said, "I don't care. I am leaving
tomorrow."

"Really? To where?"

"Home, Nigeria. I am tired of fighting. I want to go home,"
I said and I felt tired and I was actually crying like a small boy.
He put his hand on my shoulder and said, "You can't go, for
two reasons: one because there's a war out there, and two,
because you can't leave the girl. You saved her life, now she
belongs to you . . . it is an old Chinese custom."

"But I am not Chinese."

He laughed and said, "I was speaking figuratively."

In the night five of the soldiers left—they just take their
guns and left. That left me and the professor and the journalist Charles and the girl and the American and two other soldiers who didn't want to go and said I am now their
commander. I told them I am not a commander, I just want to
go home. I remember the day the American died, it is one week
after I kill Kutubi. We brought him out to the veranda and laid
him on a camp bed, he said he wanted to look at the hills and
trees and to feel the air of the mountain. The girl was seated
beside him, taking care of him as always, the other soldiers
were somewhere in the garden, looking for food, because most
of our food is finished now and we are just surviving anyhow
we can. The truth is I am staying because of the girl, and she
is staying because of the American, he is like her only family
now. I don't know why the professor is staying, though there

are many books in the house, and he is always in the library reading. The journalist was restless, he chain smokes all the cigarette in the house, he said he had to rejoin the MSF people before the rains began seriously because the rivers will become flooded and impossible to cross. It has already rained for two days now. It seems the war is coming nearer everyday, sometimes we can hear the sound of big guns over the hill.

The professor and the journalist are at the end of the veranda arguing—they are always arguing about politics, the professor said he is educating the journalist. I can hear the Professor saying to the him, ". . . .so tell me, Charles, tell me all about the book you are going to write when you go back—if you go back—to France."

"What book, Professor?"

"About how you came to Africa to save the natives from themselves, about your heroism in the face of fire, about being kidnapped . . . you'll have a bestseller on your hands. Isn't that why you came?"

"I am just a journalist attached to the Médecins sans Frontières, I report what I see. There are many like me, Professor. Some of us die in the process; it is something we believe in. It is hardly about personal profit," Charles replied calmly.

"But it is all about profit, my dear. You are looking at the smaller picture. I want you to look beyond your naïve ideas, look carefully then you'll see that the war, this war, any war, is one big market place. It is your government, the capitalist governments of the world, that always benefit." Now the professor sounded excited, this is his favorite topic. He put down his old copy of The Art of War *and stood up and begin to pace up and down as he spoke. "Who makes the guns? The West. Who influences our foolish politicians and pits them against one another so that their followers will kill each other? Whose media gets its raw material from these recurrent wars? The West. Who sells the MSF the drugs they use in their work?— it is your companies. So don't tell me about humanitarianism.*

Just write your book, make your money, give lectures about your time in Africa, because if you don't many others will. . . ."

I am confused by their constant arguments.

I was looking at a group of wood pigeons that were picking for food not far from me, so I didn't hear the girl when she come out and sit down beside me.

At first she is quiet, with her chin on her knees, all these while we have never talked, never exchange more than one or two words. I think she hate all of us, after all we took away her father and destroy her life, so she is right to be angry, and not even my saving her from the major is enough to pay for all the damage. We sat staring at the pigeons for a long time, and everything is so peaceful, as if no war is going on behind the hills, and the American is not dying, and I have my eye, and her father is still alive. Then she say, "I want to thank you."

And I replied, "You don't have to."

"You are different, I have been watching you . . . you don't enjoy killing like the others. Why would somebody enjoy killing other people and destroying their whole lives?"

I want to tell her that is how war is, sometimes you kill without thinking, but it won't make sense, it don't make sense to me even though I have been fighting for many years now. So I simply said to her, "We have to think of leaving here soon. We can't remain much longer."

The American died that night and I bury him in the garden early in the morning beside the grave of her father. It was just me and her. The others—the professor and the journalist and the two soldiers—have already left, they say they couldn't wait any longer. The journalist he had to let his people know he is still alive. It is very peaceful here now with only two of us and of course the graves. It is the peace that made us stay a few more days, and also because she said she wants to be with her father a few more days. Those were the best days I have ever known in all my life, it is as if I am back home again, the only sadness is the graves in the garden and how she will be crying

when she sees them. There was some food in the other house,
her own house and I even had her father's trousers and shirt to
wear, I threw away my old army uniform and I cut my hair.
When we lie down at night to sleep she will touch my empty
eye in the dark and she will say how both of us are wounded
and now all we have to do is to cure each other. Sometimes we
will stay awake all night and we will make plans of how we
will live our lives once the war is over. But I always reminded
her that we can leave now, there was a pickup truck in the
garage, and we can go over the border to the next country and
start our lives all over again. I also tell her about you and all
the books you are reading and she wants to meet you one day.
I finally convins her to leave after three days alone. We follow
the direction the professor left for us—it is not hard, just to
look for the river and after that about 25 miles in the next
town where the journalist said there is a permanent MSF
camp which is where we will find them. We took the old
pickup from the garage early in the morning. Now it is sad to
see all the electronics things the major had put in the back of
the Land Rover lying there in the veranda where the professor
and the journalist had dumped it when they took the Rover. I
can see Bintou taking a last look at the farm that has been her
home all her life, which she know she was never going to come
back to. With the bad roads and dangers on the road, we esti-
mate to get there by nightfall. But we are hardly been ten miles
out of the farm when we saw from far the Land Rover in which
the others left three days ago; it was stuck in a hole close to the
river. It have crashed into a tree, and when we got there we see
how the windshield is been shatered, and the bullet holes in
the door and blood on the seats. We discover that they have
been killed and also the bodies in the bushes beside the road.
The professor was sitting under a tree and his back leaning
against it with his book torn and wet from rain water at his
feet. Charles the journalist have made it farther into the bush
and he lie on his back in a thick grasses, his eyes and nose are

eaten away by vultures, his fingers are digging into the mud by his sides, as if to stop himself screaming from the pain. Insects and flies were crawling out of his eye sockets and open mouth. We didn't find the other bodies, because they have got away perhaps. They must have been ambushed by rebels because there are many of them going about with nothing to do, just to loot and shoot at anything they find.

It was not hard finding the MSF camp at all once we got into town because we simply follow the trail of the wounded and dying people. They are mostly women and children. They dragged themselves in the dust road, some are carried on strechers by family. I saw a woman standing by the road and she is streching out a bundle in rags towards us, the bundle was her dead child. "Stop, stop. Let's take her with us," Bintou said to me. But I don't because if I do all the people will come and we will have to shoot them to move forward. The clinic is been set up in an abandon primary school compound, a wire fence run around the buildings. There are many sick people, all bloody and groning, they are like one creature with many legs and hands which is twisting and groning in pain always. A white man came to us immediately and start asking questions, he looked into my face closely.

"Are you with news from Monrovia?" He kept turning from me to Bintou. Before we could speak he went on, "Are you with us, I don't know you. Yes?"

"No," I replied quickly because already a circle of hungry looking women and children have form around us. "We came because we have nowhere to go."

He look at me as if he could not understand what I was saying. "This is wrong place to come—wrong place. What am I to do? You know how many wounded we have here. . . ." He raise his hand and point at the people, and started to speak in French then in English. "You count and tell me. Thousands. Already we are on the verge of a cholera epidemic. And the fighting is moving this way. If we don't leave here in a day or

*two, we die. They will come and kill even the sick. How many
workers are here? Just two doctors and three assistants, no food,
no drugs, only rehydration solution. That is what we give
them, salt and sugar. How can we cure bullet wounds with salt
and sugar, tell me."*

*"Is there any way we can help?" Bintou asked. The man
looked into her face as if he have not heard then went on with
his complian. "We are cut off from our office in Monrovia, no
communication. Bad. Soon the rebels will be here, and I tell
you, they don't care who they kill. They rob the sick and shoot
the dead. Can you imagine that? Shoot the dead. One month
now since they took our journalist, with guns. No word up to
now. Rebels."*

*"We have news of Charles. That is another reason why we
came."*

*Once more he look into Bintou's face, but now he has kept
quiet, as if he is thinking of the words just spoken and not
understanding. Then he said, "Come with me." Now he walks
and we follow to the staff room which is serving as a clinic. We
fought our way through the clutching hands and the bodies
lying on the steps. The other doctor is a younger man with a
tired look on his face and he was inside standing in the center
of the room staring at a lamp on a table.*

*"This is Dr. Laborite. And I am sorry I did not introduce
myself before. I am Dr. Jean-Marie Nicolas. This is my seventh
month in this country, but this is my worst crisis." He was sad
and is stopping himself from saying more of his troubles once
more and said, "What do you know about Charles?" He turned
to Laborite and spoke in French before turning back to us.*

*"I am afraid the news is not good." I told him about
Charles's attempt to return to this camp and about the ambush
that we saw. The two doctors remain silent for a long time.
Laborite sat on a wooden chair.*

*"What can we do now?" Doctor Nicolas spoke slowly, mak-
ing me to feel really sorry for this people.*

"You can move this camp to our farm, there's no one there, and it is not too far from Monrovia, so you can easily contact your office for assistance . . . there's a phone there, and a generator and water." I was impressed by what Bintou was saying even though I didn't think of it before, I was looking at her without saying anything. The doctors were over happy by the sugestion and they called all the assistants and are making plans of how to move the very sick. "I am going with them," Bintou said. She had made up her mind to become a nurse and she wanted me to go with her. I had nowhere to go, so why not attach myself to this people where I can be of some use? I noded and took her hand and said, "I will not leave you."

I became a driver who helps with moving the sick people and bringing supplies between MSF camps, this can be dangerous but it is not more dangerous than fighting war anyway. We returned to the farm that night, on the way we stopped and the two doctors collected Charles's body and wrapped it in oilskin; it was later taken to Monrovia and from there to France to be buried at home. He was a nice young man and I remember how he promised to get me a glass eye after the war even though he didn't have to. I think he just wanted me to be happy because I was very depressed about losing my eye.

We have been here now back at the farm for over six months, everyday the fighting got worse and more sick people come. We enjoy working for the MSF, but soon we must all leave here because it is becoming more and more dangerous and the rain has cut us off from help. The doctors are talking of moving to Monrovia, but we will not go with them. We have decided to follow other refugees to the neighboring Guinea where Bintou will meet her mother, then we will see what we can do for our lives there, and maybe I will be coming home soon.

This is your brother,
LaMamo

PS

The skech below is of the house at the rubber plantation.
You can see the hills and the trees, and the small house at the
back. I have made the skech to show you how this place
remind me of the hills at home.

Mamo slowly folded the letter and put it on the bedside table. A car passing outside backfired, causing him to instinctively raise his hands to his ears. He always found the city too loud, too busy, and now, after his fourth day, his nerves were almost in tatters.

"The girl sounds nice, like she and he could go on to have a life together," said Zara. She sounded wistful, drowsy. "I imagine them together, somewhere in another country. I imagine them married and happy together."

The room was in semidarkness. They were both lying on their backs in her bed, staring at the ceiling. The only light was from the bedside lamp, which Mamo had used for reading the letter. "The letter was written over six months ago, so I assume they are in the Guinea already," he said. He reached down and picked up his trousers from the floor and slipped into them before standing up. Though they had been going out for over three months now, and had been sleeping together whenever they had a chance, he still found it hard to stand naked before her. She, on the other hand, loved to lounge naked around the house, with the curtains drawn; sometimes she'd cook a whole meal dressed only in panties, her full breasts swinging whenever she turned or bent down to open a drawer. He loved to stand behind her, with his palms on her breasts and his nose in her neck, inhaling; she had a distinct smell: soapy, musky, and fresh, as if she were just stepping out of the shower.

"What does your father think?"

"What?"

"About the girl. Would he like her as an in-law?"

"What's there for him to like or dislike? He doesn't know, anyway. I haven't shown him the letters."

"Why?"

"Why? Because he doesn't care. He is too busy with his widows and politics."

"Perhaps you should show him."

"No. I won't. Not now anyway. . . . When I am ready."

Last week Zara had finally turned up in Keti after a whole month of silence, looking exhausted, defeated. She had silently entered his room and sat down on the bed beside him; he had been reading a book, which he now dropped, and sat up with his back against the wall, staring at her tired face, and the heavy pouches under her eyes.

"Hello."

"Hello."

After a while he said, "I went to your place two days ago."

"My place, where?"

"In the state capital."

"No, you didn't. I was indoors all day two days ago."

"I suddenly decided to go and see you . . . because I hadn't heard from you since the school closed and I missed you very much. . . . But when I stood at your door, I was suddenly gripped by a crazy fear. I thought, what if you had another boyfriend and you were right now inside together? I panicked and turned back."

"Is that what you think of me?"

When he gave no answer she said, "There's no one but you, really, no one."

He managed to say, as lightly as he could, "I guess it was my insecurity showing once more."

But she didn't laugh; she bowed her head and fiddled with her key ring. At last he said, "But what did you want me to think? You were gone for a whole month."

She stood up. "I'll explain on the way."

"The way to where?"

"Let's go to my place in the capital . . . if you want."

She drove slowly, and occasionally cars coming up behind her at high speed would honk angrily before overtaking them. As the arid, dry-season landscape outside approached and receded beside the road, she told him about the past four weeks, how she had tried to get in touch with her ex-husband to discuss sharing their son's custody together, how she had gone to his office in the army barracks three times, and each time she had been kept waiting for over two hours before being told that the captain was busy and couldn't see her today, and how in desperation she had decided to travel to his parents' house in the village in Benue State, and how, when she got there, her husband's brothers had insulted her and called her a whore and told her to get out of their house, and how the parents had looked on without saying a word, and all of this in front of her son. She had taken the case to court; last week there had been a preliminary hearing, and there would be another hearing in two weeks. Mamo listened without saying anything, for he knew that whatever he said would be too little. He simply reached out and placed his hand on her knee. He turned away from her because he didn't want to see the raw pain that suffused every inch of her beautiful face, and the tears that streamed down as she talked on and on determinedly, at the end almost screaming out the words, "Why, why is he doing this to me?"

The first two days they didn't step outside the house: they ate and slept and made love and read and made love and ate and slept and made love again. On the third day she went grocery shopping, leaving him alone, sleeping. That was the day he came across Reverend Drinkwater's *A Brief History of the Peoples of Keti*. He found it when he went poking around in the guest room; it was tucked away in a corner of a forgotten desk drawer. The apartment had two rooms: the main bedroom, which Zara occupied, and the guest room, which had been turned into a store-room for the odds and ends left by Naomi, Zara's friend, who was the real owner of the place. There were also Zara's books stacked in boxes and cartons, left to her by her father, which she had never got around to reading. When she returned she found Mamo in the guest room, engrossed in the book, sitting on top of the dusty desk in whose drawer he had found the book, still in his boxers and a T-shirt.

"What are you reading?" she asked from the door, her hands heavy with paper bags full of groceries.

He looked up at her absently, his eyes eager to return to the slim book in his hand. "This . . . is a book of our history, by Reverend Drinkwater. I didn't know he had written a book like this. . . . Is it yours? Where did you find it? I have to borrow it from you."

"You sound excited," she said, looking at him curiously. "It is just one of the books I inherited after my father's death."

"Well, have you read it?"

"No, why should I? History is not one of my interests."

"Then I am sure you didn't know that no one has ever written our history before . . . well, only in bits and pieces. A few have done their degree essays on aspects of it, I have seen a book or two in my uncle's office that tangentially touch on it . . . but this is a whole book."

"It can't be more than a hundred pages," Zara said, passing on to the kitchen.

Mamo followed her. "That is not the point. This man actually interviewed a lot of old men . . . back in the 1920s, all of them are dead now . . . and it is interesting . . . despite his obvious handicaps. . . ."

"What are they?"

"For one, he was a missionary, and for another, he was a foreigner. . . . I might've liked the book if he hadn't wasted too much time telling his imagined home audience how really backward our culture is. . . . His first three pages are dedicated to comparing our geography to that of his native Iowa, and he seems to blame us for having only two seasons instead of four, and for not having snowfall, can you believe that? And here a whole chapter is wasted on trying to expose the fraudulence of our traditional healers. . . ."

While Zara cooked, Mamo quickly finished reading the book, then he started all over again, this time with a pen in his hand, underlining whole paragraphs and making extensive marginalia. Occasionally he'd stand up and go to the kitchen to read out entire paragraphs or pages to Zara, and then he'd elaborate on why he liked or disliked that particular passage. Now he was following her to the fridge, then to the cooker. "I like the opening: *As background to the theme of this volume, a brief characterization of the Keti people's environment, history and social organization may be here set forth.* I like that. He has a stiff, but straightforward style."

He went on, "Listen to this, it is an interview with an old man called Kashere ... I know that name. I know the family. Listen:

The old man cleared his voice and said: "Long ago upon a certain day, one of our people, a leader, Kunglung by name, musing on the unsatisfactory conditions of their dwelling place, opened his mind to one of his trusted helpers, a man of the clan of Pargatak, and said: 'This land is no longer a fit home for us. When we farm the ground the yield is bad. Go out and find us a dwelling place.' The man of Pargatak set off on his journey. When he was within sight of this region, he turned himself into a lion (as the men of his clan are all able to do), and made his way directly to one point of vantage after another until he reached a hill overlooking the whole inhabited valley. He . . . leisurely took observation of all that the people were doing, spying out also the great Njomjom, the inspired leader of the people. These observations taken, he retraced his steps.

"Not far from home, Pargatak became a man again. Reaching home, he reported to Kunglung. Kunglung called for one Kolwi, and when this man came, the man of Pargatak gave account of his journey. . . . Kunglung then commanded Kolwi to call other sectional leaders to a conference, at which he declared all that the

man of Pargatak had seen in his journey, and asked for suggestions of methods to be followed in the attempt to take the place for themselves.

"The man of Pargatak said, 'The people are great and many, and what can we do?' Kunglung said, 'Watch, and I shall show you my suggestion; if you do not agree, you may say so.' Then, lifting himself, he threw himself on the ground, and snakes ran all over the place: he had turned into snakes. Quickly becoming a man again, he said, 'If I do that and go out and in among the people, biting ten here and ten there, could I not quickly finish them off?' The man of Pargatak said he would not finish them. 'Let me,' said he, 'become a lion, so that night and day I shall mangle the people and tear their roofs and walls to pieces.' 'That will not do,' said a man of Lame. 'Just wait and let this man of Layange do his.' Then the man of Layange turned himself into an eagle and flew up and cut the air, alighting once more. The man of Lame said, 'Let us use that.'

"The great army set forth, the elders in front and the fighters in the rear. They slept at one place on the way and resumed their journey on the following day, and reached a spot near where the attack was to be made. The man of Pargatak then gave orders to the man of Layange, informing him that when he should advance he would see a large ram staked under a certain tree, where also would be a great company sewing roof grass. Thereupon the man of Layange raised himself and threw himself to the ground and, turning into an eagle, rose up into the air, through which he flew until he settled on the hillside. From there he watched for the people. Presently one came out from a house drawing a ram to a point under a tree, where he tied it to a stake. The man also had a mat on which he would sit to do his sewing. The man of Layange, now an eagle, said, 'Good! I will snatch the ram and make off with it close to the ground, and then when they see me they will follow me, thinking to snatch back the animal when I shall have alighted close.'

"Presently a large crowd gathered at the place and fell to

*sewing roof grass. Then the man of Layange rose and swooped
down upon the ram and, tearing it from the rope, made off with
it close to the ground. The men sprang up from their work, and
from every quarter in the town the people, hearing the yells,
rushed to join in the pursuit. 'See,' they cried, 'it is close to the
ground, let us follow and snatch the sheep.'*

*"The crowd was immense and growing larger every moment,
while the eagle led them on and on until he brought them into
the middle of an ambush of the invaders, ranged in the form of
three sides of a square. The men on the two sides waited until all
were in the square, whereupon the men on the end fell upon their
victims, the men on the two sides closing in upon them, making
a great and merciless slaughter. They then overspread the town
and found that they were in complete possession. They looted the
place and returned home enriched.*

*"In due time they came and settled west of the valley, and only
after some years made the abandoned towns their own. The passage of time was deemed advisable so that the defilement or bad
luck of the original inhabitants should no longer be found clinging to the place. . . ."*

As she listened Zara's face became more and more thoughtful.
She had never seen Mamo so excited about anything before; he
was like a kid being given a treat, waving the book about as he
made a point, his voice full of assurance.

She interrupted him, saying, "Why don't you write about it?"

"What?" he asked, raising his eyes from the page.

"A review, about this book. All these comments you are making, write them down."

"I can't. You only review new books. This book was published
in . . . let me see . . . 1970, by Drinkwater's son, from papers left
by his father who died in 1952. . . . No newspaper would publish
that."

"But what of journals and specialized magazines? There are
tons of them . . . and you don't have to write a review as such,

you could write about our history, about misrepresentations by foreign historians, using this book as your example."

Now Mamo looked thoughtful. "You mean a sort of revisionist essay. . . . But . . . "

"But what?"

"I don't know. . . ."

"I know the person to send it to," Zara said. "My professor at my alma mater."

"But your professor doesn't know me."

"It doesn't matter. Her name is Professor Chundum Chuwan. She will send it to all the history journals in this world if she likes it."

"But"—Mamo made one final desperate excuse—"who will type it?"

"I will."

"You can type?"

She nodded. She led him to the guest room and opened one of the cartons. Inside was an old Remington typewriter. "There."

That night he did not sleep. He began the essay tentatively, and then as the ideas began to flow freely his hand flew over the papers, filling them with bold blue characters, then crossing out lines or paragraphs, or squeezing up a sheet and throwing it away if he didn't like it. Zara lay on the couch with a novel, occasionally pausing to flash him a smile of encouragement, but finally she fell asleep with the book over her face. He finished as the hands on the clock said five A.M.: he had twenty usable pages. He left them on the table where Zara could see them when she woke up, and staggered to the bedroom.

the return of lamang

THE DAY he returned from the state capital Mamo found the entire road that passed before his house blocked with cars and pickups bearing the Victory Party logo, and a huge crowd milling about between the cars, listening to a man on an overturned oil drum. It was Lamang. He was talking into a microphone, waving his arms and pounding his chest; the crowd cheered, but Mamo didn't get to hear what he was saying because the speech was just ending. Lamang was now being helped down by Asabar and other youth wing members. When he was down he turned to a man beside him and they embraced, and the crowd gave a roar.

"Where have you been?" Asabar asked later when Mamo finally had a chance to speak to his excited cousin. They were standing beside the youth wing pickup. A couple of cars away Lamang was deep in conversation with a group of men and they were all laughing and clapping each other on the back. One of them was Lamang's erstwhile adversary, Alhaji Danladi.

"I went to the capital."

"Oh . . . to see your woman. Well, you missed it all." Asabar was looking across at Lamang as he spoke, a worshipful expression on his face. It seemed earlier in the day the party officials had suddenly appeared in a convoy of cars and pickups with speakers on their roofs blaring out party campaign songs, driving slowly, gathering a crowd of children and curious layabouts as they drove through the village's mahogany-lined streets, and they finally came to a stop in front of Lamang's house. A few of them went inside and had a long discussion with Lamang, and when they came out about an hour later Lamang was with them and they all had big smiles on their faces. An impromptu rally began when Danladi climbed a drum to announce to the crowd the good news of Lamang's return to the party. After that a few other party officials made speeches, prophesying great victory in the coming elections, and then finally Lamang climbed the drum to reassure the crowd of his loyalty to the party—that was the part that Mamo had witnessed. And now the crowd was dispersing. Lamang stood in the middle of the road waving goodbye; a discreet distance away from him stood the widows in their best dresses, waving to the crowd as vigorously as Lamang was doing.

The next day Lamang stopped him in the living room and said, "I heard that you went with your uncle to see the Mai."

Mamo nodded. He was returning from the bathroom, with only a towel around his waist; he felt at a disadvantage standing before his father, who was fully dressed to go out, relaxed in his favorite seat, his car keys dangling from his hand.

"Yes," Mamo replied. "It was about the school."

"Yes, the school. Which neither you nor your uncle bothered to tell me anything about. Perhaps you thought because I was out of the party I had no influence. Do you think the Mai knows more people in the capital than I do? Ha-ha. You saw what happened yesterday, didn't you? How they came all the way from the state capital to apologize, to take me back into the party? Those people you saw yesterday, they are the who's who of this state, they make things happen. Right now I am on my way to see the governor. Tell your uncle I will mention the school to the governor, to see if anything can be done about it."

Mamo listened, thinking, *What is it about my father, that even when he tries to help, his effort still comes across as self-glorification?* Mamo recalled what Uncle Iliya had once told him about their childhood, how Lamang used to be their father's favorite because his mother was the favorite wife, and how whenever they went to the farm Lamang would only work for an hour or so and then would be allowed to relax under a tree while the others worked in the hot sun.

But surprisingly, Lamang did deliver—two weeks after that conversation a letter came from the Ministry of Education saying that the KCS had been struck off the list of schools under review.

"This is a surprise," Uncle Iliya said, reading out the letter to Mamo, who only nodded and didn't bother to mention the conversation he had had with his father. "There is no explanation, just like that. Someone in the state capital, in his capacity as God, has decided that we are to be spared this time."

The school was reopened one week after the letter arrived. The staff all returned, new interns were sent, and the students looked happy to be back. In class Mamo read out extracts from his essay on Drinkwater's *A Brief History of the Peoples of Keti*, the students listened with enthralled eyes, trying their best to follow his arguments; everything seemed fine, the school's dark days were apparently over, but for some reason Mamo did not feel any joy in his work anymore. He mostly felt tired, depressed. Zara was the first to notice.

"What's wrong?"

"Nothing."

He felt powerless and trapped and almost desperate. He imagined his brother in whatever country he was now, free and happy. That day he left work early and took a long walk in the bush; he only returned home when it was dark.

send us more, please

THE NEXT day two letters came for Mamo, one of which was to change his life forever.

The first was from a London magazine called the *Empire Review*, and it was signed by the editor himself. The letter was typed, and it went straight to the point: *We really enjoyed the piece, "A Review of Drinkwater's* A Brief History of the Peoples of Keti,*" but we regret that the subject does not suit our particular demand at the moment. However, if you have other pieces that address such issues as the AIDS scourge, or genital circumcision, or other typical African experiences in a challenging and progressive way, we'd like to take a look at them.*

The second letter was from Uganda, from a journal called the *History Society Quarterly*. They loved his article and they were publishing it. There was a full-page letter from the editor, a Professor Batanda of the History Department, Makerere University.

Dear Professor Lamang, the letter began. Mamo laughed aloud when he saw the title. He shook his head and read the letter: the editor was delighted to get a submission from as far away as Nigeria; this was the first and he hoped it wouldn't be the last, because he wanted to make the magazine really international, and he was especially delighted with this piece because of its "relaxed tone"; he personally thought that most historians had now become too forensic, more scientific than the scientists, which was sad; and this particular piece would come out in the next issue; the author would of course be sent a complimentary copy; and, finally, would the author care to write a follow-up piece? Since this piece effectively argued what good history writing was not, would the author care to write his own opinion of what good history writing was?

Mamo looked at the back of the envelope as if to see if it was his address on the front, if there hadn't been a mistake. It seemed while sending the essay to her professor Zara had also sent along Mamo's address, which the professor had used as a return address.

He wished he could rush out to Zara's to show her the letter, but she had gone to the state capital for the weekend, as next Monday was her second court hearing. He decided to pen a reply immediately, which he began by explaining that he was not a professor, just a twenty-seven-year-old ex-university student, secondary school teacher, and that he was not a professional historian, just an amateur—he said he was explaining this to clear up any misconception about himself. Then he wrote a very long paragraph on what he hoped to write about in his follow-up essay. He said as far as he was concerned a true history is one that looks at the lives of individuals, ordinary people who toil and dream and suffer, who bear the brunt of whatever vicissitude time inflicts on the nation. He said if a historian could capture these ordinary lives, including their recollections of their own family's past, then he might come close to writing a true "biographical history" of a nation; for when we refer to a nation, are we not really referring to the people that inhabit that nation, and so isn't the story of a nation then really the story of the people who make up that nation? He said most histories spend too much time on the weather and the landscape and the constitution, and in the process they forget about the people.

He posted his letter that very day and began to wait for the reply, and while he waited the clocks and the earth all stopped turning.

But for Lamang the clock moved faster than ever before. Things had not worked out as smoothly as he had expected—after the reconciliation visit from the Victory Party officials, since the chairmanship was now irrevocably lost to him, he had expected to be offered another important position in the party or, even better, to be made the party's candidate for the post of chairman for the Keti local government, but no such offer came. In annoyance he wrote a long letter to the party complaining of how he had been maltreated, and that this time he was leaving the party for good—unless he was made the candidate for the office of chairman. No reply came. Lamang left the party, for the second and—as he explained to the widows—the final time.

A week later a delegation came to Lamang with a proposition—but this time the delegation wasn't from his own party, but from the opposition party, the New Victory Party, NVP. The delegation came to him in the night. They talked in whispers, offering him the same position he had been denied by his former party: the chairmanship.

The very next day Lamang held a big meeting in the courtyard to announce his move to the NVP from the VP, and to discuss strategy for the coming elections, for what sweeter revenge could he aim for against the party that had betrayed him than victory against it at the polls? A goat was slaughtered and the widows were on hand as usual to cook and serve and to make Lamang look good. The compound filled with faces: new faces belonging to the new party, and some old faces that had simply come for the feast.

Mamo, returning from work, decided to go straight to his room to escape the noise. His father was in the living room, talking to Asabar—they were standing in the center of the room, their heads close together, whispering. Lamang had one hand on Asabar's shoulder and they looked so close, so intimate, that Mamo couldn't help feeling a twinge of jealousy as he thought

that if things had been different between him and his father, he
would have been the one standing there, with his father confid-
ing in him. Later, Asabar met him in his room, looking happy and
full of energy. He announced that Lamang wanted him to be the
youth wing leader, just like before, this time in the New Victory
Party. He had started growing a thick mustache, which looked
rather out of place on his thin, sensitive face.

"Shame on our enemies. They thought we were down and out
and gone, but look at this gathering, just look, the whole village
is here." He opened the window and poked his head out, smiling
all the time.

"I doubt it. This compound couldn't possibly contain the
whole village," said Mamo, then he quickly changed the subject.
He knew if he so much as indulged him, Asabar could go on for
hours on politics and victory.

"I've heard from LaMamo."

That got Asabar's interest. He turned around and pulled a
chair from the reading table and sat in it. His face lit up. "What
did he say? Where is he now?"

"Somewhere in Liberia."

"Is he coming home soon?"

"He didn't say. He has met a girl and he is thinking of getting
married."

"I hope he comes home soon. This is the right time for him to
be here."

"Why?"

"To enter politics, of course. The party needs people like him
at this time, real soldiers who are . . ."

Mamo sighed inwardly and stopped listening. Asabar now
lived and breathed the party; clearly those months when Lamang
was in limbo had been like purgatory to him, and it showed in his
every feature: he was scrawnier, his combat jacket and trousers
had a few tears and hung on him in folds, his eyes were red and
shifty from increased marijuana intake, and when he spoke he
waved his arms about absently, not completing his sentences, as

if he had forgotten what he had started out saying, or had simply lost interest. Last month Mamo had witnessed a fight between Asabar and his father that had led to Asabar moving out. It seemed Asabar had gotten the neighbor's daughter, a pretty thing called Jummai, pregnant and his father wanted him to do the honorable thing and marry her, but Asabar said he wasn't interested. And now he was facing his father squarely in the center of the living room, shouting, "Don't tell me what to do with my life."

"I'll tell you what to do as long as you live under my roof and I am feeding you. You do nothing from morning to night but sit with your drunken friends and smoke marijuana and drink and brawl in the village. I am getting tired of that."

"Don't worry; I am moving out of your house." And with that Asabar had pushed past Mamo, who was still hovering at the door, and went out of the compound. Mamo had rushed after him, urging him to think and not to act rashly. But Asabar's mind was made up; he led Mamo to the nearest beer parlor and ordered a bottle and finished it in one go. "I am moving out of my father's house." He did, the very next day. With the help of his friends he built a round hut near the foot of the hills, far away from the nearest neighbor, and before long the place became a hangout for the youth wing party members. That was when Asabar began to sell marijuana on the side to his friends.

"Listen, Asabar—" Mamo began. He wanted to say to his cousin, *Can't you see my father is only using you as a common thug, to do his dirty work, and does it give you that much prestige to drive around drunk in a van, intimidating people? Don't you know this is only going to end up one way, in disaster?* But even before he opened his mouth he knew it was futile; Asabar wouldn't listen to him. He had never fully recovered from his dreams of becoming a soldier, his failure had always haunted him, but now as leader of the youth wing he had his own personal army—the party had made him an instant general.

Mamo sighed again.

"What?" Asabar asked, waiting for him to speak. Mamo reached out and touched him on the arm. "I was just thinking of that day at the abattoir and how things would have turned out for us if . . ."

Asabar still waited. "Yes, yes," he said impatiently, "if what?"

"How is Jummai? Have you been to see her parents yet?"

"I am waiting," said Asabar with a wink. "I am waiting to see if it is a boy, then I will go; if not, I am not interested."

"Just be careful," Mamo said again as they parted. Asabar nodded and left the room, giving a brief military salute.

the example of plutarch

Dear Mr. Lamang,

Let me begin by apologizing for using the wrong title on you in my last letter. I did so not out of mischief, but because of the great quality of your writing, which, as far as I am concerned, is worthy of any professor. I note in your last letter the comments you made about not being really qualified to be called a historian. Allow me to differ. History is not only about paper qualifications; if it were so, then most of the old men we depend on for oral accounts of the past would be disqualified from calling themselves historians. Have you ever wondered how most historians got their material, especially those early experts on Africa? Most of their historical accounts were based on papers left by colonial officers and their wives' diaries, and explorers' journals and missionaries' accounts, etc.—and if those people could be called historians, then why not you? And so, do not say you are not qualified to write history, or on history. Remember only that a historian must avoid unnecessary subjectivity—I say "unnecessary" because all history entails a certain degree of subjectivity, and this is not bad if it doesn't lead to a disregard for facts—he must be humble, and his only interest will be to shine a light on the past for the future.

I am also intrigued by your idea of a "biographical history." Have you ever considered doing this seriously, I mean writing history—or even better, writing biographies? Let me explain why I think biography would be more in your field: some points you mentioned in your essay, like history's need to inspire by emphasizing only our glorious moments—I am afraid that that is not for history to do. History should neither praise nor condemn, as that will amount to bias, and isn't that the very thing we criticize in the colonial histories? History only states what is, or what was, in the way it was, and by this I mean both chronologically and factually. Now, biography is totally different—it deals with the human element, it gives us the freedom to ruminate, to be subjective, and so to philoso-phize, to examine character, and to condemn or to praise (remember it has within its rubric the panegyric).

Of course, it uses the technique of "historia," of inquiry into the past, but it avoids history's constraints and limitations, it realizes more than history does that we are all human and fal-lible. Most importantly, it selects what people to write about, what events to highlight, what events to downplay—in short, it is more of an art than history. I have included a book, Plutarch's Parallel Lives, a classic of the genre, to illustrate what I mean. There is a long introduction about the author in the book, so I need not say more about Plutarch himself. Let me know when you can what you think of my suggestion, and of the book itself.

I have also included two complimentary copies of the Quarterly with your first essay in it.

I look forward to reading your second essay.

> Yours,
> Professor Batanda

The reply from Uganda took a month to come. Before then, to pass time, Mamo had made a draft of his follow-up essay, with the title, "A Plan for a True History of the Keti People," which he now completed after reading Batanda's letter. It was twice the length of the first piece, mainly because he used a lot of local

myths and legends to illustrate his point—they were the same
myths and legends used by Drinkwater in his *Brief History*, but
with a different reading to emphasize what he called "malevolent
manipulation of history," which he countered with "benevolent
manipulation of history."

This time there was no Zara to help him type his essay; she had
left to spend the weekend in the capital. Mamo was too excited
to wait for Monday. He knew of only two places in Keti to get
access to a typewriter at such a short notice—the church and the
KCS—but the KCS was out because he happened to know that
the school's old typewriter had broken down and Uncle Iliya was
still trying to raise money to buy another one.

He met Pastor Mela at home. The pastor mostly spent the daylight hours seated in his spacious veranda which overlooked the
road, listening to the radio from which he got most of the material for his "scientific" sermons. He loved to make notes as he listened to the BBC, or the Voice of America, or the German Africa
service, which he would later feed to his wide-eyed flock, per-
plexing them with words and concepts like "heart transplant,"
"satellite," and "artificial insemination" (which he was against).
But he was more famous for his sartorial daring. This fame had
started on the day of his ordination as pastor, when he came to
church wearing a jacket and a collar, an attire totally unheard of
in a place where the pastors went to church dressed simply in
their Sunday clothes, with nothing to distinguish them from their
flock.

It seemed the Drinkwater sisters, locally known as Kai and
Malai (they were born in Keti and still lived there) and both great
fans of the pastor, had suggested that he would strike a more
imposing figure if he wore one of their late father's jackets with
a collar. And so Pastor Mela arrived looking like a washed-up
musician in a black jacket that was almost tearing at the seams
over his muscular shoulders and a collar that was so tight he

could barely breathe under its vise-grip around his throat. He
sweated and his eyes bulged as he gave his sermon, but from
then on, sartorially speaking, he never looked back. From jackets
and collars he graduated to long colorful robes, the type worn by
Roman cardinals, when he came back from a church ministers'
meeting in Lagos, where he had fallen under the influence of the
rather flamboyant Lagos ministers. Soon other pastors in the Keti
area began to copy him, and he in turn became more and more
innovative, introducing a new design of robe almost every couple
of months.

Now he read Mamo's published essay with the enthusiasm of
one specialist discussing an esoteric subject with a fellow specialist. He said he found the essay almost "scientific" in its
directness and logic. Mamo said he could keep that copy, as he
had another one at home, and explained about the second essay,
not going into detail. The pastor kept nodding after every sentence, making notes, and he seemed particularly impressed that
it had Drinkwater as its center (in Keti's hierarchy scale,
Drinkwater came second only to Jesus Christ Himself). Today he
was dressed in an "informal" robe, distinguished from the formal
ones by its short sleeves.

"Come," he said at last, "let's go to the church office. I will get
the church secretary to assist you. The Lord is clearly using you
to do His work." Before they left, the pastor knelt down and
prayed.

The next Sunday, to Mamo's surprise, a copy of the published
article he had given to Pastor Mela was pinned prominently on
the church notice board, right next to the door in the view of
every villager who attended church and could read, and later, in
his sermon, the pastor asked the congregation to pray for Mamo,
Lamang's son, the headmaster's nephew, in his "great fight to
spread light and understanding," so that he may "not be swayed

by the devil and the powers of darkness that are rampant in the
air like disease viruses."

Mamo sweated in his seat in the back row; hands reached out
to shake his in congratulation and admiration. But that was just
the beginning, for unknown to him, his career as a biographer
had already begun. The next day he got a visit from Robert
Wanga, a former secondary school classmate of his who was now
the leader of the Keti Youths' Union. He wanted Mamo to come
to the union's next meeting to give an address.

"Address, about what?" he asked, partly amused by Robert's
reverential manner.

"Anything you want. About history, and about how to write,
and . . . anything you want, just to encourage the young people.
We are really proud of what you have achieved and everybody
wants to ask you questions about it."

"What I have achieved?"

"Everyone in the village is talking about your essay, and the
youths especially will be really, really glad if you could spare an
hour to talk to them."

Mamo said he would think it over. Robert gave a little bow as
he shook Mamo's hand before leaving. After Robert a few other
villagers came to see him, among them old men who hadn't the
faintest idea what the essay was about. Partly encouraged by the
pastor's words in church, and partly by what they had heard from
those who could read, they came to discuss "history" with Mamo.
Most of them wanted to see if he could tell a story very well, for
to them history was more than just an account of the past, it was
an art, and most of the artistry was in the telling. They masked
their disappointment well after discovering that Mamo couldn't
really "tell" history. But before departing they'd inevitably have a
point they wanted him to stress in his future writings, a point
about a certain battle, or the origin of a certain word or tradition.
Auntie Marina proudly played the usher, announcing each visitor with a flourish, waving them into the living room where
Mamo often sat, trying to read or watch television.

"See what you've started?" Mamo said to Zara. It was Monday; they had gone straight from work to her place and they were now seated in the living room.

"I just posted your essay, that's all," she said. Her face had glowed with pride when he showed her the essay earlier in the staff room. She had taken it around the room, showing it to the other teachers. Some of them had already seen it on the church notice board, but they now flipped through the pages as they tried hard to hide their envy.

Then she dragged Mamo to his uncle's office to show it to Iliya, who hadn't heard of the essay before now because he wasn't in church the day Pastor Mela mentioned it. Before she gave Iliya the essay to read, Zara first told him how Mamo had miraculously discovered the book at her apartment, and how he had written the essay in one sitting.

"No one in this village has done this before. This is great—you have put us on the international map. Now you have to go on and write a book," Iliya said proudly after he had read it. "We'll make a copy and put it on our notice board. I'll also send a copy to the local government chairman and to the Mai's palace. This will show them the caliber of teachers we have here, and if they are smart they will see how important education is to our village."

"No, no need for that," Mamo protested, turning from his uncle to Zara.

"Why not?" Zara asked.

"It is just an essay," Mamo said, pleased, but still feeling that the essay didn't deserve to be fussed over the way everyone was doing.

His uncle stopped in midsentence and turned to him. "What? Only an essay? But who has done it before in this whole village? No one. Certainly not me, with all my years of teaching. Ah, you are young. You take your education for granted. Don't. Keep writing, keep writing."

Mamo told Zara how, when he had shown his father the essay, Lamang had quickly flipped through the pages and dropped it on the table. "I'll look at it later—I am in a hurry right now."

She squeezed his hand. "Maybe he is busy."

Elections were coming up in a week's time and Lamang was on the campaign trail with his party candidates and his youth wing members and his party officials and his women. He was in his element, the cynosure of attention.

"Maybe."

the waziri

MAMO WAS in class teaching when a student entered and announced that the headmaster wanted to see him urgently. Earlier, through the window he had seen a car arrive and come to a stop before the headmaster's office, but he had not paid it much attention. Now as he walked to the headmaster's office he noticed that the car bore the Keti Traditional Council's logo on its doors. In the office a palace guard stood in front of the headmaster's desk in his multicolored uniform, his customary whip in his hand, his kola-filled mouth busy.

"It seems they want you at the palace," Iliya said as soon as Mamo came.

"Is everything all right?" Mamo asked, looking from the guard to his uncle.

"You will find out at the palace," the guard said. "We really have to go now."

"Come and see me when you return," Uncle Iliya said, walking Mamo to the car. On the way Mamo tried to guess why he'd be wanted at the palace so urgently, but after a while he let his mind go blank and watched the kids playing under the mahogany trees and waving and running after the passing car.

At the palace Mamo was surprised when, instead of going straight to the Mai's lounge, the guard took him to another wing of the palace. They went down a corridor lined with doors. The guard pushed one open without knocking and they entered. There was a short passage with a single chair against the wall, a passage that served as a waiting room and led into a big office. Mamo was asked to wait in the passage while the guard went into the office and almost immediately came out again, motioning for Mamo to enter.

The Waziri was sprawled in a swivel chair behind a huge table. There was nothing on the table except for a huge water flask and a glass beside it. The air conditioner hummed loudly in the background, fighting against the heat that had already started to rise even though it wasn't yet midday.

"Ah, Mamo, you are here. I have something to show you," the Waziri said, coming around and taking Mamo by the hand before Mamo could open his mouth or think of sitting down. The Waziri led the way in his long white robe, which practically dazzled in the brilliant sun, his tall thin frame seeming to float as they passed down the long veranda before the row of doors. On the other side was a small courtyard covered profusely with a variety of plants, from grass to short flowering trees, and behind the plants was a hall that Mamo guessed would be a conference room. The Waziri opened one of the doors with a key from his pocket, and they entered. It was dark and hot and musty, and it obviously hadn't been used recently. The Waziri went and opened a window and drew aside the dusty curtain, and light and air entered. The window overlooked the Palace Square. Mamo had memories of the big, rectangular square from his school days when he had stood in line with other kids in the scorching sun to listen to the Mai, in his huge flowing robes and his giant turban, deliver a speech on school holidays. The Waziri turned on the ceiling fan. They both watched patiently as it creaked into life, ruffling the sheets of paper on the table, churning up the fine dust, nudging the hot heavy air into motion.

He turned to Mamo and offered a big smile which made his beard shake and his forehead crinkle.

"Sit," he said, pointing expansively to the plush seat behind the huge dusty table. "This is going to be your office."

"I don't understand," Mamo said, totally flummoxed. He

remained standing next to the open door. The Waziri was standing in the center of the room, his robe gathered in one hand
behind him so as not to pick up dust from the floor. He slowly
took off his hat, exposing his clean-shaven head from where
streams of sweat rolled down to his face—he rolled his head
under the fan, enjoying the cooling effect.

"Sit, first of all, we have a lot to talk about. Young man, the Mai
likes you." The Waziri pulled out a chair for himself and touched
the surface with his middle finger. He looked at the dust on the
finger, and then changed his mind about sitting down. "Let's go
back to my office. It is too dusty here."

"I know this is all happening too fast for you," the Waziri said,
swiveling around in his leather chair, a benevolent smile on his
lips. His bad eye appeared to be staring at a point behind Mamo
while the good one was fixed on his face.

"I am afraid I . . . don't understand." Mamo wasn't sure which
eye to focus on. Through the window he could see the guard pacing up and down the veranda outside.

"It is simple. The palace secretary died last month, God rest
his soul, and now the Mai has decided to offer you the post—if
you want it, that is."

"But . . . just like that?"

"Not just like that." The Waziri smiled. "I persuaded him."

"I am so surprised. I never . . ."

"You see, after reading your essay, the Mai said to me, 'But this
young man is too good to be wasted away in a village classroom.
Why don't we bring him here to replace Lanjo?' and I said,
'Exactly, Your Highness, let's do that.' And so here we are, here
you are. And . . ." The Waziri raised his hand as Mamo opened
his mouth to speak. "However . . ." His hand rose higher. "However, I have a very important task for you. Tell me, will you be
willing to write a book on the personal history of the Mai and his
ancestors, a royal history?"

"I don't know . . ." Mamo began to say, then he stopped, and

tried to look confident. "I have a job . . . my uncle's school . . .
besides, I don't know anything about writing a book of history, a
biography . . . and I will need a lot of material, and interviews,
and—"

Once more the Waziri raised his hand peremptorily, silencing
Mamo. "You see, exactly one year from now the Mai will be celebrating his tenth anniversary. It is going to be a great day in Keti,
the greatest day in Keti. Your book will be presented that day; it
will be the crowning event of that day. Now, I don't know how
books are written, but after reading your essay I said, if anyone
can do it, someone from our village, it is this young man. You
have one year to do it. Can you?"

"Well, I have my theory about biographical history . . . but it is
not exactly the same as—" Mamo began, and once more the
Waziri raised his hand. "Why don't you take some time to think
it over, talk to your father, or your uncle? I assure you all of them
will tell you to do it. Do you have any idea how famous you will
be after this book? How old are you?"

"Twenty-eight, almost."

"Well, think, by this time next year you will be the most
famous of all your peers in Keti. The Mai himself will be your
patron." The Waziri had a big smile on his face as he said this,
and he looked expectant, as if waiting for Mamo to stand up and
genuflect in gratitude.

On the way back, in the same car that had brought him to the
palace, Mamo's mind went in all directions—he thought how
uncanny it was that only days ago Professor Batanda's letter had
urged him to think of taking up biography, and now here he was
being offered a chance to write the Mai's biography. This was not
the biography he wanted to write, true. What he wanted was to
write the story of ordinary people, farmers, workers, housewives,
and through their stories to arrive at a single overarching story.
But he knew that the Waziri's offer was not one to be scorned; it
offered him a chance to launch his ambition into the strato-

sphere, a chance at last to get fame. And writing the Mai's biography, whether he believed in it or not, wouldn't necessarily preclude doing the other biographies; in fact, he'd consider the Mai's story simply as part of a bigger project. How he wished his brother were around to see how everything seemed to be working out for him. Suddenly he was no longer the awkward, bumbling idiot his father had so mercilessly derided. He felt strong and unafraid, he had somehow outwitted his sickle-cell anemia, it had been over a year since he'd last fallen sick, and his odds of staying alive could only improve with each passing year. He felt like screaming out aloud, *I am alive and I am useful and everything will work out fine!*

When he got to the school there was a black Peugeot 504 with the Ministry of Education number plates parked in front of the headmaster's office. In the staff room the teachers were massed up against the thin cardboard partition that separated the staff room from the headmaster's office, eavesdropping on the voices from the next office. The voices were loud and angry.

"It is the state commissioner for education himself," Mr. Bukar whispered by way of explanation, beckoning Mamo over. Zara was the only one still in her seat—Mamo went and stood beside her.

"Trouble?" he asked. She was shaking her head, and there was anger as well as bewilderment on her face. "They are closing down the school."

". . . you are not the only ones affected, so don't feel victimized," came the confident voice through the wall. "The country is going through a phase of change. No more private schools."

"But we are not a private school, this is a community school," Iliya shouted angrily.

"Please do not raise your voice to the honorable commissioner for education," another voice said.

"But we got this letter from your ministry just a month ago telling us we are not being reviewed—"

"That is not important. Forget about the letter, things have changed now, no more private schools, or community schools, no more bogus schools. From now on education will be handled by government only. Our children are our future, we can't take chances with our future."

"You don't understand, Mr. Commissioner—"

"Honorable."

"What?"

"You must address me as Honorable Commissioner for Education, or Honorable Commissioner, or simply Honorable, but not Mr. Commissioner. We must respect our public officers." For the first time the voice was raised a pitch higher.

Zara's mouth fell open. Mamo could imagine the exasperation on his uncle's face.

"Honorable Commissioner for Education . . ."

"Go on."

"Let me point out that this is not a normal school; it is a special school, started by the community, to help dropouts, to give them another chance. If you close down this school—"

"I have made my point clear, I hope, Mr. Headmaster. We are not closing down this school or any other school. We are taking them over and improving them; we are turning them into model schools. If you have any complaints, please write to my office and you will be attended to. I can't understand why you are complaining—it is the community that will benefit in the long run. Do you want to deny the whole community this great chance? There will be more funding for you, more teachers. His Excellency the governor is making education his first priority. Mr. Headmaster, I was a teacher myself. I am also a humane person. I could have sent you an official letter, but I decided to come myself."

Chairs were abruptly pushed back. "One week, you have one week to put your affairs in order, then the government will take over."

The teachers found Iliya slumped in his chair, staring blankly at the door, as if expecting the visitors to return and say they had

changed their minds and that the school wouldn't be closed
down after all. He sat up and squared his shoulders when he saw
the teachers. He waved them in with his good hand, pointing at
the chairs before his desk. They all squeezed in; some sat, and
some stood.

"You must have heard us through the partition," he said. "They
are closing down the school at last."

Ms. Lipstick elected herself spokesperson. "We heard everything, sir. We must fight them, sir. I have said this before. You
have worked too hard to let it go like this," she said, her eyes
shining, her shrunken breasts pushed forward combatively.

"It is not about me, it is about the school, the community."

"But if the government is going to increase funding and build
more infrastructures, shouldn't we . . ." Bukar didn't finish, he
practically shriveled under Iliya's withering stare.

"Give them one year and this school will be nothing but a sta-
tistic on paper. Are you that naïve? Can't you see what is happening? If you think the military were inefficient, well, you have
seen nothing yet. In one year, no, six months, everyone will have
forgotten there was once a school here. There will be only grass
and lizards and goats in the classes and crumbling walls. Mark
my words, just mark my words."

Although he didn't say it, Mamo knew that his uncle was
aware of the real reason the school was being closed down. The
school was being used as a pawn in the battle between Lamang
and his former party, the Victory Party. Elections were only days
away and this was a direct warning to Lamang, whose relentless
campaign for his new party was beginning to get a following, and
any villager who might be tempted to vote against the ruling
party, to think twice.

After the meeting, Mamo walked Zara home—her car had broken down and Yam had taken it to the mechanic's. It was late in
the afternoon and already the farmers were returning from the
farms, whole families walking in a file, the father in front, the

male sons following him, then the females, usually with large piles of firewood on their heads, all walking slowly, their eyes glazed with hunger and their minds looking forward to rest. Recently the rains had been slow in coming, and everywhere the air was dry and hot.

"What do they think of? Do they have dreams, do they ever think of leaving this place and going somewhere?" Zara asked. She sounded sad.

"We all have dreams," Mamo answered.

"When I was a child, whenever we came home for Christmas with my family, I'd dream of one day becoming super-wealthy and sending all the village kids to school and building houses for their parents."

She had said nothing when he told her of the offer from the palace. She had simply hugged him and said, "I am so happy for you." But her voice had sounded distant, preoccupied. Now they were passing near the tamarind tree that had the shape of a human torso. He pointed at the empty space next to the tree and said, "An old woman used to live here a long time ago. We used to be so scared of her, and when returning from school we'd pass her house at a run. Then we killed her dog."

"Why?"

"We thought we could see spirits through the dog's rheum. I guess we were just bored."

He left her at the gate. He wanted to go to his uncle and chat. The day had brought too many sudden changes and there was a lot to talk about, but first he decided to take a walk to clear his head.

election day

MAMO WOKE up late. Yesterday he had spent a great part of the day hanging around Zara's house, waiting for her to show up, but she hadn't. She had left for the city two days after the school closure, promising to return for the weekend, but he had waited with Yam, in vain. He had returned home and read till the early hours, listening to thunder rumbling in the sky, and then he had slept till midday.

Now he met a deserted house when he came out to the veranda. His father would most likely be out with his party's candidates, rallying voters and monitoring events at the polls. Auntie Marina would also be out campaigning—she was part of a church group called "Vote for Jesus" that had decided to make sure as many Christians as possible won the elections by appealing to all Christians to vote. Her group wasn't concerned what party a candidate belonged to as long as he went to church. They went from house to house, praying and singing songs and quoting relevant Bible passages about duty and the virtue of having godly men in high offices. The only person in the house apart from Mamo was little Rifkatu. She was a distant cousin and a new addition to the Lamang household—Auntie Marina had brought her from one of the neighboring hamlets to live with her. Rifkatu's father had three wives and over twenty children; farming them out to relatives or whoever was willing to have them as cooks and wash maids and farmhands was his only means of catering to their needs. Rifkatu, ten years old, was one of the lucky ones: Auntie Marina treated her like her own daughter, fairly but firmly, she had enough to eat, she slept on a mat in Marina's room, and she went to school, but most importantly, she wasn't overworked.

"Good morning, Uncle," Rifkatu called to Mamo with a little curtsy as she came out of the kitchen.

"Where's Auntie?" he asked.

"She has gone to the voting."

"And you, aren't you voting today?"

She smiled shyly at the joke and shook her head. "I am too young."

He decided to walk to Asabar's house; it was the best place to get news of the elections, not that Asabar was likely to be at home—he'd most likely be with Lamang, rallying voters and making sure nothing went wrong. But Mamo decided to go anyway. Recently, Asabar had asked Jummai to move in with him after she had given birth to a boy—this would be a good chance to see both mother and child even if Asabar wasn't home. The compound stood by itself, yards away from the nearest house. Asabar said he preferred it that way, for privacy, but Mamo knew that the real reason his cousin wanted privacy was because he was still selling marijuana on the side. The police had twice raided him, and on both occasions Lamang had bribed the police to let him go. Now Mamo smelled the acrid smoke of marijuana even before the house came into view behind the mango and neem trees that shaded it so well from sight. Pumpkin branches and leaves twined themselves around the fence posts, giving the straw fence more girth and further shading the house from casual view. Asabar was at home. The party's pickup, with its logo of a crowing, victorious rooster, and its speakers on the roof, was parked before the house as usual, and as he stepped into the compound Mamo could hear voices coming from the bedroom.

After Jummai and the child had moved in with him, Asabar had added two more huts to his one-hut compound. One of the new huts served as the kitchen; the other one, smaller and removed from the other two, was the toilet. The old hut remained the bedroom, and now its thin zinc door was shut, but a window, from which the marijuana smoke streamed out, was open. Mamo knocked on the door. The zinc rattled and amplified the knock, giving the sound an angry timbre. After a while the door opened a crack and Asabar's face appeared. He pushed the door a few inches wider when he saw it was Mamo.

"Are you alone?" he asked, a ribbon of smoke curling out of his mouth.

"Are you hiding something?" Mamo asked.

"Come in and find out."

There were three men seated on a mat on the hard mud floor. In the poor light of the room, worsened by the dense cigarette and weed smoke hanging in the air, Mamo could see the sweat rolling down their faces and into their shirts. He had never seen them before, but he guessed they were part of Asabar's youth wing posse.

"Bad for your health," he said to them, trying to adjust his eyes to the dim light. He sat down on the saggy spring bed beside Asabar. He soon noticed that the three youths had grown silent and were watching him intently, and then turning their gaze to Asabar, their faces tense. He understood why when he realized what was going on. There was a bundle of cards on the mat before the youths, and when he looked closer he saw that they were ballot cards.

"These are . . ." he began, turning to Asabar. He picked one up and lifted it to the window to see more clearly. Asabar had a smug, superior smile on his face as he took the card back and handed it to his friends.

"Get back to work, we have to finish this in an hour."

"What are you doing?"

"We are voting already," Asabar said with a laugh. The three echoed his laughter as they dipped their thumbs into a blotter of ink before pressing them on the white square space next to the rooster logo on the ballot cards. They worked silently and fast, passing a thick joint from lip to lip. Mamo watched in silence, and then at last he asked, "So what are you going to do with the cards?"

"You don't want to know that," Asabar said, but then he went on almost eagerly. "We will take them to the polling stations and put them in the ballot boxes. That's how you win elections. I am sure our opponents, the old Victory Party, ha-ha, are right now somewhere doing the same thing."

"But how, where did you get them . . . ?"

Asabar waved his hands dismissively. "It is not important. We have over ten thousand cards here. If we can distribute them to the different polling stations on time, then the local government chairmanship is ours, after that the governorship—"

Mamo shook his head. "No, you can't do that."

"Oh, why?"

"What you are doing is dangerous."

The men on the mat laughed out loud and patted each other on the back, repeating Mamo's words. Asabar looked at him with narrowed eyes. "Not a word to anyone," he whispered, clapping a hand on Mamo's shoulder.

Mamo stood up. "Come outside, I need to have a word with you."

The men on the mat looked from Mamo to Asabar suspiciously, but Asabar stood up and with his usual swagger nodded reassuringly at them and said, "Carry on. I'll be back."

Outside, Mamo furiously turned on his cousin and said, "You could go to jail for that, do you know that?"

Asabar laughed out loud and took a drag from his joint. "You don't understand how these things work, Mr. Teacher. We have the police in our pockets."

"Yes, but so does the other party, which happens to be the ruling party and so has more clout than you. Think. You know how desperately they want to punish my father for going over to the opposition party. They are watching closely and waiting. Don't let yourself be a victim of their power game. Already the KCS is closed because of my father and his politics. Think."

"Think about what?" Asabar shouted, his red eyes growing narrower. "This is what I do for a living. This is nothing; I have done riskier things for the party. You don't know anything, you and my father and your school and books. This is the real life. You can't tell me anything, just go."

Mamo looked into his cousin's narrow, sensitive face and saw how dull it had grown and he knew how impossible it'd be to reach across to him. But he tried again. "Where is Jummai and the baby? I actually came to say hi to them."

Asabar waved his hand disinterestedly. "I sent them to her parents' for the day."

"Well, think about them before you do anything stupid. You have a family now."

Asabar laughed again till he began coughing. "This is funny. I can't believe you are trying to give me advice on this—this is my life." He beat his hand on his chest and pushed his face into Mamo's face. "I am the youth wing leader, remember, the youth wing leader. You think it is easy?"

"Okay, I'll go, but tell me one thing before I go: does my father know about this?"

Asabar tilted his head to one side, as if thinking, then he smiled and said, "What do you think?"

"Does he?" Mamo asked again.

"Ask him."

On the way home Mamo passed groups of people standing under trees and in doorways discussing the elections, but he hardly saw them as his mind boiled with anger against his father. Asabar was stupid and headstrong, but he didn't deserve to go to prison because of Lamang's ambition. Of course, he knew that election-rigging was the norm, which was not his concern; his concern was for his cousin. He thought of different methods he could use to stop Asabar from going out with the ballot boxes, one being to get Uncle Iliya to go and talk sense to him, but Mamo knew that Iliya would most likely shake his head and say something philosophical like, *We all choose our paths in life. I can't live his life for him.* And besides, that would be reporting his father to Iliya. He preferred a more indirect way. He found a solution just as he was about to enter the house gate. He saw a police car slowly cruising past with two policemen seated in the back, holding rifles between their legs, and suddenly he remembered what his cousin had said, that they had the police in their pocket.

"Of course, the police," he said to himself and quickly ran into the house. Neither his father nor Auntie Marina was back yet. He went to his room and hastily drafted a letter addressed generally to the Keti Police Command. He kept the letter short and direct.

> *Dear Sir,*
> *I am a concerned citizen and it has been brought to my notice that ballot papers have been illegally procured and transported to the house of an NVP member with the intent to rig the ongoing elections. I am notifying you so that you could go and bring this nefarious deed to a stop immediately. The papers are in the house of a certain Asabar Lamang. Hurry before it is too late.*
>
> > *Thank you,*
> > *Concerned Citizen*

Mamo read the letter again, changing a few words. He was happy with it—it sounded mean and stupid enough to be convincing. His hand shook as he put the letter in an envelope, and all the way to the police station he felt as if everyone he passed were looking at him accusingly, as if the word "Judas" were branded on his forehead. More than once he stopped and almost turned back, asking himself if he was doing this really to help his cousin or because he wanted to frustrate his father. But he repeatedly told himself that his motive was pure. His plan was to get the police to arrest Asabar and keep him away for a day or so. He was sure Lamang would spring him after the elections. It was a risky plan, but it was definitely safer than allowing Asabar to go out, doped out of his mind, and fall into the hands of the opposition party and the Election Commission. He didn't deliver the letter himself. When he got near the police station he gave the letter to a young boy passing and gave him some money and told him to take the letter to the policeman behind the counter.

"Don't answer any questions. Just give him this and run back here."

# of mice and men

"I AM too old for this," Uncle Iliya said, shaking his gray head from side to side. He was wearing a faded sky-blue caftan, and the empty left sleeve flapped about as he moved. "A son in the hospital, and a brother in detention, and all for what, for politics?"

They were at the Keti General Hospital, where Asabar lay, for the third day, in a critical condition. The doctors said he would live, even though a bullet had shattered his spine, paralyzing him from the waist down, and he'd never walk again. They were in a large anteroom, a sort of visitors' waiting room, next to the main ward where Asabar lay on a narrow bed by the window. Only one visitor at a time could go in to see him. Auntie Marina was now with him, probably saying a prayer over him. Mamo had been in there earlier. Asabar could see and hear and talk, but he couldn't move; he lay straight on his back, staring up at the weak fluorescent tube over the bed, his body full of painkillers. His mouth was slack, his eyes were weak and unfocused, as if he still couldn't understand why he was here, or why everyone was making such a fuss over him. Mamo had stood beside him for a long time without speaking, just watching the tall thin figure under the white hospital sheet, and for some reason his brother came to his mind—he imagined him on the battlefield in some strange country, fighting strange enemies, exposed to danger. The image deepened his feeling of guilt and he turned away to the window. In his mind he was still trying to fathom how his simple and clever plan had resulted in this. His ears still replayed Auntie Marina's screams as she burst into the house with the news that Asabar and his friends had been attacked by the police.

"But what . . . what happened?" Mamo asked, coming out to the veranda and sitting beside his auntie who had her head in her hands. Rifkatu stood in front of the kitchen, also holding her head, echoing Marina's screams.

"The police, they attacked them. They said they found them with ballot papers . . . and . . . and now two of the boys are dead . . . and they said Asabar might not last the night, shot, he was shot." Then she stood up abruptly as if just remembering that she had something to do. "They are in the hospital. . . . I am on my way there."

Mamo walked with her to the hospital. On the way sympathetic friends stopped them and offered words of encouragement. Mamo walked and his mind was a big hole; the only thought that echoed and re-echoed in the hole was, *I am a murderer. I've killed my cousin*. But Asabar did not die; he remained in a coma.

That same evening the police came and took Lamang away to the state capital for questioning.

No one seemed to be sure exactly what had happened, no one had the time or the presence of mind to find out; there was too much pain everywhere. Mamo pieced together what he heard with what he knew—his terrible secret which he couldn't tell anyone, not even his uncle—and came up with a plausible scenario: After he had alerted the police with his letter, instead of them coming to Asabar's house and arresting him as he had envisaged, they had followed him as he left the house with his friends and then they had ambushed him before he got to the polling station. Two of the youth wing members were killed by the police, a policeman died on the way to the hospital, and Asabar took a bullet in the back.

Uncle Iliya was seated in the only chair in the anteroom, a broken plastic chair with only three legs; it was propped up against
the wall to give it balance. Iliya sat balanced carefully on the
edge, fidgeting restlessly. The room was filled with visitors bearing food in plastic containers and paper-wrapped loaves of bread
under their arms; they were mostly women, thin, wiry peasants
dressed in their Sunday best to show respect to the sick and
dying. Their faces were somber, and they looked up with apprehension whenever a nurse or a blue-uniformed hospital worker
entered. It was midafternoon, the room was hot, airless, and the
single fan above was static because of the constant power cuts.
Mamo was next to the window and he often poked his head out
to take huge gulps of fresh air—the smell in the room was close,
pungent.

"Has anyone contacted you since the arrest—the police, or his
party colleagues?" Iliya asked.

Mamo shook his head. "I went to the party office yesterday, I
met the deputy chairman and he promised to do something
about it, but I haven't heard from him up to now."

"Typical. They won't do anything."

Mamo knew his father had no true friends among the politicians. His former friends from the Victory Party, who were still in
power, having won the elections again, were still angry with him
and would do anything to make sure he went to prison, while his
New Victory Party colleagues wouldn't want to associate themselves too closely with him because of the ballot paper scandal.

"I was thinking of going to the palace tomorrow," Mamo said
slowly.

"That is a good idea. Do you want me to come with you?"
Uncle Iliya asked.

Mamo said no. He still hadn't given a final answer to the
Waziri's offer—things had moved so fast since that day at the

palace. And now here was a chance for him to make use of his palace "connections." He'd make his father's liberty a condition of his accepting the offer. If anyone in Keti could intervene successfully with the authorities on his father's behalf, it was the Mai. Of course, everyone knew that the palace was not free of politics, and its loyalties would most likely be with the powers that be, and that meant the Victory Party, but it was worth a try. Not that Mamo was particularly bothered about his father's liberty, Lamang deserved his punishment, but Mamo saw this move as a step toward making right all that he had made wrong—not that there was any way he could totally make things right: Asabar would never walk again and those who had died were gone forever; this knowledge would be a pain he'd bear like the mark of Cain. Maybe someday, when the time was right, he'd confess to everyone, and their disgust and condemnations would be the fire that might begin his purification.

And surprisingly he found a sympathetic ear at the palace. He didn't even need to see the Mai. After listening to his story, the Waziri came around to where Mamo was seated and, laying a hand on Mamo's shoulder, said, "But why didn't you come earlier, on the very day your father was arrested? We could have finished everything that very day. This is a very small matter for the Mai. Remember, the palace takes care of its own. Now, don't worry about your father anymore. Let's talk of more important things. When can you begin work? The Mai has been asking after you."

"Thank you, sir—" Mamo began, but the Waziri raised his hand, stopping him.

"Like I said, the palace takes care of its own. Don't thank me."

Mamo nodded. He felt on the verge of tears. The events of the past three days had shaken him more than anything had ever done before—and now he was further taken off balance by the sheer kindness emitting from the Waziri's face; even the crooked left eye shone with benevolence. "I'll come as soon as my cousin is out of the hospital."

"Good. Now go, the driver will take you home—"

"There's one more thing," Mamo began quickly, impulsively.

"What is it? Tell me, don't hesitate."

"It is about the school. It is still closed."

"Ah, the school. First, I want you to know that the school is as much a source of pride to the palace as it is to your uncle and to the community. There is no length we wouldn't go to . . ."

Mamo's heart sank as the words kept tumbling out of the Waziri's mouth; it was like anesthesia, preparing him for the wicked cut.

". . . but unfortunately, no reply came. We think there are some powerful people behind all this. My advice is wait till after the elections. For now we are powerless."

Mamo nodded.

"You look exhausted. Go and get some rest. The driver is waiting for you."

Lamang was released from detention exactly one week after his arrest. He came home early in the morning, alone in a taxi, hunched in the back seat, looking very small. He had bruises on his face and on his arms, and Mamo was sure there were more under his once-spanking-white shirt. The first thing he did was take a shower. He was over an hour in the bathroom, and when he came out he took another hour to dress. Mamo went and sat with him in the living room, but after the first perfunctory greetings nothing more was said, and they sat in silence, Lamang seeming to be lost in thought, and Mamo feeling frustrated at his inability to say something casual to his father, until he reminded himself that it takes two to make a conversation. His father didn't look as if he was interested in small talk right then; in fact he looked as if he'd rather be alone. After a while Mamo left him and went to see if Zara had come, as it was a Friday.

Mamo watched his father gradually lose his swagger. Lamang
had expected something of a hero's welcome after his release,
but apart from the widows, and a few neighbors and close relatives, no one came to welcome him back from prison. He'd sit in
his favorite seat in the living room, placed so that it faced the
door, and he'd wait, pretending to be reading or listening to the
radio—but no one came. After a week of this he began to fret,
and pace, and look for things to do. A day after his release he had
visited Asabar at the hospital, then he had gone to offer his con-
dolences to the families of the two youth wing members killed
in the police ambush, then to the palace to thank the Mai for
interceding with the authorities on his behalf, and now he was
out of places to go. So he waited, and waited. What he really
waited for was a delegation from his party to come and welcome
him officially and perhaps organize a reception for him, but after
a week, when it became clear that the party was maintaining its
distance from him, he got into his car and went to the party
office at the village market. Strong words were exchanged
between him and the new chairman, his former deputy, and he
returned home in a huff.

A week later he decided to sue the party for abandoning him to
his fate after he had served it so diligently. Such abandonment, he
claimed, was tantamount to character assassination. He maintained that he was innocent of any allegation of vote rigging, and
that it was his former party, the VP, that was still trying to ruin
him, and now his own party, from whom he had expected support,
was an accomplice in his harassment. The whole village turned
out for the first hearing. Mamo sat in the audience, not far from
the widows, who had been the first to arrive, dressed in their Sunday best, their head scarves defiantly pointing at the unceilinged
roof. They seemed to be the only people in Lamang's corner, apart
from Mamo. The other side was crowded with the party loyalists,
some of whom were Asabar's youth wing members. They had

arrived in hired pickups with loudspeakers on the roof playing the party's song. The case lasted for two weeks and Lamang lost. In his final ruling the short, bearded judge looked sternly at Lamang and thundered in the silent courtroom, "Mr. Lamang, you are lucky no one has brought a charge against you. Men have died, and directly or indirectly, you have blame to bear."

After the decline came the fall, and when it did, it was sudden— and literal.

When he returned from court after the defeat, Lamang sat in his seat, silent, his face dark and sullen, shifting his bulk once in a while, tapping his foot on the bottle-green carpet, then picked up a pen and paper and started a letter. When he read the letter afterward Mamo saw that it was addressed to the party leadership; it was full of fresh accusations and threats, and ended with Lamang's formal resignation from the party. When he had finished writing it Lamang stormed out of the room and stood at the head of the veranda steps and shouted impatiently for the little girl, "Rifkatu! Rifkatu! Where are you?"

When she appeared wiping her hand on the edge of her wrapper, he shouted at her to run to the store and get him an envelope. Then he fell before he completed the sentence. The girl's scream brought Mamo running out of his room to see his father sprawled at the foot of the steps, his face in the dust, his legs on the last step—his body was twisted awkwardly and his legs were twitching. Mamo thought he had lost his step and fallen, but when he went to help him up he saw that he was unconscious, his jaw was twisted, his tongue was bitten in half, and blood was oozing out of the side of his mouth.

It wasn't a fall; it was a stroke.

Auntie Marina sent the girl to call the neighbors and together she and Mamo got Lamang into the back of his new Honda. Mamo drove them to the hospital—it was his first time behind a wheel, but he managed it, in fits and jerks. Auntie Marina sat in the back with Lamang's dusty and bloody head in her lap, praying all the way. Beside Mamo in the passenger seat sat Sanda the barber, a neighbor, who kept sucking in his breath sharply whenever the Honda jumped forward and swerved to the opposite side of the road.

Lamang was in the hospital for a whole month. He was discharged on the same day as Asabar, and they all went home in the same car, Zara's car. She had been coming regularly to the hospital since the stroke, and often she and Mamo would just sit in the car in the hospital parking lot, holding hands, not talking much. Now they sat in the living room with Lamang, who looked alert and even tried to make small talk with Zara, but his words came out all faint and jumbled through his crooked mouth. He later fell asleep in his chair, his head hanging toward his chest, a trickle of saliva making a thin line down his chin. Together they took him to his room and laid him out on his bed.

"Once," Mamo said to Zara as he walked her out to her car, "I hated him so much I could have killed him. Now I feel sorry for him."

"Just remember he is your father, he will always be your father."

IN THE end only the widows remained.

The TV viewers trickled down to a handful of urchins who would stand at the door and whiningly ask Auntie Marina for the TV to be brought out; one day she simply told them to go away. "Go home and sleep. There will be no more television from now on." But the widows still came bearing food and drinks and behaving as if Lamang were still the dashing eligible bachelor they had once set endless traps for. Mamo, who had always avoided them whenever possible, now began to sit with them when he came back from his office at the palace and even laugh at their humorless jokes. Sometimes he dropped them at their houses with the car when they stayed late. They loved to tease him about Zara, asking him, "When are we going to pay the bride-price?" And then they'd playfully vie with each other over who would be Mother of the Day at the wedding.

"Choose, now," they'd chorus, cornering him, pulling at his hand, batting their eyes at him coquettishly.

"All of you together," he'd tell them, surprised at how much he was enjoying it all.

"Another politician," they'd shout, turning to Lamang. "He is as hard to pin down as you."

Lamang died in degrees. The doctors had said he would recover, but he didn't. Mamo knew that his father's continued deterioration was a deliberate act of will. Lamang wanted to die. Often

when they were alone and in the living room and when his father
had drifted off to sleep in his seat, which he did more and more
often, Mamo would study his face: the mouth which had become
permanently crooked, and the gray which had become more pro-
nounced now that he had given up dying his hair, and the lines—
the lines were like cracks in a wall, zigzagging and interlocking
and rendering the face so fragile, and he would say to himself,
*Can this be the same man, my dreaded father, the sometime King
of Women?* Often he had to carry him to his room and lay him on
his bed and, averting his eyes from his father's genitalia, undress
him and change him into his pajamas.

Lamang was dying because his sun, around which the whole
world had once revolved, had suddenly lost its shine. His vanity
was now a knife, stuck in his back, twisting and torturing, making his mouth more crooked as he contemplated his helplessness
and all the ill fortune that had recently dogged him. He neglected to take his medications unless pressed to do so by Auntie
Marina—it was as if he were daring God to finish up what He
had started. He grew thin and gray and bent, and sometimes,
when he fell asleep in his chair before the TV, tears and saliva
would drip out of his eyes and mouth, and when he attempted to
walk on his own, even with his walking stick, his hands would
shake and the stick would wobble and fall to the ground, and
then he'd collapse back into his chair and wait for assistance.

Mamo would sit and watch TV with him, making general comments, still unable to address his father directly. The first time
they began talking was when his father brought out a pen and
paper and asked him to write a letter for him, complaining that
his hands shook and his eyes were blurry. He dictated and Mamo
wrote. It became a routine, and they tentatively opened up to
each other. The letters were mostly to his business partners and
former party colleagues, and once or twice to the newspapers.
Afterward they would discuss the letters, and sometimes he even
asked for Mamo's opinion. Later, he only gave the gist of what he
wanted written and Mamo would form the words and arrange the

argument. Lamang would put on his glasses and read the letter and tell Mamo he had a gift for words, and that he had put it better than he, Lamang, could have. Mamo felt unaccountably sad the first time his father complimented him.

When Lamang talked he rambled from subject to subject, from his father, to his mother, to his business, to his youth, as if he were trying to make up for lost time, as if he knew it was futile but he was trying anyway. It was his way of saying he was sorry, though he could never bring himself to say so directly.

One day they were seated in the living room and for no reason Mamo felt a flash of anger, something from long ago, the kind of restless energy that had driven him and his brother to poison the old witch's dog. In his mind different thoughts ran and crossed each other like naked wires, throwing up sparks. He thought of his childhood, of the feeling of abandonment he and his brother always felt when, after waiting for weeks for their father to return from one of his trips, he'd walk in only to pass them on the veranda with barely a glance; he also thought of his cousin Asabar, confined to a wheelchair for life, and how he was condemned forever because of his role in bringing that about.

"Tell me about my mother," he said to his father. His voice was low, almost casual. But in his head the anger pounded, making his mouth bitter.

His father looked at him, surprised. He sighed. "Your mother . . . what's there to say . . . she was so young, and frail. She died so young. . . ."

"Is that all?" asked Mamo. He stared hard at his father's face: the tired eyes, rheumy, the lips, still crooked from the stroke's twisting. Mamo wanted to press further, to bombard his father with questions, to harass him for answers. He could do it—he could stand up before the frail, slouched old man, look into his pain-suffused eyes, stride up and down before him, stand right on top of him and hurl the questions like fists at the soft, unprotected body. He could go on and on till the old man squirmed and broke down and confessed to his cruelties to the young, disillusioned girl, his negligence of his own children.

"She was so young . . . there's really nothing much to say. She died," Lamang repeated. His voice was frail, flinching; it was as if he could see the violence in Mamo's head. Mamo averted his eyes and slumped in his chair. The tight knot of tension went out of his back. *What's the use?* he thought, unconsciously repeating his father's words. *What's there to say?* He stood up to leave the room, then he stopped at the door and turned, and almost casually he said to Lamang, "I informed the police about the rigging. I met Asabar in his room, thumbing ballot cards, and I wrote to the police. I guess that's why Asabar was stopped, and you were arrested."

Mamo wasn't looking at his father as he spoke; he was looking at the plaque on the wall: THE SILENT LISTENER TO EVERY CONVERSATION.

"You didn't," said Lamang, his voice hardly audible.

"What?" Mamo returned slowly to the center of the room.

"Wait. I'll show you," Lamang said and struggled to his feet. Mamo watched, not moving forward to assist. He watched his father shuffle to his room, and when he returned he had a piece of paper in his hand. He handed it to Mamo.

Mamo recognized his handwriting immediately. It was the letter he had written to the police. He went and sat down. Now he was the one shaking as if with palsy. He looked at his father and said, "What happened?"

"The policeman who was given the letter . . . he knows me. He works for me. . . . I pay him."

"And you've had it all this while . . . why didn't you show me? I thought I was responsible for Asabar's injury . . . why . . . ?"

But Lamang had closed his eyes. He appeared to be asleep.

"Every day I wake up with the guilt heavy on my shoulders, and whenever I looked in the mirror I hated myself for what I thought I had done to my cousin." Mamo spoke slowly, almost whispering to himself. "And all this while . . ."

He squeezed the letter with both hands until his palms ached.

Lamang opened his eyes briefly and said, "We all have our secret pains, our personal anguish. It is life."

In his fluttering, almost inaudible voice he told Mamo how Asabar and his friends had left home too late to get the cards to the polling stations. They hadn't left Asabar's room till late afternoon and by then the voting was over and the ballots were already being counted. Asabar became really desperate when he found out that in all the early results coming out the Victory Party was leading. His chairman, Lamang, wasn't around to advise him on what to do with the over ten thousand cards in the back of the party pickup, and so he decided to use his own initiative. The remotest ward in the Keti local government, Pandi ward, had still not brought in its votes. Asabar's dope-driven plan was simple: ambush the election officials bringing in the Pandi votes and switch their ballot boxes with his own.

He got a handful of his most trusted lieutenants and set out. It was fast getting dark, and it was raining. They picked a suitable spot eight miles from town and waited in a ditch by the roadside, hidden by trees and shrubs, their machetes and clubs tightly clenched in their hands. They kept up their courage by swigging in turns from a bottle of cheap gin and smoking weed. When at last they saw the approaching Election Commission car with the election officers and ballot boxes in it, they were so drunk they couldn't think straight—they came out running and screaming, slashing their machetes against the windshield and through the window. The two policemen in the car came out shooting, and two of Asabar's men were killed instantly. Asabar was shot in the spine as he tried to escape into the bush; one of the policemen had his artery sliced open by a rusty machete and he died on the way to the hospital.

After his father had finished speaking, Mamo stood up and went to his room and came back with LaMamo's letters, which he quietly gave to his father. He watched the shock on his father's face as he opened the letters and saw the name and then the dates on them.

"All this while .. . ." Lamang whispered hoarsely.

How does it feel? Mamo wanted to scream. He wanted to reach out and grab his father's heart and break it into bits.

Lamang quietly retired for the night.

Early in the morning Mamo was woken up by Auntie Marina knocking on his door.

"Come," she said to him and turned and headed past the living room and into his father's room. Lamang lay on the bed, face up, his eyes closed. The room was in semidarkness, illuminated by a bedside lamp with a red shade. The red glow gave the room a surreal feel, and Mamo felt himself shiver for no reason. On the table beside the lamp were LaMamo's letters, and on top of them were his father's reading glasses. Lamang looked as if he were sleeping—his arms were folded over his chest, but his chest was not moving. Mamo turned to his auntie and in her eyes he saw the deep sadness; her eyes were red with pendant tears. Despite his shortcomings, her brother had occupied a special place in her heart because he had taken her in when she had nowhere to go. For the first time Mamo noticed how like his father she looked, the same set of jaw, the prominent nose and the wide forehead. He knew what was required of him. He nodded and stepped forward, putting his hand on his father's body tentatively, first on the arm—it felt cold already, and he had never noticed before how hairy his father's arm was, thick with bristly undergrowth. Then he touched the face, putting his fingers over the nose, but there was no breath passing. He stepped back, and turned to her. He felt no emotion, just a vague hollowness in his chest, but no tears fell from his eyes. He watched his auntie step forward and raise the sheet in a single motion and cover the body with it—he thought absently how like a wing-beat the sheet sounded descending over the body, the wings of death's angel.

They left the room together. He went to his room, and she went out to the veranda, her face calm and collected. But as soon as she stepped outside she gave a long ululating wail, which went on and on, like a song, rising lazily over the roof, curving like a scythe over the mahogany trees outside, going from house to house, where the women—just about to light the fire for the morning meal—would hear it and answer with their own wails. The women would leave what they were doing and come to answer death's imperative call. For the next two days friends and relations would troop to the house. They'd come from Keti and from the neighboring villages bearing gifts: a chicken, a goat, a measure of corn. The women would gather in the compound, crying and knocking their heads on the ground and against the walls, while the men would sit outside under the trees, playing cards, moving their mats whenever the shade shifted. Two days for death, and then life would resume.

In his father's biography Mamo would describe the burial as surprisingly well attended. He mentioned the huge baobab trees that formed a row at the foot of the hills, looking like mute, giant guardians watching over the graves. The sky was dark with rain clouds. Pastor Mela, in a new robe with a strange hoodlike collar, gave a long graveside sermon about death and hellfire, then he mentioned resurrection and paradise grudgingly at the end. Uncle Iliya gave a brief and pertinent speech on behalf of the family. Mamo was asked to pour the first handful of sand on the coffin, and, he wrote:

The sound of the sand on the wood was so final, so conclusive. I moved back and I watched the people: Father's friends, some who had avoided him only recently, now standing in the front row with handkerchiefs to their eyes; there were relations from the neighboring villages and hamlets, some I had never seen before, but all bearing a generic resemblance to Father and Uncle Iliya and I guess to myself too. The men stood around the hole, staring intently at the disappearing coffin as if its image were some precious keepsake they'd take home with them. The women were far away to one side,

I could make out Auntie Marina standing with her head high, and her eyes were red and her lips twitching. Next to her were the three widows, standing together, holding each other and crying. They had grieved more than anyone else in these past two days; at first I thought they were overdoing it, but now I realize that they were not only grieving for my father, they were also grieving for themselves. While he was alive my father had given them one gift no one else had given them in a long time: he had looked at them not as aging mothers and hopeless widows, but with desire. While he was alive he had stood between them and abhorrent age; now that he was gone, their one protection against reality was gone too.

leaving you, baby

FOR SOME time now he had felt her slipping away from him—
he couldn't tell exactly when it had started, only that he had
recently become conscious of it: there were long awkward
silences that had once been comfortable and companionable
silences, and even the lovemaking had become perfunctory and
unexciting.

He had seen her only once since the burial two weeks ago. She
came the day after and they sat together in his room, saying nothing, and the silence towered between them like a wall, like a
weight pressing down on their tongues—he had thought it was
the weight of grief, her grief for his loss, but now he realized it was
simply silence, they had run out of things to say to each other. But
so great was his fear of losing her that he dreaded her next visit,
when she might tell him she was leaving him. She was unhappy,
he knew—the court case had ended in her husband's favor and
though she tried to make light of it he could see her eyes, red with
crying, and her silences, which pushed her light-years away from
him, from everyone. Once, in the midst of one such long silence,
she had sighed and said, apropos of nothing, "I read somewhere
about a species of rodents called lemmings. They have amazing
mannerisms. Sometimes, out of a strange and mysterious compul-
sion, they mass themselves on the edge of a cliff and then jump
into the water below to drown. Weird, isn't it?"

He had taken her hands in his, saying nothing.

But now he realized that the silence did not only emanate

from her. He had contributed his own share of it too. After
Asabar's unfortunate clash with the police, Mamo had withdrawn into himself, and more than once she had asked him if he
was ill, but he had only shaken his head. More than once he had
wanted to confess all to her, but he had held back, and even after
his father had told him the truth of that incident he had still not
told Zara about it. And the distance between them had widened
and slowly a wall had sprung up between them and now they
were both shocked at how high the wall was.

△▽△

Last night, unable to sleep, he had decided to begin work on his
biography of the Mai of Keti and he had written down all he
knew of the Mai's history, starting from Mai Bol Dok, who had
started the present line of Mais. Like most people in Keti, his
knowledge came from popular tradition: gossip, legend, myth,
and what little history there was in books. Now he handed it to
her when she came into the room. She had just arrived from the
state capital. He had been asleep when she entered. She opened
the window and the light, piercing through the murky undergrowth of his sleep, woke him up. He looked at her standing at
the window; she was facing him, and the light fell on her hair,
obscuring her face, her head tilted to one side. Her perfume
filled the room. He felt so happy to see her. "Come," he said,
opening his arms. That was when he gave her the essay. He
wanted to preempt the topic of discussion—if he kept her talking about the essay, about history, about anything at all, then the
moment wouldn't come when she'd tell him, *I've been thinking
about us, about our relationship*. . . .

He left her reading and went outside to brush his teeth. When
he returned she said, "What is this?" Still reading, not looking up.

"Something I wrote yesterday, I couldn't sleep."

"There are . . . almost thirty pages here," she said with surprise.
"You wrote them all last night?"

"I finished this morning, actually. I couldn't sleep. I want to make the Mai's biography simply a part of the other biographies I told you about—so this is really one of the ten, fifteen biographies I will eventually compile to form a biographical history of Keti. That's what history really is, people and their lives, no matter how we try to manipulate it. It is the story of real people with real weaknesses and strengths and . . . not about some founding fathers and . . . even if we want to write about the founding fathers we shouldn't privilege them, we should place them on a par with other ordinary folks because really who is to say . . . I am babbling."

She was listening to him, looking at him, her head to one side. "No, you are not. But let me finish this. It is beautiful. Go out, give me ten minutes, please," she said, pushing him toward the door. He sat on the steps outside, looking so apprehensive and miserable that his auntie stopped before him on her way to the kitchen, a calabash of rice in her hands, and asked, "Is something the matter?"

"She is going to leave me," he said with certainty.

"Who?" Auntie Marina asked.

"Zara."

"Oh, a quarrel. It happens. Talk to her. Beg her a little, women love that. Don't just sit here. Come on, go in," she said, smiling encouragingly, pointing at the door with the calabash. Auntie Marina had a new jauntiness to her steps in the past few days. Her ex-husband, who had come ostensibly to pay his respects after Lamang's death, had completely broken down before her afterward, confessing what a hard time the other woman was giving him, how she openly kept boyfriends, and came and went as she wanted, and how he himself was out of a job, and his farm lay uncultivated because the other woman just wouldn't touch a hoe.

"But why don't you do the farmwork yourself?" Auntie Marina had asked him, a mischievous twinkle in her eyes.

"But I am the man of the house. Besides, you never complained about these things, you understood that as a man I had other things to do."

"Like what?" she went on almost gently. "You mean like drinking and lazing under the council tree, and chasing other women?"

"Well, meeting my friends for discussions, important discussions. . . ." he stuttered, visibly shrinking into his skin. He looked old and bent and dirty, and most of his front teeth were missing. It was at that point that she burst into tears, dancing and laughing at the same time, singing a church song about how the Lord had delivered her from Egypt.

Now Mamo wanted to ask her why she hadn't responded to her ex's petitions if women wanted so much to be begged and cajoled, but he only nodded and stood up and went back inside. Suddenly he thought of the last time they had made love passionately, how Zara had given herself to him, crying as she held him and kissed him, saying she didn't know what she'd do if she ever lost him. He stood at the door. Zara looked up, smiling, waving the papers, opening her mouth to make a comment, but the smile went away when she saw the look on his face. She put the papers down.

"Don't leave me, please," he said.

She turned to the window and he could see her forehead crease, her lips pucker.

"I have to. I am going away, for a while. To South Africa. I didn't know how to tell you, because there's also a man involved."

Mamo sighed. She went on talking, still looking out of the window.

"We were in school together, he is South African, we . . . we used to go out, but just for a short while. I met him again last month at the university, at my professor's office, you remember the prof—"

"I remember."

"Well, I went there about a job and he was there to collect his

certificate. We started talking and he told me about this orphanage he is running in Durban. It is such a noble thing to do, to
work with children, some of whom are sick and dying. I told him
if he needed assistance or anything . . . Well, he did. I am going
with him, Mamo. I have to."

"To South Africa, just like that?"

"Yes. I fear that if I don't go, if I don't get outside myself, my
troubles, I will do something I will regret, something crazy."

He sat down on the bed and said, "There's something I need
to tell you, something I should have told you long ago."

"What is it?"

He told her about Asabar. He brought out the letter and
showed her and then he said, "Now you understand why I
appeared so distant and disturbed at times. It was a big weight
on my mind, I hated myself and I felt ashamed. Now all that is
over, we can start afresh. I have the job at the palace, we can
even get married. Of course, with my sickle cell we might not be
able to have children, but you already have a child, and—"

But she was shaking her head and looking at him sadly. "It
won't work. We can't marry, it won't work, not so soon after my
divorce, and you . . . you have so much on your mind, your
father's death, and your brother. I know you still think about him,
you just don't talk about it, and because you don't talk about it,
it still weighs you down. And now you have this new job . . . you
don't need to be tied down. I have so much on my mind too. If
we don't lay our ghosts to rest, we will only make each other sad.
I'd rather be sad somewhere alone than to be here and drag you
down. I love you, Mamo, I do. But we need time alone. . . ."

"But there might not be another time," he said. "You might
finally fall in love with your friend. He sounds like a saint. And
maybe I will meet someone."

She shook her head, not looking at him. "I don't know, maybe
you are right. But all I know is that I need to see things from a
different angle, with more clarity; right now I can't see at all.

Sometimes I feel as if I am losing my mind. If not for you, if not for the time we've had together, I don't know what I'd do. I have to go, I do."

Before she left, she put her arms around him and held him tight till he could feel her heart pounding and the heat from her womb, but he couldn't seem to be able to lift his arms and return the hug—they hung by his side, weighted with tons of concrete, and it was all he could do not to buckle under the weight. She pulled back and stood with her head bent, stuffing the papers into her bag. "I haven't finished reading this. I'll take it with me. I'll post it to you when I am through."

"It is rough," he said, not very interested.

"I'll type it, if you want, and check the spellings."

As she was about to leave, he asked suddenly, "What is his name?"

"Themba," she said, and the word came out heavy and sad, like a sigh.

When she left he went to the living room and sat before the television screen, staring at the images, not really listening to what they were saying. He felt so hot suddenly, an internal heat, like the onset of one of his sickle-cell attacks, though he hadn't been ill in almost a year. After a while the fever abated. His immune system had grown stronger the older he got—it was capable of bearing most things now, mosquito bites, sudden fevers, maybe even heartache.

part three

leaving monrovia

September 1990

Dear brother,
*I haven't written in a long time, but first I want to say that I
am outside Liberia now, and things are more better than they
have been so far. When the war became too much to bear Bintou and I left for the neighboring country of Guinea. It was not
easy escaping because the rebels have now taken over much of
Liberia and have divided it between themselves. We wanted to
go on foot with refugees sneaking across the border but the
French medical workers helped us because they now have
another camp across the border where it is safe so we went with
them as their assistants which we are in reality and now we are
here safe and it seems as if all the fighting and the killing that
have been the major part of my life since I left home has been
only a dream. But I still see the people we pass on the way as
we were coming here. Their were families mostly women and
children with their bundles of things on their heads, sometimes
it is food or cloths but sometimes they even carry the dead bodies on their head because they don't want to leave it on the way
for animals to eat. Bintou was crying all the way and begging
the drivers to stop but it was not possible because we have all
the sick people from the house with us and even us we are only
clinging to the truck with our hands, but she kept saying we
can stop for just one, just one person.*

I remember my friends who have died in Mali, then Samuel Paul and the professor and how I have lost my eye, but I have to thank God that I am alive because many have died. Our camp here is just by the border of Liberia with Guinea and there are thousands of people and we all sleep on the ground but more forein aid workers are arriving to provide tents and other shelters and me and Bintou can now sleep in a tent because we still work with the MSF me as general assistant and sometimes as driver while she helps with the patients to prepare them for surgery and so on, but mostly the people are just hungry because many have not eaten for weeks. It is not easy to survive here because everyone is sick and even the healthy ones fall sick because of epidemic, but mostly people are without one leg or hand or ear or like me with only one eye. But I am not too worried because one of the doctors said when I get the glass eye it will really look like a real eye and nobody will know, only me because I can't see with it, but I still think I am lucky because many have died while I am still alive.

From here we plan to go to the capital, Conakry, because Bintou have relatives there, her mother and aunties, and people say one can survive there because there is diamond smugling where one can make a lot of money. Bintou has many plans and one of them is to go back to school, she wants to study agriculture and she wants me to school too. I will think about it, but first we have to save the money and take care of ourselves. We are even considering to marry because it is not easy living like this here together and people keep asking us if we are brother and sister. But Bintou wants to meet her family first before we marry, for their blessing, and she is also still sad over losing her father. So next time I write to you I may be a married man. Maybe you are married too because that will be good. Next time I write I will have a permanent address in Guinea and you can write to me, or communicate somehow. For now I am fine and I hope you are fine too and *every one at home. My regards to Asabar and other friends and families.*

This is your brother,
LaMamo

PS
I have included a rough skech of the refugee camp in which we are now staying. See the tents and it is circled with wire, and sometimes it feel like prison. But sometimes at night it is peaceful and quite and it reminds me of home.

lives and times

MAMO HAD hardly recognized his office the next time he went there after the first introductory visit with the Waziri, and one of the ubiquitous guards lounging in the courtyard had to assure him he was in the right room. The dust that had covered the windows and chairs and table and had sent the Waziri scuttling back to his office that first day was all gone, the loose papers strewn on the floor and falling out of the rusty filing cabinet were now neatly packed in a folder and stacked in a corner on the floor—the filing cabinet itself was gone. The window was open, the fan was turning without a creak—someone must have climbed up and oiled it—and even the square outside looked radiant with the morning sun in the trees and a few boys kicking a ball up and down. Mamo took that as a portent that everything would be fine.

After Zara had left him he had thrown himself into settling his father's affairs, seeking through activity to make his mind numb and not dwell on his loneliness. True, he had always been a lonely person, even when he was with Zara—the only time in his life when he had not felt lonely was when his brother was around—but after Zara the loneliness had turned into a raging pain that almost had him howling like a maniac. It was not the dull ennui he had felt after LaMamo's departure; this was fire, it burned. It was anger, anger that she had left him for another person.

And so he had traveled daily to the state capital to meet with

bankers, and to the neighboring villages to meet with cattle owners from whom Lamang had bought his cattle. At one point he
had even considered going into the cattle business, but after the
meetings—a whole month discussing nothing but how to turn
cows into money—he had decided that he might not be suited
for that line of work. His uncle Iliya supported his decision to sell
everything—the trucks and the warehouses—and to pay off the
drivers and assistants and put the remaining money in the bank.
He also sold his father's Honda after deciding that he really had
no need for a car. Only after he had finished doing all these
things did he realize that what he had done was erase all traces
of his father as soon as possible so that only intangible memories
remained, and impersonal banknotes locked away in the bank
vaults.

But now, after all the activity, he found his mind swinging
again to Zara, like iron to a magnet. She had typed his essay and
posted it to him, and now even the words on paper reminded him
of her. And just then, as if to take him outside himself, the Waziri
breezed in. He sat down in the chair facing Mamo and took off
his turban, and then he stretched out his legs and looked round
the room, nodding with approval.

"Good morning sir," Mamo said, pointing around the room.

"Good, good. Do you like the office; is there anything you
need? I told them to clean it and make sure you are comfortable,"
the Waziri said, and then before Mamo could answer he leaned
forward, placing both hands on the table, and abruptly changed
the subject. "Tell me, how do you intend to begin?"

Mamo had spent most of the time, when he wasn't thinking
about Zara or settling his father's estate, thinking about this. "I
see the photo albums and files you sent—I'll go over them as
soon as possible. I've also started making rough notes, mostly
introductory . . . a mere guideline. I'll need to do interviews,
preferably with the Mai first. He is my primary subject, so I'll talk
to him first—whatever I gather afterward from others, and from
documents, will be used to support his story."

The Waziri leaned back and closed his eyes, as if to assess what Mamo had just said. He stayed like that for over a minute, beating a tattoo on the table with his fingers, and then he opened his eyes and pulled at his long wispy beard. He nodded. "Good idea. I like your enthusiasm. I like your eagerness. Remember, if there is anything you need to clarify, come to me first. I know more history than almost any other person in Keti. I was the Waziri to the Mai before this one. I have seen history being made right in front of my eyes. So, ask me anything, interview me." He waited, an expansive, indulgent smile on his thin, narrow face, the off-focus eye swiveling about.

"You mean now?" Mamo asked hesitantly.

"No time like now," the Waziri said. "I can tell you about the early Mais, the ones that ruled before the present line began. Take Mai La Kei, for instance, he was deposed by the first district officer, Mr. Graves. . . . I am sure you've never heard of Graves—oh, you have? Good, good."

"Well . . . thanks, about the interview, sir . . . but I'll need to think about it, to write down the questions. . . . I wouldn't . . . want to waste your time with inconsequential things."

The Waziri considered this for a while, looking a bit disappointed, but he nodded and stood up. "You are right. I am a very busy man." He put on his turban and strode to the door. "The Mai will see you for the interview in a day or so."

Mamo nodded.

"In the meantime, let me know if you need anything. Ask me any questions, anytime. Have a good day, secretary."

Odd, Mamo thought, that the man would thrust himself forward so forcibly to be interviewed. Was he trying to police what went into the biography, or was he only trying to ensure that he got a mention in the book? If the Waziri was trying to snag himself some mention in the book, some gratuitous immortality, then Mamo could certainly understand that. In books and stories the vizier's lot had not always been an envious one—he was forever doomed to reside in the shadow of his king, getting whatever renown or benefit he could only by association, and so he was always depicted as envious and conniving, and in some cases downright mutinous. The stories often stereotyped his physique as crippled and twisted, a figure of fun that could never compete in any way with the more imposing figure of the king. But of course, once in a long while came the wise benevolent counselor to the sometimes haughty and arrogant king—a rarity: the wise vizier whose self-effacing judgment saved the kingdom. Mamo wondered what kind of vizier the Waziri was—his shifty eyes, his repulsive, serpentine demeanor all screamed evil, but so far he had been nothing but the opposite. A sheep in wolf's clothing; or a wolf in wolf's clothing. Mamo decided that one of the things he needed to do alongside his research into the life of the Mai was find out as much as he could about the Waziri.

mamo's notes toward a biography
of the mai

The present Mai, whose name is Alhassan, is the fourth in the line
started by his granduncle, Bol Dok. Bol Dok was the first Mai to be
officially recognized by the colonial district officer, Mr. John B.
Graves, in 1918. This was also the year the missionary Reverend
Nathan Drinkwater first arrived in Keti. Drinkwater was actually
brought to Keti by Bol Dok. The two had met in Jos, where Bol Dok
was living as an exile. He was forty at the time, and he had been in
exile from Keti since he was twenty.

 The story of how Bol Dok got sent into exile by the village elders
is as follows. His cousin had killed a man from a neighboring clan
over a farmland dispute. The murderer, whose name was Sanda,
was over sixty and clearly past his prime. He was an unpleasant,
confrontational character. After the murder the elders had sat
together to deliberate on whom to punish, as in those days the elders reserved the right to choose whom to punish, and it was not necessarily the culprit, but anyone from the culprit's clan. The
intention was to make the punishment as exemplary as possible,
and so the most productive member of the clan was often selected
and given the option of death or banishment. Many chose death
over exile.

 In this case the elders didn't find it hard to choose whom to punish. They all chose Bol Dok, because at twenty Bol Dok had already
distinguished himself far ahead of his peers. His name, Bol Dok,
meant "One Blow." He got it during the annual end-of-year hunting

expedition. This was the most important event of the year for the young men, a time to prove their skill and bravery, and it was a rehearsal for the battlefield. They hunted in a pack, setting fire to the dry November grass to flush out the animals, then setting the dogs on them and chasing them till they were exhausted before spearing them.

At that particular event, the hunters had been out for two whole days and so far they had only managed to kill a few squirrels and rabbits. They were all hungry and dispirited. Then suddenly the cry went up—a deer had been sighted. The dogs gave chase, but this was a buck in its prime, too fast and too strong for the exhausted dogs. The men watched helplessly as it bounded around the side of a small hill, heading for a dense bush. Bol Dok was quick as lightning; he raced up the hill and placed himself behind a boulder in the buck's path. He waited till it was right on top of him before he jumped out, and without time to think, he clubbed the big buck with his fist, blindly, wildly, hitting it smack in the nose, and so great was his strength that the deer fell down dead on the spot. That was how he got the name Bol Dok, One Blow. But hunting was not his only sphere of excellence—he was also a champion farmer, and when it came to dancing, no one could move more gracefully than him.

When he was informed of the elders' decision, he chose banishment over death. In his heart he was convinced that as long as he was alive, he would see Keti again. He was escorted by two of his peers for a distance of two days' travel, in a direction of his choice, and then left there. He survived the bush and the dangerous animals, and eventually he turned up in the big city of Kano. The days turned into weeks, into months and years, and he remarried and begot children, but he never forgot his dream of returning to Keti someday. After ten years in Kano, he decided to move to Jos, closer to home. In Jos he went to work in the tin mines. The days passed, his family grew, but his resolve remained strong.

Then one day, in the twentieth year of his banishment, his chance came when he overheard the white supervisors at the mines asking for anyone who had knowledge of a village called Keti, in the Gombe area. A white missionary, newly arrived from Lagos, wanted a guide. Bol Dok didn't hesitate, he stepped forward and said he knew the area, he also spoke the language well.

And so, in 1918, after twenty years in exile, he returned to Keti with the Reverend Drinkwater, who set up his mission in the evil forest where the villagers used to dump their twins. When, later that year, Mr. Graves, the district officer, decided to install a chief over the people to ease his problem of tax collection, Bol Dok was strongly recommended by the Reverend Drinkwater. It was an easy choice for Mr. Graves, the colonial officer: at forty Bol Dok was still a very impressive figure—over six feet, and unbowed by his years in the mines, he also spoke fluent Hausa, a smattering of English, which he had picked up in the mines and had been polishing with Drinkwater's help, and of course he spoke Keti, the local language. Graves was further convinced Bol Dok was his man when he later learned of the circumstances of his banishment twenty years ago. Graves was a tireless modernizer, a vigorous campaigner against all "backward" aspects of Keti culture. The rather arbitrary manner of meting out punishment by the elders was one example of such "backwardness" he had set himself the task of combating.

That was how the official chieftaincy began. Bol Dok ruled for only twelve years, dying at the age of fifty-two. Two of his sons ruled after him. The first, Kilang, died of stab wounds after ruling for fifteen years. The next one, Hamdi (he had changed his name to El-Nafati after converting to Islam—the story goes that he had lost his temper when the missionaries advised him to send away two of his three wives, because only the first one could be recognized by the church), died of smallpox in his thirties after ruling for only five years. He was the last direct descendant of Bol Dok. There was a protracted tussle between the cousins and nephews before the present Mai, Alhassan, a civil servant and the most unimpressive of the contenders, assumed the throne nine years ago.

the mai in pictures

IN A corner in Mamo's office was a huge pile of notebooks, photo albums, and files, which the Waziri had sent him from the Mai's library. They were the Mai's personal papers and they contained papers and pictures dating from colonial times and the very infancy of the Bol Dok line. They didn't look like much: from the files, papers yellow with age spilled out onto the floor, some of them torn and stained. Mamo transferred the pile to his wide redwood table. He sat down and picked up the topmost file—an official flat file with a metal-tipped ribbon at the top holding the papers together—and began to flip through it. It was full of correspondence between the palace and the Culture Ministry, and the letters bore the Culture Ministry's logo at the top of each page. The sentences and paragraphs were riddled with the stilted, polite phrases of officialdom. He pushed the files aside impatiently and turned to the photo albums.

There were four of them; the transparent cellophane that pinned down the pictures had lost most of its gum and the pictures fell out as he opened the pages. There were pictures of Mai Alhassan as a young man, tall, looking optimistically into the future of his reign; the Mai as a civil servant (secretary to the local government council—his last post before becoming Mai); the Mai as a child with his brothers; and the Mai as Mai; the Mai on horseback returning from the mosque on an Eid day, surrounded by his councillors and servants.

One of the albums was entirely dedicated to a presidential

visit. Mamo remembered the occasion. Eight years ago the military president had stopped briefly in Keti on his way to the neighboring state capital. The pictures showed schoolchildren lined up by the roadside, in the sun, waving little pennants, singing the national anthem. Sirens had rent the air; outriders had driven madly through the town's narrow main street forcing back the eager crowd who waited to catch a glimpse of the leader. The president had spent only an hour before passing on to his next destination, but the memory of that visit had taken firm root in Keti lore. People still talked about it in detail, and many children born in the month of the visit had been named after the president.

There was only one picture in the album that showed the president actually shaking hands with the Mai. He looked carefree as he surveyed the crowed, his gap-toothed smile lighting up the picture, not looking at the Mai as they shook hands. The Mai towered over the president, but he looked ill at ease, totally out of his depth, as if wishing that the president would return to his car and leave with his entourage before something went wrong.

But the picture that got Mamo's attention and suggested a way forward for his research was in the next album. It was one of the Mai with two elderly white women standing on either side of him, smiling brightly into the picture. Mamo recognized the Drinkwater sisters. They were dressed in colorful tie-and-dye wrappers and *buba*, their heads covered in head scarves, and each held a parasol against the intense midday heat. They were called Kai and Malai by the villagers, and Mamo wasn't sure if they had other names. He didn't know much about them except that they had been born here and had lived here all their lives, and they taught Christian religion studies at the Women's Teachers' College, played the organ in church sometimes, and after the church service always had tea with Pastor Mela. They'd sit out on the pastor's veranda overlooking the street, sipping tea in the hot afternoon, exchanging greetings with passersby. Mamo carefully took out the picture and put it in his pocket. He decided to go and see the sisters.

He went to them in the evening when the sun was red and low over the hills. He was sure they'd be home—where would they go to, two elderly women in a strange country? But then he reminded himself that this wasn't a strange country to them, they had lived in it longer than he had. On the way he mentally reviewed all he knew about them, about their father, and once again his recourse was to popular village tradition. There was a brief account of the life of Reverend Drinkwater by his son, the Reverend Michael Drinkwater, in the preface to *A Brief History of the Peoples of Keti*, which did not differ much from popular tradition—the only addition was the account of Reverend Drinkwater's early life in his native Iowa, and how he got his calling to become a missionary.

Two of the first things the villagers would tell you about Drinkwater were: one, that he had died on his knees praying before the altar, and two, that he had seen visions. He saw his first vision at eighteen. He was working on the farm with his father—he came from a farming family in Iowa—when a sudden blinding light appeared to him, and with it a voice telling him to leave home and go to New York. Only after the light had disappeared did he realize that he was on the ground, knocked down by the terrible power of the vision. He told his family, all of them strong believers, that he had received a message from God, and that he was off to New York to do the Lord's bidding. He was in New York for three weeks, living on his meager resources, unsure what to do next, but certain that God would appear to him again with further instructions. On the last day of his third week in New York, the very day his money ran out and he was thrown out of his lodging, he was delivered by a *deus ex machina*: he met Reverend Angus Williams—an old missionary just returned from India—who had been directed to that street also by a vision. The old missionary became his mentor, inspiring him with tales of his divine exploits in India, and how there was urgent need to go to

these "dark" places to spread the word. The young Drinkwater
then studied for two years at a missionary institute in New York
before embarking on his trip to Nigeria in 1911. He had decided
on Nigeria after reading the biography of the Scottish missionary
Mary Slessor, also known as the "Queen of the Cannibals," who
worked in Calabar. Before leaving New York he tied the knot with
Angus's daughter, Hannah. He embarked on his first missionary
journey alone, however, leaving behind his wife, who was pregnant with their first child. The first trip was purely exploratory,
and he returned to New York after one year. By now he was
beginning to fret because no second vision had come.

After nine months he left his wife for Nigeria again—she was
again pregnant—and this time he did not come back for two
years. That was how long it took before the much-awaited second vision came. He had been working in a Baptist mission in
Lagos, with a large body of American and Canadian missionaries
who were working with fishing communities in Yaba. He was
standing by the sea, looking over the large expanse of water and
the bobbing fishing boats, when suddenly the light appeared
again, and the voice, but this time it did not knock him down,
and rather curiously, the words were spoken to him in Yoruba (by
now he had developed a rudimentary mastery of the language).
The voice told him to go to northern Nigeria, mentioning Keti by
name, and also telling him that that was where he'd live and work
and die. Some of his fellow missionaries openly expressed their
doubts about the accuracy of this vision, especially when they
heard that the voice had spoken in Yoruba. They told him, "No
one has gone that far into the Sudan before. The farthest you can
go is Jos. Forget the northeast. Maybe one day your children will
go there, or your grandchildren, but certainly not you."

But Drinkwater had no doubt about what he had to do. He
went back to New York and returned with his wife and two sons
in 1914, just before the outbreak of the world war. From Lagos
they traveled by a Royal Niger Company boat to Lokoja, and
from Lokoja they took the train to Jos. It was a grueling trip—

especially for the wife and two sons. They all fell ill with malaria, but all recovered, except for the youngest son, Christopher. He died in Jos and was buried there. The day Drinkwater met Bol Dok in Jos was actually the day after his son had been buried. They set out for Keti a month later.

To the reverend's surprise, and to his wife's relief, they discovered that they were not the first white folks to arrive in Keti. The colonial government already had its flag firmly planted there by Mr. J. B. Graves, an ex-ivory buyer for the Royal Niger Company, now turned colonial civil servant. He had arrived a year earlier with his soldiers and had conquered the village for the Crown by the simple expedient of firing his guns noisily into the air.

Drinkwater set up his mission almost immediately, symbolically using the site where twins were dumped to die. Hannah was to give birth to two more children in Keti, Kai in 1922 and Malai in 1925. The reverend never left Keti again and he died there in 1953. His wife returned to America briefly in 1942 with her son Michael, but she came back after the war, alone. She died in Keti, a week after her husband.

geriatrics, orchids, and roses

THE DRINKWATER sisters were in the garden, side by side, bent over the flower beds, removing weeds, watering the yellow and white African orchids and red roses that blossomed luxuriantly in the heat, their colors appearing loud and sudden against the dull brown earth. The garden was a large space at the back of the little house, encircled by a wall of fat, succulent cacti, which cut off the flowers from outside view. A small zinc gate with a latch formed the entrance. Mamo stood at the entrance and called out, "Hello."

They looked up, their hands covered in elbow-length garden gloves, their heads by thin wispy scarves, and their feet in heavy gum boots that made their movements clumsy and slow.

"Hello," the one nearest to him answered with a polite smile on her face. The other one stood with her watering can half raised, her eyes squinting. She was Kai, the one who wore glasses, Mamo thought, even though she wasn't wearing them now. Malai was the one who had spoken.

"Hello," he said again, unsure how to proceed. "My name is Mamo. I came to see you. . . . I need to ask you some questions."

The two women looked at each other, and Mamo saw what could be described as interest register on their wrinkled faces. Apart from the squint the sisters looked so much alike, almost identical: they had the same matronly figure, the same wrinkled, tanned-leather skin, the same color of hair, which must have been originally brown but was now burned white by sun and age.

They would be in their late sixties. They straightened up and began to remove their gloves.

"Come in, just push aside the gate," Kai said.

Mamo followed them to the little veranda at the back of the house. The garden began where the veranda stopped, and a gravel path ran from the veranda through the middle of the garden. Two easy chairs against the wall faced the garden.

"Sit down. We won't be a minute. You came when we were just about to break for tea. We'll make a cup for you."

Mamo thought it was too hot for tea, but he smiled and nodded. "Thank you."

They disappeared into the house. The house was surrounded by fruit trees, mainly mango and guava, which formed a buffer zone between it and the neighboring houses. A heavy silence shrouded the house, broken occasionally by the chirping and warbling of birds. Mamo tried to imagine what it would be like to live in such seclusion, with only trees and birds for company. Who did the sisters socialize with, apart from the pastor on Sundays, and perhaps their students on weekdays?

Kai, now wearing her glasses, came out with the tea on a tray. She put it on the table between the armchairs. Malai came out with another chair and positioned it against the wall next to Mamo. He imagined them sitting here every evening after work, contemplating the garden or talking—no, not talking; surely they would have run out of interesting topics ages ago? Most likely reading, or knitting, or dozing like most old people, their mouths slightly open, their heads lolling on the back of the chair, coming awake with a jerk every once in a while, but too lazy, or not bothered enough, to go inside. He imagined them reading and answering letters from family and friends in Iowa—but would they have friends in Iowa, which they had never visited? Maybe just family, cousins and nephews and nieces who had seen them only in pictures, and of course there was their brother, Michael, and his wife. The Reverend Michael Drinkwater, the dutiful son who had perpetuated his father's memory by carefully compiling and editing his papers and publishing them. Mamo had seen him once, many years ago, on his last visit to Keti. He had come for the dedication of the new church, with his thin, pale wife and his two freckled children, a boy and a girl named Nathan and Hannah after his parents. He had been to Keti three times before: his first visit was in 1978, on the twenty-fifth anniversary of his father's death, the second in 1984, to lay the foundation of the new church, and the last a year later, to dedicate the church.

The sisters had lived together all their lives, and they had never married. *What is it like to never have sex?* Mamo thought, staring at the small film of down on Kai's upper lip as she made small talk. Malai had a few wispy hairs on her chin. He could see the veins beneath the skin of their arms, blue and sinuous, pulsing in the heat.

"Pastor Mela showed us your review. We thought it was wonderful, didn't we, Heather?" Kai said.

"Yes, Agnes, we did," Malai answered. Agnes and Heather—their English (or was it American, or just Christian?) names, hinting at another life, another world. On their living room walls there might be pictures of that world: a flat Iowa prairie, with tall and green cornstalks swaying in the wind, and a river running through it (the Iowa River, perhaps), with trees on its bank and through the trees the clear flowing water. He wondered if they had dual personalities: an American Agnes–Heather–Ms. Hyde that they only brought out when they were together at home, and an African Kai–Malai–Dr. Jekyll that came out when they played the organ in church and drank tea with the pastor on Sundays.

"We have sent Michael a copy of the review. You know he published the book from our father's papers."

Mamo sipped his tea, mostly listening, fascinated by their small talk, how they addressed each other by name with each statement. They had a way of asking each other for confirmation of even the most obvious things; he watched their lips close over the tea mugs, the gullets moving as the liquid descended. At last Heather, the quiet one, the younger one, asked him a direct question, taking him by surprise when she switched to the Keti language.

"Are you a journalist?"

"No, not really. I am just . . . a contributor."

"I see," she said, looking uncertain. But then she asked, "Are you working on anything at present?" Her pronunciation was faultless, a bit nasal, but she sounded rather formal, as if she were reading the words from a book.

Mamo, after a slight pause, nodded. "Yes, that is in fact why I came to see you. I thought you might be able to assist. I have been invited to write a biography of the Mai. Your father, I believe, was good friends with the first Mai, Bol Dok, and you have known the present one for a long time."

They nodded. He showed them the picture. "I came across it in the Mai's palace today."

"Oh," Malai said as she took the picture, showing it to her sister, laughing girlishly, covering her mouth with her hand. "This was a long time ago."

Kai took the picture. "Five years ago, it was, when he came on a visit to our school, on National Literacy Day," she said, also switching to Keti.

"Yes, yes," her sister assented, holding the picture.

"We will help gladly," they said together.

"Well, I was hoping for something personal, like your father's diary, or papers; anything at all from those days will be helpful."

Michael had taken away all the papers on his last visit, they said. They took him to the garage, which they had converted into a storeroom since they had no car. It was dark and airless—the spiderwebs on the ceiling and in the corners jumped into sharp focus when Malai opened the thick iron window. Old furniture: a jumble of wooden bed frames and chairs and trunks took up most of the room. Malai opened one of the trunks and showed him the old, moldy clothes inside.

"Our parents brought these with them when they first came." She took out a moth-eaten mosquito net that had once been

white but was now a green-brown moldy color. She pointed at a
dismantled Tilley lamp.

"Father used to write all through the night with this lamp. I
remember the villagers would gather outside the mission gate to
see the light—new to them, it was, fascinatingly so."

Sometimes Mamo had to strain his interpretative powers to
follow the order of the words, now that the sisters were pouring
them out thick and fast, their faces flushed by heat and memory.

There were thick walking boots, and rain boots, Bombay
bowlers, walking sticks, more mosquito nets, a toilet seat, and
other odds and ends. Mamo admired and handled them—all the
time observing the sisters, who had now begun to assume individual identity: Kai was the stern, no-nonsense one, the one with
a bad case of erythema, the one with the chin wisps, the one with
the glasses. Malai must have been the beauty once; she had the
girlish laughter and showed more enthusiasm in bringing out the
old stuff. Now she was holding up a dress, a wedding gown complete with tulle and lace and train. It looked shrunken and
impossibly wrinkled—there were holes in it made by ants and
termites.

"This was used in the first church wedding in this village. It
was my mother's; she came to Africa with it. She was born in
Bombay, our grandfather was a missionary there—she lent the
dress to the bride, LaMonje LaMemi. She is still alive. We have
the wedding picture, if you want to see." Malai had lapsed back
to English, abandoning the tortuous Keti in her eagerness to
impart this bit of information. She held up the dress against her
matronly body.

In the living room they showed him their pictures. There were
pictures of them as young girls with their parents, and for the
first time he saw what their mother looked like. She looked to be
in her early thirties in the picture, and she stood with her head
bowed against the sun. She was a beautiful woman, with long
hair and a long neck and delicate features—rather like Malai
must have once been—and her hat was placed squarely on her

head. She held Malai with one hand and with the other embraced her husband, while he held Kai with his free hand. The brother stood next to Kai, on the outside. There were pictures of other people, other places, flat and green, which Mamo assumed to be Iowa, and on the wall there was a prairie landscape, with a river running through it.

"My uncle Iliya told me that your father, during catechism classes, used to teach his students stories of the lives of the saints, and that he'd also ask them to write their own biographies. There must be lots of such biographies somewhere. You wouldn't know where they are, would you?"

They shook their heads. "Michael has them. If you want, we could ask him to send them over, to make copies for you."

"Thank you."

They were back on the veranda. The sisters were flushed with the exertion of showing him their stuff, but they seemed to have enjoyed it. Malai patted him on the knee as she said, "You must return again soon."

Kai said, "Yes, do, please. We may not be in Keti for long now."

"Are you thinking of moving elsewhere?"

"It's not our idea," she said with a sad sigh. "Michael thinks we need to return to Iowa soon, for health reasons." She spoke softly, staring into the garden at the flowers. In the corner of his eye he saw her sister reach out to take her hand. "We are not young anymore."

"But this will always be our home."

"Our heart and soul will always be here," Malai said in English, with a tremor to her voice.

"I am sorry to hear that you are leaving," Mamo said. He felt their sadness. He sipped his tea—it was cold. He put it down.

"I am afraid I came today without warning. Next time, I'll need to interview you, if that is okay, and perhaps borrow some of your pictures for my book."

"Of course you may. Sorry we couldn't help with any of Father's papers—Michael has them all."

"But if you want Mother's diary, you can have it, can't he, Heather? Not that there's anything interesting it. It is mostly grocery lists," Kai said.

"Your mother left a diary?"

"Yes," she said, sounding happy to be of help. "Wait, I'll go get it."

She went into the house and returned with a small notebook, about fifty pages thick.

Mamo took it and opened the pages, running his eyes over the neat curlicues—the pages had once been white with blue-ruled lines, but now they were yellow and crinkly at the edges. The cover was soft, brown, and it had a hand-drawn fleur-de-lis gracing the top left corner.

"I am afraid it is not much. She kept a diary for only one year, while Father kept one all his life. He actually encouraged her to start one, but she gave it up after a year, in 1928. She began another one in 1942, which was the year America entered the war. That was the year she returned to Iowa with Michael. But I don't know what happened to that one. You can go take this one, but bring it back when you are through."

"I will. Thank you."

the blessed child

"YOUNG MAN, you look familiar. Have we met before?" the Mai said to Mamo. The Waziri was seated at his usual whispering distance to the Mai; his face was expressionless save for the occasional twitching of his bad eye. When Mamo turned a perplexed face to him, he smiled reassuringly and whispered to the Mai, "He is your biographer, Highness. He wants to ask a few questions about your childhood."

Mamo had found a note on his desk when he arrived at the office, asking him to come immediately to the Mai's lounge for the interview. He had hurried over, surprised that the Waziri had been able to arrange the interview so expeditiously, just a day after their last meeting. But now the Mai continued to stare at him with dull eyes and slack face. Mamo was seated on an ottoman, not too far from the Mai's sofa, and his notebook was open on his lap, his pen poised to take notes. The Mai's dull yellow eyes were looking directly at him, expectant, as if waiting for him to confirm that he was indeed the biographer.

"Your father was well known to me, God bless his soul. He was a good man, even though his politics were confused," the Mai spoke at last. There was a quaver to his voice, an infirmness that usually accompanies old age, but the Mai wasn't that old—he couldn't be more than sixty.

"Yes, sir," Mamo said, not sure what to add. The Waziri was looking at him encouragingly, as if willing him to say something clever. A sweet perfumy smell issued from the Mai's voluminous robe; beneath the perfume there was another, vague smell: unpleasant, soporific, making Mamo feel enveloped and breathless.

The Mai continued to stare, his eyes growing duller and duller. Mamo turned his gaze to the wall mat where Eve was trying to cover her rather voluptuous breasts with an arm. He opened a fresh page in his notebook. At last the Waziri said in an oily, ingratiating tone, "Perhaps, Highness, you may wish to tell him about your childhood in the palace." Then without pausing he turned to Mamo and, with a smile, went on. "His Highness grew up with his uncle, the last Mai. He was seven when his own father died and the last Mai adopted him because he had no male children of his own. At first he was just another young boy in the palace, running around with his cousins and nephews and nieces, then something happened that got him the attention of the Mai, and from that day everyone knew he was going to be the next ruler."

"I had a dream."

Mamo looked up from his notebook. Yes, it was the Mai. His face was still slack, but now his eyes were on Mamo, as if he had finally realized what was going on. His voice was hoarse, still shaky. "I saw a woman covered in a black gown, from head to foot. She was burying something at the door to my uncle's quarters. I woke up. It was late, around midnight, and the whole palace was asleep. I was in the young boys' quarters, you see. . . ." He stopped and his eyes grew distant, as if he were able to see physically into that past he was trying to recapture with words. "There are different quarters in the palace, the young boys', the young girls', and of course the wives'. . . . So, early in the morning, I went to see the Mai. I was bold; in my heart I knew no fear. I was a blessed child, you see." For this statement the Mai lowered his voice like a conspirator, all the time continuing to stare at Mamo with his dull yellow eyes, as if waiting for an answer to a question. Mamo continued to scribble in his notebook.

"A gifted child," the Waziri echoed encouragingly, his dodgy eye swiveling wildly, and the Mai resumed.

"He was in court, surrounded by his councillors, but I knew no hesitation. I stood before his throne, directly where he could see me, and I said, 'I had a dream.' It was a great moment. He didn't doubt me, because in my voice there was no hesitation. He and his whole council went and dug up the pot the woman had buried—it was there, a deadly charm, wrapped in blood-soaked cloth. The charm was made with the skull of an infant. Someone wanted to kill him. Now, my uncle was a cunning man, he knew it was no use making threats, so he promised amnesty to whoever came forward and confessed voluntarily before the day was out. He let everyone think that he knew the perpetrators of this great evil, but that he wanted to give them a chance to confess. At the same time he warned that if by the end of the day they refused to confess, they would be exposed and beheaded." Now the Mai paused and closed his eyes as if to rest from the rigors of recollection, but after a while he began to snore. Mamo turned to the Waziri.

"It was the youngest wife, and she confessed." The Waziri took over the narration without a blink, his voice smooth. "She had enlisted the service of a Hausa woman to kill the Mai so that her son from another marriage would inherit the throne. You may go. We will continue next time."

After this rather short interview Mamo returned to his office and spent the rest of the day doodling and browsing through the files and photo albums, unsure what to do next. The Mai, his primary source, was clearly not going to be of much help. Suddenly he felt helpless, inexperienced, and a bit desperate. The Waziri seemed overenthusiastic, perhaps underestimating the amount of work involved in writing a book. At last Mamo went home, thoughtful, tired, but determined to forge ahead—this was a chance he was resolved to exploit even if it killed him. On the way he encouraged himself by sending his mind into the future,

to when the book would finally be finished. He reminded himself of the Waziri's promise that the book would make him the
most famous of all his peers. He reflected on the irony of life:
how his illness, which had stopped him from pursuing his childhood dreams of martial glory, had pushed him to become stu-
dious and this had now opened for him other avenues for fame.

Mamo already had his own plan of writing himself into the
limelight, into history. He knew how easy it'd be to get forgotten
once the book was written. That was the peculiar trouble with
biography; more than other kinds of writing, it focused attention
only on the subject, and often the author was forgotten, cast
aside, as if the book had written itself. Mamo would weave himself unobtrusively into the book in the form of a foreword, in
which he would leave detailed accounts of his investigative
endeavor, nothing too obvious, just coded hints. Then upon
reflection he decided that perhaps a foreword might be too
attention-grabbing, too obvious; an afterword might be better—
more discreet, but still doing the same job. It showed more class.
He could get someone else to do the foreword, someone really
high up—say, the state governor. It was not impossible, and that
was the beauty of this project, of working for the palace; anything
was possible, the only limitations were that of imagination.

Thus much cheered by his thoughts of impending fame,
Mamo immediately went back to work when he got home. He
picked up Hannah Drinkwater's diary and began to read—he had
gone through it once already, but he had done so cursorily, without making notes. Now he sat down at his reading table, with
pen and paper.

Apart from providing him with exact dates and some insights into
how the Drinkwaters ran their daily lives in the mission—what
food they ate, how it was procured from the natives (mostly by
barter: old clothes, mirrors, gewgaws, and other useless stuff for
food)—there wasn't really much that was useful in the diary. Bol

Dok, who was referred to as Drinkwater's "native guide" and later "assistant," was mentioned only three times. There were accounts of how the Drinkwater children spent their days, anxieties over unknown symptoms and rashes, more anxieties over delays in the arrival of vital household supplies and medicines from Jos and Lagos. There were also entries dealing with church activities, long disquisitions on how to start a married women's prayer group, and how to help the reverend prepare the Communion on Communion Sundays—certain berries had to be used in the absence of wine. The following was a typical entry:

Monday
Today I bought a lamb from Ngendi, our nearest neighbor and one of our few converts in the village. He wouldn't accept money but requested to be paid with some of Nathan's old khaki pants. Now I have to find a way to store a whole carcass in this humid weather—the best way is the native way: remove the offal and vital organs, which must be eaten immediately, then salt and smoke the flesh. It can be stored suspended from a tree branch, or from the roof in the kitchen. I prefer the roof; the smoke from the hearth helps to quickly dry it. It lasts a whole week before it begins to spoil.

But there was a long entry about the district officer, Mr. Graves, on a day when he came to the Drinkwaters' for dinner—lengthy discussions were paraphrased; there were also direct quotes from Graves. It was clear there was a wary distrust of Graves by Mrs. Drinkwater because Graves was "an indifferent Christian." She often referred to him as the "cunning Englishman." He came to dinner once in January 1928. That day's entry ended with a summary of the dinner table conversation, about whether the native had a soul. Mr. Graves wasn't sure, Reverend Drinkwater was sure. On the next page was a long quotation from Graves's dinner table wisdom—it was about his vision for Keti:

It is not enough to conquer their land; we must conquer their minds as well. And to do that we must use more than gentle Christian persuasion, more than books and schools. We must break their spirits, we must break their backs and throw them down into the dust, as it were, then slowly raise them up again—but this time as gentler, more useful beings. Then they'll be grateful to us in the future. They'll become our loyal co-workers in the huge task of civilization.

Mamo tried to conjure up the woman, and the kind of life she must have lived. Alone, with only her children and her house chores to distract her. Of course, sometimes missionaries on their way to other remote missions would drop by and spend a day at the Keti mission, but those moments were rare. She must have had an extraordinarily active mind, or believed strongly in her husband and his mission, not to have run stir-crazy. She had returned to America only once since she'd left, during the Second World War, and then she returned to die here and be buried beside her husband.

whiskey and wheelchair

ASABAR HAD sunk lower and lower into drink and drugs since his return from the hospital. The few times Mamo had been to see him in his house at the foot of the hill he had been drunk and incoherent, and halfway through each visit he had fallen asleep in his wheelchair, snoring loudly.

Today he was lively and full of chatter, surrounded by his still-loyal friends. Mamo sat to one side, occasionally chipping in a word to their conversation, which was mostly political. He never ceased to be amazed at the veneration with which his father's name was spoken in this circle—they still referred to him as the "Chairman," and they each had a personal story of his munificence to which Mamo listened as if it were about a stranger. Sometimes, overcome by drink and weed, Asabar would start weeping over some memory of his hell-raising days, and then he'd bang his hand, or his whiskey bottle, against the metal of his wheelchair, and once Mamo had seen him throw himself violently off the wheelchair and roll about in the dust till his friends restrained him and carried him to bed. When the discussion became too incoherent or too loud—sometimes it degenerated into fistfights—Mamo would quietly slip away, but first he'd stop at the kitchen, where Asabar's wife, Jummai, was busy with one chore or the other. She was used to her husband's ways and had adjusted her expectations with the typical equanimity of the peasant woman. The son, Markus, would be with her, playing

among the pots and pans, pausing to stare silently at Mamo. He
had his father's sensitive poet's eyes.

"Tell him I'll call again, soon," Mamo would tell the woman.
He'd note how, though she was only twenty, she already looked
tired and dirty, and her eyes had developed the sort of dull,
uncomprehending film through which most of the village women
viewed the world around them. Mamo would slip her some
money before leaving. "Buy something for the boy."

△ ▽ △

The church secretary brought him Zara's letter (most of the villagers, Christian and non-Christian alike, used the church's
post office address). It had arrived that afternoon, the secretary said. It was a postcard, and Mamo recognized the writing
even before he saw the name. The picture on the card showed
the Durban waterfront: a blue-green sea dotted with faraway
sails and ships that filled most of the background; in the fore-
ground were tiny surfers flying on the waves, their arms
opened, like wings, for balance. Across the picture were bold
gothic characters saying simply, DURBAN. On the back were
the date and her address in Durban, and a short note in her
slanting hand.

Mamo,
Wish you were here, so much is happening. Yesterday we witnessed the swearing in of Mandela as president. It is really
great to witness the dismantling of apartheid's structures right
before one's eyes. Take care of yourself, and please write soon.
I miss you.

Love,
Zara

The letter doesn't give much away, he thought, letting the
card droop from his hand like a limp petal from a stalk. He

imagined her in a procession in Pretoria, or in Johannesburg—
the letter didn't mention where they went to see Mandela
being sworn in —in a sea of a thousand other faces, black,
white, colored, bearing placards, singing songs in the street.
Happy.

"DO YOU have documents here dating back to colonial days?" Mamo asked the thin, rheumy-eyed librarian.

"Documents? Colonial times? I don't know," she said, looking up guiltily, as if caught *in flagrante delicto*. She was peeling an orange and reading a book at the same time. "I don't know," she said again nervously, looking at him curiously. Although the diary hadn't provided much information on Bol Dok, it gave Mamo the idea of going to the local government secretariat the next day in the hope that the library there might have archives containing documents from colonial times—letters and memos and pictures. The library was situated at the back of the secretariat, far away from the offices, next to the parking lot and the toilets—the smell of urine wafted into the open door of the library on the strong midday breeze. He was sure no one had visited this room in a long time. The girl continued to stare at him, her mouth half open. Suddenly Mamo smiled and said, "You are Ladi, aren't you? Bulaa's sister?"

She relaxed and smiled. "Mamo, I didn't recognize you."

He had gone to school with her brother. "I didn't know you worked here."

"I just started," she said. She was a veritable bookworm and, in his early teens, when he was going through a romantic phase, Mamo used to borrow Mills & Boon novels from her. She had them in boxes. He wasn't surprised she had ended up a librarian.

The room was rectangular and gloomy—the windows were

shut and the heat was trapped in the space between the wooden bookshelves. Lizards hung lazily from the old and broken ceiling, looking at the humans with their characteristic sidelong glances.

"Bulaa now works in Abuja—he was home last month," Ladi said. Then, pleasantries over, she asked him curiously, "What did you say you wanted? I only started working here last month and I don't know where everything is. No one ever comes here, you see. But there are cartons there, with papers in them. Some of them are ruined by rain—the roof leaks." She pointed to the roof.

Mamo went to the cartons and began to rummage through the old and tattered files, often pulling back to allow insects and little lizards to scurry out.

"Can't we open the windows?" he asked Ladi. "It is so dark here."

She went and opened the window next to him—the smell of urine grew stronger, but at least the room was now brighter, and he could breathe. She gave him a chair and he shared her hard, narrow table; after a while he was able to ignore her fixed, curious stare and concentrate on the files.

A few of them dated back to the days he was interested in, between 1917, when Mr. Graves, the first white man, conquered Keti, and 1960, when the country became independent and local civil servants took over from the colonialists. Three colonial district officers served between these dates, and some of the documents were copies of correspondences between them and their divisional commissioner in Jos. Most of the letters were damaged by rain and were illegible, entire pages were eaten away by insects, and some had just grown old and stiff and had crumbled to bits. Most of them were from Mr. Graves—he had served the longest of the three district officers, from 1917 to 1928. Mamo went through the letters slowly, straining his eyes to decipher the faint typewritten characters.

One letter, dated 1918, propounded on the need for a new Mai in Keti:

*We must install one as soon as possible, they've been without a
natural ruler for one year now, the last one I had to remove
because of his high-handed style of administering justice. The
need for such a chief is of course obvious—the people are more
loyal to their own kind, if he has the charisma and the
authority—of course backed by our authority. This will greatly
enhance the efficiency of tax collection, and the administration of justice, both of which I now have to do myself with the
help of a few trusted native assistants, and I must stress the difficulty of finding such trusted assistants.*

*Now, my proposal is to make such a chief paramount over
the other chiefs who rule the smaller villages — there are about
twelve of such said smaller villages, and each speaking a different tongue, and seeming to have no allegiance to the other,
always warring amongst themselves. If we can use our authority to yoke them together into a single federation, this will solve
our problem of administration, tax collection, and the like.
The chieftaincy of course must be developed on a slightly different model from that which I met when I came. The last
chief, or Mai as he was called, and whom I had to depose for
his high-handedness as I mentioned earlier, was only a sort of
first among equals, and his duties were part religious and part
administrative, but he never took decisions without the con-
sent of his council of elders (apart from the last high-handed
decision for which I had to depose him). The new Mai must
be totally distanced from such priestly duties.*

Here Mamo was forced to stop because the remaining part of
the letter was blotted out by rain. He put it to one side and
picked up another letter by Graves to the same divisional administrator; the date had been eaten away by termites:

The Divisional Administrator
Dear Sir,
Today I begin work on the project of which I referred to in my

*last letter to you. I hope to lay the building's foundations before
the advent of the rainy season three months from now.*

*At first I depended solely on the new chief, the Mai, for the
supply of labour, but after the first year progress on the project
was going much slower than I had foreseen, so I had to step in.
My solution was simple. I moved my office (I have been using
a tent for that purpose since I came here, which is one of the
reasons why I need to complete the building project as soon as
possible) to the top of the hill, a naturally advantageous site
and one that is perfect for such a building, and once there, I
made it known that whoever wanted to see me for any reason,
especially for justice, since I spend a large part of my administrative hours settling disputes between this rather litigious people, I decreed that anyone coming to be heard must bring with
him a granite boulder roughly twice the size of a human head.
Soon a huge pile was heaped up on the building site, and more
keep coming. The piling of boulders has now become a kind of
sport among this rather easily amused people.*

*So today we began the foundation. Soon there will be an
office, and a modern guesthouse of two bedrooms and a living
room. I will keep you updated on the progress of the work as it
develops.*

*Yours etc.,
Mr. J. B. Graves*

Finally the heat and the stench of urine got the better of
Mamo and he asked Ladi if he could borrow some of the letters
to read at home. She nodded happily, sucking on her orange, still
staring at him curiously. She asked him to sign for the documents
and as he signed, she finally plucked up the courage to ask, "I
heard you are going to write a book on our history, is this what
you need the letters for?"

Mamo nodded, too weak to explain. He felt as if he had been
cooked in a cauldron of hot oil. "Yes. Thanks for your help."

"Come back anytime," she said happily.

mamo's notes toward a biography of the mai: mr. graves

Mr. Graves first came to Nigeria in 1896. At the time, of course, the vast land stretching from the Atlantic in the south to the Sahel savannah in the north wasn't called Nigeria. To the Western eye it must have seemed like a vast nameless and trackless collection of villages and towns and cities and kingdoms, chaotic and innocent and reeling from the ravages of tribal wars, but also rich in agricultural products and mineral resources just ready for the taking. But whoever was going to take them must first contend with malaria, and the warlike tribes, and the local slave raiders. If he survived all these, there was still the French and the German trading outposts to compete with. These must have seemed very exciting prospects for an eighteen-year-old Yorkshire farm boy looking for adventure.

Graves came to work for the Royal Niger Company as a buyer of ivory. He did that for a whole year, and was based at the company's headquarters in Lokoja, but soon he got tired of buying dead elephants' teeth and shipping them down the Niger to Calabar and Lagos. When he heard that the company was raising an army to fight the recalcitrant emir of Nupe in 1897, he volunteered to go along. The expedition had a force of 1,500 Hausa soldiers, drilled and trained by the company, and led by thirty white officers—some of whom were lent for the occasion by the War Office in London. The troops of course made short work of the emir's bowmen, who fled at the deafening roar of guns. Not surprisingly, they had never heard the sound of a gun before. When, in 1900, the vast territory, now known as Nigeria, was transferred from the Royal Niger Company to the British Crown, Graves decided to also change masters. He applied to join the colonial service and he was accepted based on his extensive experience in the interior towns and villages, and in pacifying recalcitrant chiefs and emirs.

His work took him the length and breadth of the territory north of the River Niger, and he was only thirty when he penetrated and subdued the northeastern villages around Gombe, finally settling in Keti as district officer. But he soon discovered that the business of subduing was one that was never done. Little unforeseen, unsettling things kept cropping up to disrupt the balance. First, there was Mai La Kei. He was a charismatic and influential leader, but one who kept undermining Graves's authority at every opportunity. I don't know how Graves managed to dethrone Mai La Kei, but he soon did, and in his place he installed the more amenable Bol Dok, servant to the American missionary, Drinkwater. After this victory over La Kei, he turned his attention to building an office and a guesthouse. He finished that in 1925. Then, using the same forced labor methods, he next built a prison—it was the biggest and most secure prison in the whole Gombe area. Since all the rivers and the hills and even the trees already had names, he decided to leave his mark by redesigning the village roads—he drew a grid plan based on his memories of the streets of his village in Yorkshire. This was toward the end of his life when, the story went, he had begun to lose his mind. He had suffered too many malaria attacks, had been beaten by too much sun and wracked by too much loneliness. He demolished compounds, shifted houses, and lined the new roads with mahogany trees—his own village had oak trees, but they wouldn't grow in the African weather. In the first year of the trees' lives he made the schoolchildren of the new primary school pay their school fees by watering them every morning before going to class.

Graves died in 1928 at the age of fifty, attempting one more conquest: to climb the highest peak in Keti, the Kilang Peak, described in Reverend Drinkwater's Brief History as a "mountainous contour like a lion couchant." It was three thousand feet above sea level, and *about two thousand feet above the surrounding plain. He lost his footing and plummeted to his death. Some stories in the village insisted that he committed suicide over a local woman—the Mai's youngest wife, some people said, a great beauty, who spurned Graves's surreptitious advances; she later ran away from her husband's house to Jos with a young sweetheart.*

the avenger

THEY TALKED of the military coup. It had happened suddenly, unexpectedly a week ago. The civilian state governors and local government chairmen had been replaced by military administrators, and as often happened after such takeovers, promises had been made, expectations had risen, most of Mamo's father's old enemies and friends were now in prison for "economic crimes," but still nothing much had changed.

"Another important thing. Keep your ears open, now that we have a new government, maybe things will change—I mean regarding the school," said Iliya.

They talked of the teachers, with whom Iliya was still in close contact. Mamo hadn't seen any of them, apart from Zara, since the school was closed. Now he learned that Mr. Bukar had finally achieved his dream of going to the university to study psychology. Ms. Lipstick had found employment in another secondary school in a neighboring village.

"What of Zara? She used to stop by. I haven't seen her in a while."

Iliya was seated by the window in his living room, on a rocking chair; a book lay on the table beside him. Mamo had found him half dozing and half gazing out of the window to where Asabar's empty hut now stood; in the distance beyond the hut, the walls of the classrooms of the community school could also be seen in the clear sunlight.

"She is in South Africa. She said she . . . she works in an orphanage."

On one of the seats, Markus, Asabar's little boy, slept soundly, his breath whistling through his nose, his round belly rising and falling softly beneath his T-shirt. When Mamo remarked how like his father the boy looked, Uncle Iliya replied: "The mother brings him here every day. She says she brings him to visit us, but really she comes to get some food to take home." He sighed and turned his gaze to the school in the distance. His eyes had bags under them; his chin was covered in white bristles.

After a while he added gently, "Maybe Zara will come back. It is good to travel, because it sometimes reminds us of the precious things we had left at home." Then, changing the subject, he asked, "So, do you enjoy working at the palace?"

Mamo took a long time to answer. "I don't know. I have only been there a few months now."

"It is okay. I know they will feed you a bundle of lies. But I have no fear that you will write only the truth."

"I will. The Waziri—"

"Ah, the Waziri," Iliya interrupted. "He promises more than he delivers."

"I understand he was also the Waziri to the former Mai."

"Mai Hamdi, the one that later became El-Nafati after converting to Islam. The one that was poisoned."

"I thought he died of smallpox."

"He was poisoned, but no one will tell you that, not even the elders. These are royal secrets. The Mai before him, Mai Kilang, was stabbed while he slept. Let me show you, I have a picture of him somewhere. . . ." He got up and disappeared into his bedroom. After a while, he returned clutching a black-and-white photograph. He handed it to Mamo. It was a daguerreotype, a bit dulled by time and handling. It showed Mai Kilang seated in a chair under a neem tree, staring straight ahead, looking a bit nervous; his robes fell stiffly over his shoulders like broken wings, his turban rested on his head like a sack.

"This picture was taken by one of the American missionaries who came after the death of Reverend Drinkwater."

"Why was he stabbed?" Mamo asked.

"It was all a continuation of the power tussle that began when Graves, the first district officer, deposed one of the early Mais, his name was La Kei, by accusing him of murder."

"Did La Kei really commit murder?"

"No. He was merely enforcing the traditional law—you see, in that time it wasn't necessarily the man who committed a murder that got punished; the Mai and his council usually punished the most productive member of that family. And so, when an old man committed murder, the elders decided to punish his brother. The brother chose death over banishment—he was hanged to death in front of the Mai's palace. And that was when Graves pounced. He had been waiting for a chance to deal with Mai La Kei, whom he found too arrogant, and of course Graves was the kind of man who didn't take any challenge to his authority lightly. And so Mai La Kei was accused of murder, and was exiled to the land of the Yorubas, Ile-Ife, to die alone." Here Iliya paused and his stare grew distant, his voice becoming whispery.

"The story was current when we were growing up. They said after the hanging a quiet had descended on the whole village; people stood outside their huts as Graves passed with his policemen—he was a rather short man, with a big mustache, he always wore a bowler hat, which seemed a bit too big for his head. He had a stick in his hand, and a smile played on his lips as he led the men up the path to the Mai's house. The villagers followed cautiously from a distance. The story had gone out that Graves was going to arrest the Mai. The Mai was waiting for him; he was seated with two of his sons and a few councillors in his front room where he received visitors. When Graves arrived, he stood outside the hut with his policemen and shouted loudly to Mai La Kei to come out. 'I am arresting you in the name of the King,' he shouted. La Kei did not come out, but one of his sons did. He came out running, a spear in his hand, aimed at the white man. But before he got even halfway to him, Graves brought out his pistol and shot him in the chest. He fell down. The crowd sent up a wail. That was when La Kei came out. He stood over his son, his head bowed, and then he turned to the white man and said, 'Let's go.' He was led through the village, his hands tied behind him, to the new lockup. That night the whole village did not sleep. Many people thought the Mai's friends would invade the lockup and set him free, but nothing happened. The next day he was taken away to the state capital, and that was the last the village ever saw of him.

'Bol Dok was made Mai in his stead. But a part of the La Kei family still felt cheated, and one of them, a woman named La Monje, swore that she'd one day bring the family back to power. She didn't get a chance to do it, but her daughter, also named LaMonje, did get a chance. This was over twenty years later, when most people had forgotten about La Kei. Her chance came one day when Mai Kilang, who was now Mai after Bol Dok, went to one of the neighboring villages on his tax-collecting outings and had to spend the night in the village head's house. Now, unknown to him, the village head's wife was this same LaMonje, and that night, while Mai Kilang slept, she and her husband went to his room and stabbed him to death and in the morning they accused the guards of the deed. The guards ran away to the neighboring village, but unfortunately LaMonje and her husband never got to enjoy the fruit of their crime. They both went mad. It was said that from the night of the murder neither of them was ever able to sleep again; they kept seeing Mai Kilang's bloody ghost in their bedroom. LaMonje would run out naked into the streets screaming, 'Blood, blood on my hands!' and making scrubbing motions. Her husband committed suicide and she spent the rest of her life in the madhouse. There used to be a song about them—it was quite popular at the time."

their fathers before them

EARLY ON a Monday morning Mamo was informed almost casually by the Waziri that he was to take the minutes at the next council meeting—which was beginning the next hour. It would be part of his routine duties as palace secretary.

The council chamber was next to Mamo's office; it was a huge hall with heavy draperies that cast the room in primeval shadows, as if guarding the secrecy of the decisions taken there. The Keti District Traditional Council was made up of the heads of the twelve villages that made up the district, with Mai Alhassan as the chairman. Already the Mais were making their way into the chamber, slowly, laboriously, taking what seemed to be hours just to settle into their seats.

The seats were arranged around a huge rectangular table. Mamo was introduced by the Waziri as "the new secretary, a distinguished historian who is at the moment working on a magnificent history of our land, our culture, and our rulers," and was given a seat at a small writing table not too far away from the central table, just behind the Waziri. He had never taken the minutes at a meeting before and his greatest fear was of leaving out something important. But his fear dissipated as soon as the Mai started his opening remarks. He found himself often waiting for minutes before the Mai's rambling words could form themselves into a sentence. Today the Mai was dressed in a huge white robe over a sky-blue dashiki, his turban resting on his head like a burden. The Waziri, beside him, was, as always, sharp of dress and shiny of beard.

"We all know why we are holding this meeting. You can see from the papers before you, the agenda today is my tenth anniversary which is coming up ten months from now." Here the Mai paused to elaborate on the guest invitation list. The president himself would be the guest of honor. He talked for over ten minutes on that. The table listened in silence, a few of the turbaned heads began to nod, some were holding side chats, and then finally the Mai ended his digressions with, "Now let us hear your comments. Remember, we must make this a big event, the biggest this town has ever seen. We will invite all the governors, the ministers, and all the local council chairmen." Applause.

One of the Mais, the most senior after the Mai of Keti, stood up and pledged his support; the other Mais all stood up in pecking order and repeated the same words of support, verbatim, only replacing the name of the preceding village with theirs. Then finally the Waziri spoke, and when he did everyone listened. He was in charge of preparations for the big event, and he had all the facts and figures at his fingertips—he broke down how much money would be needed, and the possible ways of generating it. Mamo noticed that almost all the money for the event was expected to come as grants from the state and federal governments.

After the Waziri's speech the meeting broke up for lunch. The Mai retired to his quarters and did not return for the post-recess meeting. The Mais returned looking rather animated—Mamo soon found out why when the discussion turned to the issue of sending a "welfare delegation" to the state governor. Each of the Mais wanted to be a member of the delegation, five were finally chosen—the rest of the day was spent briefing the delegation on what to tell the governor. It seemed each Mai wanted a new car for himself, and money to repair his crumbling palace walls, and more money for the upkeep of his large family. . . .

As he listened to the chatter, Mamo found his gaze wandering to the window. Through a crack in one of the drapes he could see the square outside clearly—under the trees were a line of cars that had brought the Mais to the meeting; their drivers and aides waited patiently to take them back home after the meeting. Absently he thought how a few generations ago the Mais' ancestors must have sat with Mr. Graves under the council trees, eagerly discussing how to increase the taxes on their poor subjects—instead of cars they'd have gone to that meeting on donkeys and horses and on foot. He had read of how mercilessly they had dealt with whoever was unable to pay his hut tax: tying him up in the hot harsh sun, without water or food, in front of his hut, his family, his wife, his children, so that the whole village would learn from his mistake. And he asked himself almost derisively, *What really is there to write about their lives? Their combined lives wouldn't be worth more than a chapter in a decent book.* And he thought of his brother, who now had only one eye, and he said to himself, *I could write ten books about his life and times without the need for any padding.* He also thought of Zara in South Africa, standing in a crowd, watching Mandela being sworn in, after he had spent twenty-seven years in prison, and he muttered to himself, "I could write a thousand books about that moment, that minute that he lifted his arm to take the oath of office." He also thought of his uncle, seated by the window and staring at the deserted hut where his only son once lived, but who was now estranged from him, crippled by life, and the school building that was visible just over the thatched roof of the hut, and he thought, *Of my uncle's silence I could write many books. Even my father's selfish ambitions had more nobility in it than these frauds have in their whole lives.* For the first time he was brought face to face with the duplicity of his own position. His uncle had said to him, "I know they will feed you a bundle of lies. But I have no fear that you will write only the truth."

He knew that, were he to be honest to his heart, he'd right now put down his pen and walk out and never again return. But what of fame, he reminded himself, what of immortality? People don't achieve all that because they interpret the truth literally; there is always a point where they grit their teeth and do what has to be done. One looks only at the bigger picture. In the afterword there would be a chance to say a word or two about the hard choices he had to make, the compromises, to show that he was not unaware of the finer issues involved. But first he must write the book.

When he returned to writing the minutes, however, he noticed that his hand was not as steady as it had been earlier.

The disquiet grew every day inside Mamo. Every morning he'd look around his office and feel as if he were in the wrong place, as if a million eyes were watching him and asking him, *What are you doing here?*

Finally, to silence his conscience, he decided to make a bold suggestion to the Waziri—to propose a fundraiser for the village.

"Sir, I have a suggestion," he said to the Waziri; he was standing in the center of the Waziri's office. For the past couple of weeks, since the meeting, the Waziri had been avoiding him, pretending to be busy whenever Mamo approached him to remind him of the need for another interview with the Mai. Now the Waziri waved him into a seat, saying breezily, "How is the book coming?"

Mamo mumbled an answer, and then went on to his suggestion: "We really need to generate publicity about the anniversary long before it happens, starting from now."

The Waziri kept on looking at him, saying nothing, but a flicker of interest was beginning to register in his good eye now that the anniversary had been mentioned. Mamo had counted on that. He wanted to couch his proposal in words that would deflect attention from its real reason, which was to try to do something for the village, the people.

"I think if you involved the people you'd make more progress."

"What people?" the Waziri asked.

"I mean, organize a fundraising event, something that would involve the people. Invite the youth clubs, the farmers' clubs, the traders' unions, the church and mosque groups—they all have the Mai as patron, don't they?"

"You mean a form of taxation? I am afraid that simply won't work." The Waziri waved the suggestion away impatiently.

"Not that exactly. The money raised will be used to build something useful in the villages, say drilling a well in each of the twelve villages; surely the people will be happy to contribute to that?"

"I thought the whole purpose of this was to generate publicity for the anniversary," the Waziri said.

"Yes. We will generate publicity—but we have to go about it the right way. We will organize a fundraising event and get the people to come and contribute money, but the point is that most of the money will be donated by the state and the businesses that we will invite, not the people."

"Then what do we do with the money—that is, if we are able to get the money?" the Waziri asked skeptically.

"We build something with it for the village, like drilling a well. The new governor and his commissioners will definitely come to the fundraising because this is the kind of thing they like to be seen doing, and of course we will make sure the media are there to cover it. Even the minister for culture will be happy to come. After that the whole country will be talking about Keti, the papers and the television stations will be lining up to interview you and the Mai, and we will make sure to mention the coming anniversary in all the interviews."

But the Waziri didn't seem very keen on the idea, and so Mamo didn't expect to hear any more about it, but then to his surprise the Mai, at their next interview session, a month after the council meeting, brought it up.

"Secretary, do you know any youth clubs, soccer clubs, and things like that?"

Mamo stood before the Mai, unsure how to answer. He looked
to the Waziri for help, but the Waziri looked away, his hand fin-
gering his beard.

"Yes, sir, I do know some clubs in the village."

"Good—the Waziri here has an exciting idea. He thinks we
should involve the people in our fundraising—you know, the
president and the ministers are coming here for my anniversary.
We could drill a well or two and get publicity from that. Clever,
very clever, don't you think?"

Mamo was still standing with his notebook and pen in hand.
The Waziri wouldn't look at him; he was picking off an invisible
piece of lint from his spotless white robe.

"I think it is a good idea, Your Highness," Mamo said.

"Sit down, secretary. Tell me more. Is this possible, is it really
possible?"

Mamo sat down. "Yes, it is possible. All it needs is careful planning. A committee should be set up to look into it; we must invite
the town elders, the club leaders, the local government council,
perhaps a representative from the governor, and set things
rolling. But first we must decide what time we want to hold the
fundraising event. I suggest we do it three months from now; that
should give us enough time afterward to drill the wells and to
commission them well before the anniversary itself. The success
of all these, of course, depends on how many wells we are able
to drill."

"Good, but we must not forget that this is not only about wells
and villagers, it is about my tenth anniversary!" the Mai shouted,
turning to the Waziri as if for support. The Waziri smiled and
nodded reassuringly. The Mai smiled and waved his hands impatiently, urging Mamo to continue speaking. The Waziri looked
on, a secret smile twisting his lips.

"The aim is to have you in the public eye, the nation's eye, till
the very day of the anniversary. Then, to cap it off, on the day of
the anniversary there will be the presentation of your biography."

"Tell me," said the Mai, looking from the Waziri to Mamo, "this biography, what is it all about?"

The Waziri leaned forward and whispered, "Your, Your Highness. It is your family history, remember, we started the interview last month."

"Ah, you are the biographer. I knew there was something familiar about you. Where have you been all this while? I have a lot to tell you. Today I will tell you about my childhood, how I foiled a plan by one of my uncle's wives to poison him. Now, this is what happened: I used to have dreams, and they always turned out to be true. I was a blessed child, you see. . . ."

part four

the mai's durbar

THE FUNDRAISING durbar proved successful. The crowd started gathering in the Palace Square from the early hours of the morning, and by late noon, when the event was billed to begin, the square was overflowing and most people had to find standing space in the roads and in house doorways. Dancers from all parts of Keti and the neighboring local governments came in busloads, each vying to outdance the other. Schoolchildren stood in lines in their uniforms and sang songs to the governor and the Mai.

Mamo sat in the third row behind the Mai and the Waziri and the military governor, enjoying the spectacle, happy that the event was proving a success. He had had his doubts at moments during the organization, and even today he had not deemed the event a success till he saw the governor arrive with his entourage of commissioners and secretaries, sirens wailing, then he had turned to the Waziri and smiled.

The "durbar" angle came from the Waziri, who suggested a horse race in the square in front of the invited dignitaries and villagers to lend an air of competitiveness to the fundraising. Now the Waziri nodded as if to say *I told you so* as the horsemen came out in their colorful robes and raced right up to the front row, throwing up their spears and catching them again, all the while chanting praises of the Mai and the governor. The equestrian display proved to be the day's pièce de résistance—even the governor couldn't help waving his swagger stick in appreciation.

After the spectacles and the speeches, a sum of over fifteen

million naira was realized, most of it from the state government,
more than half of it in promises.

Later that evening the Mai hosted the important guests at a private party in the government guesthouse. This was the guesthouse originally built by J. B. Graves; it now belonged to the local
government council. Over the years more rooms had been added
till it was now a big rambling house, taking up much of the space
on the hilltop. From that height most of the village below was in
view: the lights from the houses and shops and moving vehicles
shone dully through the trees and the dust from the untarred
roads.

   Inside, Mamo sat in a corner with a glass of juice in his hand,
watching and listening. Most of the faces in the room were
guests from out of town: they stood in little groups, whispering,
backslapping, drinking, networking. There were young men who,
through their connections, had risen high in government; they
talked the loudest, about big government contracts, about the
ministers and governors they knew personally. There were
women in stiff, towering head scarves and colorful *buba* standing
hand in hand with the potbellied, fat-jowled, slit-eyed "big men,"
into whose ears they whispered while their eyes feverishly
scanned the room for their next mark. Figures in millions
dropped carelessly from lips to hang in the air.

   The Mai, still in his grand robes, sat in a group with the military governor and the Waziri. Before them there was a small
queue of people waiting to be introduced to the governor. After a
while the Mai's group stood up and went around the room, shaking hands. Mamo saw the Mai's usually dull eyes sparkling and
his hands moving up and down in grand gestures. Mamo moved
toward them and stood next to the Waziri.

   "Where have you been? The governor has been asking to meet
you," the Waziri whispered to him, taking him by the hand and
tugging him forward. The Mai turned and saw him and a smile
lit up his face.

"Your Excellency, here he is, the man who organized every-thing, my personal scribe," he said.

The governor, still dressed in his colonel's uniform, looked even shorter up close than he had looked earlier at the square; his epaulets sparkled with brass, his beret slanted at a rakish angle on his head, and all the while he tapped the floor with his swagger stick.

"Well, well," he said, stretching forth his hand. "At last, the elusive secretary. Everyone has been talking about you. How did you do it?"

"I . . . did not do . . . it alone, sir," Mamo stammered, his hand still in the governor's tight military grasp.

"Mai, I didn't know he was so young. I thought all Traditional Council employees were old men," the governor joked and waited for the obligatory laughter. Then he went on, "You really shouldn't keep such talented people hidden away in the village. You must send them to work for me in the capital. We need them."

"Ah, Your Excellency, I must disagree. We need them more than you, otherwise how can we hope to lure you to the villages every once in a while?" the Mai retorted, and there was more laughter; a few career sycophants even clapped their hands and loudly repeated the Mai's witticism to each other. The group was standing in the center of the room. Mamo, standing next to the governor and the Mai, felt like an animal caught in a car's head-lights. He wiped the sweat from his forehead. Now the governor turned to an alert-looking young man behind him—Mamo thought the man looked vaguely familiar—and said, "Captain, give him my card. Mamo, you must come to see me at the state-house. I have heard about the biography you are writing; maybe after the Mai's you will do mine, eh?"

The aide handed Mamo a card.

"Thank you, sir."

After the governor and the Mai had moved on, Mamo remained surrounded by a few curious men who took the governor's card from his hand to admire it and to copy the phone numbers.

"I should be more careful with that if I were you," a man said, taking the card and returning it to Mamo. He was a tall military-looking man, about Mamo's age. He extended his hand. "I am Major Hamza, the new local government administrator. I am surprised we haven't met before—though I only got transferred here a couple of weeks ago." He had a Fulani accent. Mamo shook his hand.

"I am Mamo," he said. The Waziri joined them and said, "I see you two have met. Mamo, since you have started making important connections, better ask for the major's card. He might prove more useful to you than the governor himself."

The major laughed self-deprecatingly and said to Mamo, "Has the Waziri told you about the party we are having here next week?"

Mamo shook his head.

"Saturday evening. Why don't you drop in? It will be great. Waziri, I hope you will make sure he comes."

The Waziri clapped a hand on Mamo's shoulder, his bad eye twitching. "Of course. I will bring him myself."

"I will be expecting you," Hamza said and moved to another group. Suddenly Mamo felt tired. It was a delayed reaction to the weeks and months of grueling exertion to which he had subjected himself in organizing the durbar. His legs felt weak, his head ached, and for a moment the familiar panic that he might be going into a crisis gripped him, but then the dizziness passed. He felt his senses heighten, he could hear the voices and see the people around him with hyperclarity: a woman to his left was crushing him, her huge breast dug into his arm, he could even smell her sweat; the ceiling fan overhead squeaked as it revolved; the Waziri's sweaty face showed every pore, every hair. He also remembered why the governor's aide had looked vaguely familiar. He had seen the man in a picture where he was holding a sword, cutting a wedding cake, arm in arm with Zara. He heard her voice, clear, bitter, telling him, "My ex-husband's name is George, everyone calls him Captain George."

"Excuse me," Mamo said to the Waziri, "I need to get some air."

He escaped the room and went out to the veranda. The party was gradually breaking up, the Mai had left, but the governor, an inveterate party animal, was still around, surrounded by a group of admiring women. The Waziri and Major Hamza were also inside, waiting to catch the governor's eye. Mamo breathed the warm night air and felt glad that today had been a great success—now he had to address the task of writing the book. If only he could write a book that would both satisfy his conscience and please the palace—but he knew that was going to be impossible. Crickets chirped in the night air, fireflies glowed in the grass and flew over the line of cars parked before the gate. One of the cars, a Peugeot 505, was his, placed at his disposal by the Mai himself, to ease his transportation needs. The interior light in one of the cars suddenly flashed as its door opened and a woman jumped out, loud music blasting out after her, drowning out the loud curses she was hurling into the car's open door. She slammed the door and staggered away, rearranging her dress; she brushed past Mamo, still cursing, and went into the room. After a while a man came out of the car, zipping up his fly, dragging on a cigarette. He came and stood on the veranda next to Mamo. It was the captain, George.

"Hello," Mamo said, turning to the aide-de-camp and offering his hand.

The captain turned, frowning, and then he smiled when he recognized Mamo.

"Did you see that? The stupid bitch would rather have unprotected sex than suck my dick. Can you believe that, in this time and age?" The captain sounded surprised.

"I can believe that," Mamo said. The captain looked sharply at him, blowing smoke into his face. Mamo coughed, waving the smoke away with both hands.

"I was going to offer you one."

"Thanks. I have sickle—" Mamo began, and then he stopped. "I don't smoke," he said. The captain inhaled and said, "Wise decision. They are impossible to stop once you've started."

After a long silence Mamo took a deep breath and said, "I know your ex-wife, Zara."

The captain threw away his cigarette and came closer to Mamo, peering at him as if he were nearsighted. He stank of booze and cigarettes. He said theatrically, "Don't tell me you are also screwing her. Ha-ha!"

Mamo said nothing for a while, but suddenly he felt sad, and good at the same time. Sad because Zara had had to spend almost three years of her life with this jerk, sad because she'd actually had a child with him, but happy because she'd had the courage to walk away.

"We were colleagues. I understand she is in South Africa now," Mamo went on.

"Yeah, she is married to her South African at last. But I bet you she'll soon leave him. That bitch can't stay married to anyone— I give her a year, six months, hell, three months and she'll be back, begging me to have her back."

"She got married?" Mamo tried to keep his voice neutral, but he couldn't have succeeded, because George looked at him curiously and said, "Hey, what's all this interest in Zara? You are not related to her, are you?"

"We are distant cousins," Mamo lied, thinking, everyone was related to everyone else in Keti if you dug far back enough. He wanted to ask George if he was really sure about his facts, if there was a chance he might have been misinformed about the marriage.

". . . very important," George was saying. Mamo had missed most of the speech. "Just don't lose the card. I think he likes you, and you can turn that into money, I mean serious money. Just ask for me when you come to the statehouse."

But Mamo was walking away. He wanted to be alone, at home.

He was tired and the morning was only hours away. He got into his car and drove away.

△▽△

When he went to bed he could not sleep. He watched the false dawn grow dark again and finally change places with the real dawn, he listened to the cock crowing with all its heart, and he thought, *If only we could bring to our lives half the conviction that cock brings to crowing, then . . . then . . .*

Inside he felt small, insignificant. He had lost his passion—it seemed at every turn something waited to thwart his optimism, his hope. He did not go to work in the morning—he remained in bed, reading. Nothing seemed important today, not the office, definitely. He had moved into his father's bedroom two months ago. It had been locked up, unoccupied since his father's death, and two months ago Auntie Marina had told him she was moving his things to the room, that she was sure he'd be more comfortable there because it had bigger windows than his own room. But throughout his first week there he had slept poorly, unable to get used to the huge four-poster bed. Then the next week he had removed the big bed and brought in his old bed. He also repainted the deep indigo walls sky blue—the indigo reminded him too much of his childhood and the day he had woken up sick in this room, with Auntie Marina seated next to him.

Now she knocked on the door and after a while she came in.

"Are you all right, Twin?"

"I am fine," Mamo said, trying to sound light, cheerful.

"Are you not going to work today?"

"I am taking the day off," he said.

"Are you sure you are all right?"

For a moment he felt tempted to tell her about Zara, but he stopped himself. This was a personal pain, a personal disappointment. He'd sit in a corner alone, like a wounded dog, and lick his wounds, gradually rallying himself for another climb, another leap. That was what life was all about anyway, wasn't it, one hill after the next till finally you came to the hill you couldn't climb, or you were just too tired to try—like his father, like Mr. Graves, like his uncle Haruna. And Zara, had she also met a hill that was too high to climb, too wide to circumvent, and decided to give in? *But,* he said to himself, *why do I go on flagellating myself over something I knew I had lost a long time ago? For surely from the moment she told me she was going to South Africa with a former friend I knew I had lost her.*

This was the time to let it go. Finally. Let it all go, life's river would bring more in a second. He took a week off from work and spent the days sleeping and reading and going for long walks in the evenings. At night he sat out on the veranda with his auntie beside him and together they'd stare anxiously into the dark, cloudy sky—all night long the clouds would pass, raising hopes of rain, but by morning the sky would be clear again. This was the second month of the rainy season, but the rain had still not fallen.

party people

IT WAS a birthday party for Major Hamza's girlfriend at the hill-top guesthouse. The Waziri said to Mamo as they drove in, "This place is perfect, no one comes here who is not invited. We come here most evenings to relax, you know what I mean?"

Mamo said he knew what he meant. But what the Waziri meant became even clearer when they went in. The party was already in progress at the open courtyard behind the main house; music blared from a huge stereo in the veranda, and it seemed the whole courtyard was filled with young giggly girls—none of them seemed to be older than twenty—trying desperately to look cool and sophisticated. Sprinkled among the girls were a few men, most of them elderly, though there was another group of young military types standing to one side—Major Hamza's colleagues, most likely. Most of the guests were already seated in plastic chairs under broad-leafed umbrella trees from whose branches colored lightbulbs blinked into the night. The entire compound was surrounded by huge brick walls studded with barbed wire and broken bottles. As the Waziri and Mamo took their seats, some of the men came over to the Waziri to pay their respects—some of the faces Mamo had seen before while organizing the durbar: they were councillors from the local government, and a few contractors who made their living from contracts awarded by the local government. They handed Mamo their cards as they shook hands. Their girlfriends clung to their arms, as if to keep their balance on their high heels.

Major Hamza came out of the house and shook hands with them. "I see you are able to make it," he said, pumping Mamo's hand enthusiastically as if they were long-lost friends reuniting. Then he pulled the Waziri to one side and they whispered for a long time.

"There is never a shortage of girls at these military parties. I never miss them. Ha-ha," the Waziri said as he returned. A young girl came over and sat in his lap as soon as he had taken his seat; he turned and winked at Mamo with his good eye.

"Get one of your friends to keep my friend here company. A beautiful one. Good clean girl," the Waziri said to the pouting, gum-chewing girl in his lap. The girl remained seated, clinging more tightly to the Waziri. Mamo was served food, but he was not really hungry; after a few bites of the chicken he pushed aside the plate. The girl who had served him, and who had been watching him from across the courtyard, approached him and said coyly, "Don't you like the chicken? I cooked it, you know."

"It was excellent, I just wasn't hungry," he explained.

The Waziri leaned over and whispered in his ear, "I think she likes you."

Mamo turned and looked fully at the girl. She was young, like all the other girls, not more than eighteen; her hair was braided and the tail rested on her shoulders; she had a nice smile and wide, disarming eyes. The Waziri stood up and clumsily dragged his girlfriend to the central clearing, where a few couples were dancing to a new song from the stereo. Some of the men cheered when they saw the Waziri bravely attempting to follow the fast-paced hip-hop beat.

"Would you like to dance?" the girl asked Mamo.

"No," he said, "I am not good at that, I am afraid. Why don't you drag a chair over and we can talk?"

She smiled and nodded. She placed her chair so that it touched his. Her perfume floated in the air, sweet and a bit too mature for her young age.

"What is your name?" he asked.

"Julie," she said. "What is yours?"

"Mamo. What do you do, are you a student?" To Mamo's surprise, she took his hand and burst out laughing.

"What is the matter?"

"You," she said, still laughing. "You sounded like my father, the way you asked that question."

"Tell me about your father," said Mamo, his smile uncertain. Now everyone was taking their seat. A table was being set in the central clearing.

"They are going to cut the cake," Julie whispered to him, making her lips deliberately brush his ear, her breath hot against his skin. She held his gaze when he looked at her, her eyes bold, unblinking. The cake was brought in ceremoniously by two girls—it was on a silver tray and covered in white cloth; everybody clapped when it was uncovered. The cake stood pink and huge and incandescent, with eighteen candles on the surface.

"Actually she is twenty, and this is not her birthday at all. She just wanted a party," Julie said, giggling into his ear.

"Is she your friend?"

"My cousin," Julie corrected, clapping like everyone else as the celebrant stepped forward and stood before the cake, a group of her friends around her. She was petite, chirpy, dressed in a skimpy pink evening dress, with matching high heels and bag. She waved impatiently at someone in the shadows. It was the photographer; he ran forward and stood before the girls, his camera poised, but suddenly the celebrant shrieked, looking around her wildly. "Wait! Wait! Where's Julie, where's Julie?"

The others echoed the cry and Julie stood up, a pleased smile on her lips. She squeezed Mamo's arm and whispered, "I'll be back."

After the cutting of the cake, the girls danced and the men showered money on them—Mamo watched as the notes cascaded down and formed a carpet on the grass.

"Well, well," the Waziri said, leaning over to Mamo, his hand caressing his beard, his eyes glinting animatedly. "I see you have

already found company." Mamo caught a whiff of gin on the
Waziri's breath. On the table before the Waziri was a two-liter
bottle of spring water mixed with gin. As the evening wore on,
the effect of the gin showed more and more in the Waziri's
speech, in his eyes, and soon he grabbed his girlfriend and, waving goodnight to Mamo, staggered into the house. After midnight
the party moved into the huge living room, since the courtyard
had grown chilly.

"I'll have to call it a night now. Do you want me to drop you
somewhere?" Mamo asked Julie.

"What is the time?" she asked, standing up, taking his hand.

"Almost one A.M."

"Why do you have to rush away? Don't you want to hear about
my father? Remember, you asked me about my father." Her lips
were on his ear, her arms around him; she was laughing, her eyes
a bit dulled by drink. When they went in she dragged him right
past the dancers in the living room to one of the bedrooms.

"There are seven bedrooms in this house," she said, sprawling
out on the bed, kicking off her shoes, and rolling onto her
stomach.

"Do you know that a president once slept in this house, probably in this bedroom, on this bed?"

"Who told you that?" Mamo asked, sitting beside her.

"One of the men, Major Hamza."

"The president couldn't have slept here—he was in Keti for
only an hour."

"Oh." She squeezed up her face.

She began undressing, starting with her *buba*, then the wrapper, till she was in her underwear. Now she looked at him, and
her eyes were suddenly clear. She wasn't really as tipsy as she had
made out.

"You will stay the night, won't you?" Her hands were behind
her, unhooking her bra. Her voice had gone sultry, seductive.

"I . . . am so tired," he said. He lay on his back beside her, staring up at the ceiling. She stood up and went on undressing, bob-

bing on the bed: the bra came off, then the panties. She towered over him, her legs on either side of his body, her arms akimbo— she looked magnificent in her nakedness and she knew it. Her breasts peaked like twin spears; her hips curved and flowed flawlessly into her thighs.

Slowly she descended onto him, spreading the full length of her body over his, covering his mouth with hers.

When he got home, still early in the morning, he was overwhelmed by a sudden need for air. His lungs felt constricted, his body felt hot and feverish. He put on his thick walking shoes and took a path into the fields. He walked in the dry grass and brambles for a long time, feeling the twigs break under his soles, passing the farmers who picked determinedly at the dry, rock-solid earth, occasionally glancing up into the sky as if by dint of willpower they could make the clouds gather and the rain fall.

He walked until he grew tired; in his mind images of Julie's young, supple body with her legs twined around his waist kept appearing and reappearing. Sometimes the face on the body changed to that of Zara, causing him to start suddenly and to look behind him, as if expecting her to appear out of the air.

Let it go, he told himself, *let it all go*.

the young pretender

THERE WERE more parties, mostly at the same venue, mostly with the same people, and mostly for the same reasons: birthdays for girlfriends. With the success of the fundraising durbar, Mamo found that his life had almost imperceptibly entered into a new, sociable phase. Strange women began to drop in at his office, introducing themselves as contractors, or agents for contractors, asking for news of the wells that they heard were soon going to be dug in all the villages. When he told them he really didn't know anything about that, that he was only a secretary, they'd laugh knowingly, press his hand and look meaningfully into his eyes, and tell him they'd "take care" of him once they got the contract.

They were mostly middle-aged women, the direct opposite of the birthday party girls, who might well be their daughters. Some of them were not without charms, some were married, some single, but all implied they were available for business or pleasure. They gave him invitation cards to more birthday parties and housewarming parties in the state capital, invitations which he never honored.

The Waziri said, laughing, "Accept their invitations, have your liaisons with them, then tell them, sorry, you are not the one in charge of the contracts, but that you will put in a word for them with the Mai. You have worked so hard since you came here, you must also learn to relax."

"But there is still so much to be done. When will work on the wells begin? Has the Mai said anything yet?"

"Young man, you have done your part; the rest is in our hands. I want you to know that we, the Mai and all his councillors, care for the people more than you'll ever know. Don't forget, his whole life as Mai is dedicated to serving the people."

Mamo nodded. "Yes, I guess so. . . . I just want to be sure things are going according to plan, because the next stage, which is the publicity, will depend on how soon the wells are completed."

They had formed a core group consisting of Major Hamza, the Waziri, and some contractors and councillors. A few of Major Hamza's military friends occasionally drove down from the state capital to spend their free evenings at the guesthouse, partying or just watching movies with the girls.

Some days, like today, when it was too hot to stay indoors, or when they were feeling restless, they'd drive into town to the barrooms and restaurants that had started springing up all over Keti. On such occasions the Waziri always stayed back with his girlfriend and his bottle of spring water mixed with gin. "I must maintain some level of decorum. I can't be seen in barrooms with women," he'd say.

They drove in a convoy of three or four cars, playing soft music, the girls all dolled up and chattering loudly in the back seats. The hotel managers would come out to the cars to meet them as soon as they arrived, effusively leading them to a special section in the courtyard covered in trees and dim lights, away from the noisy, crowded main hall. A waiter would hover around to attend to them throughout the evening.

The girls always drank wine, the men drank ice-cold beer with goat-head pepper soup; Mamo was the only teetotaler, always nursing a bottle of soft drink, and enduring the other men's jeering comments. Major Hamza and the councillors discussed contracts and their impending trips to London or some other foreign capital, while Mamo listened. Julie was cuddled up against him, surrounding him with endless chatter about things she had bought on her recent trip to Lagos. She dealt in jewelry and shoes and bags; she bought them cheap in Lagos and sold them to the socially ambitious housewives in Keti and the surrounding towns. Most of her clients had only seen such dresses or shoes or jewelry in the Lagos society magazines, or worn by someone at a wedding, and wanted to look like them.

"So, where do you get your capital from?"

"From my father," she answered shortly. She didn't like it when he talked like that. She never asked him for money. He was glad for that because he wasn't sure how he'd respond if she did. He bought her gifts when he could, nothing expensive, for which she always showed extravagant appreciation. Often he tried to interest her in school—she had a good mind, and an amazing head for figures, but her studies had ended three years ago when she graduated from secondary school.

She turned to the other girls, who were waving frantically to a tall, dreadlocked youth in a yellow Bruce Lee tracksuit; he had emerged from behind the trees and was headed for the drinking hall.

"Prince, come and play for us!" the girls shouted. Now Mamo saw that the young man was carrying an acoustic guitar slung over one shoulder. A cigarette dangled at an angle from his lips.

"He is really good," Julie said to Mamo.

The young man stood before their table, his cigarette sending smoke into his eyes, forcing him to blink. He appeared to be quite popular with the girls—he was handsome in a rugged, unkempt way. They gave him money and cigarettes and soon he was strumming away, his back propped against the umbrella tree under which they were seated. He sang a couple of reggae tunes in a hoarse, manly voice. After he had left, Mamo asked, "Who is he?"

"You don't know him?" one of the councillors, Lakuturus, asked, belching loudly.

"Should I?"

"You should, you are the Mai's biographer."

Mamo waited patiently, but finally the story came out: the man had appeared in Keti about two months ago, with his guitar, claiming to be the real heir to the throne of Keti.

"Tell me more," said Mamo.

"Well, a long time ago a Mai was deposed by one of the white district officers. This Mai then went into exile to Yoruba land. He died there—you do know that, don't you? Ha-ha! This boy, Prince, claims to be that Mai's grandchild; he even has some papers to prove it. But no one believes him. Some people think he is mad, he smokes marijuana, but he is harmless. He sings in barrooms and is really popular with the girls, as you have just seen."

From his position Mamo could see clearly into the bar hall. Prince was going from table to table, shaking hands, accepting drinks, and strumming on his guitar. He stopped when he got to a large group. A request was made; Prince nodded and began to sing, throwing his locks into the air, skanking madly, his eyes closed. The group clapped and threw money at him.

"The engineers," Julie told him, following his stare.

"What engineers?"

"The water engineers, the ones digging the wells. They have been around for weeks now . . . but surely you must know about them, you work with the Waziri, and people say that. . . ." She stopped and shook her head.

"Why did you stop—what do people say?"

"Nothing."

He took her hand. "Julie, tell me."

She shrugged, looking at the others, who were pretending not to be listening. "Well, people say that the engineers are really not good engineers, and that the Waziri and . . . you . . . hired them just to find an excuse for embezzling the money from the fundraising . . . and . . ."

"People say that?" Mamo asked, feeling his mouth go dry, but trying to smile, to appear nonchalant.

"I don't believe what people say—really, I don't. But you know how people talk."

Mamo said, "But I didn't even know work had started on the wells."

"Hey!" Major Hamza said, patting him on the shoulder. "People will always talk once you are in a position of influence. If it is not the wells, it will be something else. It is what we call the PhD syndrome."

"Pull Him Down syndrome. Ha-ha," the others chimed in, laughing, breaking the tension.

Mamo watched the engineers through the door. One of them, fat and short, had jumped to his feet and was dancing to Bob Marley's "Get Up, Stand Up," the strains of which were coming clearly to them under the tree outside. Mamo felt numb and all he wanted to do was go home, lie down, and think. His mind had totally shut down and he couldn't think. That was all he wanted to do right now, think. He pushed Julie away as she leaned forward to rub her lips against his. Inside the hall the corpulent man danced with a girl on each arm, once in a while dipping his hand into his back pocket and throwing money at Prince. He left his friends at the bar and drove home, his eyes blinded by anger. That night he drafted a short, angry resignation letter addressed to the Waziri. Only then was he able to sleep.

△ ▽ △

"I saw the water engineers yesterday," Mamo said to the Waziri early the next day. He had arrived very early and had waited for the Waziri in his office. His hand was in his pocket, waiting to bring out the resignation letter. "I didn't know work had already started on the wells."

"Oh, yes. I was going to mention it to you, but I didn't want to bother you. I know how time-consuming your writing is," the Waziri said calmly, swiveling around in his seat. Mamo felt the anger rising in his chest, denying him speech.

"But surely I should have been informed, seeing that it was me who first raised the idea of the fundraising, and the wells—"

"Calm down. Calm down. I understand why you feel left out. It is natural. Don't think I am trying to steal credit from you . . . but you know the council works by committee. You were not around the week we met, remember? You took a week off. By the way, all the Mais spoke highly of you at the meeting . . . we all decided that the sooner we began the project, the better. We decided to begin with the money that has started coming in . . . of course not all the promises made publicly at the durbar will be honored . . . but we decided to begin work immediately with what little we had. You see, we are aware of the people's trust in us, and of how money has a habit of getting sidetracked into other ventures. So we said, let work begin. First in Keti, then, when more money comes in, in the other villages. . . ."

Mamo listened, and as he listened he kept his eyes on the Waziri's smooth, skinny face, getting more and more convinced that he was being lied to. But there was nothing he could do about it.

"You do understand, don't you?" the Waziri asked, ending his long speech.

"People say the engineers are not real professionals—" Mamo began, but the Waziri cut him off short with a wave of the hand.

"I hired them myself. I have seen other projects done by them. Of course I have heard what people say, but don't let that bother you. They will eat their words soon."

Mamo changed the subject. "I saw a man yesterday, called Prince. He claims to be an heir to this throne?"

The Waziri waved his hand dismissively. "Ha-ha, I wondered how long it would take you to run into that madman. He is just a disturbed young man who wants to look important by making these ridiculous claims."

"So you have investigated this claim, and there's no truth in it?"

"Absolutely none, so don't bother yourself about it."

"Does the Mai know about this man?"

"My dear talented scribe, I am surprised that you still haven't realized that there's very little that goes on in this town that we don't know about. The town elders you see coming here daily, they are more loyal to the throne than they are to their pastors, or imams, or even to their own families. They tell us everything."

"Well," said Mamo, "I am surprised no one told me about this. I found out by accident, just like I found out about the wells." He waited for the Waziri to comment, but when he said nothing, Mamo went on. "I will still need to meet this guy, to hear what he has to say—it will make an interesting side story."

"No, don't do that," the Waziri said sharply. When Mamo looked surprised at his objection, he gave a little laugh and said, "Don't bother yourself going to him, he is not that important. We know where he stays. I'll have him brought to your office and you can interview him here. Just tell me when."

"Thanks," Mamo said, standing up. Now he was utterly sure he couldn't trust the Waziri. As he was about to step out, the Waziri called after him, "How is the book going?"

"Good, very good."

"Remember, we have just a few months to the anniversary."

Back in his office he slowly tore up the resignation letter. It'd be stupid to resign now. The best thing was to stay and find a way of either blackmailing the Waziri to do the right thing, or if he wouldn't, to expose him; only by doing that would Mamo be able to clear his own name.

He wanted to talk to somebody, to vent his feelings, and perhaps get some advice. He went to his uncle, but his uncle wasn't home, he had gone to the state capital and wouldn't be back till early the next day. Mamo drove around aimlessly, finally ending up at the site where the Keti well was being dug—it was by the roadside, not too far from the old abattoir. The site seemed to be deserted, apart from a single old pickup truck and a rig half buried in the ground. A toolshed made from zinc and wood stood open and a short stocky man sat at the entrance; he gave Mamo a bored look.

"Are you the guard?"

The man nodded lazily.

"I am looking for the engineers."

"You may look, but you won't find them."

"Why, where are they?"

"They have gone to the state capital."

"When will they be back?"

The man shrugged, yawned, and closed his eyes.

In the afternoon he went looking for Prince. Not knowing where he lived, Mamo decided to ask Julie if she knew. He met her at home—she was just waking up. He had been to the house once before, and now he knew that she had no father, her father had died many years ago, and she lived with her mother, who was a secretary at the local government secretariat. He had never met the mother; the only time he was at the house he had met only Julie and a group of her friends, chatting in the living room, applying makeup and nail polish while watching a Nigerian movie. He met the same group today—they all seemed to be just waking up from sleep. Julie was in a long flower-patterned night-gown, yawning and blinking, when she met him at the door.

"I know where he lives, but I can't go out now. Come back later, in two hours, after I have taken my bath. Or you can wait here with the girls."

"I'll give you an hour. Hurry up."

"But I am hungry, I'll need to eat first, then—"

"I'll buy you lunch."

He went home and brought his recorder and a camera, all the while thinking up questions to ask the young pretender. Julie was waiting for him when he returned, dressed in a skirt and a blouse. He followed her directions and soon they were at the house—it was really a single mud hut by the roadside. The thatched roof was held down in places by huge rocks and pumpkins that looked as if they'd roll down any moment. When he knocked on the wooden door it swung open, the hinges creaking loudly, to reveal an empty interior.

"Are you sure this is where he lives?" he asked Julie.

"I am sure," she said. They went in. It was dark and musty inside, but clearly no one lived there anymore; an empty iron bed frame stood in a corner, newspaper pages and cigarette butts littered the hard mud floor. As they turned to go, Julie pulled at his hand and pointed at a woman standing before the entrance of a neighboring compound, holding a child firmly by the hand, staring at them with a bovine intentness. They went over.

"Hello," he said to the woman. She didn't answer.

"We are looking for Prince. Does he live here?"

"Prince is gone," the woman said after an obvious debate with herself. "He left early this morning. Some people came to see him and he left afterward."

"What people?" Mamo asked. The woman didn't answer. Julie knelt down and handed the child a fifty-naira note, tickling it in its protuberant belly. The woman's face softened and she said, "They were from the palace. I saw the guard's uniform. Prince always said that he knew people at the palace, but we never believed him, till today. They took him to the bus station in their car. I have to go now." The woman abruptly turned and disappeared into her house, dragging the snotty, runny-eyed kid after her. Mamo was thoughtful all the way back, trying to make sense of what he had heard, but finding no sense in it anywhere.

"What was that all about?" Julie asked him, yawning, reminding him of his promise of lunch.

"I am not sure, but it is very important. Listen, you must forgive me, I can't take you to lunch. I have to go home now. I have work to do."

She pouted and refused to speak to him. When he dropped her at home she mumbled, "Will I see you at the guesthouse tonight?"

"I doubt it."

a brief history of the waziri

AFTER MAMO had told him about the well scam, and about Prince, Iliya said, "Unfortunately, I don't know much about the Waziri's history—all I know is that he is from the Pandi clan, and that he is distantly related to the Mai," Uncle Iliya said.

"I didn't know he was related to the Mai."

"Not many people do. You see, a Waziri is not supposed to be related to the Mai—this is to ensure that he does not use his position to influence the kingmakers after the Mai's death to become Mai himself. Only the Mai's blood relations can contest for the throne."

"But why was this Waziri's case an exception?"

"Well, he became Waziri at a very difficult time—it was during the reign of Mai Hamdi, who reigned before this one. The Mai before Hamdi, Mai Kilang, had been killed brutally in his sleep, and everyone believed his Waziri had a hand in it, and so when Mai Hamdi assumed the throne he chose this Waziri as his vizier because he felt he could trust him, being his distant cousin. Of course, Hamdi himself later died of poisoning."

Mamo was thoughtful. After a while, he asked, "Was the Waziri ever suspected of foul play in connection to the poisoning?"

"No, they were really close. Cousins."

Uncle Iliya stood. "I know one person who can help you with more information. He must be over a hundred years old, but his memory is phenomenal."

They didn't walk very far—the old man, his name was Kopi, lived a few huts away from Uncle Iliya's compound. They found him sitting on a log outside his hut, chatting to passersby. Kopi was something of a legend in Keti. He was blind. There were many stories about his mysterious powers; he was said to be descended from the original inhabitants of Keti, the Komda, who had been routed centuries ago by the present settlers. Kopi was descended from one of the two families spared by the newcomers to instruct them on the secrets and rituals of the old Komda. These families became the religious priests and seers—they knew every medicinal herb and tree, every ritual and magic necessary to avert evil. Though blind, Kopi could wander the maze-like village pathways and even climb the hills alone and without a stick. He said the wind spoke to him, and the trees on the hills, and that the very earth on which he walked guided his steps.

It was said that once a missionary came to him and tried to convert him to Christianity. "I heard that your Christian God is famous for making blind people see again. Will he return my sight if I become a Christian?"

"He will forgive you your sins, and that is better than regaining your sight."

"But I never sinned against him. Why should I seek his forgiveness?"

"We are all sinners . . ." the missionary went on, but Kopi had stopped listening. "Keep your religion, I'll keep mine," said he when the missionary had stopped speaking.

Now he cocked his head and stared with his opaque eyes in Mamo's direction and said, "Lamang's son? Are you the soldier or the one who writes history?"

"I am the one who writes history," Mamo replied.

"We need to know about the Waziri," Iliya said.

"Well, how come a historian doesn't know about the past? Ha-ha." He cackled and hit the ground with his stick; his cackle grew into a chesty cough, which ended with the expelling of a stream of phlegm. Then he went on, "Waziri La Kalla. I am sure you didn't know his name, did you, did you?" He rubbed his shrunken calves with thin bony hands as he waited for Mamo's answer, his head cocked. His mouth was open, exposing his toothless gums—they were dirty pink beneath the black caving-in lips.

"La Kalla indeed, that's his name," Iliya said. "Tell us about him."

The old man was silent for a long while, as if cranking his old brain into action, and then he began a long lecture on Keti families and lineages, and finally concluded with, "Most people don't know that the Waziri La Kalla's father and Mai La Kei's father have the same grandmother. They forgot about poor La Kei as soon as Bol Dok became Mai. No one speaks of him anymore. He died in Yoruba land alone and lonely. But he was a good man. He was only doing what was right. . . ."

"When you said he died alone, do you mean he was sent into exile alone, without his wife and children?"

"Yes, he had two wives and two daughters, but the wives remarried after he had gone, and their children became adopted children, bearing new names. No one remembers who they are now."

As they turned to go after thanking him, he called after them, "Come back next time and I'll tell you how La Kalla's eye got the way it is now. He wasn't born that way, you know. He loves other people's wives, and one day an angry husband surprised him in his own bed. Ha-ha. . . ."

"Well, I didn't know the Waziri was also related to La Kei," Iliya said.

"If La Kei remarried while in exile, then the boy Prince might actually be who he claims to be, and that makes the Waziri his great-uncle."

"All this doesn't make any sense . . ." Uncle Iliya said. They were back in his living room, and he was leaning back in his chair, looking exhausted from all the brainstorming.

"First, the Mai hired me to be his biographer and—" Mamo began, but his uncle interrupted him.

"Was it actually the Mai who hired you? I should think the Waziri was more instrumental in that."

"You are right. But how on earth is the Waziri going to benefit from that? Is he hoping that the book will reveal something about the Mai that will force him to abdicate, and then Prince will step in . . . . ?"

"So we are assuming that he invited Prince to Keti. But Prince will make an unlikely contender for the throne. There is something more, I am sure, and I think the biography has something to do with it. . . . Did he try to influence you in any way in the writing?"

"He did offer to be interviewed a couple of times. But I still can't see how the biography is tied to all this."

"Well, let's forget the book for a moment. Let us look at the facts: The only way Prince, or anyone else, can become Mai is if the Mai is removed, or dies. I am not sure if you knew that this Mai has no male child. He has no direct heir; when he dies there is going to be a big fight for the throne, all the cousins and nephews will come out."

"But the Mai is not dying soon, is he? He is not ill, unless . . ." Mamo looked at his uncle. "Unless the Waziri knows for certain that the Mai is dying soon . . . but how?"

Iliya shook his head. "One can't tell. But then, to people like the Waziri such things are not as horrifying as they are to you and me. It is just a means to an end. All I can tell you is be careful. He is a very evil man, and if he suspects you of trying to thwart his plans in any way, he won't hesitate to remove you. I suggest you resign, tell them you don't want to write the book anymore, or better, just go away somewhere quietly," Uncle Iliya said.

Mamo was shaking his head. "I don't think running away is the answer. Besides, we don't know if we are right or just speculating."

"Just be careful," Uncle Iliya said, looking very agitated. "Promise to let me know before taking any step, and whatever you do, don't confront the man."

Mamo promised and went back home.

△▽△

Zara took him by surprise.

When he got home, Auntie Marina handed him a handwritten note. "I was just going out. Your lady friend left this."

He did not look at the note—he was sure it was from Julie—till much later, after he had taken his shower and was about to go out. That was when he glanced fully at the note on the table where he had dropped it and for the first time noticed the unmistakable capital *E*—it was Zara's handwriting; she always wrote her *E*'s in capitals, even in the middle of a word. He read the two lines:

> *Hi Mamo,*
> *I came to say hi, but you weren't home. Look me up at the dispensary later if you have time, from midday.*
>   *Zara*

He rushed out to the neighbors', looking for his auntie to verify if it really was Zara who had left the note. It couldn't be, because Zara was in South Africa, married to Themba the South African. He didn't meet his auntie, but it was almost noon anyway, so he decided to drive to the dispensary right away. On the way he wondered why she wanted to meet at the dispensary. He hoped she was not ill. He drove fast over the narrow, dusty road, sometimes braking suddenly to avoid children playing. The dispensary was not too far from the church compound—it had started life as a little clinic run by a Scottish doctor, but later the local government had taken it over. Now it was run by Dr. Njengo and an old retired nurse. It opened daily, minus Sundays, from nine A.M. to midday. It was mostly empty—except in the rainy seasons when the mosquitoes bred and malaria fever became rampant. Emergencies, such as snakebites and problematic childbirth, were very rare, and when they did happen the doctor routinely referred them to the general hospital.

Dr. Njengo, now in his seventies, usually sat dozing in the veranda, the radio beside him broadcasting the news in Hausa. Today looked like a typical day at the dispensary: there were only two women with their two kids waiting out on the veranda. They were seated on a bench gossiping. They stopped when Mamo parked his car and approached them.

"Good day, Twin. Are you ill?" one of the women, a close friend of Auntie Marina's, asked.

"No, I came to see a friend, but she doesn't seem to be here," he said, unable to hide his disappointment. But just then the flimsy curtain covering the clinic door parted and Zara appeared. She stood with the curtain bunched in one hand. The other hand held a file from which she read out a name: "Lantana, you are next."

She hadn't seen him; she turned to go back inside.

"Zara," he said, coming up the veranda steps, smiling. She was wearing a sort of nurse's uniform, only it wasn't white; it was blue, with white stripes. She looked different, slimmer, thinner, her face looked tired, and there were lines around the forehead.

"Mamo," she said, a smile breaking through her weariness. "I am almost through, these two are the last, you can come in and wait. You don't have to go now, do you?"

He opened his mouth to ask a question, and then he decided to save it for later. He went in. The dispensary was made up of a single room. He remembered it very well. As a kid he had been a regular visitor here. The same heavy mahogany table with used syringes and ampoules lying carelessly on it, and against the wall was a row of neatly labeled tins full of tablets; the labels carried

the usual names: chloroquine, Panadol, aspirin, Piriton. He sat
down on a bench and watched Zara attend to the patient. It was
a child of not more than five; the mother held her in her lap as
she answered Zara's questions. Zara read from the card the
woman handed her and asked the woman a few questions, then
she spooned out tablets from one of the tins and put them in a
transparent sachet and handed it to the woman.

"Give her two in the morning, two in the afternoon, and two
before going to bed. She should be okay in about a day or two, it
is nothing serious."

When the woman and her daughter went out, Mamo asked
Zara, "Where's Dr. Njengo?"

"He is not feeling well today. He left early."

"I didn't know you were also a nurse."

"I trained, in Durban, for three months. I needed to because
of my work with the children—I know enough to read prescrip-
tions and to change bandages and wash wounds and give injec-
tions, nothing too challenging."

He watched her clean up the next patient, a girl of about nine,
covered in puke, feverish, scared, and struggling wildly. He
helped the mother hold the kid as Zara injected her. The room
was hot and by the time they were through they were all
sweating.

"That was the last," she said. "I'll wash my hands then we can
go."

"I have a car, I can give you a lift home," he said as he waited
for her to lock up.

"Good. Saves us having to walk, I am really tired."

"How long have you been in town? When did you begin to
work here?" he asked as they drove over the bumpy road to her
house.

"One week," she said, "I—"

"You've been in town one week?" Mamo said, taking his eyes
off the road to look at her.

"Careful. Yes, one week. I heard the doctor needed a nurse—

the other one is ill, she is my auntie and she got me to volunteer till she can return." Her voice was weary, hoarse, as if she were just recovering from a fever, or as if she hadn't been using the voice for a long time. As they passed the community school she said, "I see the school is still closed."

"Yeah. Remember the commissioner that came that day to close down the school?"

"Yeah, the one who wanted to be addressed properly."

"He died—he was shot by the soldiers when they took over power. They went to arrest him and he resisted."

Zara's house was as he remembered: the big gate; the one-eared gatekeeper, Yam—grumpy as ever, but wearing a thick beard now as if to register the passage of time, or maybe just to cover his missing ear; the living room with its big windows and the pictures on the walls, but he noticed that the wedding picture was not there anymore. Zara left him in the living room and went to the bathroom to clean up. It was hot in the room despite the open windows and the overhead fan—the fan only circulated the same hot, stale air. He went outside and sat on the steps. The sky was gray and dull as usual, as if it would rain at any moment. At night the clouds would descend low over the hills, lightning would flash and thunder rumble, and when it seemed as if rain were inevitable, the wind would grow strong and fierce and chase the clouds beyond the hills to reveal a clear, starry sky. A few farming families had started moving to neighboring towns where the rainfall was more regular.

The Mai had called for prayers and fasting in churches and mosques; some religious ministers were agitating for all brew-houses and barrooms in the village to be closed down to lessen the evil that they believed was the cause of the drought.

"The sky looks overcast today," Zara said. She was standing right behind him; he hadn't heard her come out.

"Should we go back in?" he asked.

"No," she said, sitting beside him, "it is cooler outside." Her feet were bare. She had changed into shorts and a T-shirt. Her hair, which had once been long and cascading, was now cut short. But the greatest transformation was in her face, in her eyes. They looked as lovely as ever, huge and round and expressive, but not as open as before, there was something guarded about them. The lips had a set to them that implied determination, but a bitter, almost desperate determination. She ran her hands through her wet hair, staring up into the dull sky.

"Where should we start? We have so much catching up to do." He didn't want to bring up the issue of her marriage to Themba; he wanted her to broach it first, to explain why she hadn't written to him about it. He noticed that there was no ring on her finger, but that didn't mean anything; some married couples don't wear rings.

"Let's start with you," she said a bit too quickly. "Everyone is talking about you—about the fundraising, and the wells. I am so proud of you. Are you happy at the palace?" She looked directly at him when she asked the question, her voice low, gentle. It was an unexpected question, one that he had not considered before, one that he didn't have a ready answer to.

So he said, "I met your ex-husband the other day. Captain George."

"Oh, where, when?" She did not sound very interested. She was staring in front of her, at the gate. He could feel the sadness emitting from her in waves and torrents.

"Over a month ago. He is the governor's ADC. We met at a reception, after the fundraising durbar. I recognized him from the picture I saw here. I told him you and I were colleagues."

"What did he say?"

"He told me you were married, to the South African, and that the marriage would soon crumble anyway, because you couldn't stay with one man long enough . . . and . . ."

She turned and stared at him, looking him squarely in the eye. "Go on, why did you stop?"

"Because that's all."

She remained silent for a long time, staring at the gate, then after a while she took a deep breath. "I guess I owe you an explanation. . . ."

"No, you don't."

She went on, as if he hadn't spoken. "I married Themba for practical reasons. My visa had expired and the only way I could remain in South Africa was to marry him. I felt it was worthwhile because of the work I was doing there, and we both agreed that it wasn't a real marriage, it was for the job, the children needed me. The home was going through a difficult period. We had started expanding and accepting more orphans, some of them AIDS orphans, and if I left, even for a short while, the work we were doing would suffer. And so I said yes; we got married."

Mamo waited to hear more, but she was quiet. He said, "And now?"

"I left because he started wanting more. He wanted it to be a real marriage, but I told him I wasn't ready for that. I wasn't interested in him, not in that way, but he became very sad, distracted from the work. I felt angry for letting myself get into that kind of situation. What I wanted to avert began to happen, the work began to suffer. He said he was in love with me and he couldn't go on that way. So I left. I came here straightaway. I spent only one night in the state capital, to let my mother and sister know that I was back."

"But why didn't you come to me?"

"I don't know. . . . Now I really have to rest." She stood up abruptly and went inside. Mamo stood up and followed her. She was sitting on the sofa by the window, crying. "Please go. I really want to be alone now."

He turned to go, and then he paused and said, "I'll come again tomorrow."

Zara seemed much calmer the next day, though she looked as if she hadn't slept much. She said she hadn't been to the dispensary; she had taken the day off. It was late afternoon and very hot inside, so they sat outside on the steps again, and it was as if they hadn't moved from this position since yesterday, and when she began to speak, she did so without any preamble, as if they hadn't broken off since yesterday.

She said, "As a kid I was afraid of the dark, of being alone in the dark. But I outgrew that with time. Then in school I feared not being liked by the other girls, but I outgrew that with time also. After school it was the fear of failure—I still fear failure, but for a different reason, a more mature reason. I fear it for myself. I don't want to fall below my expectations for myself, that'll be so unbearable, only that at times I don't even know what my expectations for myself are. . . . I seem to keep mixing them up with other people's expectations of me. When does one stop growing up and become really grown up?"

It was a rhetorical question and Mamo did not attempt to answer; he didn't know the answer. She went on, "I remember what you once told me: you said the world is as new today as it was when first created, remember?"

He nodded.

"Well, I want to believe that. I really do."

They sat watching the shadows move beneath the trees. They talked about the drought, and he told her about Kai and Malai. "Let's go visit them now. I have to return the diary I borrowed from them anyway."

"Okay."

For a moment they pushed to one side the raw pain of yesterday and established a hesitant, probing *entente cordiale*.

The sisters were in the garden, having their afternoon tea.

"This is Zara, a friend," he introduced.

After much digging the sisters discovered that they knew Zara's father.

"Of course, Lamemi, we knew him well," Malai said, putting her hand over Zara's. This led to the sisters bringing out their early photo album and showing a picture of themselves and a group of local boys at the mission school. Mamo watched in silence as they talked. He watched Zara's eyes become animated; he saw how easily the sisters warmed up to her. She was that kind of person, he told himself, she had that kind of effect on people. The sisters were seated on either side of her, their fair heads framing her dark head.

"This one is your father." Malai pointed him out to Zara, who shook her head in amazement, turning to Mamo.

"I can't believe it, look at Daddy. He looks so small and scruffy."

"We have heard of his death. Sorry, child."

"It was a long time ago, almost ten years now."

The sisters sighed, perhaps contemplating the passage of time. This turned the conversation to their coming departure; the date had finally been set. They didn't seem very happy.

"Michael insists. It is best for our health, he said. But in His hands God has everything."

They stayed for over two hours, watching more pictures of the Drinkwater family. When they got to the mother Mamo asked suddenly, "Did she ever want to go back to America?"

"Oh, but she did. She went during the Second—"

"No, I mean, to take you all back. Never to return."

The sisters looked at each other and sighed. "It was the only point of misunderstanding between my parents. She wanted to go back, but he believed God had ordained for us to live and die here," Heather said, speaking softly.

As Mamo and Zara left, the sisters made Zara promise to visit again.

"I will," she promised, hugging each of them in turn.

In the car Zara sighed and said, "She has such sad eyes."

"Which of them?"

"I mean the mother. She has such sad eyes. I wonder what her story is. Married to a preacher—"

"A fanatic."

"Far away from her friends and her homeland, and one of her children died. She must have been a broken woman."

at the guesthouse

THEY DROVE about in silence, aimlessly, passing the houses by the roadside. They found themselves in a quiet, almost sad section of the village, with people seated in groups underneath trees, making rope, or gossiping, or just waiting for night to fall so that they could go in and sleep. Then, as if she couldn't bear the silence, Zara pointed at one of the houses and said, "See that house? That is my auntie Saraya's house. She is ill; she's always been ill since I knew her. Her daughter, Abigail, is a nurse in Brunei."

"A long time ago my father used to be in love with a woman called Saraya. Her husband died in a car crash or something. He was a truck driver."

"Really? My auntie's husband was a driver, and he died a long time ago. I never saw him."

Mamo almost laughed out loud at the coincidence. "It must be her. I've seen her only once, from a distance. I was only ten then. What's she like?"

"An angel. Maybe that's why your father loved her so."

"Maybe," Mamo said, surprised that he still felt a twinge of bitterness against the woman—it was a knee-jerk reaction carried over from his childhood.

"Now I'll introduce you to a few friends of mine," Mamo said, suddenly taking a turn and heading back to the village center.

"Who are they?" Zara asked as they drove up the hill to the guesthouse.

"Some people from the local government office. We meet here in the evenings to kill time. You don't have to return home immediately, do you?"

There was no car in front of the house; the guard opened the gate when he saw Mamo.

"A president once stopped here for a quick nap, on his way to the next state."

"It looks like someone's love nest," Zara said, looking at the heavily draped windows, the tall hedges in the driveway. Once they were inside, she wandered around the living room, peering at the pictures on the wall: There was the sole administrator shaking hands with the state governor. Next to this picture was the Mai in his full regalia, holding his staff of office, his owlish eyes looking wise and focused on the camera. And next to that was a picture of the first district officer, Mr. Graves.

Zara was pensive as she walked around the room; she finally went and opened the window, pulling aside the drapes. "It is hot today."

"I can turn on the a.c. if you want," he said, going to the fridge to take out a bottle of orange juice.

"No, let's leave the window open. Come, see the hills from here, aren't they lovely?"

He joined her, standing close behind her, opening the curtains wider with his hand. The sun had started its descent over the hills, slowly assuming a darker, reddish color. He turned away from the view and watched the smile on her face. On impulse he bent forward and kissed her on the neck. The unexpected move startled her and she almost jumped, then they burst out laughing.

"Sorry," they both said at once, staring into each other's eyes. He took her in his arms and buried his face against her neck. After a while she pulled back, holding him at arm's length and staring into his eyes.

"Let's watch a video—are there any Nigerian films?"

"Yes."

They watched the film in silence, leaning against each other, not bothering to turn on the light when the room grew progressively darker. As the film came to an end a knock sounded on the door, and before he could stand up the door opened and a female voice said, "It's so dark in here."

He recognized the voice immediately, even before the lights came on to illuminate Julie at the door, one hand still resting on the light switch, a smile on her face. The smile wilted when she saw his partner.

"Hello, Julie," he said brightly, but his mind was thrown into confusion. She advanced slowly into the room, her eyes fixed curiously on Zara.

"I saw your car."

"Julie, this is Zara. Zara, Julie."

Julie continued to stand, her hand tapping the back of a chair. She was dressed in jeans and a T-shirt; she had a wig on her head beneath which her real hair peeked, making her look even younger and more immature than her years.

"Won't you sit down?" he asked.

She sat down and turned her eyes to the TV, crossing and uncrossing her legs. Once in a while he saw her steal glances at Zara.

"The film is finished, won't you turn off the TV?" Zara asked.

Mamo turned off the TV and the VCR. Julie announced loudly, suddenly, "I have to go now."

He walked her to the door, and as soon as they stepped outside she broke into tears. "Who is she? Why did you bring her here?"

"Julie, go home. I will explain later," he said wearily.

"But I love you," she went on, the tears now streaming down. He looked at her in surprise; the fact that she might be in love with him had never occurred to him. How could he tell her that he didn't love her, that what he had for her was mere adventitious desire that would wither away as soon as he stopped see-ing her?

"Look, I can't talk now. Meet me in the office tomorrow," he said as gently as he could.

When she finally left he stood for a long time staring at the far-away hills before returning inside. Zara was standing in the cen-ter of the room, facing the door. He stopped. They remained like that, facing each other. On their faces a million fleeting expres-sions came and went: sorrow, pain, doubt, regret, love, even fear.

Zara spoke first. "What will you tell her when she comes to your office tomorrow?"

He shrugged. "I don't know. The truth, that I don't love her."

"Listen, I am sorry about everything, about Themba, about leaving you that first time . . . about so many things." She stopped, took a deep breath, and blurted out, almost in a whis-per, "It would never really work, would it, you and I?"

He said nothing.

"Maybe we love each other too much," she said. Still he said nothing. "You are still angry with me, aren't you?"

When he still said nothing, she started toward the door. "I have to go now. This is goodbye, then, I guess."

"I can drop you at home if you want."

She shook her head. "No, I'll walk. The air will do me good."

Her musky perfume brushed his nostrils as she passed. He lis-tened to her footsteps on the veranda, then on the gravel, and then there was silence.

a walk in the night

HE WENT and sat down. He didn't know how long he remained seated like that, silent, his head bowed, his eyes fixed on the dead TV—but he was roused by the arrival of Lakuturus, the councillor.

"Why are you seated alone, staring at the dead TV? Are you waiting for someone?" Lakuturus asked, taking off his *babban riga* and draping it on the back of the sofa. Mamo looked up and said nothing.

"I desperately need a drink," the councillor went on. "It's been a very busy day today."

He went to the fridge and took out a bottle of beer. Dumbly Mamo watched him, and it seemed as if his words came from afar. He came and stood over Mamo, staring at him curiously. "Is something wrong?"

"No."

"You don't look good."

Mamo did not answer; he merely stood up and started for the door, staggering a little. His legs felt weak. In his mind all he could see was Zara's face as she passed him at the door, her head high and proud.

"Are you sure you can drive? I'll drop you if you want," Lakuturus called after him.

"I am okay. Thanks."

He had been driving for almost thirty minutes, taking random turns, before he realized he was lost. His senses had grown dim,

like a light switched off, and he felt as if he were floating on
cloud—a dull, gray, and endless ocean of clouds that threatened
to engulf the car and drown the splash of light it threw on the
dark road. His eyes kept closing on their own, and minutes later,
when he opened his eyes, he was in a ditch. The car had veered
off the road and one of the front wheels was stuck in the open
roadside gutter. He opened the door and crawled out, but as soon
as he attempted to stand up he fell, his legs like jelly. He finally
pulled himself up by holding on to the car; he went and sat down
on a culvert, hoping that someone would come along to assist
him. But then minutes, or hours later, his body acting almost
independently of his mind, he found himself walking away from
the car. He walked and walked, stumbling into the dry grass
clumps by the roadside, often falling down, knocking into trees
and rocks. Fear gripped at his heart; he didn't know what was
happening to him. This was a manifestation of his illness that he
had never experienced before. Everything looked hazy—it was as
if a huge wall of wool had been erected around him and he kept
bouncing back when he tried to go through it. He had no idea
where he was.

He looked around to see if anyone was passing, but all he saw
were trees looming in the darkness, looking ominous, like scav-
engers waiting for him to cease struggling before swooping in. He
walked faster, now breathing in short painful gasps, then far away
he saw a light and he almost cried out with relief; he started
toward it, half running, half walking, but the more he walked, the
farther it receded. He walked on, his breathing getting worse and
worse, forcing him to clutch at his chest, to rest against trees,
and sometimes to sit down. At last he was close enough to hear
voices coming from the direction of the light: faint, multiple,
raised as if in a song. Once more he started toward the light,
weaving and stumbling and falling. Finally, he stood in front of a
huge, warehouselike building, its wide doors standing open, a
single lightbulb burning over the doorway. The voices came from
the dim interior, polyglot, jabbering, but one voice always rose

above the others, orchestrating the cacophony, howling out the name "Jesus" in a sort of demented ecstasy.

He walked in and dropped heavily into the first seat he found. He remained like that, bowed as if in prayer, oblivious to the noise around him, to the bodies that brushed against his in their prayerly fervor, and some that fell at his feet muttering in many languages at once and foaming at the mouth. It was minutes, or hours, or seconds later, he couldn't tell, when he slowly returned to his senses. The screams and chants had now decrescendoed into low hums and moans and groans. He lifted his face and saw all around him the disheveled hair, the foreheads made bloody by banging against walls, the faces clawed to bloody welts by passionate nails. His own body was also covered in dirt and grime and vomit and blood. He couldn't remember throwing up.

"Tomorrow we will go to the hills! We will pray and the Lord will send down the rain," a voice chanted. It was a tall, broad-shouldered man standing behind the altar, waving his Bible at the now-silent congregation, his face illuminated by the candles on the lectern—his eyes reflected the light, making his pupils glow like fireflies. But now Mamo, feeling much revived, slowly got up and made for the door. Outside, he became vaguely aware of where he was—he was in the quarter known as New Town, where a rash of new radical churches and mosques had sprung up. He was a long way from home. He faintly recalled driving his car into a ditch, and before that . . . Zara. He glanced at his watch and saw that it was broken. Its hands stood at a quarter to midnight—that must have been when the car went into the ditch, or after that when he fell against the rocks by the roadside. It must be much later than that now.

He headed in the direction of home, shivering, pulling his flimsy shirt tightly around his thin frame. His head felt heavy, he felt hot, nauseous—he knew what was happening, there was no doubt about it, though he hadn't had one in a long time. He was going into a crisis. He stopped, paralyzed by fear—if he collapsed here, exposed and alone, he'd be dead before morning; his body was already weak. He turned and headed back for the church. It was his best hope. But after a few steps he couldn't walk any-more, and sank slowly into the middle of the path, flat on his face; minutes later he was able to drag himself to a tree by the side of the road. He propped his back against the trunk, staring up into the clear sky above him. And all he could think of was how beautiful the stars looked, there must be millions and mil-lions of them up there, and how ironic it was to be dying on such a night, and whether it was true that good souls rise up to become stars after the body dies—he hoped he might be consid-ered a good soul. He shivered and sweated at the same time, drifting in and out of consciousness. Gradually he gave up hope; detachedly he watched his spirit leave his body to hover over him, unable to bring itself to finally walk away.

the riots begin

HE WOKE up in a hospital room. Auntie Marina was seated next to him, her eyes fixed on his face, anxious, patient. He was gripped by déjà vu: this had happened before, ages ago in another life, the walls had been indigo then, and his father had been there in the background talking to a doctor, and his brother . . . where was LaMamo?

"Mamo, thank God you are awake," Auntie Marina said, the lines on her face relaxing. He thought, *How old she looks. Recently the lines have thickened and multiplied on her face. It is age, or sadness.* . . .

She was speaking to him, "Can you hear me, Mamo . . . ?"

"I can hear you."

There were other beds in the room, other patients and their families. Yes, he had been here before, to visit his father, and Asabar, and his uncle had been there in the waiting room. There was a big window beside his bed and he could see the huge field outside, far away there was a fence, and on the other side was the highway that led to the bridge on the way to the state capital.

"Some men found you on the road . . . they were coming back from an all-night vigil in a church. . . . It was a miracle . . . your car was far away in a ditch . . . and . . ."

He closed his eyes, and thought, *Death is the miracle. A human's body is designed to survive against the stiffest odds, his cells to repair and regenerate themselves. His body merges effortlessly into its surroundings for protection, and the very atmosphere, the air, is*

food to his cells. It takes the most extreme kind of violence to kill us,
and of course old age. It is not life that is miraculous, it is death.

He laughed aloud.

"Are you sure you are all right, Twin?" Marina asked anxiously.

"I am fine. Really." He opened his eyes and tried a smile at her.
He felt sad and exhilarated at the same time. She tried to get him
to eat, but he pushed aside the plate and instead accepted a bottle of water and drank and drank.

"How long have I been here?"

"A whole day. One of the nurses came to the house to tell me
you were here. Another miracle—what if she hadn't happened to
be on duty when you were brought in? It is the Lord's doing, we
must be thankful. . . ."

Later the doctor came in and asked him how he was feeling.
He was an elderly man with thick glasses resting on his nose; he
had long upper incisors that lent his face a probing, severe
expression.

"Not bad," Mamo replied truthfully.

"Good, nothing is really wrong with you. Your auntie told me
you have sickle-cell anemia . . . nothing I can do about that, and
you must be more careful of your health, what you eat, and drink."

Mamo nodded.

"We'll keep you for another twenty-four hours, just to make
sure no complications develop."

Auntie Marina left soon after, promising to return tomorrow
with a taxi to take him home.

△▽△

She did not return because the next day the riots began.

In a bid for divine intervention the Keti Christian community,
regardless of sect, had decided to go to the top of the hill early in
the morning to pray for rain and to persevere till their prayers
were answered. Auntie Marina, never one to miss a chance to
pray, went along. The group sang as it went, growing in number.

On the way the singers stopped at the houses of all known Christians to persuade them to come to the hill with them.

The trouble began when their path took them past the village mosque, which was in the section of Keti known as Hausa Quarter because most of the people living there were originally from the Hausa cities. Though the Muslims had lived in Keti for many years, intermarrying with the villagers, they never really assimilated; they still kept their religion and their Hausa traditions.

The singing drew the Muslims out of their mosque and beds, and when they discovered that the Christians were going to the top of the hill to pray for rain, they decided not to be outdone. They went back into their houses and mosques and brought out their prayer mats and beads, and chanting "Allahu Akbar!" they also made for the hill. For many hours later the trees and rocks rang with the shrill sounds of Christians and Muslims praying, and so great was their rivalry that neither group was willing to quit before the other; the morning changed into afternoon, and the afternoon to evening, but still they prayed, without eating or drinking. Some fainted, all grew hoarse; the skies darkened, thunder rumbled, lightning flashed, but no rain fell.

Then, in frustration, the two groups began to jibe at each other, and the Christians said to the Muslims, "Pray harder, perhaps your God has grown hard of hearing!"

And the Muslims responded with, "No, you pray harder, perhaps your God has gone to the market, and you must shout harder for Him to hear you!"

But who cast the first stone—one of the jagged, fist-sized stones so plentiful on the top of the hill? No one knew, but soon they were whizzing through the air and connecting with faces, arms, legs, and chests.

△ ▽ △

"The fighting descended into the village, into the streets, into houses, before the riot police came. Churches and mosques are

on fire, there are dead bodies on the streets—I saw many with
my own eyes," a wild-eyed, arm-waving man said to a group of lis-
teners standing next to Mamo, who had been discharged hours
ago. He had sat patiently in the waiting room, waiting for his
auntie, wondering what had kept her. But now news of the fight,
with some of the casualties, had started arriving in the hospital.
People stood in groups at the hospital gate to hear the news from
the increasing number of people fleeing the fights. The hospital
was one of the obvious safe places. He saw women coming in
through the gate, their possessions rolled up in bundles on their
heads; others had children strapped to their backs, and as they
ran they kept looking back over their shoulders. The injured were
brought in by pickups and off-loaded unceremoniously in front
of the casualty ward.

Mamo stood in the crowd by the gate, feeling bodies bump into
him, and eyes unseeingly staring into his. Fear was palpable in the
hot air, and a sort of low, ceaseless humming came from the
women who surged forward whenever new refugees arrived, looking into the faces, checking for news of loved ones. They weren't
even aware they were giving up the continual humming noise.

Mamo felt weak and numb; the news was so sudden, so unexpected. Somehow he knew his auntie would be in the congregation on the hill. He went and sat on a bench by the entrance to
the casualty ward, waiting. Not far from him a child of about
three stood alone, lost, crying. The light was dying; soon it would
be night. More people trooped in through the gate, and now the
whole space before the wards was filled with groaning, tired bodies sitting and lying in the dusty earth, a few nurses in white
going about with bandages and cans of water.

They could now hear faraway gunshots: the police, keeping
the peace. Near him a man, perhaps the same wild-eyed man
who had earlier brought the news of the fight, was talking about
how the police had gone from house to house, beating whoever
they found indiscriminately, untying the goats and chickens and

throwing them into the back of their trucks, and all the time shooting into the air, keeping the peace.

Mamo spent the night on the bench, hungry, his arms wrapped around him to keep warm, listening to the babies crying and their mothers moaning continuously. In the morning he made his way into the emergency ward, looking at the bloody faces. Some he recognized, but none was his auntie. Next he went outside to the center of the crowd, men and women sprawled out on the dusty ground, but still there was no sign of his auntie. A group of young men were making their way out of the hospital gate. A security guard stopped them and began to argue with them, trying to dissuade them from going out. "The police are still out there, shooting."

But they went anyway.

Mamo went with them. They were about five in number, and many times they were stopped by gun-toting policemen and told to lie flat on the ground while they were searched for weapons; but at last he got home. He found the little girl, Rifkatu, sitting on the steps alone, tears running down her face.

"Where's Auntie?" he asked.

"She went out to the hill yesterday and she hasn't been back."

He went to his uncle's house and that was where he found out that Auntie Marina was among a group of people arrested by the police. Mamo felt his body slowly relaxing, untensing. She was alive.

"But is she all right, did you see her?" he asked his uncle gently, fearfully.

"No one knows anything for certain, there's so much confusion. . . . I am going to the police station later to see what is going on."

"I'll come with you," Mamo said immediately.

When they got to the station they were surprised by the size of the crowd waiting to hear word of their families. Suddenly there were no Christians and Muslims, just anxious people eager to see their loved ones. They stood before the station, facing two policemen standing on the steps with rifles pointed at the crowd.

After a while a potbellied inspector came out of the station to make an announcement. The crowd went quiet. "I am going to read out the names of the people we have here—there are forty of them. If you hear your relation's name, then you may bring him food, but you cannot see him or her. They will be held here for their role in the riots; they will be released after they have been interrogated. Do you understand?"

The crowd murmured an answer, the inspector proceeded to read out the names, and one of them was Marina. Mamo turned to his uncle. "What do we do now?"

"We do what he says. We'll go home, we'll get her some food, we will wait. I am sure it will be all right in the end."

the unmasking

THAT EVENING the Waziri came to see Mamo.

"You weren't affected by the fights, were you?" he asked, coming up to the veranda where Mamo was seated on a chair. Mamo stood and offered him the chair. He went inside and brought out another for himself.

"This is a big surprise, sir."

"Yes, I am sure it is. You didn't expect to see me here, did you? Ha-ha. But it is okay. I am going about to make sure that everything is okay, to talk to the people and show them the folly of violence. All the mosques and churches and most of the shops and barrooms are still on fire. This is folly, sheer folly. And the dead—they are still discovering bodies. Over ten dead, so far. You weren't affected, were you?"

"Not personally, but my auntie is in detention."

"What? But why didn't you come to me immediately? Don't you know what brutes the police are? And their stinking cells? Arghh. . . . " The Waziri put his hand over his nose. "It is not a place for an old woman."

"I wasn't around. I was in the hospital. I just got back today."

"Oh, were you ill?"

"My car ran into a ditch," Mamo said without elaborating.

"Yes, I saw it outside. Dented. It wasn't very serious, was it? It's not going to affect your writing, is it? Or have you finished the book already?"

"No, I haven't finished the book."

The Waziri waited for elaboration, but Mamo kept silent, turning his eyes away. Then he turned back and blurted, "Waziri, I want to talk about the wells. . . ."

"What, not that again?" The Waziri stood up and began to pace the tiny space of the veranda; his face was thoughtful, expressive of his displeasure.

"I went to the site the other day, and there was no work going on at all. Why don't we get other engineers? Surely money is not a problem now that—"

The Waziri sighed and sat down; he pulled his chair closer to Mamo. His face retained its patient, long-suffering expression, and when he spoke, it was like Einstein explaining $E = MC^2$ to a child. "You really don't understand how these things work, do you? I told you we work by committee, and did you think the committee works for nothing? I will be open with you. They have to be given something, their share of the fifteen million, and these are the Mais we are talking about here, so you don't give them small money. And so at the end of the day, what remained for the wells is not as much as you'd expect. Do you understand? I am being blunt here."

"You mean the money, the fifteen million that was raised for drilling wells so that the people could get water, was shared among the Mais and nothing is left for the original project?" Mamo asked. Now it was his turn to speak slowly, patiently.

The Waziri's smile slipped, then returned. "Not all the money. Did you think we forgot about you, our talented scribe? Ha-ha. No. You will give me your account number, and I will put in something for you."

"How much?" Mamo asked.

"Let's say a hundred thousand naira? You deserve it. But the book must be finished soon. It is very important."

"But what of the people? Don't they get anything at all?"

"Come on, secretary. I know the people, I represent the people. It is my work to know the people. Do you think they don't know how these things are done? They do. And you know what—

I am sure this is what you didn't realize before—this money shared by the Mais, it will eventually find its way back to the people. These same people will come to the palace with their list of problems, medicines for their children, school fees, hunger, and do you think we turn them away empty-handed? Never. So in the end, the people benefit more than anyone else."

As he listened to the sweet, Mephistophelean voice, Mamo noticed that despite the Waziri's squint, he had a predator's keen gaze, and he seemed to be always waiting, patient, trying to out-guess his interlocutor—and the breath, why hadn't he noticed the foul predator's breath before now? Or was it just that he had preferred not to notice? Why had he not walked away from the council chamber that day when he had looked out the window and had realized that there was nothing of dignity to be written about the Mai? And later, there had been other opportunities, but he had not taken them. Suddenly he thought, *LaMamo would have walked away. Does that make me a weaker person than my brother, both physically and morally?*

"But," said the Waziri in conclusion, "let's not waste time talk-ing about the obvious. What is more important at the moment is the book. You must finish it soon, then we will start talking of printing it. How many copies will be sufficient? I want every household in Keti to own a copy. Think, soon your name will be in every household, on every table."

"Tell me, sir. Why is the book so important to you?"

"No, no, not to me. To the Mai, to the anniversary, to all of Keti."

"Perhaps I am not the right person to write the book. . . ."

"Why do you say that?"

"There are so many things I don't understand. For instance, why did you hire me to write the Mai's biography and try to make it seem like it was the Mai's idea to hire me?"

"Young man, the Mai himself ordered—"

"No, Waziri, he didn't. But we could ask him at the palace if you insist."

The Waziri was silent for a moment, and then he said, "Does it really matter?"

"At first," Mamo went on, "I was puzzled when I met him for interviews and he'd appear surprised to see me. But then later I said to myself, what if he didn't hire me at all, what if the Waziri hired me and led me to believe that the Mai did? At first it didn't make sense, because why would you do that? I even tried to explain it by believing that your only ambition was to get a good mention in the book. But soon other things happened to open my eyes to what was really going on. I came across the young man, Prince. You remember the day you promised to bring him to me for an intcrview? Well, I suspected, rightly, that you wouldn't, so I went to him, only to discover that he had been bundled out of town by palace servants. Servants sent by you, so that I couldn't get to interview Prince. But again, why? I didn't have an answer, but by then I knew that you were desperately hiding something—something you didn't want me in particular to know."

"And what might that be?"

"I am coming to that. I found out, also, that Prince had been bragging to his neighbors that the palace invited him to come to Keti from Ile-Ife. You had played the same trick on him as you had done on me. You invited him, but made him believe that it was the Mai that invited him. But again, I asked myself, why would you do that? Could it be that you wanted him to become the Mai after this one? But surely you knew that no one would take a dreadlocked, weed-smoking busker seriously?"

"Ha-ha," the Waziri said. "You do have a great imagination. Go on, I am enjoying this."

"Indulge me," Mamo said dryly and went on. "Your plan is so clever because on the surface each phase of it appears to be separate—for instance, no one can see the connection between Prince and yourself, or between you and my book—they all appear to be separate. Unless, of course, one is in a position to see a pattern. And that person is me—I am in a good position to

see the shape formed by these disparate pieces. And this brings
us to the book. You want me to write a book that will apparently
celebrate the greatness of the Bol Dok line, culminating in the
present Mai. But the more I researched, the more I discovered
there is nothing to celebrate. All my book can do is the opposite,
which is to heap ridicule on the Bol Dok line by showing how it
was the beneficiary of the violence on our culture by the colonialists, and therefore not a true representative of our people. All
the evidence will be in my book. This will only make the people
want to get rid of the Bol Dok line, and perhaps desire a return
to the earlier La Kei line, especially if there is great unrest in the
land, perhaps due to the broken promises over wells. The people
are desperate and hungry and in no mood for a long contest over
the throne. Once confusion begins over who really deserves the
throne, you will be there to advise the kingmakers to begin to
seriously consider a return to the La Kei line, which will of
course be the will of the people."

"And who will their choice be? Prince? You just said he can't
be taken seriously."

"But that is the beauty of your plan, isn't it? You are actually
his great-uncle, so you are as eligible as he is to be La Kei's successor. And that will make you the perfect compromise candidate
for Mai, because not only are you related to La Kei, you are also
related to Mai Alhassan."

"I'll forgive you, because I am sure you didn't know that a
Waziri cannot succeed his Mai."

"Anything is possible where there is a will, and means. The
kingmakers, under your guidance, wouldn't find it difficult to
waive the rule that says a Waziri could never succeed the Mai.
You'd make sure they did—you will make their decision easier
with generous money gifts, perhaps the very money raised at the
durbar. After all, who is there to challenge you?"

"Well, well, secretary. At least I was right about you. You do
have a lively imagination."

Mamo stared directly into the Waziri's good eye, and despite the Waziri's light, bantering tone, he could see in the eye that he wasn't amused.

"What," the Waziri said slowly, "if I offered you more money?"

Mamo laughed. "You seem to forget that my father left me a lot of money, more money than I need. But thanks for the offer. I just want you to dig the wells like we planned."

The Waziri was silent for a long time. He stood up as if to go, then on the last step he turned rather theatrically and said, "What if I told you that all these things you've said are figments of your imagination, that I am a loyal subject of the Mai, and my only ambition is to see his memory preserved in your book? Would you believe me?"

Mamo shook his head. "You shouldn't have deceived the people over the wells."

The Waziri shrugged. "You leave me no choice, then. I heard that all the arrested rioters would be taken to the state capital for questioning. How long will an old woman last in that kind of situation? How old is your auntie? Sixty, sixty-five? But if you want I can get her out in a minute. Her life is in your hands. Think about it."

fire on the hills

LAMAMO CAME at night when the hills were on fire.

The police had set the hills aflame to flush out rioters who were still hiding there from capture and brutalization by the police. Mamo was seated on the veranda, watching the hills burn. The Waziri had left hours ago, but Mamo had been unable to move from where he sat. The girl Rifkatu had asked him if he wanted something to eat, but he had waved her away impatiently without even looking at her. He knew he should go to his uncle and discuss what had transpired between him and the Waziri. His uncle had warned him not to tackle the Waziri over his suspicions, but he had done it, he'd had to do it to regain his dignity, but it seemed he had now ensnared himself with his own mouth, and the only way out was to agree to write the book.

He couldn't bring his limbs, or his brain, to function. He felt physically tired; his body hadn't yet recovered from its recent ordeals. And he realized he hadn't eaten anything since yesterday. His head ached, and his eyes were blurry from hunger, and so when the gate opened and a man with a bag slung over his shoulder came in, Mamo thought it was his eye imagining things. He waited for the figure to become recognizable, and when he saw the eye patch his mind told him it should mean something. That was when he recognized his brother, but when he opened his mouth to speak, no words came out. He was so overcome by emotions, and confused and saddened by the eye patch, that he felt tears come to his eyes. His brother was standing at the foot of the steps looking up at him, a bit hesitant, uncertain, as if waiting for Mamo to make the first move. At last Mamo stood up and said hoarsely, "LaMamo."

"Mamo," said LaMamo. "For a moment I feared I had entered the wrong house."

He came up the stairs slowly and the brothers embraced rather formally, then they both sat down. Both looked at the floor, and then at the faraway hills, and then at the compound walls, but not at each other, as if they found looking at each other too painful. Mamo was conscious that he looked thin and tired and haggard, and LaMamo's eye patch looked so strange on his face that Mamo felt like leaning forward and pushing it aside to see if underneath the eye was really gone.

"I saw buildings burned down, and the people hiding. I passed by the church and it was still smoking," LaMamo said heavily.

Mamo nodded. "There's worse. A lot of people have been arrested by the police. Auntie Marina is with them."

"And Father?"

Mamo looked sharply at his brother. LaMamo saw it in his eyes, but he waited to hear it. "Father . . ." Mamo said slowly, clearing his voice, "he died. Almost a year ago."

LaMamo was silent for a long time, and then he said, "I felt as if I had lost my way coming up from the bus stop. This wasn't what I dreamt of coming back to. I told Bintou about the green hills and farms and valleys. . . ." He stopped talking and gave a little laugh, looking down at his hands. A thin beard covered his chin, and in the weak light he looked rugged, burly; the eye patch added to the rugged look.

"Bintou. Tell me about her," Mamo said. And without a word his brother reached into his pocket and took out his wallet; he brought out a picture and slid it across the table. It showed a young and pretty face, determined, optimistic.

"How old is she?" Mamo asked. He really didn't know what else he might ask.

"She will be twenty-five this July. She is three months pregnant." Mamo turned the picture around and around in his hands; the card had lost some of its gloss and stiffness, like pictures do when they are kept for long in a wallet, or when handled too often. He imagined his brother bringing out the picture and showing it to people, friends, or casual acquaintances on the bus, in a barroom, how he'd say—careful not to appear too proud— *She hopes it will be a girl. Me, it doesn't matter, a boy perhaps, but it doesn't matter. It might be twins; I am a twin, actually.*

"Is she coming to join you soon?"

LaMamo shrugged. "I don't know. After she became pregnant I started thinking about home, and things like that . . . and she encouraged me to come and see how things are, hoping that one day we might . . . But now . . ." He shrugged. "She has her degree now, you know," he added proudly.

His voice had a certain twang to it, which Mamo guessed would be a Liberian twang. "And you mentioned going back to school yourself, in your letter. Did you?" Mamo asked.

"I did. I got a diploma. . . . It wasn't easy. But I did it."

Suddenly, as if talking about his wife had restored his appetite, LaMamo said, "I am hungry. I haven't eaten anything since I left Lagos this morning."

Mamo stood. "I doubt if there's anything prepared. I could wake up Rifkatu to prepare something for you."

"Who is she? You are not married, are you?"

Mamo smiled and shook his head. "No, just a cousin staying with us."

LaMamo descended the stairs and headed past the kitchen toward the chicken coop.

"Does Auntie Marina still keep chickens?" he called back to Mamo.

"Yes."

"Good, why don't we have roast chicken? Start the fire, I'll be right back."

Mamo shook his head and made for the kitchen. Suddenly it seemed as if the worries that had weighed on his shoulders, squashing his entire horizon only hours ago, were now lifted. His appetite came rushing back. He went into the kitchen and felt around for the matchbox. The electric bulb in the kitchen had died months ago and Auntie Marina hadn't bothered to change it. He struck the match and with its light he found the kerosene and poured it onto the wood in the triangular hearth. He threw the dying match onto the wood and the flames whooshed into life.

Soon LaMamo returned with the chicken. He had slit its neck with a pocketknife; its legs were still kicking. His hands were covered with blood—the blood looked black in the poor light in the kitchen. And suddenly Mamo recalled his brother's letters, about how he had killed the major who tried to rape Bintou. He tried to imagine what the room would have been like, and how the blood would have flowed on the carpet, and the terrible sound the gun must have made when the shot was fired.

They sat on low stools before the hearth, waiting for the kerosene to burn off and for the wood to begin to burn properly. LaMamo's hands quickly, effortlessly plucked the chicken's feathers, revealing the plump skin underneath.

"How did Father die?" he asked. He pushed his knife into the center of the chicken's rib cage and cut it open from chest to anus, and then he began to pull out the entrails. The blood dripped onto the pile of feathers on the mud floor. He pierced the chicken with a thin, sharp stick and suspended it over the glowing fire. Mamo told him about Lamang's political defeats, of the subsequent violence and arrest, and of Asabar's paralysis. The conversation was desultory, and often they'd fall silent and stare into the flames on which the chicken was roasting. The fire threw their shadows against the wall; their heads looked distended, bowed close together like card players, or like conspirators.

"How did you cope with him?" LaMamo asked, shaking his head, turning the spit, squinting his single eye against the heat and smoke. Now the chicken had started to give up a sweet smell and Mamo felt the juices quickening in his mouth. He rummaged about for the salt and pepper and soon they were eating, cutting huge chunks of the soft flesh and dipping it into the salt and pepper.

"He wasn't so bad toward the end."

LaMamo shook his head again.

"The widows helped, in a way," Mamo went on.

"Those shameless old women."

"Again, they weren't so bad toward the end."

"But they—" LaMamo began, but his brother interrupted him.

"People are just people. The widows actually helped me survive some very dark moments. I still see them sometimes, when I can."

LaMamo shrugged, and then he changed the subject. "What do we do about Auntie Marina? Should we go to the police tomorrow?"

"It is more complex than that," Mamo said, and then he told him about the Waziri's ultimatum. "Now I am not sure what to do," he concluded.

"There is no doubt about what you should do. You must not give in to his blackmail."

"But what can I do?"

"Tomorrow we will go and pay him a visit." LaMamo's voice was so confident that Mamo found himself feeling optimistic suddenly.

"What will we do when we go to him?"

"I don't know, but we must never let him win. People like that must be opposed no matter what. Surely you can see that, can't you?"

It was almost midnight now. They were both sleepy, but neither really wanted to go to bed yet. "Let's go inside," Mamo said. They went inside.

to the palace! to the palace!

MAMO WOKE up late to find LaMamo waiting for him in the living room.

"How was your night?

LaMamo shrugged. His eyes looked red and puffy, as if he hadn't slept well. He brought out a piece of paper and laid it on the center table. "This is yours? I found it in a drawer." His voice was stiff, and his eyes roamed over Mamo's face as if looking for some clue. Mamo bent down and picked up the paper. It was his letter to the police. He must have left it in a drawer when he moved to the master bedroom.

"Oh. I wrote this when—" he began, and then stopped when he noticed that his voice was hoarse. He cleared his throat. He was unable to meet his brother's eyes as they continued to travel over his face.

"You don't have to explain anything," LaMamo said. Mamo was surprised by the disappointment in his brother's voice. He quickly reached out and held LaMamo's arm. "Let me explain. This is not what it seems. . . ."

"I said you don't need to explain. This is your affair." Now the disappointment in LaMamo's voice had deepened into hostility. Mamo withdrew his hand.

"I am going out. I am going to see Asabar," LaMamo said, heading for the door.

"We will talk later," Mamo said, and watched his brother stride out of the room.

Mamo thought of following him to Asabar's place, but then changed his mind. He washed his face and sat on the veranda till the sun rose high in the sky. He had often thought of planting flowers before the veranda, just beside the steps—but he had never gotten around to it. Besides, water was a big problem. But in his mind sometimes he could actually see the flowers growing, like now. He closed his eyes and imagined them sprouting out of the ground, their leaves and petals wet from the rain, the earth muddy beneath his feet. He smiled, caught up in the ecstasy of his imagination.

He remained like that for hours, till he was jolted back to reality by shouts from the street. And for no reason at all his heart skipped a beat and he said aloud, "It is LaMamo."

He stood up, and then he sat down again. His legs felt weak. He told Rifkatu to go and see what was going on. She came back, breathless, and said, pointing toward the noise, "They are fighting outside."

He went out and was surprised at the huge crowd. For a moment he thought the fights had started all over again, but then he saw that there was no fight actually going on. The people were moving up the street toward the market, shouting, "To the palace! To the palace!"

"What's going on?" he asked one man.

"The people have chased away the water engineers," the man said, "and one of them is dead. They've burned their trucks and they are now going to the palace."

"He knocked down a policeman, I saw it," another man said excitedly. "Now he is leading the people to the market."

"Who?" Mamo asked.

"I don't know, he is a soldier. They say he just came back from Liberia. He is leading the people to confront the Mai."

"But . . . are you sure . . . ?" was all Mamo could say, but the man was already moving away with the crowd. Mamo watched the crowd, undecided. He went back into the house and mechanically put on his shoes and changed his shirt. He knew he had to follow the crowd to the palace; maybe he could still manage to speak to LaMamo. He felt dizzy and he sat down abruptly. What he would love to do now more than any other thing would be to go out and take a walk, follow the path into the parched, rock-hard fields, and feel the hot air on his face, to just walk and walk, to clear his brain. But he got up and went after the crowd. They were now past the market, and as he went he found out more: LaMamo had met a fight on his way back from Asabar's house. A group of villagers had accosted the water engineers, who had just driven in on one of their rare appearances at the drilling sight, all five of them, in a car. The villagers had been waiting for them. One of them, pulling his daughter along, had accused the fat engineer of impregnating his daughter. The tearful teenage girl had pointed out the culprit, who was behind the wheel. But the engineers had only laughed at the villagers and threatened to run them down if they didn't get out of the way, asking the girl if she hadn't been paid enough money. That was when the incensed villagers had pulled the engineers out of the car—the fat one was killed instantly, the other four barely managed to escape. The drilling site was pulled down, the pickups were set on fire. A lone policeman on patrol had come across the scene and had pulled out his gun to shoot when LaMamo, passing by, sprang up behind him and knocked him down. Now the villagers, returning to their senses, faced with a dead body, were about to slink away when LaMamo rallied them and told them that it was too late to run away, and that the cause of all their problems was not the engineers but the palace.

"Who hired the engineers?" he shouted, looking them in the eye, from face to face.

"The Mai!" one shouted.

"The Waziri!" another one shouted.

"And Mamo, the son of Lamang!" another one shouted.

"No! You are wrong there. Mamo was deceived like the whole village was deceived, he planned the fundraising, and his only concern was to see that the village got a well, but the Waziri went behind his back and hired these . . . these . . . pigs. And in case you don't know who I am, my name is LaMamo, Mamo's twin brother. Now, who wants to come with me to the palace to tell the Mai and his Waziri what we think of them, and to demand the immediate release of our family from the police cells?"

The dead engineer's body was thrown into a donkey cart and the crowd swelled as the procession passed through the village center. Most of them didn't know why they followed the one-eyed leader, but their minds were still fresh with images of yesterday's police brutality; there was also the drought and the imminent famine, which added fuel to their anger, and they felt that anything was better than the frustration and the hopelessness of their existence. As he followed, short of breath and almost choking on the dust raised by the myriad soles, Mamo kept looking around, surprised that the police hadn't yet appeared shooting. He was sure they were out there somewhere, biding their time, or perhaps they were right now at the station, arming.

He pushed through the crowd with all his might, shouting at the top of his voice, "LaMamo! Stop! Listen!" but his voice was drowned by the din. LaMamo was right at the front, behind the cart, a switch in his hand with which he urged the donkey on. Surrounding him was a mass of angry-looking youths, all shouting at the top of their voices. Whenever Mamo got close to his brother, the angry youths would jostle him back, the dust blinded him and blocked his nostrils, and now it was all he could do to remain on his feet. He slowed down and moved to the outside of the crowd, coughing, breathing through his mouth.

They passed through the market and soon they were before the palace. The crowd filled the square, where not long ago horses had galloped and the governor had given a speech and money had been raised in the name of the people. And now what Mamo had hoped for did not happen; he had hoped that the crowd would sober up as soon as they came face-to-face with the palace, and might then turn to LaMamo for inspiration, and he in turn might give a speech, at which point Mamo would jump forward and warn the crowd of the danger of what they were about to do. But it didn't happen. The youths, with LaMamo at the front, broke into a run as soon as the palace came into view. There was a brief struggle with the elderly palace guards, who formed a human shield at the arched entrance, but soon the young men prevailed and the crowd surged into the palace. LaMamo was the first inside.

Mamo followed the crowd into the familiar passages and doorways, looking around for his brother. The crowd had now broken up into groups; some were bashing down the office doors, others were throwing huge rocks to break down the glass doors of the Mai's lounge, and yet others had melted into the myriad doorways that led into the main compound. Mamo stood in the doorway of the waiting room, undecided which way to go. Bodies pushed past him, knocking him about. The air was filled with the shouts of "Get the Waziri, get the Waziri."

Soon there was smoke billowing out of the office windows. Galvanized by the smoke, he ran to his office. The door was open and three men were inside, pulling out the drawers, tearing down the curtains. Mamo could smell kerosene on the carpet. One of the men looked at him and smiled, exposing brown rotten teeth, and asked, "Brother, do you have a match?"

Mamo turned and headed for the Mai's lounge, and that was when he saw LaMamo, just coming out of the lounge—they saw each other at the same time. Mamo's anger and relief and frustration vied to dominate his face. He took his brother's arm and shook it roughly. "Are you crazy? What do you think you are doing?"

LaMamo opened his mouth to speak, but Mamo raised his hand, silencing him. "Let's go home immediately. There's no time. The police will soon be here."

LaMamo pulled away. "No," he said, "this has to be done."

Both spoke at the top of their voices; now they could feel the heat coming from the fire burning in almost every room of the palace. The sweat poured down LaMamo's face, soaking his black eye patch.

"Think of your wife, and your unborn child," Mamo shouted desperately.

"I am doing this for them."

"But there has to be another way . . . this is senseless violence. People will die."

"It is not a waste if people die trying to be free. Yesterday, when I came, I could see the hopelessness on the people's faces. There was no light of hope anywhere. I felt as if I had lost my way, as if I had entered some crazy town where the sun never shines. . . . I can't bear that. This is the right thing to do. My friend the professor once told me that all wars are unjust, except the one people fight to liberate themselves from injustice."

The twins stared into each other's eyes silently.

"Listen, the letter—"

"Asabar explained everything."

Mamo looked around helplessly. That was when he saw the Waziri and the Mai coming out of a side door. They must have been hiding inside the compound with the women. They were dressed in ordinary shirts and trousers, and no one recognized them till they had entered one of the cars parked against the wall and had started the engine. Then the shout went up, "It is them. Waziri! Mai!"

The Waziri was behind the wheel. He panicked when he saw the men running toward the car, brandishing clubs and knives. He engaged the gears and the car shot forward, ramming into another parked car, then it straightened and made for the exit. Stones and clubs bounced off it as it went, men hastily jumped out of the way. LaMamo went after the car. Mamo walked out of the palace, heading for home. He hadn't gone past the market when he heard gunshots. The police had arrived. It was too late now; before the day was over, there'd be dead bodies laid out in the square.

Later he heard of how the car with the Waziri behind the

wheel had gotten stuck in a ditch not too far from the palace, and how the rioters had dragged the two noblemen out through the windows and stripped them down to their underpants. The Waziri was killed instantly when he threatened the people with arrest and prosecution, but the Mai, when he rolled on the ground and begged for his life, was spared.

blood on the bedsheets

LATER, IN his book *Lives and Times*, Mamo would write that he knew the instant when his brother was shot; he felt something go out of him at that moment, as if his vitality had been halved instantly. He was seated in the living room then, looking at the open doorway, waiting. He had sat like that for hours since he returned from the palace in the afternoon. He watched the sun go down, all the time his ears cocked, listening to the faraway gunshots coming from the direction of the palace.

LaMamo came as night fell. His arrival was heralded by Rifkatu's screams. Mamo remained seated, his eyes fixed on the door curtain, which shook in the light wind blowing from outside. He waited to hear voices, or more screams, but nothing came. Then he heard heavy footsteps on the veranda, and his brother's voice say, "Let's go in." He still sat, his head bowed, then the curtain parted, revealing LaMamo supported on the shoulders of an unfamiliar young man, both swaying from side to side as if drunk. Mamo got up slowly, and for no reason at all he looked up at the clock—the time was seven P.M. His legs felt heavy as he moved forward to help support his brother, who was bowed and almost falling to the floor. LaMamo's left hand was clutched tightly to his stomach and now Mamo saw the blood seeping out between his fingers and dropping to the floor. They all stood in the doorway, saying nothing, and for a moment everything came fully into focus before Mamo's eyes: his brother's sky-blue shirt turned black by the blood, and the green carpet

turning black wherever the blood dropped on it, and the girl with
a wooden bowl in her hand, her mouth and eyes open wide in
terror. The sweat ran down the young man's grimy face, his nose
flared with exhaustion as he half carried, half supported
LaMamo.

Mamo took his brother's other arm and led the way to
LaMamo's room. They laid him on the bed—the bedspread was
white and fresh, LaMamo must have laid it this morning before
going out. Mamo wanted to ask if they shouldn't change the
white sheets because of the blood, but it seemed a silly and triv-
ial thing to say, so he stood aside, unable to say anything. He felt
a sharp pain in his stomach at exactly the same spot where his
brother was clutching his. He watched the young man unbutton-
ing LaMamo's shirt and dropping it to the floor. There was a long
strip of cloth wound around his body, covering the wound; it was
black with blood. LaMamo started coughing and blood trickled
down the side of his mouth.

"We must get him to the hospital," Mamo said at last. His
words shook; he had started to shiver and the sweat dripped from
his forehead.

"No, we can't do that," the young man said. Mamo turned to
him and saw the agitation in his eyes. "The police will be there,
waiting. They are out on the streets and they are shooting. We
only got here after hiding for hours and moving from cover to
cover."

"Who are you?"

"Samaila," the young man replied.

"How are you feeling?" Mamo asked his brother, who was staring up at him, on his lips a weak, apologetic smile.

"I . . . I . . . I am not too bad. I am just numb. I've seen people
shot five times and they still made it—" He broke off and began
to cough.

"Shh," Mamo said, "stop talking. You'll be all right. I'll get the
doctor, just rest now, rest."

He turned to the girl, who was standing by the door as if ready

to bolt, the calabash clutched tightly to her chest. "Go and tell
Dr. Njengo to come. Tell him my brother has been shot. And be
careful, take the back paths."

He sat down on the edge of the bed and placed his hand over
his brother's where he was clutching his wound. He could feel
his brother's stomach moving as he breathed, and the warm
blood rising to cover his fingers. LaMamo opened his eye and
smiled, and then he closed it again.

"What happened?" Mamo asked Samaila, who was standing in
a corner, absently making washing motions with his hands,
which were crusty with dry blood. His terrified eyes were fixed
on LaMamo. He opened his mouth and, his eyes still fixed on
LaMamo, began to narrate how he had found LaMamo unconscious in the grass; that was after the police had arrived and had
started shooting at the crowd. The palace and the square had
been covered in tear gas, men fell from bullets, and the young
man, blinded by tear gas, had dropped behind a clump of grass
not too far from the palace, and that was when he saw LaMamo
lying on his back, covered in blood. He recognized him because
of the eye patch—he had seen him earlier leading the donkey
cart to the palace. He dragged him to a nearby house where he
knew the family. The family sheltered them and helped him tie
up LaMamo's wound. When he came to, LaMamo wanted to
leave immediately, but they stopped him because outside the
fighting still went on. They waited till nightfall before leaving the
house. The young man spoke as if by rote, his voice without emotion, but as soon as he had uttered the last words he sat down
abruptly on a chair beside the bed and began to weep. He was
really young, not yet twenty, Mamo guessed; perhaps he had
never seen so much blood before.

"I owe him my life," LaMamo answered. His eye was open,
staring at the young man. "He is very brave."

"Shh," Mamo said, taking his hand. "You must rest. Rifkatu
will soon be back with the doctor. Just rest. Just rest."

But LaMamo went on speaking, his voice growing fainter. "Do

you remember that time when I fell from the flame tree and broke my arm?" There was a small smile on his sweating face as he stared at Mamo. For some reason Mamo had also been thinking of that same day.

"It seems like yesterday," Mamo said.

"Yes," LaMamo breathed. "I . . . want you to know I am not scared of dying. . . . My only regret is now I won't see my child." He gripped Mamo's hand, his grip surprisingly firm. "Promise me you'll send for Bintou when things are back to normal. . . . I want my child to grow up here . . . beneath the hills, like we grew up. . . . I know everything will be all right."

He got up on his elbow and reached into his pocket and brought out his wallet. He took out the picture and handed it to Mamo. "Promise."

"Of course I will. But everything will be okay. The doctor will soon be here."

LaMamo relaxed back onto the pillow and closed his eye. He died before the doctor came; his face looked peaceful, his hand tightly gripping his brother's.

after the gunshots

My Dear Mamo,

I must first apologize for taking so long to reply your last letter, which I received almost a year ago. But so much misfortune has befallen me since then and I am sure you will forgive my tardiness when I tell it to you. Before I go on to weigh you down with my sad stories, though, let me first say that my sadness is now in the past and (even though I am over sixty years old) I look to the future with some optimism. Let me also say that I hope you and your dear ones are fine, and that the sun is shining on you as brightly as it is shining here this morning.

As you can see from the address on this letter I am no more with the university—I retired over a year ago and moved to the village where I have a farm. My wife died six months ago, and since her death I have been rather lethargic and neglectful of my other responsibilities. But this morning I reread Plutarch's letter of consolation to his wife after the death of their two-year-old daughter. I came across these lines and I felt as if they spoke to me directly: "For each person takes grief in of his own accord. But once it has fixed itself with the passing of time and become his companion and household intimate, it will not quit him even at his earnest desire. We must therefore resist it at the door. . . ."

But let me not bore you with my ramblings, the ramblings of an old man. I write all these only because I imagine you as someone like myself. Someone who lives mostly in the imagination—

we are sooner or later going to have to face life, come face-to-face with experience, and that would overwhelm us. In the imagination things are more manageable, we can think up a million solutions in our minds—without fear of loss of dignity, or having to lower our aims. But in real life these things almost crush us, and we realize how like everyone else we really are— there is nothing really special about us. We must lower our expectations, learn humility like everyone else, and move on from there.

But now, let us talk about you.

Have you done anything about your ambition to write biographies? This morning I reread your essay, "A Plan for a True History of Keti," in which you propose to model your work on Plutarch's Parallel Lives *and thereby achieve a truly human history of your people. I hope you have. I have already mentioned it to a few friends of mine who are in the publishing business and they have expressed their keenness to see it. I am not writing this to rush you into finishing your book, just to encourage you on a worthy ambition. Write soon and let me know how you are doing.*

I remain yours,
James K. Batanda

PS
Unfortunately, we couldn't publish your essay, "A Plan for a True History . . ." because the Quarterly *was scrapped by the university due to lack of financial resources. But I took the liberty of sending it to other history journals that I am sure will want to publish it.*

△ ▽ △

For three months after his brother's death Mamo sat, mostly out on the veranda, and stared into space. Things had moved fast since the riots. The Mai, after his close shave with death, had

ordered the release of all the detainees—he said he didn't want
anything to spoil the anniversary celebrations. But unfortunately
things had not worked out as planned for the celebrations—the
ministers did not come, neither did the military governor. It was
a lacklustre affair. The villagers were too busy looking at the sky
for signs of rain, or mourning their dead relatives, to attend. Only
the police, with their rifles alert for any sign of threat, formed the
audience. In the evenings Mamo would stare at the hills when
the sun hung over them, red and dying, and he'd imagine the
graveyard beneath the hills, just out of sight, with the baobab
trees rotund and tall, their huge, velvety, pear-shaped fruit—
which the Reverend Drinkwater called "Monkey Apple" in his
relentless search for equivalents to the world he knew—and
think of how all the houses at the foot of the hills lay in the graveyard's shadow. Then he'd say to himself, *All my life I've lived literally in the shadow of death*. When he looked back on his life he
saw the headstones lined up like milestones. Sometimes friends
and neighbors came to visit, and would try to take his mind away
from his morbid thoughts—but he mostly listened, and only fit-
fully talked to them. He wanted to tell them that he was not sitting like this out of sadness, or in mourning for his brother. He
had come to terms with his loss; what he was doing was simply
measuring his life, putting it on a scale to see which way it tilted,
if so far it had been worth anything at all.

His uncle Iliya had visited him yesterday and they had sat side
by side on the veranda. He had come up with a new scheme to
get the authorities to reopen the school. He was collecting signatures; his aim was to get the signature of every single citizen of
Keti, and then send the signatures to the military administrator.
Mamo said it was good idea. His uncle was over seventy, but still
a fire burned in him. As he was leaving he had put a hand on
Mamo's shoulder and said, "This is life. There's nothing more.
The trick is never to give up."

More than once Mamo had tried to whip himself up into some
sort of writing frenzy, and he had gone as far as jotting down the

things he would write about, the people he would interview. In his mind he was now clear about what shape his book would take—it'd be in fifteen to twenty chapters, and each chapter would cover the life of one individual. He'd talk with the people, go into their houses, into their hearts, to write about their secret desires and aspirations. He wouldn't be seeking for parallels between lives, like Plutarch did, because he saw that as already given: all lives are already parallel; each life is comparable to another life regardless of circumstance. People desire the same things; they only differ in how they allow their aspirations to be modified by the dominant values of their society. All aspire to be happy.

He didn't know if the result would be a true history; he didn't care. In the final analysis he'd be writing the book for himself. The first name on his list of persons was his father: because he still didn't know who his father was, or what had driven him and others like him; then his brother, because if he really understood his brother, then he'd also come to understand himself, they were one person; then his uncle Iliya, because he saw the way forward and was unstinting in his push for it; his auntie Marina, because she was the mother he never had, and if he could understand her, then he'd come to understand all mothers; Zara, not only because he loved her, but because she remained rooted to Keti and could see all that was beautiful in it, but at the same time she kept her arms open to other people and other ideas and places, because of her generosity; Drinkwater, because in a way he owed him his life; the Mai, because Mamo had already gathered so much material on him, and because if he could demystify him, and others like him, then he could understand the limitations of tradition, and also its possibilities; the Waziri, because he was evil and every book should have at least one evil person in it; and Graves, because he would like to know what ran across his mind as he fell to his death from the Kilang Peak; and Kai, and Malai, and Pastor Mela—but first he'd start with his uncle Haruna. What sort of demons would drive a man to kill himself?

Yesterday Auntie Marina complained that she had seen Haruna's ghost in her room, trying to talk to her.

"He looked unhappy," she said. Mamo had tried to calm her down, saying it was perhaps her imagination, or her ill health. Since she came back from the police cell two days after LaMamo's death she had been sickly, had suffered a mild stroke, and had spent days in the hospital. And now she was seeing ghosts.

He'd write about that too. But for the moment he had to overcome this ennui.

△ ▽ △

Soon after the burial he had written a long letter to LaMamo's wife, telling her of her husband's death, explaining the circumstances, concluding rather feebly with, "Do not mourn too much. I know how hard this request is. But your pain will be eased by the knowledge that he died fighting not for himself, but for others. The people here will always remember him as a hero. The whole village turned out for his funeral." He told her that LaMamo's last wish was for her to come to Keti. As he waited for her reply, he tried to imagine what kind of person she was, how she'd adjust to life in the village. Often he'd take out her picture from LaMamo's wallet and stare at her young, determined face. Auntie Marina was more nervous than him, and every day she'd ask him if the reply had come yet, and what kind of food Bintou might like, and what room to put her in. They had bought a new mattress and other bits of furniture for LaMamo's room where they had finally decided to put her.

"I hope when she finds out that he actually died in this room she won't be too upset," Marina said.

So he sat and waited, like he had done most of his life, waited for the dark patches to make sense, for the jigsaw pieces to form a pattern. Sometimes, when the door opened, he would look up, hoping it would be Zara—he hadn't seen or heard from her since that day at the guesthouse. Maybe she had gone back to South Africa, or maybe she had met someone new and married again— as her ex-husband said, she had a talent for that.

△▽△

"What are you peering at?" Marina asked. She was walking around the room, and at the moment she was at the other end by the bed; she grunted as she bent and tested the bedsprings by pressing hard with both hands on the mattress. She pulled off the sheets and frowned at them.

"Something in my eyes," Mamo replied. He was staring into the mirror, looking into his eyes for telltale signs of death. He knew the signs, he had seen them in his brother's eyes just before he died, and also in his father's eyes, and, though he had been too young to recognize them, he had seen them in his uncle Haruna's eyes a day before he hanged himself from the flame tree. It was a shadow, like an eclipse, around the brows, a lack of focus in the eyes, as if they were gazing at some shifting, preternatural shore, far beyond life itself. But his eyes were normal.

"Don't you think we should repaint the room?" Marina asked. Bintou's letter had arrived early in the morning today, and now they were getting the room ready for her—the letter said she would be arriving in a week. Auntie Marina ran her hand on the wall and examined it under the light, trying to see if the paint had come off on her fingers.

"Nothing wrong with the paint," he said.

She asked for about the hundredth time, "Would she like okra, do you think, or maize with baobab-leaf soup? Of course eggs. . . ."

Mamo reassured her that there was nothing to worry about. "Just make sure she gets a lot of fruits. She is pregnant."

He went and stood by the window, staring out into the mango

grove.

It was almost dark outside; the last light of the evening hung over the mango leaves in weak orange patches. The mosquitoes coming in through tiny holes in the protective gauze buzzed around his eyes and nose; he waved them away impatiently. A huge piece of the grove had been cleared and now a concrete structure, already at lintel level, had replaced most of the trees; he could hear voices calling from inside the structure, children playing hide-and-seek.

"Don't forget to close the window," Auntie Marina said as she left the room.

bintou

MAMO FIRST noted that she was sensibly dressed: she wore a
light cotton gown that fell to just above her ankles. Her head was
covered with a thin silk scarf. She gathered the gown in her hand
as she got out of the taxi, her pregnancy making her move slowly
and painfully. She would be almost seven months pregnant now,
Mamo calculated as he went forward to meet her. She raised her
hand and covered her eyes against the blinding afternoon sun.

"You look much younger than your picture," he told her as he
led her into the house. When she did not respond immediately
he realized how unsuitable his words had been for the occasion.
This was their first meeting, and she was perhaps as nervous as
he was; his intention had been to make the atmosphere less awkward, more welcoming. A few neighborhood kids were struggling
with her bags, arguing about whose turn it was to carry them.

"And you look exactly like your brother, only you are thinner
. . . and taller," she responded after a while. Her voice was soft
and low; her English had the same Liberian accent that
LaMamo's had had. He was glad to notice the lack of formality
in her direct and unremitting stare. She sat down as soon as they
entered the living room and kicked off her shoes. Her face was
lined and there were bags beneath her eyes, as if she had not
slept in a long time.

He went and threw open the window. "It is so hot today."

Auntie Marina came in with a cup of water; Rifkatu came in
after her with a bottle of Fanta on a tray.

"This is my aunt," he said, still standing, unable to sit down. "LaMamo must have told you that our mother died the day we were born. Auntie Marina is the one who brought us up. She is our mother."

Auntie Marina went to the visitor and took her hand in hers, smiling into her eyes. "You look tired," she said in Hausa.

Mamo translated into English, "She said you look tired and you must rest now. She will show you to your room. Your bag is already there. There is so much to talk about, but first rest. If you need anything just call me, I'll be in the living room."

"I'd like to see the grave, please."

"We will do that tomorrow—" he began, but she didn't let him finish.

"No, today, please."

He nodded. The women left the room hand in hand.

In the evening he took her to the burial ground. The path from the house wound up through the mahogany trees to the foot of the hills where goats grazed on the dry, almost nonexistent grass. Most of the graves were plain mounds of red earth under the baobab trees with no headstones on them. LaMamo's grave was next to Lamang's, but Mamo did not bother to point out his father's grave to Bintou as she knelt before the concrete headstone bearing the simple words, LAMAMO LAMANG 1963–1994. She had brought with her a wreath of red carnations whose petals were already wilting in the heat; she must have bought it in the state capital. Now she carefully laid it before the headstone, then she ran her hand over the words, muttering some silent, private words of goodbye. Mamo stood a little distance away; close by under a baobab tree a group of children stood watching them curiously. The burial ground—goats, trees, people, headstones, and mounds—was tinted red by the setting sun, which could just be seen on top of the hills. Her shoulders began to shake silently, and when she finally stood up he saw the tears. He took her hand and helped her straighten up—he felt her pain, yet he did not know what to say to comfort her; they were strangers, even though she was now family, his brother's widow. She looked so frail; her hand in his felt light, so thin.

"He said he would be gone for only two weeks. I waited and waited and waited, and then I got your letter. It was terrible, terrible. I did not know where to turn or what to do . . ." she sobbed. He patted her hand silently. He wanted to tell her, *Everything will be fine*, but he kept quiet.

That night, after the evening meal, they sat out on the veranda. It was not yet eight P.M., but already the night had grown silent; occasionally voices from outside could be heard passing. The light from the bulb in the veranda shone dully into the huge, dark compound in front of them, illuminating the square patch of ground that Mamo wanted to turn into a garden—when the rains returned. Auntie Marina, after fussing over Bintou's meal and ensuring that she had everything she needed for the night, had gone to bed. The girl had gone out to play.

"How peaceful the village is," Bintou whispered, as if talking to herself. Mamo listened to her voice, trying to discern from it what kind of person she was—he could do that easily with most people, but he found Bintou difficult to read. Her eyes, her voice, her gestures were polite and sufficient, never excessive.

"He never really talked much about his life before we met. But he talked about you all the time. . . . He said how much he missed you."

"We had a rather lonely childhood," Mamo said softly.

She was listening to him attentively, as if expecting him to say more, and when he didn't, she said, "Please tell me more. That is why I came here, to find out more about him, all the things he never told me. I don't know why, but I have to know."

"There are things I want to know too, about you, about Liberia. But first I will tell you everything," he said. He looked up as if for

inspiration. The hills were black, ominous hulks in the night—
the fires had long since stopped burning on them. A month ago
the police, perhaps having decided that the village had been suf-
ficiently pacified, had suddenly pulled out and returned to the
city, but not until after they had indulged in one final orgy of gunshots and house-to-house intimidation.

Mamo hardly knew where to start—he was not particularly
fond of talking about himself, and to talk about LaMamo would
definitely be to talk about himself. He took a deep breath and
began. "You could say we were the perfect twins, almost. We
complemented each other—what I did not have my brother had,
and what he did not have I had. I was always ill and weak, my
brother was the opposite, he was healthy and bold and reckless.
I listened, he talked, I was introverted, he was extroverted. . . .
He was the one who always stood up to our father—"

"But . . ." Bintou interrupted, and in the gloom of the veranda
he could see her shaking her head as if in confusion, "those were
the things he said about you. He said you were the bold one, the
one that always stood up to your father."

Mamo shook his head. "Time had blurred his memory, or perhaps he was just being kind to me." He stretched out his hand,
laughing. "Look at my hands, do they look strong and bold? No,
I was born with a sickle-cell disease; I am lucky to still be alive.
But anyway, that is neither here nor there. . . ." He paused, as if
he had momentarily lost the thread of his narrative, then he went
on. "Despite our dissimilarities we had the same dream, which
was to leave home as soon as we could. You know what our
favorite pastime was? Spotting planes. We'd go to the top of that
hill and wait for airplanes to pass; whenever they did we'd shout
and scream and pretend it was us up there. 'There, there we go!'
we'd scream. We'd imagine ourselves en route to some faraway
place, on some important assignment. Then we'd return home to
read, and make plans for how we'd one day depart. We even had
a map of the route we'd take. . . ." The more he talked, the easier it became, and he could feel a lessening of the heaviness in

his heart, as if a huge stone he had been carrying were gradually being eased off his shoulders. They talked far into the night, he doing the talking and she the listening. By the time he finished it had grown chilly outside and they retired for the night.

Mamo waited to hear Bintou's story, but instead of opening up she withdrew further into herself, spending her days locked up in her room. Whenever she was obliged to be sociable—mostly when the neighborhood women and their kids came to greet her, or to bring her gifts of food, or to simply gape at her—she'd sit quietly in their midst, not understanding the language, nodding vaguely whenever a statement was addressed to her directly, but her expression always remained lost, faraway. Mamo often wondered what was on her mind, if she regretted coming to Keti, or if she was still trying to make sense of her loss. Auntie Marina said it was normal for pregnant women to be moody. In the hot afternoons she loved to lie on a mat under the flame tree with a book. This was after Mamo had told her that the tree had been planted on the day they were born, and about LaMamo falling from it and breaking his arm. From then on the tree had taken on an almost totemic significance for her, it became her tree. He did not tell her about his uncle Haruna hanging himself from the same tree. One day she snapped when she came upon two men cutting off its branches—Mamo was with them, giving them directions. She rushed to him, her bright, loose-fitting print dress flapping around her legs—she had about a dozen of such dresses, she said they made her feel cool.

She took his arm; it was the first time he was seeing her so overwrought, her eyes were full of tears. "Why are they cutting the tree? Tell them to stop immediately!" The men stopped working and stared at the angry, wild-eyed woman.

"They are not cutting it down; if they were, they would be hacking at the trunk, not the branches. They are trimming it—

we do this to all the trees in the dry season, it helps them conserve water. New branches will sprout with the first rain, you will see," he assured her.

Sometimes she followed him on his evening walks; she walked slowly in a kind of waddle, her belly looking impossibly huge. Most of the time he had to wait for her to catch up with him. He took her to the abandoned community school and showed her the now roofless classrooms, the broken windows, the cracked walls on which lizards lazily sunned themselves.

"I used to work here—this used to be a great school, run by my uncle Iliya. Now it belongs to the government."

"It is abandoned," said she.

"They are still trying to decide what to do with it."

From there he took her to the hills, following the footpath that zigzagged lazily up to the summit—they rested often, but at the end they got to the top of the smallest hill, with a clear view of the village below. To his embarrassment he found that he was more out of breath than she was. She took his hand. "Let us sit down—see, there is a tree."

To their right the taller peaks rose sharply, leaning as if about to fall toward them. The ground around them was covered by ash and soot and charred branches from the brushfires. This was where the religious fights had started; some of the rocks still had blood on them.

He told her about the last Komda man. "When the Keti people took this place after routing the original inhabitants, killing most of them, they began to see a mysterious fire every night, up there." He pointed at the tallest peak. "One day a few warriors decided to climb up there to find out who was lighting the fire. They found that it was the last surviving Komda man and his family—some say two families. They begged to be spared and promised to teach the new settlers the mysteries of the village, the religious practices, which were really more advanced than those of the new settlers. That was how we got our gods and shrines. Some of the shrines are still in use."

"The town looks so green," she said.

"It only looks so from here. More than half of the village's trees have been lost in the last ten years—cut down for building or for firewood, or lost to drought. In the next ten years most of the remaining trees will be gone. Look, see that long narrow white strip—that used to be the Keti River, the one next to the abattoir. Look, gone."

She followed his hand pointing at the winding dry riverbed running from north to east of the town. The white sand of the riverbed looked like a huge scar on the earth's surface.

They stared down in silence—the people from this far looked like ants; they were returning from their farms, which they had stubbornly refused to abandon even though the rains still hadn't come.

Bintou's face looked all puffed up from the pregnancy, giving her a rather mischievous, cherubic look. He had gradually come to discover why his brother had been so in love with her: she had an intelligent, questing mind; to be with her was never to be bored.

"Tell me about the trees—who planted them in perfect rows like these?"

"A colonial officer named Graves. He wanted to re-create the streets of his native village here in Keti." He added gently, "Was your home in Liberia a bit like this?"

They were side by side, their shoulders almost touching, staring down into the village; they could see the smoke curling up from kitchens; and how the branches of the mahogany trees on the sides of the road met overhead and formed a crude triumphal arch, as if waiting for some triumphant general to pass through. He felt her recoil at the question. Her face darkened, and he immediately felt guilty: guilty of spoiling the ineffable, idyllic peace of the evening.

She shook her head. "No, not like this." Then she added, "Shall we go now? I need to rest."

Nothing changed till a week later. Early in the morning he stood before her door, a carton full of papers in his hands. She opened the door. Her eyes looked puffy.

"Can I come in?"

"Yes."

He went in and stood by the window, looking outside. He heard the bedsprings groan as she sat on the bed. He sighed and turned around. "He died on this bed. There was blood all over the sheets, and the only thing he thought of was you."

Her shoulders began to shake as she cried. He went and sat down beside her, putting his arm around her shoulder. After a long time she stopped crying. He pointed at the carton. "These are some of his papers—nothing important. Just childish jottings and sketches. I was going to burn them, but have a look first."

Later, they burned the papers together, under the flame tree. She knelt before the fire, watching the flames rise and fork in the air, send up bits of black, filmy sheets. He stood at the other side, watching the tears in her eyes, and he thought, *I hope someday, when I am gone, someone will mourn for me like this.*

the woman in the back room

THE VISITOR came in a car. He looked young, not more than thirty. His youth became more glaring when he introduced himself as a doctor—most of the doctors Mamo knew, beginning with Dr. Njengo, were grim-faced, portentous old men whom he always associated with death and illness. This one was dressed in a light suit, black. The suit, and the fact that he spoke in English, marked him out as a stranger. The locals did not wear suits; their preferred formal wear were caftans and dashikis, whose loose, spacious fit worked very well against the heat.

They sat out on the veranda; inside was too hot. Recently the skies had started darkening again with clouds. In the night the air was heavy and motionless, which was a good sign because the strong blowing winds often chased away the rain clouds.

"I came from Zara," the doctor said. "She said you are a friend of hers." He spoke with a distinct Yoruba accent.

"Zara?" said Mamo, his surprise showing. "Where is she?"

"Here in Keti. She is ill. Her mother and sister are with her."

Mamo looked away from the doctor's somber face (how true to type he had turned out to be despite his deceptive appearance) to the far end of the compound, near the outhouse, where Marina stood with a hoe in one hand and a weed in the other. She had been idly weeding the almost weedless compound all afternoon; a cluster of chickens followed her expectantly, pouncing on the worms unearthed by her hoe. Mamo wondered what she might be thinking as she stood motionless, staring at the weed and obviously not seeing it. He had read somewhere about signs and their interpretations: how in some Asian theaters a dab at the eye with a handkerchief by a woman represents great tragedy, death perhaps, or a flood, even the destruction of a whole city. Nothing vulgar like Hollywood—just a gentle, elegiac bowing of the head and a dainty dab at the corner of one eye with a handkerchief. But of course one needed to be trained in its semiotics to understand the enormity of the pain behind that gentle gesture. Like a person staring absently at a weed for minutes. Perhaps she was thinking about her life: her wicked ex-husband, the children she had never had, all that could have been—all that had shriveled up like the weed in her hand. Mamo wondered if the doctor, who had appeared so innocuous at first, was some sort of sign, a harbinger of doom. Was that why he was clad in black?

"She is not dying, is she, Doctor?"

The doctor seemed taken aback by this sudden question, but he soon regained his aplomb. He even smiled. "No. Nothing like that."

Mamo sighed in relief, but he noticed that the doctor still hesitated to say what he had to say. At last he said, "Tell me, what do you know about mental illness?"

"Nothing. One of my uncles committed suicide; I am afraid that's the closest I ever came to mental illness. But I don't see what—"

"She is suffering from acute depression, nothing too dangerous in itself, but if allowed to go on it will intensify and cause injury to the mind. She is highly unstable and most of the time she is either speechless or crying. I just came from her. Her family contacted me last week; they had been referred to me by another doctor that they had been seeing for almost two months now. I have a practice in the capital and this is the second time I've seen her. The first time she was brought to my clinic she wouldn't even speak to me. She just huddled in a corner and sobbed, and then she suddenly turned and went on and on about her son. She

believes he is in some kind of danger, and that she is to blame for
neglecting him. I recommended that they take her somewhere
peaceful, where she would be calmed by the surroundings, so
they brought her here, to Keti. It has already started working.
Today she was calmer. But for some reason I don't think the presence of her mother and sister is helping matters. Do you know
anything about their relationship?"

"They don't get along." Mamo stood up and began to pace the
veranda. "Excuse me, Doctor, but I can't sit still."

"I understand. Tell me more about her relationship with her
family."

"It is very complex. She was closer to her father. She married
her first husband after her father's death mostly to please her
mother. They had a child, the marriage later broke up. The husband's family took the child. Her mother refused to support her
in her effort to get the child back. After that the gap between
them widened. You see, the mother wants her to be like her sister, but she is different. She is more . . . complex."

"Tell me about the father."

"I don't know much about him. I never met him. But from
what Zara told me, he was something of a great achiever. He
began life as a poor farmer's son, like most of the people here,
and ended up pretty high up in government."

Mamo sat down again. His gaze was fixed on the doctor, waiting for him to speak. The doctor picked up his case from the floor
and unzipped it. "She gave me something to give you." He
brought out a thick notebook and handed it to Mamo, who took
it and looked curiously at the soft cover. It was a thick writing
pad of about two hundred blue pages closely covered in Zara's
handwriting. He recognized the peculiar *E*'s.

"She was writing a novel. She was a precocious child," said
Mamo, thinking, *We both were, but see where we ended up—I,
tired and defeated, and she, she is losing her mind.*

"I don't know if this is a good sign," said the doctor, looking at
the manuscript before handing it over to Mamo.

"Why not?" Mamo asked.

"The mind is reaching back into the past, into happier times to escape the present. What ails her is here and now, and she must deal with it on those terms. Otherwise . . ."

"Otherwise what, Doctor?"

But the doctor changed the subject. "Are you . . . lovers?"

Mamo didn't answer immediately. At last he said, "I love her, very much."

"Excuse me if I seem to be prying. But by sending you the manuscript she is reaching out to you, you are part of her happy memories. You are the only person she has communicated to . . . she wouldn't talk to her family, not even to me. I have read it, but I suggest you read it and let me know what you think she is trying to tell you, perhaps some secret message that only you might understand? Here's my card."

Mamo walked the doctor out to his car. Before he left, the doctor reluctantly allowed a smile to contaminate his somber expression. He said thoughtfully, "The mind is a fragile, sensitive thing, Mr. Lamang. It takes only a little nudge to damage it. But it also has incredible regenerative abilities. Look at all the hurt we go through every day and still manage to maintain our sanity. All we need is a little peg and we will hang our hopes and dreams on it. Why don't you go to her, talk to her?"

"It's the questions," Mamo whispered suddenly.

"What?" the doctor asked, realizing that Mamo hadn't been listening to him.

"Questions about life. Do you ask questions, Doctor?" Mamo asked. *Sometimes we seek answers where there aren't any*, he thought. *Questions fill us with fear and anxiety. We fear not knowing. Sometimes the answers come, but they don't fill us with the enlightenment we seek, and sometimes they even lead to madness.*

All afternoon Mamo pored over the manuscript. This was not the copy Zara had once shown him; it had been recopied and revised many times. It was a love story in the Mills & Boon tradition. As

he read he imagined Zara penning the words, making correc-
tions, crossing out whole sentences and pages. He read, but he
found no secret messages; frustrated, he closed the notebook,
and that was when he noticed the epigraph—he hadn't read it
before going into the story—now he noticed that the ink in the
epigraph was fresher, the writing frailer; he was sure it had been
written not long ago, most probably today. He smiled as he read
the familiar quote: *The world is as new today as it was when first
created. . . .*

This was the message.

△▽△

A car was parked in front of the house—a big Volvo with a huge
aerial sticking out of its roof. The gate was ajar and he slipped
through quietly, expecting to see the unsmiling Yam materialize
from somewhere in the compound to challenge him. But he saw
no one. He climbed the steps and knocked on the door. Minutes
passed and no one opened the door. He knocked again, louder,
rehearsing a smile.

"Who is it?" a bored voice shouted not far from the door.

"It is me, Mamo," he answered.

At last the door was opened by a tall, thin woman. His face
must have shown his surprise at the striking facial resemblance
between the woman, whom he assumed was Rhoda, Zara's sister,
and Zara. Only when she opened her mouth to speak did he see
the difference—this face didn't have the humor, the warmth of
Zara's. He thought of Ms. Lipstick. Rhoda looked at him from
top to bottom, lingering for a long time on his walking shoes so
that he began to wish he had polished them before coming. She
asked impatiently, "What do you want?"

"I came to see Zara."

Now her face lost its haughtiness and appeared undecided for
a while, but just for a while, then it recomposed itself. As she
opened her mouth to speak, another person appeared, the same

face, the same attitude, but shorter, stouter, and older: the mother. She looked at Mamo but addressed herself to her daughter. "Who is he?"

"He says he wants to see Zara."

"I heard that. Who is he?"

"My name is Mamo. I am . . ." He wasn't sure how to introduce himself. "I am a teacher, I used to be. We taught at the same school. I heard that Zara is not well. I came to see her."

"You can't see her," Rhoda said flatly, turning to her mother as if for support. Now two boys of about three and five appeared, pushing themselves forward, staring up at Mamo curiously. Rhoda's children.

"Let him come in," the mother said, turning back into the house. The children took their mother's hands.

"Come in," she said and turned back into the house. He was shown a seat by the mother, who then sat next to him. Rhoda went to the sofa by the window and stretched out in it, putting up one shapely foot on the armrest. Her children threw themselves on the floor before her. She opened a magazine and buried her face inside it.

"Who is your father?" the mother asked, looking into his face as if to discern a family resemblance.

"Lamang. He died two years ago."

"Lamang," she repeated, not saying if she recognized the name or not. Then she said, "Zara is asleep. You have to wait till she wakes up."

"Thank you," he said, trying to sound cordial. Already he could see why Zara didn't get along with her family.

They sat in silence: the mother beside him, staring forward, not talking to him, and occasionally turning to the children when they got too loud, telling them to shut up. Mamo sat with his legs straight before him, hardly daring to relax. He stared at the pictures on the wall. They had been rearranged. Zara's wedding picture was back again in the position of honor. The minutes passed. Outside, the sun descended lower in the sky. He recalled the days and nights he had spent in this house with Zara. Each piece of furniture held its own memory, its own associations: How many times had they made love on the sofa on which the sister now sat, reading? How many times had they stood arm in arm by the window, spying on Yam, the caretaker? Today the house seemed like an entirely different place, hostile, regimented, cheerless. Everything was in its proper place, the seats' armrests covered with spotless white cloths; even the children didn't seem to be as noisy and messy as other kids. Their mother remained behind her magazine, turning the pages quietly.

This calm wasn't ruffled even when a scream rang from one of the rooms down the hall. When no one showed signs of having heard anything, Mamo relaxed, thinking he had imagined it. But then after a while the scream returned, louder, followed by insistent knocks on a door. He looked from the mother to the sister to the kids. After a while the mother got up and went down the hall. A door opened, and closed. Then silence. After a long while the mother returned and resumed her seat. He looked at her, waiting for a word, but she said nothing. Night had fallen outside; the sister got up and closed the windows.

"Come," she said to the children, "time for your bath." They disappeared down the hall.

Mamo began to have a sense of unreality, as if he were in some underwater cave, or in a dream. The mother appeared to be dozing beside him, her head tilted to one side. He waited again to hear the screams, but none came, only the faint voices of the kids in the bathroom. At last he stood up and said to the mother, "I'll be going now."

"Goodbye," she said, yawning, and waved to the door.

the new interpreters

TODAY BEGAN the week-long send-off festivities planned for the departing sisters Kai and Malai. The community had drawn up an ambitious program, which, among other things, included a farewell speech by the state governor on the last day of the festivities, which was next Sunday, seven days away. Not that there was much hope of the governor coming—but he might send his deputy, or most likely his commissioner for religious affairs, which was good enough. For the past six months the Christian community had almost ruinously taxed itself and had raised a reasonable amount of money: most of it would go to food and drinks, and to transporting the sisters from Keti to the airport in Kano. The Women's Fellowship group had ordered a special design of cloth from the textile company in Kano—it bore the Drinkwater sisters' pictures on it. Beneath the pictures was the bold writing: *Separated in flesh, but together in the Lord* (2 *Corinthians* 5:8).

In the church grounds canvas canopies had already been struck up in anticipation of the capacity crowd that would gather on the grand day. But today the drama group had center stage. They were going to open the festivities with a special production of *The Coming*. As usual the stage was the concrete platform in front of the church. The building itself, still scarred from the recent riots, would provide a rather unsightly backdrop; a thick cloth had been draped on the wall to cover the broken windows and the ugly spots left by fire. Already some of the thespians had put on their costumes and were mingling self-importantly with the crowd, shaking hands and promising everyone a great spectacle.

"These children don't know anything," Auntie Marina lamented, shaking her head. She and most of her peers who had run the drama club for almost two decades had stepped aside to create space for new blood. The new thespians were mostly young married women who had understudied their roles for years. They were under the leadership of Abiyatu, the butcher's wife, whose once lithe and graceful body had inflamed Mamo's young blood and led him to feats of creativity. She was now a matron, her body transformed by repeated childbirth and house-work. Unlike the older generation, a lot of them had completed their primary and even secondary education. Some of them were secretaries in the local government, some teachers in the primary school. This was going to be their first major production of *The Coming* as a group, hence the air of expectation in the audience.

"See how they mingle with the crowd before the event? They should be inside, preparing," Marina went on.

"Maybe they are nervous," Bintou said. She was perhaps the only person in the crowd who had never seen the production before.

"It is as amateur as amateur gets," Mamo had warned her before they came. He had decided to come mainly because of her; he found the drama rather boring, and was often surprised at the enthusiasm with which each year's production was received. But perhaps today the new hams would bring some-thing new to it. He and the two women were seated in the front row of the wooden benches arranged not too far from the first steps of the stage. To one side, with a clear view of the stage, was the high table, reserved for the guests of honor, Kai and Malai, and the church elders.

Soon a buzz spread in the crowd and heads turned as Pastor Mela was sighted coming with the guests of honor. The buzz thickened as they took their seats, the pastor gallantly holding the chairs for the women before sitting down.

"She is looking at you . . . she is waving."

"Who?" Mamo asked, turning to Bintou. It was Kai. She had seen him and was now waving furiously to him, at the same time nudging her sister. Mamo smiled and waved back. Now she was standing up.

"She is coming over."

"I better go to her, then." Mamo stood up and hastened to the high table.

"We heard about your brother's death. Sorry," the sisters said to him somberly.

"Thank you. That is his wife over there, Bintou.".

"Oh, but we must meet her, you must bring her over to the house," Kai said, speaking in English, waving at Bintou, who looked back at them with a shy smile. Now the crowd had started taking an interest in what was going on. The pastor, who was on the verge of delivering the opening prayer, fidgeted impatiently with his Bible, an indulgent smile on his lips. .

"Perhaps you would like to come over and sit with us?" the pastor offered. "There are still seats at the table. Bring your sister-in-law."

The sisters nodded vigorously. The pastor stood up and began to pray as soon as Bintou had taken her seat at the table beside Mamo. The women shook her hand, beaming at her. The pastor prayed and prayed. There was a legend in the village that Drinkwater had once prayed through a Sunday sermon; that was a whole hour of prayer. The rumor was that Pastor Mela's ambition was to someday beat that record, to pray nonstop for over an hour. Now Mamo's heart sank as he thought that the pastor might be using this chance to fulfill his ambition. But the prayer ended and the actors made their entrance.

On the table were copies of the play's text—foolscap sheets stapled together—with the title, *The Coming*, boldly written on the cover. This was clearly one of the many innovations promised by the new generation of actors. Mamo picked it up and was impressed to see that the actors strictly followed the scripted dialogue, almost word for word. Another innovation was the cordless microphone that amplified their speech—but that unfortunately slowed down the action as it was exchanged from speaker to speaker. But that was not the last innovation. A loud cheer went up when the Drinkwater family appeared onstage— the actors playing the white characters had painted their faces pink and had attached some prosthetic to their noses to make them straighter. This heightened verisimilitude, especially since the audience could not easily recognize the actors behind the disguise. Beside him Bintou was clapping loudly, her eyes shining. He felt happy to see her so at ease. He felt a nudge to his right and he turned. Kai was pointing at something in the text, on the last page. He bent closer and he saw that it was his name. *By Mamo Lamang.* And suddenly what had been nagging him since he had first seen the script became clear. This was a copy from the original that he had written for Auntie Marina's drama group long ago.

"You wrote the lines?" she asked.

He nodded, and he couldn't avoid adding, "When I was fourteen."

Funny, he thought, *how something I did to pass the boring hours of childhood has proved so enduring—perhaps that is the trick to things: to do them as if we are just killing time.*

The crowd cheered as the play progressed—Bintou was laughing so hard that tears came to her eyes. The Drinkwater sisters were also clapping. Even Auntie Marina was smiling now, her frown grudgingly ebbing away. Suddenly he realized that the worst was over, they had survived, life had hurled its arrows at them and now it was out of missiles. He thought of Zara and the first time he had met her right here, watching this same play. *She should be here*, he thought, *she deserves to be here.* That day she had promised him in her assured, convincing way that because they were writers, they were both geniuses.

It was now a week since the day he had gone to see her and was given the cold shoulder by her mother and sister. Yesterday he had gone back and loitered by the gate, but at last he had walked away, his resolve to walk in and demand to see Zara dying away when he remembered the sister's sneer and the mother's grim silence. All night long the guilt had weighed on him, and he kept asking himself, what if he was the only person in this world who might reach her, rescue her, because he was the only one who really knew her?

But it was more than that, he realized suddenly: he needed her. Now that he felt strong, there was so much he wanted to do: the book of lives would be first; and then he might travel and see other places, other customs, and perhaps write about them. He was not sure how long this strength and conviction would last—but he was certain that if Zara were to be with him, she would always renew his strength for him. She was that kind of person. Suddenly he knew what he had to do.

"I am going for a walk," he whispered to Bintou. "I'll see you at home."

He resolved to go to Zara and this time no one would deny him access to her. He would reason with the mother, he would tell her how much he loved Zara. And to work up his nerve for this task, he decided to take a walk.

As he walked away, the cheer from the crowd followed him, drenching him like water, clearing his thoughts, and he suddenly realized why the people found the play so intriguing year after year, something he had failed to see before. To them the play was not about Drinkwater and his "conquest" of their culture by his culture, it was about their own survival. They were celebrating because they had had the good sense to take whatever was good from another culture and add it to whatever was good in theirs: they had done this before when they first met the Komda, and many times before that in their travels and migrations, in times earlier than even the oldest among them could remember. This was their wisdom, the secret of their survival. This was why they

were still able to laugh. And when the new thespians donned
their prosthetic faces and tried to look like Drinkwater, there was
irreverence in their posture, in their gestures, there was more
satire than celebration, as if they were saying to him: *We know
something you didn't know, something you couldn't know.* And so
each generation would bring to this play its own interpretation.
This was what he would tell Zara—it was all about survival,
about bending a little so as not to totally break. He was sure she'd
understand.

After the church fence was his uncle Iliya's house. The old
man would be inside now, staring out of the window, or reading,
or perhaps playing with his grandson, Asabar's son—Asabar, who
had once been tall and ambitious, but was now confined to his
wheelchair and was always drunk before noon. He passed the
few thatched houses between his uncle's house and the community school. Iliya still sent letters to the Ministry of Education
asking for the school to be reopened; still he received no replies.
The school's signboard lay facedown on the ground, its wood
eaten away by termites—a group of kids played hide-and-seek in
the classrooms whose doors lay broken on the ground. After the
school the open field, which had once been thick bush, began.
In Mamo's mind the thick bush of his childhood still stood, and
LaMamo was beside him, easily outstripping him as they ran: It
is early in the morning and they are running eastward so that the
warm sun rising is in their faces, through the cacti fence that
marks the perimeter of the schoolyard, into the long broom
grasses, past the shea butter trees, past the baobab trees that
look oh so sad in the morning, their thick humanoid trunks and
scanty leaves and dangling breastlike fruits, and into thicker
bushes where the brambles begin, their branches and stems cutting into their ankles and knees, and the after-rain flowers, yellow and purple, that soon will wilt when the sun is up, and the
bees and the colorful butterflies that settle and rise and hover
and settle again out of sight in the noiseless bush. Suddenly from
the little mound the view of the abattoir, alone and derelict, and

behind it the river. The fan palms that line the riverbank stretching into the distance, their leaves like arms waving goodbye in the wind—soon they'll all be gone. Auntie Marina says every inch of the palm tree has economic use: the juicy red fruit for eating, and its seed for replanting, and the wood, too precious for cooking, is used for making roof rafters, the dry palm leaves for kindling fire and their ash for seasoning. On the underside of the leaves of the wild berries locusts crouch, still sleepy, easy to catch in the quick cup of the hand—to be roasted and eaten. Afterward the long swim in the river. But only LaMamo swims. Mamo shouldn't because he might get an infection, which could mean death. On the way back the hills in the distance loom large and black from the brush fires that ceaselessly burn away the harmattan-dried leaves. Above the hills the clouds have thickened, brushing the surface of the hills. The rain will fall today.

HELON HABILA

WAITING FOR AN ANGEL

Lomba is a young journalist living in Lagos under Nigeria's brutal military regime. His mind is full of soul music and girls and the novel he is writing. Yet when his room-mate goes mad and is beaten up by soldiers, his first love is forced to marry a man she doesn't want, and his neighbours are planning a demo that is bound to lead to a riot, Lomba realises that he can no longer bury his head in the sand. It's time to write the truth about this reign of terror ...

'An exciting book. The narrative is astonishing, at once tender and embittered, humorous and unforgiving' *Daily Telegraph*

'The culture of poverty, violence and fear is so skilfully and quietly evoked that it is almost palpable ... the story is peopled with well-drawn, idiosyncratic characters. Deeply moving and memorable' *The Times*

'A telling insight into life under a modern dictatorship and a moving testimony to trials, tribulations, injustices, imprisonments, loves and deaths' *Time Out*